FINDING JUDGEMENT

Natalie Gayle

Centre Games
BOOK 2

Dedication

To Amy Lee Abrahams

(June 8th 1993 to 29th May 2003)

You made all our lives so much richer for having
known you.

I hope you enjoy reading Finding Judgement in Heaven.

For Amy

Our beloved Amy
Daughter, sister, partner, friend
A portrait so fine
How do words describe
Such beauty inside

So many things to so many people
You touched us all
A magic unique to you
With your presence so warm
Your soul so pure and bright
Your laugh so musical and light

Zeus, Ode, Dan, Pink, Noble, Phillip, Switch
Equine and canine friends
All so close to your heart
Their soft eyes and warm fur
Allowed your spirit to soar

Across the globe you spread your wings
Enjoying the best life could bring

Australia wide, Paris, New York, Florida
Just to name a few
Tamborine and Cairns
The places closest to you

Dedication, commitment and focus
To get the task done
Balanced with love, laughter and fun
The fabric you shared
With everyone

Your beautiful smiles
Would change dark to light
Family and friends meant so much to you
Always friend, never foe
You realised the value of love
And were generous with yours
Now even above, we feel your love

Our living angel has moved to another place
Looking down upon us
With all your love and grace
We'll hold you in our hearts
Until we walk together again
Forever our beloved – Amy

From your friend always – Natalie Gayle

Prologue

9:50 a.m. Team Briefing

Rory was sitting at the large polished boardroom table in the Gold Coast office of the Centre. The office had only recently been established. Apparently the powers that be decided the Gold Coast was a nice innocuous place to house a quasi-government agency. Who would expect a bunch of covert operators to hang out on the Gold Coast?

His great mate and "brother," Quade, was seated opposite. Quade was looking particularly relaxed or was it a little worse for wear? Rory didn't feel great today but he was restless. If this little shindig hadn't been sprung on him, he'd have been down the surf, catching a wave, chilling out and clearing his head. He loved to surf; it always made him feel better. More centred.

They'd all partied hard last night, enjoying the wedding reception of their fellow team member, Brayden. Before they'd got too deep into their celebrations their leader, Tom "the Boss" Anderson, had advised them he expected the three of them here for a team briefing of their next assignment. That was cruel, just plain cruel.

He'd sat through hundreds of these in his almost fifteen years at the Centre. Today was different from any other day he could remember, though. A new chapter in the history of the Centre was beginning, but that wasn't what had his skin prickling. This was the first time that any of the twelve highly secretive members of the Centre's operational team had ever gotten married. In fact, it was the first time any of them had ever had a meaningful relationship. That may seem strange to an outsider, but not if they knew the secrets the team all kept.

All twelve members of the Centre's operational team were special. Not only did they have years of specialist training that would rival many special force military operatives, the twelve of them also had a few other specialised "enhancements" to help out. The Centre operatives were the product of a highly classified quasi-government science experiment.

Their human DNA had been spliced with that of the twelve animal signs of the Chinese zodiac. They couldn't do anything kooky like shift, but what they did have were five senses that were heightened to the strength of the animal's DNA their human cells had been spliced with. Incredible strength, speed, and endurance were also extremely handy. Finally, they also had that sixth sense for danger, or when something "big" was going to happen, like when the elephants take to the hills for no apparent reason and a few hours later a tsunami crashes through the low lands.

That sort of sixth sense.

And today was one of those tsunami sort of days. Rory just knew something big was going to happen today. He didn't know what, but it was going to be big. That's what had been eating at him ever since he walked into the room and making his skin prickle. God, he wished he felt better.

Finally, Quade broke the silence. "What's up? You're like a flea in a bottle, or more like a dog with a bad case of fleas."

"Ha, ha, very funny." The guys loved to tease each other. Quade was having a subtle dig at Rory's dominant animal, the canine. "Something's up. Just got this feeling something big's about to happen today."

"Well, I hope to fuck you're wrong and it happens tomorrow and not today. Not up for anything big today." He groaned and slouched his giant frame farther into the tall backed leather chair.

Rory smirked but offered no further comment. Quade wasn't talkative at the best of times. When he didn't want to be here—best to give him a wide berth.

The second thing that struck him as being completely different in the Centre today was Dr Jazz Carter. She'd just made her way in and sat beside him, cradling a cup of coffee in her hand as if it were a lifeline. Tall, red-headed, green-eyed, and gorgeous. But that was just the packaging. She was also gregarious, sharp as a tack, and totally unpredictable.

Over the last three months since he'd met her, she'd become a close friend as well. She, too, didn't seem to be functioning at her best. Her head was cradled gently in her hand and her mouth was pulled tight in pain.

Jazz was the best friend of Dr Rihanna Mason, his "brother" Brayden's new wife. Rihanna was beautiful, smart, and a dedicated veterinarian, and Brayden worshipped the ground she walked on. Hopefully they were enjoying the start of their two-week honeymoon. They made an awesome couple and Rory was very happy for them.

Brayden had had the guts to stand up to the boss and demand his right to a relationship. All his team admired him for doing that. His actions demonstrated a huge commitment to his new wife, Rihanna. Rihanna's new status as Brayden's wife only further cemented her position in the Centre. The team were very tight knit and the moment Brayden staked his claim, they all considered Rihanna family.

This change of the status quo had also opened the gates for the rest of them when the time came. Not something to be taken lightly, if you knew the boss. Even if the guy didn't have animal-enhanced senses, he was fuckin' scary. It was rumoured he was a retired general or something. It was easy to believe. He sure treated everyone as if they were soldiers. This in itself was a very sore point for Rory. He hated being considered or associated with the military in any way, shape, or form. Not that he had anything against soldiers; he was just not keen on the parameters they worked within. He voluntarily agreed to be part of the Centre. This was a status he could deal with most of the time.

He cast a glance back at Jazz. The other thing that set her apart today was her DNA. Jazz was the run-of-the-mill type human—totally human—and she was sitting in at an Ops team meeting. This was the first time the boss had ever invited an outsider, someone without altered DNA, to an initial closed Ops team meeting. Sure, they had civilians in from time to time but never at a pure Ops team meeting. But Jazz was also part of the team now. In fact, today was her first day of working for the Centre.

Yep, something big was definitely going down. Jazz's presence wasn't it, but he'd bet his left nut that she'd have something to do with it. Sparks were going to fly, as sure as the sun would rise tomorrow somewhere in the world.

"Hung over, Jazz?" he finally inquired. His voice was filled with sympathy.

Jazz groaned. "Like you wouldn't believe."

"What? Scared of needles, honey nose? Can't believe you didn't give yourself an IV or something." Quade was playing with fire. Within thirty minutes of meeting, Jazz and Quade seemed to have immediately established this weird, combative sort of relationship that was underpinned by a truckload of sexual tension.

They went out of their way to tease, annoy, sledge, and basically terrorise each other. "Honey nose" had become Quade's immediate tag for Jazz. He was always ragging on her about how she couldn't mind her own business. But then there was the other element to it as well. Quade had taken two bullets in order to save Jazz's life. She'd then worked on him from the site of the shooting to the operating theatre in order to save his. That had added another whole layer of weirdness to their relationship.

Mmm, far too complex to ponder today, thought Rory. He simply just wasn't feeling up to it.

That was the moment the boss chose to walk in and sit down, drawing his attention from his musing. None of them felt much like being here today. They could have all used a "rest day" after the wedding.

The boss wasn't a tall man by the standards of the team. He was probably no more than five ten or eleven. But what he did have was presence. It just seemed to seep from his pores. His blue eyes could only be described as polar. And yes, that went for not only the colour but the glare he could pin you with. Total ice. Rihanna had once described it to him as the colour of the submerged ice shelves in the Arctic. He couldn't think of a more apt description.

"Good morning. I trust you're all well rested after last night's fun and frivolities," he said as he opened his ever-present notebook.

Nobody said a word. The reality was they all felt like shit and the boss knew it. Jazz was probably the worst because she didn't possess the animal DNA to rocket her metabolism to hyper speed. They all burnt through copious amounts of food to keep themselves energised but equally they were capable of tucking away vast amounts of alcohol as well—far more than a normal person.

Regardless of how crap they felt, none of them would utter a word about their respective conditions. There would be no sympathy from the boss, just a lecture on irresponsible behaviour. No thanks. Been there done that, had the T-shirt...not doing it again!

"So let's get started." The boss glanced up from his notes and cast his eyes around the three of them. "We have a new threat, people."

There were nods around the table but they all looked up and became more alert.

"LizDern Dairy Products contacted the Centre about a week ago. They found the presence of genetically modified milk in their routine product testing processes."

Rory noticed Jazz sit a little straighter in her chair. Her interest in the new threat became obvious.

The boss went on. "As you may or may not know, Australia has a policy of no genetically modified dairy cattle in this country. So that essentially means the artificial growth hormone rBGH is not approved for use in this country. Apparently this compound leads to some interesting side effects in the dairy cattle. The key one being the increased levels of something called IGF1, apparently by about twenty times. I'm not sure I have the entire medico speak on the actual side effects but I've been able to determine it's bad and we do not want this in our dairy products."

The boss paused and looked between them. "Maybe you can shed some light on what that really means in everyday speak, Miss Carter?"

Rory noted Jazz shook of any semblance of suffering, flicked her hair back and levelled her gaze directly on the boss. "My pleasure, Tom." Her voice was sweet and professional but it held another note. Rory knew what it was. It was on; the gauntlet had been laid down.

Jazz and the boss had shared a couple of momentous showdowns during the recent Hendra virus threat. Jazz had won the first two. However, given that Jazz was sitting at this table, he had to give the third head-to-head to the boss. He'd wanted Jazz on staff and it seemed he got his way. It took three months and a slight deviation to another position. But Jazz was sitting at this table. This meant she was now part of the Centre. Yep, he'd give round three to the boss.

"IGF1 is a protein that is found in humans and other animals. The problem in these genetic modification situations is the quantity in which the IGF1 protein exists. If, in fact, it is twenty times as you stated, Tom, the risk of breast, prostate, and colon cancer just skyrocketed." Jazz paused before going on. "If the risk of an increased likelihood of cancer was not enough, then the fact that this protein also blocks the body's natural defence mechanism for early sub-microscopic cancers makes it incredibly nasty. The odds just keep getting worse and worse."

Jazz looked between Rory, Quade, and the boss. There was a lot of head nodding and eyebrow raising. Quade let out a long whistle.

"So where is the source of the contamination?" she asked.

"That's a very good question, Miss Carter." The boss never used Jazz's deserved title of doctor. Rory was sure it was a way of keeping Jazz in her place. Jazz didn't let on that it annoyed her, but it had to grind. No doubt she'd worked incredibly hard for those qualifications. Jazz was a recently qualified specialist psychiatrist, to boot. In order to obtain those quals, she'd gone through about twelve years of medical study, including becoming a "normal" doctor before she could specialise. She deserved the title and the recognition that went with the accomplishment.

"Have the food authorities been alerted? What sort of track and trace protocols have been put in place?" she fired back, all business.

"That's all been taken care of. In fact, it was the Food Safety Authority in conjunction with LizDern that alerted us to the threat a week ago. But before we could act, we needed a starting point. They've now investigated and have been able to narrow if down to about twenty dairy properties spread throughout the Gold Coast hinterland and the Sunshine Coast." The boss paused to make sure everyone was still with him.

"It seems that those twenty properties are serviced by two different milk transport companies. That's about all we have to go on at the moment."

"So what's our role, boss?" Rory asked.

"Rory, you're taking lead on this one. Quade, you're to provide backup. I'm still not one hundred per cent convinced you're fully fit from the wounds you sustained earlier this year. Miss Carter, you're Quade's shadow until I advise otherwise. Your new medical facilities are currently being fitted out on the floor below. Until that time, you're going to be at a bit of a loose end. Best you learn more about field work. Quade, I'm counting on you to properly brief Miss Carter." The boss shot Quade a firm look, giving no room for argument or anything less than a top-notch job.

"So what's the first assignment?" Rory was restless and he wanted to get out of here and start moving. Maybe the strange feeling he was carrying would ease if he were moving around.

"Rory, Rheeba will be forwarding the details of the first task to your phone presently. You start immediately. I want a report later today."

"On it, boss." He rose to head from the room.

"Just a moment, Mr Southall. I haven't finished." The boss turned back to Quade, fully knowing that Rory would plonk his butt back in the seat.

"Quade, like Rory you'll also be getting your assignment shortly. Miss Carter, I'd like a word with you privately before you head out. While I do that, I'd like you two to head to the basement and check out the four new vehicles that have just been delivered. They're supposed to be fully kitted but I haven't had a report to confirm that. That's what I want from each of you before you head out. Things have been getting a little sloppy around here. Let's pick it up a notch or two."

Rory knew all of this was for Jazz's benefit. Things weren't sloppy—no way, not in the least. This was just the boss's way of making sure she knew what his expectations and standards were all about. He was flexing his muscle as head of the Centre.

"If there's nothing further, you're free to go. Miss Carter, if you wouldn't mind staying?" It wasn't a question. It was an order posed politely as a question. Rory noticed Jazz smile. She was totally onto the boss and his games. In fact, if Rory wasn't mistaken, Jazz seemed to have shaken off her hangover and was fully engaged in the game as well.

Quade joined Rory on the other side of the heavy double doors to the boardroom. They moved to the lift area and waited for the next car.

"I can't believe this shit's happening, man," Quade said, shaking his head.

He knew what Quade was getting at and it was time to call him on it.

"What can't you believe? The fact that Jazz is now working with us or the fact that you're so in lust with her you can't think straight?"

Quade stood straighter and half growled. "Bullshit, Rory. She means nothing to me."

Rory snorted. "Keep telling yourself that, Quade. See how long it lasts for. Sooner or later, you're going to wake up and smell the coffee."

"I'm telling you there's nothing there, mate," Quade protested.

Rory spun and faced Quade, forcing him to look right at him. "Right. So I didn't hear you growl when she put her head on my shoulder last night?" Rory's stare pinned Quade, and as Rory expected, Quade looked away, unable to answer. His face was enough to confirm things. The bell sounded, indicating the lift car had arrived.

"Right. Just as I thought. Let's get these vehicles checked out." The doors slid back and Rory stepped into the car.

The doors closed, leaving just Jazz and Tom "the Boss" Anderson in the boardroom.

"So we haven't really had a chance to discuss your appointment. I trust that the terms of the original contract will satisfy your needs." Tom opened a large document wallet that he had on the table and pulled a thick wad of paper from it.

Jazz immediately recognised the contract she'd reviewed only three months before. The terms were more than she could have hoped for. She was to become the resident medical specialist at the Centre, responsible for overseeing everything to do with the health, wellness, and ongoing medical management of the whole team and personnel associated with the Centre. She was also responsible for ensuring adequate medical support was organised for field operations.

It was cushy and she had free rein. But what was even better was the amount of time she would have for extra training. The contract stated she was getting advanced emergency and genetics training. Jazz loved to learn new skills and these were skills she didn't have to pay for or sacrifice part of her salary to obtain.

That in itself was persuasive but the clincher had been the freedom to conduct her own studies and research. There would be issues with disclosing the research but recognition was not what drove her—solving the puzzle was. Working at the Centre presented her with endless opportunities to solve puzzles. It didn't hurt either that her salary would be comparable to private practice. Seven figures with no overheads, flexible hours, and she got to basically do what she wanted and to work with her best friend, Rihanna.

The only negative she saw was having to report to Tom. Just as he refused to call her doctor, she refused to call him Boss as all the other operatives did. Well, she wasn't an operative. She was a doctor and that in itself distinguished her from the rest of the team. That, and the minor fact that both Rihanna and herself were the only ones not to have altered DNA.

She might have held out for three months and had a slight detour into a private clinic that she knew before she started would bore her to near death, but she was here now. And she was ready to play.

Jazz was determined to build the medical side of the Centre into the best darn facility in the country. Even if her work would be completely under the radar, it didn't really matter. Somebody very high up the food chain knew about the Centre and provided the seemingly bottomless budget. That was enough for her at the moment.

Tom cleared his throat and she realised she'd zoned out for a moment, thinking over the contract and the last three months.

"If you'll just sign here." Tom pointed to a line on the last page. "You'll be officially part of the Centre."

Jazz accepted the pen he offered and slid the paperwork in front of her. She made a show of flicking through the contract as if she was trying to verify the content.

A quick scan reassured her it was in fact the same document that she'd been presented earlier in the year. She knew it would be, but it was smart to check and she wanted to draw it out a little longer, to keep Tom on his toes.

Finally, she uncapped the pen and added her signature to the bottom line where her name was. She'd just agreed to a five-year term with the Centre. It would set her up for life and provide her with the adventure she secretly craved.

Essentially, twenty-five years of school and many thousands of hours of studying had brought her to this point. Now she was going to enjoy herself. Sure, she was happy to work hard and do the best job she could but she wanted some excitement; she craved it, and the Centre, not to mention its operators, was just the place to provide it.

Jazz recapped the pen and pushed both it and the document back towards Tom.

"Welcome aboard, Miss Carter. I'm sure you'll be happy here. I dare say working together won't be without its challenges. However, I'm sure it will never be dull."

Jazz could hear the humour in his voice. She was on to him. Tom enjoyed their sparring as much as she did.

Well, if that was the case, she wasn't about to disappoint him.

Jazz let a light musical laugh escape.

"I agree—very unlikely to be dull." She raised her eyebrows and sent him a knowing smirk.

Tom cleared his throat and went on. "Right, now that we have the formalities out of the way, let's move on to what I need you looking at immediately."

Her interest immediately piqued. "Oh, what needs to be done?"

Tom settled back into his chair and clasped his hands together in front of him on the table. Jazz could tell this was something he wasn't comfortable with but knew had to be done regardless.

"I want you to do an evaluation on Quade. I want to know where he's really at after the gunshot wounds."

"I'm not sure I understand why, Tom. He seems physically fit to me. Is he somehow not up to 'normal strength'?" Jazz raised her hands to emphasise the air quotes. "At this stage, I'm not sure what the baseline for these guys is. I'm sure you've got reports or data that I can read up on." She looked at him again and knew then she wasn't on the right track.

"But that's not what you want me to evaluate, is it?"

"No, it's not. I want you to give me a psych eval."

"Can I ask why?"

"I think there's something going on with him, and I want to know what it is. Quade isn't big on talking; he internalises everything. I want to know what's up his butt. If it's something left over from the shooting, I want it out on the table and dealt with. I need him one hundred per cent focused and on the job. There's only one caveat. He can't know you're doing this. It'd eat him even more."

Jazz forced her face to remain unchanged. *He couldn't be serious.* "Let me get this straight. You expect me to do an evaluation without letting on I'm doing an evaluation, then provide support and therapy without letting on I'm giving it, if that's what I deem he needs."

"That's exactly what I expect."

"Oh, and now for my next trick, let me show you how I pull a rabbit from a hat." What Tom was asking was near impossible and he knew it.

Rather than addressing her comment, Tom looked at his watch. "I've got to run. I expect a preliminary report in a week. I'll have Rheeba notify you on the various orientation aspects you'll need to go through."

He stood and went to exit the room before she had time to facilitate a comeback. "Oh, by the way, Miss Carter, I know it won't be easy but I have no doubt you'll succeed."

With that, the doors closed and Jazz realised she'd not uttered a word in protest. She must be slipping. Normally she'd have had numerous snappy comebacks. Oh well, she'd fight him the traditional way. There was always email.

Chapter One

TJ Walsh looked to the left, and then the right, before releasing the clutch while gently depressing the accelerator. The big old Kenworth bonneted prime mover growled as it launched forward. Once the front left tyre was almost at the edge of the road, she palmed the wheel and spun it to the right with everything her small frame had. The engine roared, looking for another gear. She tapped the clutch to disengage, slipped the gear stick into neutral, and then tapped the clutch again to slide the shifter into a higher gear.

The beast rumbled forward, picking up speed; she started to straighten the wheel as she watched the long milk tanker behind her clear the gate posts. It was an intricate dance: one hand on the gear stick, one on the massive steering wheel, both feet on the pedals, one eye on the mirror, and the other on the road.

She shifted twelve times and swapped to a higher deck before she coaxed the big prime mover and trailer up to seventy kilometres an hour. The road was far from great; it was a narrow country road. The type you had to put half your vehicle into the rough when another car passed.

It was just on dark and she was running late. There'd been a problem with the pump at the dairy for moving the milk from the various tanks. So what should have taken about thirty minutes had taken the better part of two hours.

TJ needed to get home. Her mum was not good. Not good at all. She was in the middle of yet another bout of chemo and her younger brother and sister needed some direction. TJ placed a quick call and let them know she was running a couple of hours late. She tried to be around as much as possible to help out. Not just around the house but as an adult figure. Even though she was barely twenty-four herself, sometimes she felt closer to forty.

Her mother, Rosemary, had been battling breast cancer on and off for the last eight years. The doctors were hopeful they had it all this time but they'd said that at least twice before. There were never any guarantees with cancer.

She let out a huge sigh as she settled in to navigate the roads, shifting up or down two or three gears as the terrain dictated. She was rolling across the Numinbah Valley floor, heading back into the outskirts of Brisbane to drop off the milk her tanker contained.

Oh, how life can throw curve balls, she thought. Just over two and a half years ago, she'd been about to finish up her degree in physiotherapy. Then her father and eldest brother had been killed in a truck accident. They'd been driving two-up on a long haul between Adelaide and Brisbane, close to three thousand kilometres each way.

Her father had been driving and the coroner's report said he'd been under the influence of amphetamines. She knew in her heart this was total rubbish because there was no reason for her father to have taken the drug. That's why Alan was with him—to share the driving.

Something didn't add up but there was no way she could prove it. Knowing what she knew did nothing to diminish the anger in her belly. Her whole family had suffered as a result of the accident.

And that suffering was likely to go on for a few more years yet. TJ had immediately dropped out of school and taken over the running of the trucking company, Walsh Haulage. Her father had inherited the business from his father about ten years ago and built it up from six trucks to almost twenty.

Her job now was to hang on to it for the family! Not an easy task with a million-dollar debt hanging over her head for the value of the truck that the insurance wouldn't pay out on because her father had supposedly had the amphetamines in his system. Nor would they pay on his life insurance for the very same reason.

Trucking was a tough and cut-throat game at the best of times. Having an additional million-dollar debt and one less truck just made things more challenging.

She'd been brought up on hard work, and the task didn't normally daunt her. She'd learnt to live with fear over the last couple of years. The gut-wrenching, starve you of sleep type of fear.

That was what her life had become—one big terror. She was never without it. The only thing that changed day to day was the ferocity of its hold on her gut.

She was terrified for her family, terrified about keeping the business afloat, and terrified someone would eventually see through the flimsy façade of calm and competence she was working so hard at maintaining.

But today, well, that was another thing.

She was driving "Old Faithful" because she'd given her prime mover to Bob to take on the long haul to Melbourne. His normal prime mover had blown a fuel pump yesterday and they were waiting parts, which wouldn't arrive until at least tomorrow. Old Faithful held very fond memories for her. It was the first truck she ever drove. Her father had taught her when she'd finally grown tall enough to reach the pedals.

Not that she'd grown much more. She'd topped out at the massive height of five foot two. Well, at least she'd managed two more inches than her mother's five foot.

Yep, she remembered those days fondly. It was her father who'd taught her to navigate her way through the road ranger crash box transmission, much to her mother's horror and objection. Her mother was old-school Catholic—a woman belonged at home tending the family, raising kids, and so on. But her father had stood firm. In his opinion, just because she was a woman and small didn't mean she couldn't do something or be taught to.

And make no mistake, there had been lots of crashing as she learnt the technique of double-clutching through every gear. Never once did she recall him grimace as she grated gears along the way. He'd just offer quiet encouragement. God, she missed him and that was the problem with driving

Old Faithful. It was just like having him in the seat again. Reassuring in some ways but gut-wrenching lonely in others.

Now she had more problems to deal with: The monthly grind of making ends meet. Chasing creditors. Cashflow was everything when you were sailing as close to the wind as they were. One wrong step and it could mean a situation that there was no recovery from.

Her thoughts were on just that very subject when she downshifted to take a blind corner. The wall of the valley came down to meet the road. TJ bled off speed and danced between the clutch, brakes, and throttle, dropping back four gears. She punched the large nob on the dash to engage the Jake brake, which used the engine exhaust pressure to slow the truck. It was just as an added assistance. It took a lot to slow forty plus tonne of machine and milk.

Satisfied she'd got the truck to the speed she wanted, TJ used the entire road to manoeuvre the metallic beast around the corner. On corners like these, she loved her cabover Scania. The long nose of the Kenworth just took up that much more extra room. The Scania was a pleasure to drive after the twenty-five-year-old relic Old Faithful. She passed a silent prayer skywards in thanks for there not being any other cars coming in the opposite direction.

Just as she made it through the apex of the corner and could finally see the road ahead, instinct dictated she slam the brakes on. And slam them she did, because right in front of her was a car blocking the road, its nose firmly embedded in the deep ditch that snaked the edge of the road.

She felt the back of the trailer start to break away as she kept the pressure on the middle pedal. She only hoped she'd bled off enough speed to pull before she hit the car. There was no way she could sneak past its side. Her truck and trailer were just too big.

All twenty-two wheels locked, bit, and finally screeched to a stop with just inches to spare. Adrenalin surged through her veins and she took a huge breath.

Far-out! That had been close. She'd nearly taken out the car!

Her left hand immediately engaged the hazard lights and then punched the air brakes to lock the wheels before she flicked the transmission to neutral and sunk back in the seat to compose herself before she contemplated what needed to be done next.

The question was unwittingly answered for her when her door was wrenched open and a big hand clasped painfully around her wrist and tugged her from her seat.

Gravity took hold and she fell the seven or eight feet to the ground. She landed upright but her right ankle immediately buckled beneath her and she ended up on her knees. The rough bitumen road bit into her tender flesh through the fabric of her jeans.

Excruciating pain radiated up her right leg from her ankle. Before she could focus too much on righting herself, she was wrenched upwards under the arms and was being half dragged when suddenly she was dropped again to the rough bitumen of the road.

"Hey, leave her right there." A voice rang out from the darkness beside the tanker of her truck.

"Come on, come on, get out of here," she heard gruff voices call as booted feet scuffled away.

Then she heard two doors slam and the roar of a big vehicle, probably an F truck, as it peeled away up the valley.

TJ slumped to the ground, hurting everywhere. She was trying to roll into a sitting position when she felt gentle hands lift her from the ground.

"What…" she stammered.

"Shhhhh, sweets, it's okay, I've got you," a low voice murmured in her ear.

She didn't know why but she snuck an arm around his neck and relaxed into his chest as he strode off to the rear of the truck.

Something told her she was safe.

That someone cared.

Somehow he managed to open the passenger side door of the SUV and place her on the seat without putting her down. TJ yelped as the movement knocked her injured ankle into the door pillar. The sudden light from the interior cab blinded her for a moment.

Before she could say anything, the big man who had picked her up off the ground moved into the light and recognition dawned through her.

It was the guy from the horse sales a few months back. She was almost sure of it. What was he doing here?

He reached out and brushed a stray lock of her hair behind her ear that had escaped her high ponytail in all the excitement.

"Where are you hurt, Pixie?"

Her mind went numb for a moment. *What was he calling her Pixie for?* She hadn't answered, so he tried again.

"Sweetheart, my name's Rory, and I'm trying to find out where you're hurt."

She motioned to her right ankle without speaking, still too confused about everything to really make sense of it.

He gently placed his hands on her ankle and she smothered a squeal as her body jerked at the radiating pain.

"Mmm, guess that hurts like hell, hey?" He looked at her directly then, and she saw the warm chocolate brown eyes full of concern and immediately felt even safer.

"Just stay there for a second, sweetheart. I've got to make some calls and get this mess sorted out."

TJ took a deep breath and tried to make sense of what happened. It was evident now the car in the ditch had been a setup, but why? And who had tried to drag her off, and why would they want to do that?

She didn't know why this Rory guy was here but she had to admit she was mighty grateful just about now. TJ took another deep breath and focused on what needed to be done. First off, she needed to move the truck from this corner. It was beyond dangerous. Thankfully it was a really quiet road and it was a Sunday night.

Carefully, she used the door surround to lower herself to the ground and she cautiously placed a little weight on her right foot to test it and almost crumpled to the ground. The pain was that severe. It wasn't comparable to anything she could recall.

Not at all deterred when her mind was set on doing something, TJ half hopped, half hobbled to the edge of the trailer and then used its strong bulk as she manoeuvred her way towards the cabin. She grabbed hold of the railing beside the door and was using her upper body strength to haul herself into the cabin when strong hands gripped her around the waist and she was once again in Rory's arms.

"Sweets, what do you think you're doing? I distinctly recall having a similar conversation with you last time when there was a trailer on fire. What is it with you and doing crazy things?"

He plonked her unceremoniously back in the passenger side of the SUV and looked at her in disbelief. She didn't say a word, desperately trying to smother the pain of her ankle.

"I'm guessing you were trying to move the truck with a broken ankle?"

"Yes, I was."

"Not going to happen, sunshine." She went to protest but before she could form the words, he cut her off. "I'll do it."

"Can you drive a prime mover and trailer?"

He flashed her a cheeky smile and winked at her. "I'll figure it out." And he was gone before she could protest.

Seconds later, she heard the driver's door close and the idle of the beast change as it was slid into gear. The hiss of the air brakes sounded as they were released and then she watched as Old Faithful rumbled and jerked backwards past the SUV, before smoothing out to slowly crawl back round the corner. He cautiously reversed the truck and trailer back until there was a grass verge that was safe enough for the rig to be parked on while she sorted out what needed to happen to get the load of milk delivered.

The rig pulled to a halt. The hiss of the air indicated the park brake had once again been engaged and the hazard lights again illuminated the sides of the prime mover and trailer. Only then did she realise she was holding her breath. Reversing a strange rig around a blind corner in the dark was no easy feat and he'd done it like a pro.

TJ edged her body around a little till she was sitting in the seat properly. The support of the seat back was very welcome. When he hadn't returned immediately to her, she reached up to the rearview mirror and adjusted it so she could see what was happening behind her.

Rory was bent over, placing the last of the hazard triangles all heavy vehicles were required to carry in Australia. He'd placed them correctly, alerting other drivers of the potential hazard. She didn't miss the tight stretch of denim over his butt or the way they moulded to his thighs. The man sure filled out a pair of jeans very nicely and from the way his chest and shoulders had felt against her when she was in his arms, she was pretty sure he had the whole package going on.

Her train of thought was broken when headlights sliced through the interior. She glanced up and saw him lean over, talking to the driver of the car, pointing at the path they needed to take to avoid the truck or the car. She watched the car crawl past and accelerate away.

The silence was broken by Rory's approach. He placed a hand on the dash, and leant in to speak with her. "Okay, that's about as safe as I can make it just at the moment."

"I need to get that load of milk delivered."

He threw his head back and laughed. "Why am I not surprised?" he managed to get out around belly laughs.

TJ looked at him, puzzled. *What was he on about? It was obvious, wasn't it?*

"What?" she finally managed.

"After last time, nothing surprises me."

"We're contracted to get that milk to the processor. I'm already late because of a delay at the farm." She looked at her watch. "Blast, I have to get the milk there in the next hour or I'm going to cop penalties."

Agitation poured off her as he looked at her a little more and laughed again.

"What?" she huffed out in frustration.

"Sweetheart—who says blast anymore?"

"I do. I was brought up to be a lady and just because I drive a truck doesn't mean I have to use the language of a stereotypical truck driver."

Rory put his hands up in mock surrender. "Fair enough, Pixie. I can appreciate that."

"Why are you calling me Pixie?"

"Because, sweets, you are a pixie. You're tiny, gorgeous, and well, you look like a pixie." He threw his hands up in exasperation.

"Well, I don't think I like it."

He chuckled again and shrugged. "Well, if you don't like it, then what's your name?"

She straightened her back and squared her shoulders. "My name is TJ." Her voice sounded very proper.

"You don't want me to call you Pixie but you're happy to be called TJ? What sort of name is TJ?" She could tell he was working hard to contain the amusement that this scene was undoubtedly creating for him.

"It's short for Teresa Jane."

"Well, now I can see why TJ. But sorry, you're Pixie to me."

The man was unbelievable. She huffed out a, "Whatever." She didn't have time for this; she needed to get the truck to the processing plant—time was her enemy.

"Look, Rory, thanks for your help and for preventing me from being abducted but I really need to get going now. I've got to get that rig to the processing plant."

"You're not going anywhere but the hospital, Pixie. And while we're on the topic, you're remarkably calm for someone who was almost abducted. You know who those guys were, don't you?"

His eyes pierced into her. TJ looked away, unable to maintain his scrutiny. The last few months of her life had become even tougher. The fear in her gut had reached a whole new level of pain. She had a very good idea what the abduction attempt was about but now was not the time.

"Rory, as I said, thanks so much for your help but I really need to get going." TJ grabbed hold of the handle above the door and the dash and went to lever herself out of the SUV.

"How do you think you're going to drive that monster, Pixie? I'm staggered that you can reach the pedals and spin the wheel on that beast on your best day, let alone when you have a broken ankle."

"Rory, thanks for your concern but I have no choice. I have to get that load of milk to the processor in less than an hour otherwise I will be up for stiff penalties. Penalties I can ill afford right now."

She glanced up at him for a second as she tried to move from the SUV. To be truthful, all she'd really managed to do was move closer into him. Her last words had brought a change in him. Something she'd said hit home with him.

He reached for her and lifted her back onto the seat.

Seriously—this being lifted, carried, and manhandled (albeit gently) was getting old already. It was not as if she didn't realise she was small, but one thing she knew beyond belief was that she was capable. Her father had raised her to be, even if her mother had the helpless thing down pat. Right now her sole focus had to be on making the delivery.

"Pixie, if it means that much to you, I'll help you get the milk there."

She breathed a huge sigh of relief and jumped at his offer—she was desperate. "Thank you. Glad we're finally on the same page. By my calculations, it's about a fifty-minute drive and I now have fifty-two minutes to get there."

Before she could say anything further, another car approached and pulled in behind them. Rory immediately walked back from the SUV towards the vehicle. She glanced in the rearview mirror and saw a huge man get out of the vehicle and a tall, curvy woman. Rory opened the back door and grabbed a bag out of the back seat.

How strange, she thought. *Did he know these people?* Her heart rate began to race. Something very strange indeed was going on. Were they somehow involved?

The woman almost bounced up to the door and she stuck her head in. "Hi, I'm Jazz, and I'm a doctor. Let's take a look at you," she commanded with a smile.

TJ was almost overwhelmed by the presence of this woman. She was larger than life and appeared out of nowhere to help her?

She must have looked alarmed because Rory chose that moment to reassure her. "It's okay, Pixie. Jazz and Quade are friends of mine. I called them. It just so happens it's your lucky day and Jazz is a real doctor."

"So Rory mentioned your ankle."

"Yes, it's not the best."

At her comment, she heard laughter.

"Not the best, sweetheart? I'm not a doctor and I can tell you it's broken," Rory confirmed for her.

While Rory had been talking, Jazz had gently taken her ankle between her hands. She started to slightly move it and TJ yelped in pain.

She'd tried to refrain from crying out but it just hurt so much.

Jazz stood and said, "Okay, I agree with Rory. It's most likely broken. We need to get you to a hospital for an x-ray. I can give you a shot for the pain to make it bearable before you get there. I want you to leave that boot on to try to keep the swelling down until we get you to hospital."

"No, I have to drive. Look, I don't mean to sound ungrateful but I really have to go—now."

"Arrh. Look, I'm sorry; what's your name?" TJ and Rory both answered Jazz at once. TJ said, "TJ" and Rory said, "Pixie."

Jazz just shook her head and gave them both a curious look. "Well TJ, Pixie, you can't drive with that foot. The pain factor alone would be insane."

"I've got to go—please." TJ almost begged.

Fortunately, Rory picked that moment to take control of the situation. "Okay, how about I take the truck to the processors and you go to hospital?"

"I can't leave that load until it's delivered. It's my responsibility and I have to sign the load in. I'm not going anywhere near a hospital until I have it delivered," she huffed out, frustrated.

"Okay. Jazz, can you give her something for the pain? Seems the quicker we get the milk to the processor, the quicker Miss Stubborn gets to the hospital." He emphasised the Miss Stubborn by glaring at her. She didn't know him well enough to know whether he was joking or not.

Jazz rummaged through her medical bag and came up with some pills and a bottle of water.

"Here, some Pandeine Forte—they'll help take the edge off the pain."

TJ quickly downed the pills with a swig of the offered water. The pills were a godsend. If she admitted the truth, her ankle hurt like hell; she'd never felt pain like it. She moved to the edge of the seat. "Right, let's go. Time is a ticking and we'll be lucky to make it as it is."

Rory immediately swept her into his arms again. The giant fell in beside him, still silent.

"Pix, this is Quade."

She managed a mumbled, "Hi" as Rory tried to gently carry her to the truck. She thought she heard a grunted response from the stranger.

"Quade, grab the door, mate."

Quade immediately jogged up and opened the passenger door. He turned and Rory thrust her at the stranger. "Here, hold Pix for a second while I get in and then you can pass her to me."

Strong arms enclosed her small body and she felt swamped in the massive power of the man who held her. It was as if it radiated from him in waves. A second later, she felt herself being thrust upwards and another set of strong arms encased her and gently lowered her to the passenger seat.

Her foot bumped against the floor and she let out a huge hiss of pain.

"Sorry, sweetheart." He winced at her pain.

Fortunately the cab of Old Faithful was large and roomy and easily allowed for Rory's big frame to slide over into the driver's seat.

He immediately fired up the engine. She thought to ask, "Umm, please tell me you have a heavy combination licence." The last thing she needed was further potential insurance hassles. His response was just to smile and wink.

That told her nothing, but oh what a smile. When he smiled, it changed his whole face. It was like a huge magnet sucking you into the depths of those rich chocolate coloured eyes.

TJ couldn't believe she was trusting one of her trucks to this guy, but she had to get the load to the processor and if she was being totally honest with herself, there was no way she was capable of driving. Nor did she have the time to try to get one of her off-duty drivers to get out here and move the load.

Rory shifted into gear and released the air brakes. He slowly released the clutch and increased the throttle. Old Faithful took one lurch forward and then smoothed out. He quickly needed another gear. This was the problem when you had eighteen of them, and as Rory went to shift, the gears screamed their protest by way of a ghastly metallic noise and she immediately knew he had the revs too high.

"Let the revs drop off and slide it between fifteen hundred and seventeen hundred revs. That's the sweet spot." The truck lurched again as he finally got the gear. He momentarily shot her a sideways grin and she knew by his look that her mention of the "sweet spot" had turned his thoughts into something very adult and raw.

Oh wow! That smile and what the unspoken lust in his eyes relayed sent her stomach fluttering and her female core sprang to life. Even the pain in her ankle was momentarily overridden by the spike of lust she felt for him.

Rory's changes got smoother and smoother as he finally got the truck up to cruising speed.

"Okay, where are we going?"

"Just head towards Nerang, then out onto the M1. The processing plant is at Yatala."

"Okay. That's just off the M1 south of Brisbane, right?" His focus returned to the road. She could tell he was still getting comfortable driving Old Faithful.

"Yes." She made no further comment and let him settle in. He was doing great. She didn't know anyone who didn't reshape the gear cogs the first time they drove a rig like this. These old trucks were cantankerous and had personalities of their own.

"So how old is this truck?" he asked, leaning forward to rub his hand affectionately over the dash. The only way to describe the beast was a relic. A very well-maintained one, but a relic nonetheless. The truth was any other trucking company would have retired the truck years ago but the prime mover held sentimental value to the family.

"Umm, I think Old Faithful's about twenty-five years old."

Rory burst out laughing. "Old Faithful?" He turned and raised his eyebrows at her.

"Yes, this old truck was the first one my grandfather ever bought brand-new. There's no way we could part with her. So we keep her well maintained and use her whenever we have the need," TJ explained.

"Yeah, last time I saw you, you were driving a near-new cabover Scania, if I'm not mistaken. That was a sweet truck."

She let out a giggle. She wondered whether he'd recognised her. The memory of him helping her hadn't faded in the last three months since he'd fleetingly come to her rescue the first time. "That's my baby. I call her Annabelle."

Rory let out a hoot of laughter, double-clutching and downshifting twice as he took a bend. She'd quickly learnt to brace herself against the door and the seat to avoid bumping her foot.

"So why Annabelle?"

"I could ask you why Pixie?"

"Oh, that's simple. I looked at you three months ago and Pixie immediately sprang to mind. The image hasn't changed, sweetheart."

TJ huffed. *He was impossible.* "Well, I looked at my truck, hopped in and immediately thought Annabelle. So Annabelle it is." Tit for tat.

"Fair enough. So tell me about what we're doing."

"What do you mean?" she asked, puzzled.

"Fill me in on how the run works," he said more seriously.

"Simple, really. I pick up the milk from the various farms and deliver to the processors. I sign the paperwork. Then do it again the next day. I get a payment into our account each month for the deliveries as per the contract amount and if I'm late, I have money docked." She looked at her watch and knew they would be cutting it fine. She hoped there were not any traffic issues. "Lots of money."

"How long have we got, Pixie?"

"Thirty-three minutes."

Rory was just guiding the big rig out onto the motorway and he immediately upped the pace, pushing through the gears like a man on a mission. She appreciated him trying to make her deadline.

"So a tanker full of milk—is it just from one farm or multiple farms?"

"It could be either. But in this case, the milk we have on board is all from the same farm."

He nodded his understanding.

They had thirty minutes before they needed to be at the processing plant and she needed to clear something up that had been bugging her for the last hour. TJ took a deep breath and launched in. "It seems to be too much of a coincidence that you were at the horse sales that day and then just happened to come to my rescue. Who are you working for and what's your interest in me?"

She saw something flicker momentarily across his face at her words. Without doubt, he was considering her questions and formulating his answer carefully.

For the first time tonight, the lights from the motorway were giving her the opportunity to really study his face. Yes, just as she recalled, he was seriously handsome. But when he smiled, he became something else totally. There was no other way to describe it but magnetic. And if he was the positive charge, she felt like the polar opposite negative. Uncontrollably attracted.

Rory gripped the steering wheel a little tighter at her question. He'd been waiting for her to put it all together and ask the question he was dreading. There was no easy way to tell the principle in an assignment that they were the "principle." He'd also learnt a valuable lesson recently from Brayden. It was best to tell the principle early, and come clean on things. Stringing them along just didn't work. He wouldn't tell her everything just yet, but he would tell her the truth about what he could divulge.

He glanced at Pixie briefly to judge her mood. She seemed to be patiently waiting his response. "Well, you're partially right. The horse sales were a total coincidence. Our meeting there was a purely chance thing. However, today's meeting was not by chance. I've been tailing you this afternoon."

Rory heard Pixie suck in a breath that she tried to disguise. She sat straighter in the seat and turned slightly towards him, alarm clearly registering on her face. "And why, may I ask, would you be tailing me?"

He didn't hesitate; rather, he launched right in. "I work for a government-sponsored organisation that specialises in the control and management of biological, agricultural, and environmental issues. I've been tasked with investigating your operations. We believe the milk you've been carting has been contaminated or at least produced using genetically modified dairy cattle. As you may or may not know, this is highly illegal due to the overwhelming evidence of side effects arising from consumption of the milk or the products it's manufactured into."

Rory took his eyes momentarily from the road and noticed the shock that had spread across her beautiful features. She had an innocence and freshness about her that was unique and incredibly appealing. Her cheekbones were full and high but delicately tapered to a pert chin, which only added to the whole "Pixie" package. Her nose was straight, narrow, and slightly turned up at the end. But her eyes—wow! They were perfectly almond shaped with long lashes. He knew they were blue but he couldn't name the actual shade in the muted light. That would be a question for him to answer later on. The glorious long curtain of hair he remembered as near white silk was tied up in a ponytail today, but his memory of it out and flowing had not lessened in the past months.

"What sort of side effects?" It wasn't the question he

expected but then that seemed to be the norm with Pixie. She did and said things that he didn't expect.

"Apparently cancer is the main one. Significantly increased rates of breast, colon, and prostate cancer."

He glanced sideways again and saw her suck back a further shocked look. She seemed deep in thought. Something was obviously upsetting her about the information she'd learned. Again, not a reaction he'd been expecting. He'd expected fireworks, not shocked contemplation. A few long moments went by before she finally turned to him again and asked, "So exactly what does 'investigate my operations' mean?"

"It means I need to understand and review how you go about making these deliveries. The enzyme has been found in the milk at the processing plant. The milk has to get from the dairy to the processing plant. It's my job to find out which farms are using the genetically modified cattle, how they're getting the GM drugs in the first place to create the cattle, and how we stop it."

She looked surprised. "So you're some sort of detective?"

"Not really. We're referred to by the organisation we work for as operatives or operators."

He glanced sideways and noticed she nodded her head in understanding. Pixie also snuck yet another glance at her watch and shifted restlessly in her seat. She had to be in huge pain. The pills Jazz had given her wouldn't ease the pain of a break very much. Fact was, she was hiding it well. He had a hunch that might all change when this load of milk finally made it to its destination.

He pressed down harder on the accelerator. The tachometer moved up to just below the redline as he eased the old truck up to its maximum engine rev range. He was probably pushing ten or fifteen kilometres over the speed limit. He hoped to God he didn't get a ticket. They couldn't afford the time. Surely the universe wouldn't do that to him today.

A sign flashed past, indicating the Yatala exit.

"Take the next exit. Just watch your speed on the off-ramp; it's tighter than it looks."

"Cool."

She directed him down through the streets of the industrial estates to the heavily fenced processing plant.

When he pulled up at the guardhouse, he was given a very cautious—or was it suspicious?—look from the guard inside.

Pixie must have noted the look because she yelled out and half raised herself from her seat so the guard could see her.

"Hey Lenny, it's me, TJ. Rory's just helping me out tonight. I've hurt my ankle."

The guard's face immediately changed, his voice and face not masking his concern for her wellbeing. "Oh, angel, you okay?"

"I'll be fine. Did we make it on time?"

Lenny looked at his watch and smiled up at her.

"By my watch you did."

"Thanks, Lenny. I owe you one."

"Don't owe me nothin', love. Seeing your smile is thanks enough for an old man."

Rory watched this conversation over his lap with interest.

"Oh you, old charmer you!" she joked with him. "You want this in processing two?"

"Let me check the manifests." After rustling his papers, he said, "Yep, processing two it is, angel face."

"Thanks, Lenny. Catch you on the way out."

Rory watched the exchange with interest. The concern and affection from Lenny was genuine. There was no hint of anything else.

TJ eased herself back into the seat and let out the breath she'd been holding. For the first time, he noted, she'd forgotten to mask the pain. He knew then he'd have done anything to take the pain from her. The best thing he could do was turn this load around quick smart and get her to a hospital.

He put the truck into gear and followed her directions to unload the milk. They were met at processing two by a short, thickset man.

"Why don't you stay in the cab, while I unload this?"

Rory was out of the cab and had the door closed before she had a chance to protest. There was no way she was getting out of that cab until they reached their final destination.

As soon as Rory got down from the cab, a bloke dressed in navy cargos and shirt with a florescent high-visibility vest approached him. He carried a clipboard and had suspicion written all over him as well.

Rory broke the ice by flashing him his friendly grin and extending his hand. "Rory Southall. Hey, I'm just helping TJ out tonight. She's hurt her ankle pretty bad and needed me to drive."

Just like Lenny, the man's face immediately changed as well when he heard the news about TJ. He accepted Rory's hand in a firm shake and introduced himself as Don.

"How'd she get banged up?"

"Oh, she took a bit of a misstep from the cab of the truck and rolled her ankle."

"Well, she's such a little thing, doin' more than a man's work each day. Had to happen sooner or later. I swear that girl never stops. In that truck seven days a week. Must be hard with what's happen'."

Rory's ears pricked up at the innocent slip Don had made.

"What exactly is going on, Don?" Rory asked, trying to sound as casual as possible as the two of them worked to hook up the pump that would empty the milk from the tanker. Rory could sense a story here. He knew it.

Don immediately realised his gaff and clammed up. "Not my place to say. Best be talkin' to TJ if you want to know. She doesn't like people getting in her business."

Rory nodded his head. "Duly noted. Thanks for the advice, mate."

Interesting. Very interesting. He wondered whether this, whatever it was, was the reason she hadn't been terribly surprised about the attempted abduction tonight. TJ had some explaining to do. He threw his senses out, scanning. It was an integral part of him, as if he had another limb. It dawned on him then that the unsettling restless feeling he'd had throughout the day had disappeared since he'd met TJ tonight. Now he knew exactly what the "something big" was about.

Chapter Two

TJ sat up in bed. She was in hospital and desperately needed to get out in a hurry. She swung her legs to the side and nearly ended up on the floor. The weight of the heavy removable cast on her right leg provided more momentum than she expected.

"Darn." She swore and lowered herself to the floor gently. She hobbled to the bathroom and took care of her needs. She'd been here two nights now. That was two nights too many.

Rory had brought her in here straight after they'd got the milk delivered. She'd wanted to get the truck back to the yard but he'd refused and driven her to the front door as casual as you please in a twenty-two wheeled rig. And just as surprising, he'd managed to get a break in the parked cars long enough to pull Old Faithful into. The car parking fairies loved him, evidently. She wished a little of his luck would rub off on her. She could sure use it right about now.

What had proceeded was a series of x-rays and examinations, which resulted in a trip to the operating theatre yesterday afternoon to pin the broken bones in place. Now she was the proud temporary owner of a bandaged ankle and a removable cast. Great, just more challenges!

A quick glance around the room and she found the bag Rory had dropped off for her yesterday after he'd taken the truck back for her. Since he'd turned up in time to help her out the other night, he'd stuck to her like glue, only being away from her side when absolutely necessary.

First, he'd sat with her through all the exams and x-rays. Then he'd been waiting when she woke up from the anaesthetic. She'd been very sleepy last night and hadn't felt like talking. He'd staunchly sat in the chair beside her bed, almost as if he were playing guard.

TJ was getting the distinct impression Rory had decided he was sticking close to her; she really needed to talk about that with him now that she felt a little better. In fact, she was surprised that he wasn't here in the room with her now. She was fast coming to realise he was unique. It would be easy to be overwhelmed by his charm, good looks, and downright yumminess. Despite being raised a "good Catholic girl," she liked and appreciated hot men as much as the next girl. And Rory was off the scale when it came to hotness.

As she rummaged through and pulled out the clothes her aunt had packed for her, she realised just how much she was doing things on her own. That in itself caused the familiar fear to chew at her belly.

Her family loved her; she knew that beyond doubt. They also needed her. Big time. Her mother was too affected by the chemo to do anything much at the moment. It really knocked her around. Fortunately, her mother's younger sister, Clara, was looking after her mother and making sure the house still ran. The kids still had to get to school and sports and all those things. She had to make sure the business ran and that wasn't going to happen from a hospital bed.

TJ was sitting on the bed in her panties, and just finishing buttoning up the cotton blouse when Rory walked through the door to her room. His eyes cut to her partially clothed form. The look that crossed his face left her in no doubt he was enjoying the view. She hastily moved to pull the blanket from the bed across her thighs to cover up.

"Sorry, Pixie. I thought you'd still be asleep." He turned his head away from her slightly, obviously trying to be polite but she hadn't missed the male appreciation in his eyes.

"Umm, would you mind giving me a moment to finish getting dressed?"

"Oh sure—I'll just step outside." He flashed her an amused smile and promptly walked out the door.

TJ let out a breath and hurriedly reached to pull the denim shorts over the cast. It was a struggle but with some jiggling and persistence, she managed. She zipped and buttoned the fastenings. Wow, she felt exhausted and she'd only gotten dressed.

"Umm, you can come in now," she called a little breathlessly.

Rory immediately came through the door and flashed her his thousand-watt smile. Butterflies immediately erupted in the pit of her stomach. He was overwhelming. Rory sank his large frame into the armchair beside the bed and sipped from the extra-large takeaway coffee cup he held.

"I would have got you one if I knew you were awake. You're welcome to some of this." He thrust his hand forward, offering her the cup.

"Ah, no thanks," she said, waving his hand away.

TJ reached for the call buzzer and pressed the button.

"You need something for the pain?" His voice was full of concern.

"No. I need to get out of here."

"But Pixie, the doctor hasn't even seen you this morning."

"No but I need to get to the depot and make sure everything is alright."

"Don't you have anyone who can fill in for you, at least for a few days?"

She let out a long sigh, making no effort to cover the fact that this conversation was not one she wanted to be having with him. TJ didn't bother to hide the annoyance she felt. "No, I don't, Rory. I need to make sure everything is happening as it should be."

He looked away and she could see him taking a breath and obviously trying to come up with another line of argument to stay here.

"Rory, I can't stay here. I have to check on things. The business is really struggling at the moment and I need to make sure everything is done so that we get paid."

He turned back to her, and she saw something cross his face.

"That comment you made back at the races. You said, 'It's not my life I'm worried about, but my livelihood.' What exactly did you mean by that?"

"Exactly as it sounds." TJ was shocked he remembered the comment she'd made over three months ago. Did he remember their first meeting as clearly as she did?

"Explain it to me, Pixie. How could it possibly be so bad that a couple of days could make all the difference?"

She leant back against the bedhead. "Short story is I took over the company just over two years ago when my father and eldest brother were killed in a truck crash. According to the coroner, my father had been taking amphetamines to stay awake. No way that was the case. Alan was with him to share the driving, and regardless, there is no way he'd take drugs to stay awake.

"Anyway, I had to drop out of university to keep the business running. The insurance company refused to pay out on the wrecked prime mover and trailer. Nor would they pay my father's life insurance. Since then I've been paying off the debt for the truck and trying to keep this business afloat. It's not always easy."

"How much do you owe?"

"I don't think that's any real business of yours." Her voice portrayed all the prickles she felt at talking about her family's shaky finances.

"You're right but I'm making it my business. You can either give me the information I want or I can have one of my teammates, Rheeba, run a check on you, and I'll know a few seconds after I request it. Either way, I'll get the information."

Cold embarrassment and frustration ran through her veins. People knowing her business didn't sit well with her. But she knew he'd do it. His actions over the last two days indicated that he'd be very tough to shake when he had his mind set on something. What did it matter? The state of their finances was hardly a federal secret.

"We owe close to a million on the wrecked truck, plus we have all of the normal ongoing payments for the rest of the fleet. Trucking is a tough business and the additional expense without the income it should return, have made things very tight." She let out a breath and looked away.

"How tight?"

Her voice dropped to almost a whisper. "We're running month to month. There are no reserves."

His eyes sought hers and locked on. "You're not behind?"

Talk about being put on the spot. "No, as long as I keep everything happening, we should be able to keep our heads above water. Just. I didn't need the medical bills from here, but that just seems to be my lot at the moment. Lots of unplanned expenses."

Rory drained the last of his jumbo coffee as the nurse walked in. A quick exchange followed where TJ let it be known she was on a tight time frame and wanted out as soon as possible. After protesting for a few minutes, the nurse agreed to go find the doctor.

TJ had slumped back against the bedhead, dearly wishing she could while away a couple of days doing nothing. Rory chose that moment to press on with their discussion.

"So tell me about what happened the other night, Pixie. It was obviously a setup and I have a pretty good idea you knew those jokers. What's the story, princess?"

TJ felt her temper rising. He wanted too much from her. More than she felt comfortable giving. "What is it with you that you can't use my name? Why is that?" she fumed. She used her irritation at his choice of names for her to deflect the real reason she was annoyed. She didn't want to talk about the other night. It was her problem to deal with.

Further to her annoyance, her display of temper did nothing but result in a belly laugh from Rory. If he wasn't so good-natured and attractive, he'd be a downright pest.

"Sweetheart, there is no way I'm calling such a beautiful lady by that God-awful abbreviation."

TJ was momentarily taken back. *He thought she was beautiful? Well, he'd just said it, didn't he? Did he mean it?*

"As I told you the other day—my name is Teresa Jane and I prefer TJ, and before you say anything further—yes, I was raised to be a good little Catholic girl." She knew her voice was filled with sass and attitude, but he was pushing her buttons.

His response was to flash her a devilish grin. "Mmm, I

wonder how good a girl?" as he finished his words on a chuckle and an insinuation.

"Ahh, you're impossible!" she cried.

"Don't worry, baby; you'll get used to me. Apparently, I grow on people." He smiled again at her. The fact that he was making her uncomfortable seemed the least of his concerns. "Now let's go back to the question I asked about the other night. Don't think I didn't pick up your avoidance."

TJ was desperately trying to figure out what to say when the doctor walked into the room. Ah, saved by the bell! Maybe her luck was improving?

Rory guided her into the boardroom at the new Centre headquarters. Guide maybe wasn't the right word. Truth was he almost had his right arm wrapped around her slender waist, making sure she didn't fall. Pixie hadn't mastered the crutches just yet and seemed intent to hobble along as if she were in an imaginary three-legged race. She only had to ask. He'd be more than happy to be tied down one side of her delectable body.

He contemplated that for a moment. Yeah, there was definitely something there. A fire, a flash, a spark—whatever you want to call it. And it felt damn near at ignition point, if you wanted his opinion.

His cock had been half hard for the last two days. It hadn't slipped his notice either, that the gnawing feeling in his gut had not come back. Nope, since he'd been near Pixie, he felt more centred and focused. Mmm, interesting. He had a theory about what his mate Brayden would say about all that. No doubt he'd be talking to him about it soon enough.

Once he'd graciously seated Pixie in a chair that afforded her a very pretty view of the Broadwater, he slid himself into the one beside.

"So what is this place?" she asked.

"Oh, this is our new headquarters. Our boss wanted a word with you about the tainted milk."

She nodded her acceptance. It had taken some doing to get her here in the first place. She'd insisted on going immediately to her depot upon release from the hospital. The doctor had been very unhappy about that and had wanted her to stay on for a few more hours for a little more monitoring just to make sure everything was okay.

He'd reluctantly agreed to let her go when Rory explained she'd be under the immediate care of Dr Jazz Carter. Apparently he knew her and said to pass on his regards.

The heavy double doors cracked open and the boss filed through with Jazz and Quade hot on his heels. The boss took his seat at the head of the table and as customary, opened the notebook and file he'd been carrying. Quade and Jazz selected seats opposite. Rory didn't miss the amused gleam in Quade's eye.

"Right, let's get started." The boss broke the silence. "First off, let me introduce myself, Miss Walsh. My name is Tom Anderson and I'm the man in charge of this organisation."

Pixie politely extended her slender hand in greeting and the boss returned the gesture briefly, closing his larger one around hers.

"Nice to meet you, Mr Anderson."

It never ceased to amaze Rory how people automatically defaulted to being very formal in their addressing of the boss. The only two people he'd seen buck the trend were Jazz and Rihanna.

"And you, Miss Walsh." The pleasantries out of the way, the boss ploughed on. "Right. I understand you ran into some trouble the other evening, Miss Walsh, and have sustained a nasty injury as a result."

TJ held the boss's fixed stare and confirmed his statement. "Ah, yes, I had a little bit of an accident."

The boss raised his right eyebrow and intensified his stare towards Pixie. "Miss Walsh, being dragged from your truck with enough force to break your ankle is hardly a little accident. Rory has briefed me and he is of the opinion you know your assailants. Who were those men and why were you targeted?"

Pixie immediately flashed him a glare that spelled *how could you?* without uttering a word. Rory knew he was now officially in the doghouse as far as Pixie was concerned. Oh well. At least he wouldn't have to put in too much effort to chase her with a busted-up ankle. Not that he wouldn't enjoy chasing her delectable rear end.

"I'm not sure it's any of your business, Mr Anderson." It came over very prim and proper and Rory felt his dick twitch at the tone. She'd been driving him crazy for two days.

Please, Pixie, don't, he mentally pleaded with her. He snuck a sideways glance at Quade, and he duly noted the smirk that had now joined the knowing gleam in his eyes.

The smirk confirmed what Rory already knew. Quade could smell the pheromones they were both letting off. There was no hiding attraction from another member of his team. One with their super senses, anyway.

"Miss Walsh, we can do this the easy way or the hard way. The outcome will be the same. I will get to the bottom of this. The only difference is whether you choose to cooperate willingly or we have to resort to more drastic measures. Your choice."

Rory immediately felt his hackles rise at the tone and manner the boss had used with Pixie. "I'm not sure we have to be quite so heavy handed here, boss. I'm sure Pixie will tell us everything we want to know."

The boss shook his head and pinned Rory with the steel of his glare. "Thanks for your opinion, Mr Southall. I don't recall asking for it."

Rory felt a low growl surge up through his throat and he wasn't quick enough to suppress it. Nor did he want or attempt to. He was very rarely irritated or pissed off. Now seemed to be the exception. The boss's attitude towards Pixie had shot his temper to the red line. He noted Jazz looked up in alarm but said nothing. Quade just continued to smirk.

The boss was just about to say something when Pixie got in first. It was as if she'd decided to explain rather than risk the two of them facing off any further. "I believe they're from a rival trucking company. They're keen to put me out of business and take over my contracts. Sometimes their methods aren't exactly polite."

The boss turned his attention back to Pixie and Rory felt himself relax a little. "How long has this been going on, Miss Walsh?"

"It's hard to say. I've suspected it for a while but there have been a number of incidents over the last three or four months. This is the first time I've ever been physically targeted as I was the other night."

"I see." The boss looked down at his papers and shuffled a few around. "I'm assuming Mr Southall has briefed you on our interest in your company."

"Yes. Something to do with the milk we cart potentially being from genetically modified dairy cattle."

"That is correct. We are the agency responsible for investigating and eliminating the source of the contaminant. We'll be working with the other appropriate food authorities to aid in their eradication of the product through the supply chain."

Pixie nodded her understanding of the situation but said nothing.

"I understand this is probably a major inconvenience to you but we will not tolerate the possibility of innocent people being unwittingly exposed to a significantly increased cancer risk through ingestion of this tainted product."

"I understand and fully support the position," Pixie confirmed for the boss. That took him a little by surprise but only for the good. "My mother has suffered from cancer for eight years. It is a very debilitating and horrific disease. I wouldn't wish it on my worst enemy. If I can help you stop this problem, then I'm happy to cooperate."

For the first time, the boss let a genuine smile soften his commanding features and he nodded his head. "Thank you, Miss Walsh. Your cooperation will be most appreciated and I'm sure that will make Mr Southall's job significantly easier."

Pixie shifted uncomfortably in her chair. The large leather executive chair seemed far too big for her delicate frame. "What exactly do you mean by that, Mr Anderson?"

The boss glanced up from his papers, and locked his eyes with Pixie's. "Very simply, Miss Walsh, I'm assigning Rory to be your shadow." A very audible gasp escaped her pretty pink lips. "My gut tells me these incidents you've been having are somehow connected. And until we can learn more about the threat of the contaminated milk and also the source of your troubles, I want Rory with you. The last thing we need is for another attempt, like the one made the other night, to be successful."

"But I have a business to run," she protested.

"I understand that, Miss Walsh, as does Rory. He will not interfere in the operation of that business. I have no doubt you're being targeted, nor do I have any doubt you've unknowingly carted contaminated milk, probably for quite some time. He will, however, be your shadow twenty-four seven until I'm satisfied this situation is resolved."

Before Pixie could utter another word, the boss closed the file and turned his attention to Jazz and Quade. Something told Rory that Pixie wouldn't protest any further in this forum. From what little he'd seen of her, he knew she'd been brought up to be respectful to authority and her elders. The boss represented both of those.

"What have you two got to report?"

Was that a hint of amusement Rory noted?

Rory watched Jazz glance to Quade, as if expecting him to speak. When he didn't, she prompted, "You're the operative. I'm just the quack, remember?" She'd plastered a sickly sweet smile on her face as she delivered the comment to Quade. He'd wondered how long Jazz could refrain from sounding off at Quade. She'd done well by previous standards. Her control must be improving.

"We've turned up nothing so far. The two leads we've investigated turned out to be legit." Quade cut his glare to Jazz and drew the corners of his mouth up and then dropped them immediately in a blatantly sarcastic smile. The boss ignored the exchange between the two of them.

"I'll have Rheeba send through the latest intel. I want you two out there again tracking it down—surely they can't hide

these cattle in broad daylight. Okay, people—get busy." The
boss started to stand but Rory had something further to add.

"Ah, Boss, I'd like Jazz to take over the management of
Miss Walsh's ankle."

The boss looked at him quizzically for a moment and then
nodded in agreement. "That's fine." He looked up at Jazz.
"Miss Carter, if you wouldn't mind."

"Not at all, Tom," Jazz replied to his retreating form. She
got out of her chair and moved around the table to take the
seat that Rory had just vacated. Rory stood back from the
table to allow Jazz to sit.

"Hey Q, why don't we go catch up with Rheeba while
these two go through the treatment needed on Pixie's ankle?"
Rory suggested and moved to the door. Quade said nothing
and followed him out, but not before Rory felt the tempered
amusement stalking him through the door. He knew he
wasn't going to escape the tease from Quade. Might as well
get it over and done with.

TJ spun on her chair slightly to allow her to face Jazz.
Jazz was no less of a huge presence today than when she'd
first met her briefly the other night.

"Looks like you've had a tough couple of days." Jazz
nodded at the cast but TJ knew she was referring to the
bigger picture, not just her unattractive and mobility-limiting
cast.

"I guess you could say that," she offered diplomatically,
not quite sure what to say to Jazz just yet.

At her words, Jazz broke into a musical laugh and leant
forward and patted her on the knee. "Oh, I love it! Another
queen of understatement. Rih is going to love you."

TJ studied Jazz, even more confused.

"Oh, TJ, sorry. I'm just playing. Rihanna is my very best
friend. She married Rory and Quade's teammate Brayden last
weekend."

She nodded her understanding at Jazz's words but was still confused. "Umm, I'm not sure I understand what you're getting at?"

"TJ, I have a strong feeling we're going to be seeing a lot more of you around here for a long time to come."

"Okay—I'm still not sure what you're driving at, Jazz." TJ was really confused now.

"So you're the type who needs to be bashed over the head with it—okay, we can do that, too." Jazz sighed. "Rory's got the hots for you, big time. I'd say that gorgeous hunk of a man is going to be doing everything he can to convince you to hang around."

TJ took a deep breath and sat up straighter. Jazz's words caught her completely off guard. Not only by the manner in which she'd delivered them but also the point she was making.

"Oh, I don't think so. I'm sure he's just doing his job. Besides, I've got a trucking company to run. The last thing I need is a relationship."

Jazz burst out laughing. "Well then, just use him for sex. We all need that from time to time."

TJ knew her mouth was wide open. Jazz's last comment had floored her. Was she for real? She'd meet Jazz for no more than five minutes two days ago. Now she'd spent seconds in her company and they were apparently having a conversation about her sex life. What alternate universe had she descended into?

"I'm sorry, TJ. I have a tendency to be very 'in your face.' I can only be the professional doctor for so long before I shake it off." Jazz emphasised the professional doctor with air quotes. "So let's move to less confronting territory. Tell me about what's happened with your ankle."

TJ relaxed then and filled Jazz in on the medical events of the previous days. She finished by mentioning that the doctor who had been looking after her had mentioned for TJ to say hi.

"What did you say his name was again?"

"Dr Hillier."

"Oh, Mitch." Jazz laughed again. TJ wished she felt as light-hearted and carefree as Jazz. It was evident that this woman loved her life and sucked every last morsel out of it. "Mitch is a great friend of mine. I'll give him a call and he can shoot your file over to me. He's not so hard on the eyes, either."

Before she could check her thoughts, TJ responded, "I can't say I actually noticed, to be honest."

Jazzed just smirked. "Interesting. Tell me, was Rory in the room by any chance?"

TJ wasn't quite sure what Jazz was driving at but answered anyway. "Ah yes, from memory, he was."

"God, I love it when I'm right," Jazz exclaimed, clapping her hands together. TJ could almost see Jazz giving herself a pat on the back. "I'm going to borrow one of Rory's favourite phrases and just say this—should be entertaining to watch."

TJ raised her eyebrows in surprise. It seemed Jazz enjoyed being cryptic and she got the distinct impression nothing further was going to be divulged just yet.

Jazz reassured her. "Not to worry, TJ. It'll all make sense in good time."

Yep. She'd definitely morphed into Alice and slipped down the rabbit hole. These people were very different than any she'd ever encountered and seemed remarkably content dancing totally to their own drums. The question was—what beat was hers playing?

Rory and Quade took the lift down two floors and sat around a table that faced a large flat-screen TV strategically placed on the wall. The table was situated in the middle of two rows of open-plan cubicles that all faced into the middle. Quade had grabbed his MacBook Pro off the nearby desk and was in the process of wirelessly projecting his notebook screen on the TV.

"So what's Rheeba got for us?" Rory asked Quade as he was connecting in. Rheeba was one of their other team members. She had a penchant for organisation and intelligence. As a result, she tended to run most of the background work for the assignments that the Centre undertook.

"Nothing as yet. I'll just ping her and see how long till she can shoot us the next lot of intel."

Rory slumped back in his chair and closed his eyes. He could use a little nap. Although genetically they could function on a lot less sleep than their purely human counterparts, it didn't mean he had to like it. And over the last two days, he'd had a lot less sleep than he'd normally like.

He'd kept almost a bedside vigil with Pixie over the last couple of days. She supposedly had a close family but nobody had visited or seemed to come forward. That seemed strange to him.

He'd taken the truck back to the address she'd given him early yesterday morning. The depot, he discovered, seemed to be an old cane farm down in the Jacobs Well/Pimpama area. From what he could tell, there were a couple of houses, quite a few sheds, and all the normal things you'd expect for a trucking depot. What he hadn't been impressed with was the security. Essentially there was none.

The houses were set a long way from the actual "yard" part of the truck depot. This meant from the house, you'd have very little idea what was happening down there. Even his senses would be at their maximum range to be constantly scanning the area. That in itself would be tiring for him over an extended period.

"Dreaming of your new assignment, mate?" Quade's tone was full of meaning.

Rory opened his eye. "You betcha. I've been wondering about her for three months and she just lands in my lap." Rory opened his eyes and smiled. "I told you the universe owes us, mate. About time you guys started believing me."

"Did you take a smack to the head? You've got to be kidding me, right?" Quade's tone indicated he wasn't buying Rory's theory at all.

"Nope—I'm telling you, the universe loves me."

"Well, good for you. Hope it lasts for you because where there's a woman involved, you need all the luck you can get."

"Oh, come on, Quade, what's so bad about women? Look at Brayden and Rihanna—they seem blissfully happy."

"Ha, maybe, but for how long?"

"Hopefully a damn long time. So what's eating you?" Rory had his suspicions. In fact, he'd bet his last dollar that it was being in such close proximity to Jazz.

"I can't believe the boss put me on babysitting duty," Quade grated out.

"I'd hardly call having to hang out with Jazz babysitting duty. She's smart, funny, great to look at—what's your problem?"

It was Quade's turn to get twitchy. He sat in the chair, fidgeting, waiting for Rheeba to send through the next series of intel reports.

"She just rubs me the wrong way." It was such a cat analogy. Cats hate to have their fur stroked in the opposite direction than the way it grew, and one thing for sure, Quade was definitely dominant feline. Tiger, to be exact.

"So what are you going to do about it?"

"Nothing I can do about it. The boss has assigned me to her and it was made clear you're going to be busy with TJ, so I guess I just have to suck it up."

"So when are you going to admit it?"

"Admit what?"

"That you'll feel a lot better once you've been with her."

Quade pushed back from the table with a lot more force than necessary. Yep—definitely a raw nerve, thought Rory. A thundercloud looked as if it had rolled across Quade's face and decided to take up residence. A Quade "mood" had never bothered him before and he wasn't about to start worrying now.

"Okay, so you're denying the attraction? Just in case you forgot, I can smell it. Not all the time but it's there. You want her. Why don't you stop being so hardheaded and do something about it?"

Rory was met by silence and he knew there was no point pushing further. Quade wasn't about to talk nor was he going to open up and discuss how he felt.

Oh well, at least he'd managed to turn the conversation from himself. It was an art he'd perfected years ago. Keep the party going and everyone laughing—that way they never really probed or asked about you.

Chapter Three

Rory held the doors of the lift while she hobbled in. They were finally heading out of the building that housed the Centre's offices. She felt exhausted; the people and the place overwhelmed but there was no way she'd let on that was how she really felt.

TJ shuffled to the side and leant a hand on the brushed steel railing that surrounded three sides of the lift car. Rory sauntered in and propped himself against the wall on the other side, directly opposite her. She met his eyes and he flashed her a killer grin. The temperature in the enclosed space suddenly seemed to overheat and her skin tingled in anticipation of his touch—even if only casual.

Not quite knowing how to handle such blatant male interest unnerved her a little and amped up the nervousness in her stomach. It was fear but of a different kind than she was used to. This was fear of something that you suspected would be really good but you hadn't experienced. The type of fear women had when they met a man they were desperately attracted to and didn't want to blow their chances before they'd even got started. Maybe apprehension was a better description, she pondered briefly.

One thing TJ was certain of: there was no way she could let him know that she was unsure and had a few issues. If she had any chance of coming out of this situation with her heart and mind intact, she needed to play by her rules. TJ was tenacious—some said impulsive and even reckless. She knew all these things, but it was her mechanism or armour for covering for the insecurities and fear she constantly lived with. Being five foot two, curvy, young, female, and blonde came with its own set of stereotypes.

The last thing people expected was for her to be single-mindedly determined and a force to be reckoned with. That's the façade she needed to portray in order to survive. She was doing a man's job in a man's world—nobody needed to remind her of that. That was a fact and a fear she'd lived with every day for over two years.

So rather than look away as she desperately wanted to do, she forced the biggest smile she could manage on her face and tilted her chin just a little. Enough to hint at the fact she'd picked up on his interest but not too much to seem a sure thing.

Rory's response was to let out a slight chuckle and his smile transformed into a knowing grin.

The doors opened and he shoved off from the side of the lift, and moved to take her arm and help her towards the waiting SUV.

"Come on, sweet Pixie, time to get you home and that ankle elevated."

The moment his hand came into contact with the exposed skin of her elbow and forearm, she felt the zap of electricity all the way to her toes. It was just as she'd expected when he casually touched her.

Being in his presence had all her female senses on heightened alert. Rory touched her and they jumped immediately to "action stations," hoping for an erotic onslaught.

Rory flicked the remote as they approached and opened the door for her. He took her crutches from her and leant them against the car. She was in the process of reaching for the panic handle on the doorframe when she felt his strong hands close gently around her waist. She was immediately boosted clear of the ground and placed carefully in the seat.

TJ went with her first reaction and that was to object. She needed to set some sort of boundaries.

"I'm not some doll you just pick up and move whenever you feel like it, Rory." On the one hand, she'd had just about enough of him lifting her and physically moving her from place to place. She might be small but she was capable of doing things under her own steam. Another part of her immediately started preening at his overt attention. That was the part that wanted to reach out and grab him behind the head for a mind-numbing kiss.

"No, sweetheart, you're not a doll. You're a Pixie. A slightly damaged but still gorgeous Pixie and I should warn you right now. If I'm going to be spending time with you, then you'd better get used to me helping you. You're injured, in case that slipped your notice, and I intend to make your recovery period as relaxing and pleasant as possible."

Before she could respond, he swiftly shut the door, deposited the crutches in the luggage compartment and was in the driver's seat. He'd made her recovery sound like some sort of holiday at a resort and her mind immediately dived into hedonistic things, with Rory featuring as the star attraction.

"Rory, I'm not sure what you think is going to happen but I've got a business to run. And by that, I mean I will be running it as business as usual."

An amused smile emerged across his face as he pulled out of the carpark.

"What?" she demanded, irritated by his attempt to malign the seriousness of the situation.

"We'll see."

"We'll see? I don't think so. You can do what you want. I'm running my business."

"Okay."

Ahh, he might have said okay but that wasn't what he really meant. Well, it wasn't his hide that the bank would come looking for.

She puffed out her displeasure and looked out the window.

A few moments later, Rory broke the silence that had settled. "So back to your place?"

"Yes...please." It cost her to add the please but upbringing and manners won out. She might be annoyed at him but she wouldn't compromise her own standards, and manners were one of those things she held preciously.

TJ sneaked a few sideways glances at the picture Rory presented as he drove on. He was all relaxed capability. She wondered what was going on in his head. He'd slid a pair of very sexy sunglasses on as they'd pulled out of the carpark. Yes, they totally added to the "hot" package but they prevented her from seeing directly into the dual pools of chocolate she'd become accustomed to visually sampling over the last couple of days.

"So, Pix, how about filling me in a little more on what sort of issues you've been having with your competitor?"

She shifted uncomfortably in her seat. It was speculation at best but her gut told her who was behind it. "I think we're being targeted by Q-Trans. They basically have the other half of the local milk carting contracts."

Rory looked at her disapprovingly. He was obviously after more information but she really didn't have much more to give. Just a series of random things that might or might not be related, some of them hunches more than anything.

"So when did all this start?"

She shrugged, not really wanting to talk about it. There was no clear starting point—one day she woke up and just knew she was being targeted. Kind of like waking up and knowing that you're hungry. You just know. Some sixth sense tells you.

"Pix—I'm about done with the silent, blocking treatment on this gig already. Look, I know I'm the last thing you wanted or expected but why don't we see if we can work together to sort out some of these issues you're having. I get that you're used to operating alone but at least while I'm around, that's no longer the case."

"That's all well and good, Rory, but what happens when you're gone? What happens when I've become accustomed to you helping and then it's no longer there?" TJ let out another long sigh, or actually it was more like a frustrated groan. "Thanks, that's nice of you to offer, but I think it's best that I manage things on my own."

"Pixie, there are a few things I've figured out in this life. First, none of us can fix the past; second, the best we can do is influence the future. That leaves the here and now. The present is something we can do something about and dictate what happens. So fair warning. I'm going to help you wherever I can and see fit."

She let out another long sigh. "Fine, do what you like. I figure you will anyway."

At her words, he turned to her slightly from behind the wheel and grinned. "Thanks, I will. That wasn't so hard, was it?"

"Don't start taking too much credit—you haven't done anything yet."

"All in good time, my sweet Pixie," he smiled and joked back at her.

Ahh, the man was impossible! God, she hoped this contaminated milk thing was over soon. She didn't know how long she could stand putting up with his pushy, annoying, oh so gorgeous ass.

Traffic was light and it seemed as if no time at all passed before they reached her depot and home in the flat land to the righthand side of the M1, heading north towards Brisbane. Pixie lived and worked from an old sugar cane farm. The land north of the Gold Coast on the righthand side of the highway was very flat and used extensively for sugar cane farming. It was a section of land that was prone to being wet and easy to flood. Perfect for sugar cane growing but not much else. The marshy lands of Moreton Bay meet the sugar cane fields to the east.

Rory had done a brief reconnaissance of the property when he called past yesterday to collect the clothes for Pixie and return Old Faithful. He intended to get himself fully acquainted with the area he was responsible for protecting, particularly if Pixie was staying there.

He turned off the road and headed down the gravel driveway. He peeled off to the left and approached the couple of houses and sheds that stood at one end of the property. The gravel road he'd turned off continued on about three-quarters of a kilometre to the yard where the trucks were held and managed from.

Rory drove past the larger brick house and pulled up in front of the fibro cottage that he'd discovered yesterday belonged to Pixie.

Pixie was reaching for the door when he put a hand across the seat to still her movements. "Just wait, sweetheart. I know it's hard to swallow, but I'll come round and help you down." She said nothing but scowled at him and he added, "Humour me—please."

She shook her head acknowledging her annoyance but refrained from trying to get out of the high SUV.

He helped her from the truck, and handed her the crutches. They'd slowly made their way up the five steps of the front verandah and to the door when he caught a glance of a tall figure moving across the grassed area between the two houses. The two houses sat at either end of a rectangular grassed area that was about the size of a football field. A couple of sheds also faced the rectangle but from the longer sides. His senses immediately started to tweak at the approaching figure. Something about him was off. Rory wasn't sure what yet. But he trusted his senses and they didn't have anything positive to report about the approaching figure.

"Looks like we've got company, Pix." He nodded towards the approaching figure when she looked up from the door handle.

"Ah, shit—just what I need."

Rory felt the tension immediately return to her small frame. First off, Pixie didn't swear by her own admission— so what was this about? All her muscles had tightened into hard knots. Not only could he see it—he could feel it. The contained energy flowed from her in waves.

"Who is he?"

"Ah, my stepcousin, Kelvin."

"I'm guessing you're not too keen to see him."

"Ah, you could say that."

"What's the problem?'

"Nothing—just don't particularly like the guy."

"Okay—want me to get rid of him?"

Pixie turned to him and looked up into his eyes. "I'd love you to, but better not start World War Three in the family."

Mmmm, there was a story here. Rory would bet his left nut on it and he'd get to the bottom of it.

Pixie opened the front door but left it ajar, obviously in preparation for the impending visitor. They walked through the entry into a long central hallway, which was typical of Queensland homes from this era. Rory guessed that the bedrooms would be off to the left, the lounge and dining rooms to the right. Kitchen, laundry, and bathrooms would be to the back.

They'd moved to the rear kitchen and Pixie was in the process of filling the kettle with water when the tell-tale footfalls of boots hit the front verandah.

"Anyone home?" called the voice.

"In the kitchen, Kelvin."

Rory took a seat at the scarred wooden table that took pride of place in the big open-plan country kitchen. The footfalls continued down the hallway, but his eyes never left Pixie. It was like watching a study in tensioning a spring. The closer this guy got, the more wired and tense she became. Something about this guy was setting her off. Rory intended to find out exactly what that was.

He didn't have to wait long. The man rushed to Pixie and tried to pull her into a solid hug. He immediately noted Pixie resist and started to rise from his chair in reaction to her alarm.

"Ah, TJ, how are you, my poor pet?" he said, trying to envelope her in a huge hug.

Obviously realising the plan, she stepped back, keeping her distance, making the manoeuvre seem all the more awkward.

"I'm okay, Kelvin. Just a broken ankle."

Rory took the time to quickly sum the guy up. He was reasonably tall, probably the same height as himself, so around six foot. But that was where the similarities ended. The guy had pasty skin, narrow shoulders, and a noticeable paunch forming over the belt of his khaki slacks. His dark brown hair was greasy, looking as if it should have been washed a week ago and his eyes—well, they were just the flat, beady brown of a predator. Nothing good there. Nothing good at all.

But the real tell was not what the guy looked like, but what he smelt like. And that was a serious problem. Super serious—because this guy, Kelvin, had the hots for Pixie in a big way and the pheromones he was letting off were a dead giveaway to somebody with a nose as sensitive as Rory's.

Kelvin stepped back to cover for the awkwardness of the failed embrace and hitched his hip on the bench. Rory took the opportunity to move between them and pull out a chair for Pixie as far away from Kelvin as possible. He also pulled another out for her ankle and gently helped her place it on the seat.

"Here, sweets, put your ankle up. I'll make the tea."

He felt her slightly relax at his touch but she was still on high alert. Something about this guy really set her off. Rory smoothed a lock of her hair back behind her ear and flashed her an easy grin, his way of letting her know it would be okay. It was a tender, familiar caress and he knew Kelvin would not miss it.

Rory grabbed a couple of mugs from the shelf above the kettle and nodded to Kelvin. "You want one?"

"Ah, no thanks; just had one with Aunt Rosemary and Aunt Clara."

Rory nodded but said nothing. He was waiting for the stranger to make the first move.

"So, TJ, how did you hurt your ankle? Aunt said you did it at work. I've been telling you for ages driving trucks is no place for a woman." His tone was scornful and authoritative, but far from convincing.

"Just a misstep, Kelvin. My boots were wet and I slipped and missed one of the steps. Then I guess I landed wrong and well, the result is I've busted it up."

He nodded and frowned, obviously not convinced but not pushing any further.

"So I don't believe we've met. I'm Kelvin, TJ's stepcousin

and fiancé." Kelvin thrust out his hand but thought better of it and returned it to his pocket.

Rory felt the surprise slam into his spine. *Fiancé—what the hell was that about?* Pixie hadn't mentioned anything about having a fiancé.

Before he could think further, he felt Pixie stiffen and move to rise from the chair. "How many times have I told you, I'm not marrying you! You and Uncle Max and Mum can plot and scheme all you want. I'm not getting married."

She didn't make it from the chair but the vehemence of the rebuttal was no less apparent from the reduced height of her position. Nope, the girl did not want to marry this twat. *Thank fucking Christ.* That would not have worked for Rory at all.

"But TJ, we've been through this all before. It's the best solution to everything," Kelvin almost pleaded.

"The way I see it, Kelvin, there's no problem to need a solution to. I don't love you, and I'm not marrying you. End of conversation." Her blue eyes flashed with fire. She was pissed but he also recognised something else underneath the anger. It was fear—cold, steely fear. That was something his senses also had no trouble in picking up. And her fear only served to piss him off. How dare this guy walk in and start upsetting her like this.

"But TJ, I could take on the business and you could go back to school or do nothing if we got married. You wouldn't need to keep working yourself to the bone." The sleaze all but dripped from Kelvin. Rory's skin was crawling just from being in the same room. He pitied Pixie, who the slime was directed at.

"The answer is no. Just the same as it was six months ago and it will be again six months or even six years from now. Sorry, but that's how I feel."

Rory noted that Kelvin was getting frustrated at being rebutted in front of a stranger and was edging forward closer to Pixie. Rory slightly widened his shoulders and subtly stood a little straighter, making himself far more prominent in the room. He moved to partly block Kelvin's view of her.

"Sorry, mate, the lady has spoken. As you can see, she's not at her best and I think it's time you left her to get some rest."

As Rory had intended, the son of slime moved his attention to him.

"And just who the hell are you?" Kelvin demanded, sounding more whiny than threatening.

"I'm her boyfriend—Rory. And just to clarify things—I'm intending on being around for a long time so, if I were you, I'd be packing those marriage plans with Pixie away and go find some other woman to annoy. This one's evidently not interested."

At Rory's words, Kelvin's face started to turn a beet red with rage. He'd heard a little gasp from Pixie at his words; he could almost feel relief coming from her now. That was good. Much better than the fear he'd recognised her unease to be.

"But she's never mentioned a boyfriend," Kelvin stammered.

"We met a while back. I've been away for work. But I'm back now and I'll be staying here." Rory was now standing straight, legs apart, knees slightly bent, ready for action.

Kelvin tried to peer around Rory's wide shoulders to TJ. "Does Aunt know about this? It's not right having a man living in the same house as you when you're not married. Surely she's not condoning this."

At that, Pixie lurched to her feet. She wobbled slightly and Rory immediately thrust a hand around her waist and pulled her tight to support her.

"Kelvin, I'm a grown woman who runs a business and lives on her own. If I want to have a man live with me or share my bed, then that's my decision and nobody else's."

"But it's not right. You weren't raised that way," he stammered.

"Right or wrong, it's what I'm doing and I don't need your permission. I'm feeling a bit tired and I'd like to go lie down. I think you should go."

Kelvin's faced turned even redder with rage.

"This is not finished, TJ. We're supposed to be together. You know that."

Rory felt Pixie stiffen and then let out a long sigh against his side.

"Kelvin, we've been through this time and time again. It was some stupid comment that was jokingly passed over a dinner. It meant nothing. What's more, it's not going to happen."

"I can forgive many things, TJ, maybe even a little indiscretion with somebody like him but I won't wait for much longer. You're going to be my bride."

Before Rory could say anything, Pixie jumped right in. "What do you mean someone like him?"

Rory watched Kelvin open and shut his mouth a few times before finally managing to get his words out. "Well, look at him, TJ. He's huge and you can just see he's been around and there's something arrogant and aggressive about him. He's no good for you."

Rory had had enough. He gently helped Pixie regain her chair and turned to Kelvin.

"So I guess you're everything she needs, hey mate?"

Kelvin straightened a little at Rory's words. "Yes. Yes I am."

Rory threw his head back and laughed, knowingly goading the lesser man. He moved forward and started to crowd Kelvin towards the door.

"Come on, mate. The lady said it's time for you to go."

"So what—you're throwing me out?" he asked in astonishment.

"Ah, yes—that would be my plan. Either walk under your own steam or I'll help you. And I think you and I both know that wouldn't end well for you."

"You're threatening me. See, TJ, I told you this guy was trouble," Kelvin threw over his shoulder to TJ as he edged from the room.

"Okay, Kelvin, you've tried my temper about as much as I'm going to allow. We've established that Pixie's with me and that you're nothing but the pushy stepcousin. So in the interests of ongoing family relations, now is definitely the time for you to walk out the front door and not return until invited again." Rory placed a hand on Kelvin's shoulder and applied a small amount of pressure in the kind of way that provided a large amount of instantaneous pain.

Kelvin spun his head around to Rory in confusion at the pain, as he further stumbled towards the front door—surprise and pain written all over his features. Rory just smiled and couldn't help but add, "Oh, I guess we never did get to the part where we chatted and I mentioned my interest in martial arts." Rory pushed him through the door and "helped" him down the front steps. "Word of advice. Always smart to figure out what you're up against before you go starting something you can't finish."

Kelvin half fell to his knees and then quickly regained his footing, humiliation coming off him in waves. "This is not the end of it. She's mine and I intend to make her my wife."

Rory just stood there, smiling.

"Best of luck with that, mate. Something tells me you'll be waiting a while."

With Rory's parting words, Kelvin slunk away back across the grassed area. He turned around to note that Pixie had somehow managed to join him at the door.

"Is he gone?"

"Yeah. He's gone and if he has half a brain, he won't come back." Rory flashed her his thousand-watt smile. "But I have a feeling that he'll be back."

She smiled weakly at him. "Yeah, he'll be back. He's called around every week for the last six months. And the answer has been categorically no and getting more so every day."

"Does your family know about this?"

Pixie ducked her head and he had his answer without her speaking a word.

"Why don't you tell them?"

"Because it's nothing," she spat at him, her temper clearly raging. "I can handle him and Mum doesn't need the added worry."

He nodded slightly. "I think that sentiment could be extended to you as well, sweets. From what I've learnt over the last couple of days, you've got more than your fair share of worries sitting squarely on your shoulders."

"I can handle it," she retorted accusingly.

"Never said you couldn't. Doesn't mean that it's right or that you shouldn't work towards lifting a few of those worries."

She shifted restlessly between legs; having the cast on made it difficult to stand.

"And you don't think I'm working to sort things out? Well, I am, every waking moment. I'm doing what I can to set things right."

"That's not what I meant and you know it, Pixie. What I meant is that sometimes you can't take it all on yourself. Sometimes you have to share the load and let others help you. If you're not going to talk to your family, then at least let me help you out."

She didn't say anything immediately, obviously mulling over his words. "Okay, I'll give that a try—but I'm in charge." She looked up and fixed her brilliant blue eyes on his. "Boyfriend..."

At that, he laughed, scooped her up into his arms and carried her into the lounge room, placing her down gently on the forest green leather lounge.

"Rory, I thought we discussed this thing about you moving me around."

"You mentioned something about it. I decided it was nonsense and besides, I like having you in my arms—girlfriend."

With that, he leant forward and captured her chin with his hand and joined his lips to hers in a light kiss. The moment their lips met, the energy that had been sparking between them amped up to a whole new level. His tongue slid out and lightly glazed across the seam of her lips, encouraging her to open for him. She resisted for a split second before she shifted her slight frame, changing the angle of the kiss. Before he could intensify anything, she took him by surprise and tangled her tongue with his, searching, seeking more from him.

His initial surprise lasted a mere moment before he got on board with her plan and followed her lead. She nibbled at his bottom lip and then licked her tongue over the spot to soothe and tease. It was making him harder. His cock expanded against the front of his jeans, desperate to be free and deep inside her.

He heard her moan in her throat and felt her reach her arms up to surround his neck. She was making it abundantly clear she wanted more. He took her arms by the wrists and pushed them back over her head, dropping to his knees in front of her. His lips never broke contact with hers while he sunk to the ground.

Pixie leant forward, trying to reduce the gap between their bodies. The twin tips of her hardened nipples lightly brushed against his chest beneath the polo shirt he wore. He took both wrists in one hand and trailed his fingers lightly down the inside of her arm. She shuddered at his touch but didn't move away; rather, she moved into him, seeking more.

His fingers had almost reached the slope of her breast when he pulled back and abruptly stood. She looked up at him, shocked. "What's wrong?"

"Somebody's coming." Before he said anything further, the telltale footsteps of someone walking across the wooden verandah could be heard. There was a light knock at the door. Then a feminine voice called out, "TJ, are you in there?"

"Yeah, Aunt Clara, in here."

Rory reached down and adjusted the bulge in the front of his jeans. He tried to think of anything but what they'd just been doing but it was difficult when he could smell her arousal. It was calling to him.

The front door opened and closed and then Clara appeared in the doorway to the lounge room.

"Oh, TJ—how are you feeling, dear?"

"Not too bad, thanks, Aunt Clara. Just having a bit of a sit before I get stuck into it again."

Aunt Clara nodded and turned slightly to Rory.

"Good to see you again, Mr Southall."

"It's Rory, please."

"Well then, you must call me Clara."

He smiled and nodded his acceptance.

"So are you going to be okay here on your own, honey? I think it might be best if you came and stayed at the big house."

"No thanks, Aunt Clara. I'm fine here and besides, Rory is staying as well. I'm sure we'll manage."

"Ah, yes, that business he explained yesterday. I hope this is not dangerous." Concern was evident in her eyes and tone.

"I'm sure everything will be fine. If you can just help out with Mum and the kids, it'll be one less thing I need to worry about."

"Of course, dear. Are you coming over to visit today? Your mother's not having the best of days. She's napping in bed."

Pixie nodded. "I'll come over tomorrow. Let her rest for now."

"Okay, dear. Kelvin just came back and headed off. He was very unhappy about something, dear. I hope nothing's wrong."

"Nothing at all, Aunt Clara. Just a little misunderstanding about something."

"Well, I hope you sort things out soon. I wouldn't want there to be any unpleasantness. It's important not to upset the men."

And that was enough of a conversation for Rory to confirm the picture he'd half expected. It seemed Aunt Clara and probably her mother had a rather outdated view of a woman's role in society and the family.

"Of course not, Aunt Clara."

"Well, if everything's okay, then I'll just leave you to it. Call if you need anything, dear. The guest room is the third door on the left, Rory, in case Teresa hasn't been able to show you."

"Thanks Clara. We've got it all sorted. I'll walk you out and grab my duffle at the same time."

With that, he took the opportunity to take her elbow and guide her through the front door and out onto the verandah.

"Don't worry, Clara. I'll take good care of her. My boss

officially assigned me to Teresa earlier today. So I'll be sticking with her until this is over."

"I've never been happy about her running the company. Driving trucks and working with men is not a woman's job. Something like this was bound to happen. I only hope she doesn't get hurt."

"As I said, Clara, don't worry. I'm here now and I'll sort it out. You look after Rosemary and I'll help Teresa sort out these threats."

He'd told Clara a little of what was happening yesterday, but not very much. He'd mentioned about the threats and how it had spilled over into some government investigations. He'd used the rule they always employed: stick as close to the truth as possible without actually confirming or denying anything. Was it his problem if she slightly misinterpreted something?

After he left Clara halfway across the grassed area, he returned to the house with his duffle to find Pixie had dozed off, curled up on the lounge. He smiled at the peaceful image she made all soft and cosy on the oversized lounge.

Good. Pixie being asleep gave him the opportunity to make a few calls and find out a bit more about his new friend Kelvin Walsh. "Friend" was a very loose term.

Chapter Four

Max Walsh sat out on the verandah of his thirty-second floor Main Beach penthouse. The stiff afternoon ocean breeze was refreshing as he watched the white caps roll in. He led what he called a comfortably extravagant life. Now in his mid-fifties, he could look back and be proud of what he'd achieved. Hard work, dedication, and tenaciousness had served him well. His peers would call him cut-throat and ruthless. He saw it as being shrewd and commercial. Nothing had been handed to him, unlike his older brother, Robert.

Robert had been the golden son in his father's eyes. Max had always been second best and played second fiddle. That was until he shook off the shackles of being number two when he was eighteen and joined the army. He'd spent six years learning a trade and learning he was good enough to do it on his own. The army had taken the scared young man and honed him into a hard-edged warrior with killer instincts. Things that he'd seen and done in the name of queen and country would haunt him forever. But he was tough and he refused to crumble at the hands of the things he'd seen, done, and experienced. He'd learnt to become immune to his own demons. The ultimate mark of a man.

When he'd come out of the army, he took the money he'd squirrelled away during his enlistment and the additional money he'd made at cards to purchase his first property. Hard work, skill, and a little luck had meant he sold the property six months later for double what he'd paid. Max had continued this process for the next ten years before he expanded into the big time.

Now he took on property development worth hundreds of millions of dollars and he used other people's money, not his own. He was incredibly successful in anyone's book, achieving the pinnacle in his chosen field. But he'd never received the recognition from the one person he craved the most—his father. His father had never recognised the success he'd achieved and now his death ten years ago meant he never would.

The burning need in his gut to be the best still lay unquenched. To have the last word, and to prove beyond doubt he was better than Robert would now need to be played out to a different audience. Only then would he be completely at peace.

What he'd achieved wasn't enough. He wanted what Robert had as well. And have it he would. All of it—his. Unlike his father, he'd make sure his son also had what he wanted. That was the ultimate love a father could show his son. He'd learnt that watching his father with Robert. Robert got what Robert had wanted. Now, albeit years later, it was his turn.

His thoughts were firmly on his plans when he heard the screen door slide behind him. He looked around and saw his son Kelvin. The boy may not have been his biological son but he was his true son in every other sense of the word. He'd raised him since he was a baby, when he married his mother, Anne. Max was the victim of mumps when he was a teenager and the episode had rendered him sterile—never to have his own child.

But how could Max prove he was the better man without a boy? So like everything in life, he'd considered, thought, and then acted and a few months later he was both a proud husband and father. He only had one stipulation when he married Anne, and that was that the baby be given his name and be his true son.

"Hey son, how's your day been?"

Max knew just by glancing at him that something was very wrong with him.

"I went to speak to TJ again today and she turned me down

again." Frustration was written all over Kelvin's face as he slumped against the railing.

"And what was her reason this time?"

"She told me she didn't love me and that she wasn't going to consider the idea at all." Kelvin raked his hand through his greasy hair. "But that's not the real kicker. She's taken up with some guy. Got him living there, even."

At this news, Max sat up straighter and took a sip of the aged single malt whisky over ice he favoured. "Tell me more."

"I turned up today and there they are playing house, casual as can be."

Max considered this a little more.

"And who is this guy?"

"Well, that's just it. I don't know. In fact, I haven't a clue. His name's Rory. But, Dad, he's not like any guy we've come across before."

At this, Max's ears pricked up. "What do you mean, son?"

"There's an edge to him. A toughness that makes you know he's going to follow through with what he says."

"And what exactly did he say, Kel? Did he threaten you?"

"Well, not really, but he made it very clear that he was with TJ and I was nothing but the cousin."

"So other than that, you found out nothing about this guy? Other than he's now taken up with the girl who should be yours?"

Kelvin looked sheepish and ducked his head. He knew he'd failed and let his temper override his judgement. Just like he usually did.

"I know he's very well versed in martial arts."

At this, Max's eyebrows shot up.

"And how, pray tell, do you know this?"

"Well, he kind of did something to my shoulder as he escorted me out."

Max sat and said nothing. He knew silence was a much better chastiser than anger would ever be. Finally, he levelled his stare at his boy. Sometimes it was really hard not to be disappointed.

"Kelvin, Kelvin. How many times have I told you not to provoke an unknown opponent? Always let the other man show his cards first."

"But Dad, he was in the same house as TJ. He's probably fucking her right now, for all we know."

"And whose fault is that, Kel?"

Kelvin pulled out a chair and collapsed his body into it, sighing as he did so.

"Mmm. It seems I'm going to need to step things up a bit. But first, I think I need to pay a visit to Rosemary and Clara." He pondered that for a moment. "Actually, I have a better idea. I need you to stay away from TJ and the depot until further notice. Do you understand me, son? I know you're itching to make her yours but this is not something that can be rushed. Go scratch the itch with one of the whores I keep on speed dial for you. TJ is off-limits to you until I say anything further."

Kelvin looked at his father, and resignedly nodded his head.

Five minutes later, Kelvin stormed from the building and tore away in his yellow Lamborghini. He decided to take his father's suggestion and partake in a little release. Who should he call? Oh, the choices were wide and varied, but he needed something edgy today. It was something that his appetite seemed to have been growing increasingly strong for lately.

He needed to see the whore writhe and scream in pain. Pain from his paddle, flogger, or whip. He needed to imagine it was TJ submitting to him in every way. He needed to break her impetuous spirit. One day very soon she would call him master and husband. But until that day came, he'd practice and hone his skills on the whores. Those were his for the taking whenever he chose. Those who mattered not if he marked or scarred, for they were merely objects of pleasure to satisfy his needs until he could indulge in the main event.

Teresa Jane Walsh had been his for the last six years and he had only to complete the transaction. He intended to own and master her in every sense of the word. She would bow and submit to him at will.

He'd keep his distance as his father dictated. But it would be a struggle. The thought of that guy fucking his TJ was too much to bear. His father may have said stay away from TJ but he'd said nothing about Rory. The guy needed to learn to watch his back and know his place, and Kelvin was just the man to teach him that lesson.

Chapter Five

TJ woke to a gentle hand stroking her face. Warm fingers caressed her cheek, down over her neck and back up again. It made her sleep-fuzzed brain lurch to carnal things—sensuous and pleasurable things with Rory. A moan escaped her throat and she heard a small chuckle, which served to increase her level of awareness.

"Lenny was right. You do have an angel face."

She stretched and tried to focus her sleepy eyes. He was sitting on the bed beside her. A bed that she had no recollection of ever moving to.

"Mmm, how did I get here?"

Again the low chuckle was her answer.

"I carried you, sweet pea. I came in from seeing your aunt home and you were dead to the world on the lounge. I figured you'd be more comfortable on the bed, so that's where I put you."

He was right; she was comfortable. A little sleepy still but that would fade.

"It's nearly four, sweets. If we're going to do the milk run this afternoon, we need to get moving. I let you sleep as long as I could. You can always nap in the truck if you're still sleepy."

At his words, she sat bolt upright. Gosh, they were going to be late. How could she have slept so long? If Rory hadn't woken her, she would have slept till who knows when.

She didn't miss the concern in his voice or his eyes. He truly seemed to care about how she felt.

"No, I'm fine. Just give me a minute and I'll be right with you."

He nodded his head and rose from the bed, but before he'd risen to his full height, he dipped back down and placed a tender kiss on her lips. It was quick and fleeting but it promised more and reminded her firmly of what had been interrupted earlier in the day.

"I'll go fill a couple of travel mugs with coffee to go. Black, right, with a dash of cold water?"

She looked up at him and smiled. "Thanks, that would be great."

He really did seem to be keen to help out—maybe she could use just a little of that help.

A few minutes later, Rory bundled her into the golf cart that was parked under the awning adjoining her house. It was what she used to move between the depot and the house. Sometimes she enjoyed the three-quarters of a kilometre walk but that certainly wasn't an option at the moment, and if she was honest with herself, she rarely had the time to enjoy the simple pleasure.

They said nothing on their way to the yard and Rory parked the cart under the lean-to awning off the prefabricated building they used as a depot office. She gave a quick scan to the yard, noting which trucks were in and which weren't.

Rory helped her limp from the cart to the door of the office. She was loath to use her crutches. They were nothing but an annoyance.

She tripped on the step and would have fallen if not for his quick reflexes securing her around the waist.

TJ mumbled her thanks and slumped gratefully in the chair at her desk. She'd never admit it but her clumsiness had made her ankle ache again. She could really use some more pain pills but she didn't have time for that now.

"What's up?"

"What do you mean?"

"Something's got you agitated and I'm betting it's more than the nasty rap you just gave that cast."

She looked out the window and sighed, almost hoping looking for it would make Bob and Annabelle appear.

"Bob's not back yet from the interstate run. I would have

thought he'd be in after lunch. I was hoping to take Annabelle tonight. But it looks like Old Faithful it is."

"So why's he running late?"

"Could be any number of reasons. I should have called him hours ago." She reached for her cell phone in the pocket of her shorts.

"Or maybe he should have checked in hours ago?" he logically pointed out.

Rory had a point but that wasn't how she did things. She knew she tended to baby them all but she just needed to know that things were running to plan.

"Okay, Pixie, let's get moving. You can call him from the truck."

Quickly checking her phone revealed what she already suspected—no message from Bob.

Rory had her out of the portable building and into the passenger's seat in no time at all. She noted that he didn't miss the opportunity to run his hands over her butt or give it a little but noticeable squeeze as he eased her up and onto the seat. *It would be so easy to get distracted with him!*

TJ had her phone out and was dialling Bob before Rory even had Old Faithful fired up and rolling. She tapped the toe of her left foot impatiently. *Where was he?*

Finally, just as the phone was about to go to voicemail, he answered, breathless and grumpy. "Yeah."

"Hey, Bob, it's TJ. How're you travelling? I expected you home a few hours ago."

"Would've been if I hadn't blown half a dozen tyres."

"What? What are you talking about?"

"Blew all four inners on the bogie axles on the prime mover and two inners on the trailer. Never seen anything like it in all my years drivin' trailers."

TJ winced. Inner tyres were the pits to change, particularly on trucks and trailers this size.

"Have you got it sorted?"

"Yeah, called that national tyre mob you have the deal with. They've been out but each time I've had to wait around for the best part of an hour. So I'm hours behind schedule."

"Where are you now?"

"About fifteen klicks short of Grafton."

"Damn. So you're still at least four hours away, even if you don't have any further problems. Why didn't you call me, Bob?"

"Heard about your accident, TJ—didn't want you worrying, girl."

"It's my job to worry, Bob."

"That may be the case but nothing you can do. I just got to get this rig home."

"How are you for hours on the log books?"

"I'm just about out of hours. I could dodgey the times."

"Don't you dare. Get into Grafton and rest up—head out again at first light."

"You sure?"

"Positive—you know the rules. Nobody drives tired, nor do we falsify hours on log books."

"You got it—see you tomorrow."

"Drive safe."

And the connection went dead.

TJ slammed her hand down hard on the dash—it hurt like hell but it felt better.

"Want to tell me what's going on?"

"Bob's late because he's blown six tyres, all inners. Four on the prime mover and two on the trailer."

"I'm guessing he's going to blow another four before he gets home."

She spun around in the seat, looking at him.

"What do you mean?"

"Nobody blows inners like that—from my calculations, there's only four left on the trailer that haven't been changed. Chances are they're going to go as well. Someone's been messing with your tyres, Pixie."

He was right. Somebody had targeted her truck.

"Why don't you call him and get him to get the other four on the trailer replaced before he heads out. Get him to throw the four he gets taken off into the trailer. I'll have our guys check them out and see what we can find."

She agreed with Rory. It made perfect sense. No point in delaying Bob any longer.

TJ quickly phoned Bob back and gave him the new instructions.

"Shit, this is going to cost me a motza."

Rory just chuckled.

She spun on him, fuming. "You're laughing at this costing me?"

"No, Pix. I'm laughing because this exercise is probably going to cost you the best part of ten grand and the most you can say is shit! Drop the good Catholic girl routine and swear like you really want to. I won't think less of you. If ever there was a situation that called for a good 'fuck,' this is it. Hell, you might even find it liberating. Someone's screwing with you, sweetheart, and I'm going to find out who. Come on— gimme, gimme just one little 'fuck.'"

A lot of her anger evaporated and she almost chuckled at his antics. He could be such a clown.

She tried to force the word through her lips but all that squeaked out was a weak sounding, "Faaarrrk."

Rory shook his head, grinning. "Seriously, that the best you can do?"

"'Fraid so."

"Well then, I've got some work to do."

She looked at him, confused, and shrugged in a *what do you mean?* gesture.

"Pixie, the thought of you talking dirty to me does all kinds of things to me. Guess I'm going to have to liberate you into swearing. Well, at least talking dirty to me in the bedroom."

"Rory, I can't believe we're having this conversation now."

"Why not? Good a time as any and we've got about another half an hour to kill before we get there."

"And who says we're going to end up in the bedroom?"

He turned and looked at her in mock horror. "What? I finally get a girlfriend and she's shy about heading to the bedroom. Universe, you know better than to do this to me."

"Ah, Rory, I'm not really your girlfriend."

"Ah, Pixie, do you not recall the conversation we had earlier today with your lecherous cousin? Yeah, you are most definitely my girlfriend. And that's how I'll be introducing you to everybody from now on."

TJ felt totally confused. Was he for real? Was he actually thinking of her as part of some elaborate ruse or was he wanting to explore the chemistry between them?

"Rory, I'm confused. Are you for real? Or is this all just window dressing?"

He turned and flashed her a grin. That was enough to have her heart melting and her panties dampening.

"Of course I'm for real. There's something between us that I think's worth exploring. You seem to be on board with it. You also need someone to run interference between you and Kelvin. What could be better than a boyfriend? It also easily explains why I'm in the house and trailing your every move."

She thought on his words for a few seconds. There was something so appealing about being Rory Southall's girlfriend. But was it right? Did it matter?

They'd be together for the next few weeks anyway. Jazz's words flashed through her mind. *Rory has the hots for you; just use him for sex.* Maybe Jazz had a point? At the very least, she had the pretence of being able to explore the relationship.

Geez, she hadn't had time to have a relationship in ages. In fact, from well before her father's death. How did she feel about this? It was a bit terrifying. What if she got attached to him? *What the heck*, she thought. The thought terrified her in many ways. So she went with her gut instinct when things terrified her, and dived right in. You only live once.

"Okay, Mr Boyfriend, what do I tell people when they ask what you do?"

"Oh, just be evasive, tell them I'm some sort of IT geek who works my own hours. Nobody really understands what IT geeks do anyway."

Well, that was true. She sure didn't have much of a clue about technology. She preferred to leave the bulk of that stuff to her fifteen-year-old brother Marcus. He seemed to be able to figure things out.

"Okay, I can do that."

What a bizarre few days! Her world was turning upside down and the man who had captured her dreams for the last three months rides in to rescue her. How did that happen? Was this one of those "be careful what you wish for" things? Well, her father always used to say never look a gift horse in the mouth, and she could certainly use some of the luck Rory seemed to bring. And maybe if she really let herself admit it, there was something very comforting about having a strong, capable man around to shoulder some of the load. It was probably poor judgement, but diving in sure felt better than sitting on the sidelines with the fear gnawing.

Rory double-clutched and shifted down to take the last couple of bends before they arrived at the dairy. He knew Pixie was a little off balance but instinct told him it was the right move to make. Having her on board and playing a role would make the whole operation a lot easier. Only thing was, it wasn't a role. He really did want her for his girlfriend. Nobody had ever haunted his dreams and stirred him on such a primitive level like Pixie did.

There was just something about her. She'd intrigued him since the first chance meeting three months ago. And if he was being totally honest, the image of her had kept him awake many nights. Sure, she was gorgeous: Clouds of long white blonde hair. Eyes the purple-blue of irises. Skin the milky colour of porcelain.

But it was something more. She had a strength of spirit, drive, determination and a wildness that downright astounded him. He truly believed there could be something between them, and like Brayden a few months ago, he wanted the chance to explore the possibility. Brayden and Rihanna had proved that there could be more to life as a Centre operative and he wanted that, too.

It was the same dairy that Pixie had been picking up from the other night. This was the first time he'd been here, though. Apparently the contract was to pick up here every second day and deliver back to the processor.

He eased the big prime mover through the narrow front gates and watched in the mirrors as the tanker tracked through behind with barely an inch to spare on the gate post. His admiration for how Pixie manoeuvred this rig increased. It was a very tight fit and there were no scuff marks on the posts, so he gathered she'd been handling it like the professional he'd come to believe she was.

"Just head up behind that large silver shed, the tanks are in another shed behind this first one. Don't put any wheels off the gravel because the grass is really spongy and you'll sink down to the axels."

"Great, a boobie-trapped dairy."

"It's not quite that bad but I've had a driver who needed to get hauled out with old Mr Macgregor's tractor and he wasn't happy about it. In fact, I think it's only in the last month he hasn't mentioned it and it was well over twelve months ago that it happened."

"I'll keep that in mind." He winced.

Pixie guided him around the buildings and he pulled in to park for the loading of the milk. Meeting Jock Macgregor was an experience. He was a crusty old farmer, obviously been farming for years. Just like with Lenny and Don, the first thing Jock asked about was Pixie. And his concern was immediate and genuine, to the point that he left Rory to hook up the pump and get things underway while he stood at the base of the passenger's side, chatting to Pixie.

While he was waiting for the milk to transfer from the holding tanks to the transport tanker, he wandered around a little and started cataloguing scents.

He had no real baseline to work from but if he could start to determine the various different scents, there was a good chance he'd be able to smell the subtle differences between the genetically modified cows and the "normal" herd.

He also thought it was likely he could pick up the differences in the scent of the milk. Obviously the feed that the cows were consuming and the breed differences would make the milk smell and taste slightly different. However, if he concentrated long enough and worked his way through the various dairies, there was a good chance he'd quickly be able to pick the differences.

He'd talk to the boss about it. It had to be the most logical way. After all, this was the exact reason they'd been "modified." It was supposed to all be about fighting these sorts of issues. Sometimes Rory had his doubts and was confident that they'd eventually get to the bottom of the Centre's secret reasoning for why they'd been created but that was a topic and a question for another day.

With the tank filled and the paperwork complete, Rory swung back up into Old Faithful and flashed a smile at Pixie. "All set, princess?"

"Yes. Did you secure the hoses and the pump housing properly?"

He didn't answer her, just flashed her a cheeky grin and got them underway.

"Rory, do you have any idea how frustrating it is when I ask you a direct question about something important to do with the business and all you give me is a half cheeky, half condescending grin? I still don't know if you even have a licence to drive this rig. Nor have I seen a log book." She looked at him a little disapprovingly.

Oh, she was even hotter when she was in a snit. He chuckled before answering her.

"You worry too much, sweet pea. Yes, I do have a licence. Every one of the operatives at the Centre is licensed to operate most things that can be driven or ridden. Apart from all the run-of-the-mill stuff, I can also operate earthmoving machinery, fly a reasonable sized jet, oh and I'm checked out on choppers as well. Plus we do at least annual refreshers and advanced courses on all of those vehicles that I mentioned. So you, your truck, and your insurance are all safe with me."

Pixie shook her head.

"Was that really so hard to say?"

"No, but it was more fun to keep you guessing." He chuckled, briefly turning to her before returning his gaze to the windscreen. "Seriously, Pix, I'd never do anything to put you or your livelihood at risk. I fully respect what you're doing here and how hard you work. I wouldn't jeopardise that. I'll also add that I'm more than prepared to help you defend your business from whatever threats you're facing."

Pixie was silent. She said nothing. A moment of unease settled over Rory. He glanced sideways and noticed the silent tears cascading down her porcelain skin.

"Oh, sweet Pixie, what did I say? Please don't cry." His voice was full of concern.

"You don't understand…" she sobbed. "I've been so alone since Dad died, doing everything myself. Sometimes it just gets so hard." She sniffled and sobbed again. "Thank you. You can't possibly know what it means to me for you to have said that."

He may not know exactly but Rory was far from stupid and he was very intuitive and astute. He guessed that Pixie's emotional tank was running on empty. She'd worked herself into the ground to keep everything happening, and to make the job even more difficult, now she was being targeted.

He decided to break the intensity of the mood. What needed to be said had been said; now Rory needed the mood to lighten. He chuckled quietly. "You know, if I wasn't so certain that you'd be pissed at me for stopping, I'd pull over right now and give you a big hug."

She looked over at him with a slightly confused expression on her face. She was still getting used to him joking around all the time.

"You would be pissed if I stopped, right?" he asked for confirmation.

"Ah, yeah." She might have just as easily said *der moron*. Her tone left him in no doubt about her conviction. "I like to make sure we have as much time as possible to get to the processing plant in case we have issues."

"Cool—figured that. Just thought I'd check. I was kind of hoping you might agree to me giving you a hug and then you never know, I might just get to feel up my girlfriend." He shot her a crooked smile and a little eyebrow raise.

"Rory—what is it with guys? Can't you stay focused on getting the job done before you start thinking about that stuff?"

"Short answer, my sweet Pixie—no. Those thoughts are with us all the time. Particularly when one's girlfriend looks as good as you do and smells even better."

She was sitting up there in the passenger's seat, jean shorts moulded to her thighs. The figure-hugging tank top she wore gave him a clear outline of her very feminine curves and he'd been itching to run his hands over them all day. In fact, he'd just got his hand on her when her aunt arrived. What terrible timing. His palms were still tingling at the memory of the feel of her body against them.

"What are you talking about? I'm not wearing perfume."

She had a unique smell that was nothing to do with perfume and everything to do with Pixies. It reminded him of vanilla and peaches and summer berries. Her scent had haunted him since January. Having her this close to him threatened to push his senses into overload. He had to be careful, too, in how much he disclosed. He was skating close to the wind. His nose could pick her scent up and dissect it into minute components.

"Well, then it just must be you. But whatever it is, I'm hungry to taste it."

He knew his teasing rattled her momentarily; her scent profile subtly changed and he could smell her anxiety. He could also sense the increased speed of her heart pumping blood through her veins.

Pixie tilted her head and raised her eyebrows a little. "So what sort of tasting did you have in mind?" Her words were confident, seductive, and totally in contrast to what the telltale signs her body was telling him.

She'd picked up the gauntlet and was going to play! For some reason, that made him very happy.

"Well, I'm a pretty thorough guy and I like to take my time—make sure I do things right. I guess I'd want to sample you from head to toe. But there's definitely a few places in the middle I'd like to stay a while."

A second later, his nose was assaulted by the smell of her arousal. He could just imagine how wet and dewy she was for him right now. What had he been thinking, starting down this path? Sometimes he wondered about his own sanity and now was one of those times. His cock had been semi-hard for hours. At the words of their game and the increased smell of her arousal, he'd now reached the uncomfortable point.

"Mmm," she purred, playing the role of sex kitten. "That does sound good. But aren't you taking a little bit for granted, Surfer Boy?"

He chuckled and smiled knowingly. Somebody had obviously told her his nickname. "Maybe, but honey, if we hadn't been interrupted before, I think there's a pretty good chance a few of my curiosities would have been answered."

"That may be so, but don't you think you might be moving just a tad too fast?"

"Pixie, I've spent the last three months wondering about you—consider that a form of foreplay. You've been teasing me for weeks, regardless of whether you knew it or not. I'm hoping you won't tease me much longer."

"I've got a feeling you like to be the one who normally does the teasing." To emphasise her point, she drew the index finger of her right hand over her mouth, catching the moistness of her top and bottom lips, slowly and seductively—she knew exactly what sort of reaction this would have on him. His blood felt like it was close to boiling. He wanted her badly.

"And here I thought you were a good little Catholic girl," he joked.

"Oh, but I am." Her face was the picture of sweetness and innocence. And then she let out a sultry giggle, the sound shooting straight to his hardened cock. "Just not all the time."

She was aroused; his nose told him so. But it also told him there was a strong layer of fear despite her seductress routine.

Oh God—he had a feeling this woman was going to be dangerous.

Chapter Six

Gold Coast Pistol and Shooting Range

"I still don't understand why I need to learn to shoot this thing, anyway." Jazz held the pistol in her hand with the minimum amount of contact, distaste for the weapon and what it represented written all over her face. She was standing at the end of the lane, peering down at the target in the distance.

"Fuck! Is nothing easy with you?" Quade fumed.

"I don't know why you're so pissed. I just asked a question."

"A question you know the goddamn answer to. You're here learning to handle this weapon because Centre protocol states that all operatives need to be able to handle all types of weapons."

"And that's just my fucking point," she gritted out through clenched jaws. "I'm not an operative—I'm the team doctor."

"Well, the boss said to bring you here and teach you to fire a pistol. That's what I'm doing. For once in your life, could you just cut a guy some slack?"

"Cut you some slack! You've got to be kidding me. That's the last thing I'd want to be doing. Where did I put my phone? I need to call Tom." She was starting to flail around, with the pistol moving dangerously to an unsafe position, something that Quade was watching with heightened awareness. "This is just ridiculous. I fix gunshot wounds, not create them. In case it slipped everyone's notice." She was referring to Quade's recent near-fatal gunshot wounds to the chest and thigh. She'd worked damn hard to keep him alive till the surgeons could patch him up properly, no mean feat given that she was drastically restricted in what she could medically administer to stabilise him due to his altered DNA.

"Yeah, well, right about now I'm thinking death would have been preferable. At least I wouldn't have to be listening to you whinge."

"Well, fine, you ungrateful sod. Next time you get shot, remind me not to give a flying fuck or lift a finger to help you. And just for the record, if you think this is whingeing? Ha—I haven't even started yet."

"Yeah, that's what I was afraid of."

She chanced a glance over her shoulder and threw him a sickly sweet smile. He took a deep breath to control his temper. He was hanging on to it by a thread and it felt as if that thread was about to snap. He took a deep cleansing breath, mentally telling himself to breathe the anger out—let it go. He'd try another tack.

"Honey nose, do you seriously think I want to be standing here teaching you to fire this weapon?"

"For the four millionth time, don't call me that. And if that's how you feel, well, let's call it a day then." She spun around, obviously intending to move away out of the lane. Unfortunately, her right hand was holding the pistol at chest height. Complete rookie mistake and absolutely a sin in the eyes of safety.

Before she could complete the turn, Quade stepped behind her and engulfed her in his arms. His right arm closed firmly over hers to take control of the weapon and prevent an accident. His chest and abs pressed tightly to her back. His left wrapped tightly around her body, just under her breasts.

"What is it about you and deadly weapons? You are seriously dangerous," he spat. "First the knife and now a pistol. Rory's wrong—the universe hates me," he said, more to himself than her.

"I wasn't going to shoot you. And I was perfectly capable of using a knife to cut up vegetables. You didn't need to grab the knife then and you don't need to grab me now," she snapped back.

He ignored her and continued on. "Did I just not get

through telling you to keep the weapon pointing towards the sky at all times unless you were taking aim?" Even to his own ears, it sounded as if he were dressing down a five-year-old.

She blew out a breath and her delectable ass collided with his groin. He instinctively thrust his hips backwards, not wanting her to realise just how much she affected him. The one thing Rory was right about was how much he wanted her. The problem was he didn't know whether he wanted to fuck her or strangle her. Both urges danced back and forth in his mind and each held an incredible amount of appeal.

Nobody pushed his buttons like she did. She'd been having a starring role in too many of his dreams of late. The worst problem was it wasn't just when he slept anymore. He found himself thinking about her just a little too much recently. He needed to figure out a plan. Maybe Rory was right. Maybe he should just fuck her and get it out of his system. But first he'd have to get her to agree to that and something told him that was going to be a challenge in itself.

He took a measured breath and moved their bodies back around to face the target. *Think with the big head, mate,* he told himself.

"Let's try this again. The sooner you hit that target, the sooner we call it a day."

"Ha, you said we were going."

"No, actually, you suggested it, Jazz."

"Oh fine. Let's get this done."

He eased her arm towards the target, his large frame slightly hunched to compensate for the difference in heights.

"Okay. Safety off, breathe...." Oh boy, he could feel her ribs move beneath his left hand. The curve of her breasts just glanced across the top of his forearm. Shit, it was enough just about to send him over. "Gently squeeze." She did as he asked and the bullet flew from the barrel of the weapon, hitting the mark true. The mental image of her squeezing something else sizzled into what was left of his brain like a branding   iron.

The recoil from the pistol pressed her firmly back into his

body. He braced himself and held firm; her rounded butt bumped his erection again. *Fuck, this was going to kill him.*

She turned her head around, obviously excited by scoring her first hit to the target and seemingly oblivious of his predicament. He glanced at the neat hole in the paper target. He didn't need to draw it back for him to know it was accurate. The benefits of his super sight.

"Well done," he said flatly.

"Can we do it again?" He could feel the excitement running through her and it only served to electrify him further.

"I thought you wanted to go?" He tried to ease slightly back from her without letting go of her right arm.

"Well, that was before I realised I might actually have some talent for this."

He shook his head. Only Jazz could come up with logic like that. And she was a shrink. Was it any wonder the world was so fucked up with logic like that?

"Okay, you can try it again. This time, I'll let you set up the aim."

She nodded her understanding and turned back to the target, preparing to line up her next round.

Jazz drew in a cleansing breath as he'd shown her, relaxed her shoulders and focused on the target. He withdrew most of the guidance of his right arm but provided just enough to hold steady and absorb some of the recoil she'd feel.

She squeezed the trigger and the bullet hit just beside the first a fraction of a second later.

He reached around her with his left hand and pried her fingers gently from the weapon, immediately clearing the chamber and disengaging the clip to ensure the weapon was harmless.

"I think that will do it for today."

She spun around, annoyance on her face.

"So just when I start to get the hang of it, we call it quits."

"You've had enough for today. Your arm will ache tomorrow, and you'll thank me then when you still have the use of it."

"Oh, that's such shit and you know it." She shifted her weight from one leg to the other and Quade could have sworn she'd almost stamped her foot. "You're just worried I might rival you."

With her last comment, he turned his back on her and began preparing their belongings to leave.

"Yep, knew it."

He stood to his full height and plastered his most menacing look on his face, the one he knew usually had his enemy shaking with fear.

"Knew what? Do you ever finish a sentence or make any sort of sense?"

A look crossed her face and it looked suspiciously as if she'd just figured something out. "You're worried you're going to get bested by a woman," she said almost incredulously.

At that, he let out a sarcastic chuckle. "You're joking, right?"

"Couldn't be more serious."

"You seriously think that I'm calling it quits today so that you won't improve in order to prevent you from rivalling my ability?"

"Yes, exactly, as you so succinctly put it," she said confidently.

He shook his head and a thought crossed his mind. His better judgement told him to leave it but he'd had enough. She'd strung him up too tight. Caged him too much.

He grabbed a full clip and slid it expertly into the body of the pistol. He stepped in front of her and in the blink of an eye, fired off seven rounds. Without even looking up, he knew they were all grouped within a hair's breadth of each other. He leant over and punched the button on the wall to retract the target.

While he waited, he cleared the chamber and clip again and then returned to what he'd been doing before. He could feel the hostility rolling from Jazz.

He reached up and retrieved the paper target from the wire. He didn't even look at it. He didn't need to. A perfect grouping. Anything less would have been second-rate. But he didn't miss the look that crossed her face. Was it astonishment or was it admiration?

"Well, sweetheart, when you can get them all within a palm's breadth of the target, I'll start getting concerned. Until then, I can sleep easy at night." This time it was his turn to slip her the belligerent grin.

Unfortunately there was something else intruding on his dreams and it wasn't his ability to roll off perfect groupings. He could do it with his eyes closed, quite literally, but she didn't need to know that today. No, his dreams were filled more and more with Jazz. Some erotic, some disturbing. He'd been there last time. What happened when she wandered into the next situation and he wasn't there to take the bullet for her? Truth was he cared—a fucking lot—and it made him feel vulnerable for the first time in his life. He didn't like it one little bit.

Similar to the night before, Rory had organised the unloading of the milk from the tanker while she remained in the truck. Regardless, she felt useless sitting there doing nothing, but the reality was she'd be far more of a hindrance than a help in her current condition with a cast on her leg. Maybe next week, if everything was healing well, she might be able to get a smaller cast or ditch it altogether in favour of something else. Ideally just a bandage. She didn't think that would be possible but no harm in dreaming. Maybe she could have a word with Jazz about it.

Don had wandered up and said hello to her. But he'd also said a lot more and his words meant something to her. He was a sweetie. She'd known him a lot of years. In fact, from the very first time she could remember her daddy bringing her here, he'd been part of her memories. From when she was a tiny little thing who had to climb like a monkey to make it up into the cab of the truck, Don had always been there, initially in the background but since her father's death, more prominent. He'd been there at her father's funeral and had helped her out the first few months after she took over the running of the business.

Now he'd asked her to think about getting out of the business altogether. He was worried about her and the things that had been happening over the last few months. They shared a common suspicion that her father and older brother's deaths were far from what they seemed to be. Of course, she'd vehemently refused to even consider the idea, but that was more the role she'd learnt to play rather than what she really thought would be the smartest thing to do.

The problem was there was no way out. She needed the business to be able to provide income for the family. TJ also had the situation with the debt that had been incurred. The only way she could see to eradicate that was to keep working through it. And that was about cash flow. The trucks needed to keep rolling and earning money. She also had to think about the welfare of the drivers and other staff she employed. She didn't think selling was really an option—who wanted to buy a business slowly drowning in debt?

"What're you so deep in thought about, sweet pea?" Rory asked her as he swung in behind the wheel, quickly firing up Old Faithful and taking off. He always sounded so cheerful, which was a refreshing change from her current thoughts.

"Oh, just some stuff that Don had to say," she replied a bit absently.

"And...?"

"He asked me to consider getting out of the business. I told him about what happened to Bob the last couple of days. He kind of freaked about the last couple of attacks. He's been close to the family for years. It seems like he's known Dad forever." She let out a sigh.

"How do you feel about that?"

"It doesn't really matter how I feel about it, Rory. The fact is I have to keep working the business. I don't have any other way to pay off the debts. I also have to consider all the consequences for the families who are relying on Walsh Haulage for their income."

He looked towards her briefly as he guided the rig through the exit gate and out onto the road home.

"That's a lot to take on, Pixie." He was back to being the solemn Rory.

"It is but I don't have a choice."

He nodded. "Maybe it seems that way right now. But one thing I do know is that there are always choices. The trick is making the right one."

She didn't say anything—just contemplated his words as the streetlights flashed by. Mmm, maybe it was time for a family meeting to discuss things. There was no doubt she was committed to the cause but when was enough, enough? And could she really make it work? She'd been trying for more than two years and the hole didn't seem to be getting any shallower.

They'd made it back to the truck yard quickly. The traffic was light at that time of the evening and most of the roads they needed to use were the kind that were the less frequented. Rory had pulled in and parked up Old Faithful in her designated spot before helping Pixie down from the truck and into the office. A bit of a breeze was blowing through tonight with a hint of a chill in it, the first of the season. He noticed she hadn't brought a jacket with her and he wanted her out of the cold quickly. Besides, he wanted to have a quick look around the depot before they headed back to the house.

His nose had picked up a new scent on the breeze and he didn't have a matching person for it yet. That was always a concern when there were threats lingering. He liked to know what his potential threats were. He also had to ring into the boss sometime soon. If he left it too long, he'd get an earful from the boss—that was never fun and something he tried to avoid whenever possible. The smell was faint and they hadn't been to the yard. It was coming from down towards the houses.

Darkness had now fallen and he used its security to conceal his extraordinary speed as he rushed through the daily checks and fuelling that needed to be done on the truck before the day could be officially finished for the day.

He walked through the door to the office and found Pixie typing at a computer, sitting at a big old scarred oak desk that dwarfed the portable fabricated building.

"Hey, sweet Pixie, you ready to blow this place? I'm starving."

She looked up at him with those incredible iris-coloured eyes. He could have happily drowned in them—he found them that magnetic.

"Just about. I just need to send this email then we can head home."

"Cool. Do you have any sort of security system on the yard?"

"Umm, what do you mean?"

"How do you secure this place at night?"

She shrugged. "Just lock the gates on the cyclone fencing and let the dogs out of the yard."

"Okay, I think we need to look at upgrading that, then."

She turned away from him, uncomfortable with the topic.

"Rory, I'd love to but I just can't afford a fancy new alarm or whatever you had in mind. I don't know how I'm going to make this month's payments if I don't get some backloads ordered pronto. Those tyres were just the last straw."

Pixie glanced back at him and he could see how uncomfortable this made her.

"Don't worry about it. I'll sort something out." And he would; he didn't want her worrying anymore. He'd also see what he could do about swinging some work her way.

"Rory, it's not your problem to solve."

"I said don't worry about it. I mean it, Pix. I'm sure the Centre will pick up the tab, but if not, I can get my hands on some gear that's not being used."

"Okay but you need to talk to me before you do anything." She looked at him sternly.

He smirked at her. "Oh Pix, I can't believe you think I'd do something without talking to you about it first." He put his hands to his chest in a wounded gesture. "That burns, sweets."

She giggled at him in return, and replied sarcastically, "You're so convincing—smart aleck."

He clapped his hands together and rubbed them vigorously.

"Come on, sweet pea—starving man here. Hustle…hustle."

"Right…." She tapped a few more keys and then flicked the monitor off and rose from the desk. Pixie used the desk and chair to support her moves as she hobbled to the door, where her crutches rested against the wall.

"You know, you could try using them."

She spun around and flashed him a cheeky smile. "Yeah, I could but they annoy me and hurt my arms. Besides, if I used them, it wouldn't give you an excuse to carry me everywhere."

He nodded, an amused grin on his face.

"True. Definitely not a fan of the crutches then."

Her light tinkly laughter floated across to his ears. It was good to hear. Something he'd like to hear a lot more of.

He put his arm around her waist and helped her into the golf cart so she wouldn't need to use the crutches, which he placed in the carry all in the back. Maybe she'd need them later.

"I need to let the dogs out. They're in the kennels and day yards behind the maintenance shed."

He headed the cart to where she needed to go and immediately got out and moved to the enclosure. Yesterday he'd made friends with the twin bullmastiffs. It was a cinch for him with his dominant canine DNA. He was immediately recognised by both of them as the alpha. They'd behaved like docile puppies ever since.

"Wait, don't go near them. They'll rip you to shreds," she yelled at him in a panicked voice, trying to extract herself from the cart.

He spun around, briefly flashing her a grin. "Don't worry, Pixie. I've got it all under control. Besides, I introduced myself to these guys yesterday—it's all good."

He heard her draw in breath, conflicted.

"Well, when you get bitten, don't say I didn't warn you."

He reached for the latch and opened the gate to the enclosure. Both dogs came bounding up to him, looking for some attention and affection. Rory dropped his hands and gave them both a solid scratch and pat behind the ears.

"Ah, fellas, missed me today, did you?"

He dropped lower and gave them both a half hug, half wrestle that had them playing with him. They were beautiful animals but he had no doubt they could be extremely dangerous if not managed responsibly.

"Okay guys. I need to head off. I can't keep Pixie waiting any longer. You understand how it is," he said solemnly to the dogs. He swore he could see their understanding reflected in their eyes.

He returned to the cart and hopped in, and then headed them towards the gate.

"How did you do that?"

"What?"

"That thing with the dogs. They hate everybody except me, my younger brother Marcus, and Gary, the yard supervisor."

He shrugged, deflecting the significance of what had happened. "I'm good with animals. I've always had a way with dogs." Well, it was true. He was good with dogs; his kooky DNA made sure of it.

"Sure. But that was something more. Zeus and Thor hate everyone," she challenged.

"Cool names," he said, trying to deflect her attention.

"Yeah, they are. I named them when they were just puppies. I was going through a mythology stage."

He leapt from the cart and swung the two-metre tall wire mesh gates shut, securing them with the heavy chain and padlock. Rory climbed back into the cart and headed towards the house before she could start on him again about the dogs.

He got in first, "So what's on the agenda for tomorrow?"

"Just more of the same as today. I need to go spend some time with my mum. I haven't seen her in a few days and that's crazy given we live a couple of hundred metres apart. I want to make sure she's doing okay."

"Sure. What have you got work wise?"

"All the normal stuff. I need to be back here at six to get the guys organised and away for the day. Then I'd normally do a few local runs, picking up shipping containers and stuff before I started my afternoon milk runs."

He nodded his understanding.

"I think I'll get one of the casuals to pick up my container runs, though. I don't expect you to be involved with those. It's got nothing to do with the milk issues you're interested in."

"Pixie, I don't care whether it does or doesn't—the boss cleared me to help you anyway I can and that's what I intend to do."

"Sure, I get that, but it's not your responsibility, and besides, one of the casuals would be happy for the extra hours."

"I thought you said you were tight for dollars?"

"I am but what's a few hundred dollars in the whole scheme of things? It's a drop in the ocean."

"Okay, if you say so. Your business."

"It is, and that's what I want." He didn't miss the slight edge to her voice.

He let the subject go. Just as he suspected, she was kind-hearted as well. *Could she get any more perfect?*

A few seconds later, he pulled the cart into its spot beside the house and helped her inside to the kitchen.

The feel of her satiny skin beneath his hands was getting harder and harder to ignore. He leant casually against the kitchen counter as she settled herself in a chair at the table.

"Okay, what're we doing for dinner?"

"Um, over there in the freezer, there's a heap of frozen meals. Aunt Clara stocked me up on Friday."

Dread immediately filled Rory. He hated processed food. He was a meat-and-potatoes sort of guy. Heavy on the meat, light on the potatoes. What he wouldn't give right now for a couple of kilos of prime rib fillet cooked very rare, or even better, blue. There was nothing better than a blue steak when both sides had just been "kissed" by the grill, and then taken off.

He walked to the single-door freezer that was actually in the laundry that adjoined the kitchen. Hope replaced dread as he opened the door and realised there were about twenty plastic freezer containers, all neatly marked. It was home cooking, not processed. That was at least a start.

He quickly sorted through a few.

"What do you want?" he called to her.

"I'll take a lasagne if there is any."

"Yep—got it." He grabbed a couple of lasagnes and a beef in red wine for good measure. It still wouldn't be enough to eat but he could at least be convincing with this much.

He moved back into the kitchen and set the containers in the microwave on defrost. They'd take a few minutes and then he'd need to heat them through. Lasagne was notorious for coming out of the microwave frozen in the middle.

Pixie was leaning back, eyes closed, cast elevated on a pulled-out chair. She looked delectable and tired all at the same time.

Rory moved behind her and gently closed his hands over her shoulders. He immediately felt the spark of electricity that seemed to flow between them whenever they came in contact with one another. His hands moved over her shoulders, massaging and kneading the tight muscles. She let out a low moan. The sound shot straight to his already awake cock.

"Mmm, do you like that, baby?"

She moved her head towards his arm and nuzzled against his hand and forearm. It was the sort of affectionate, touchy-feely gesture he loved with the right person.

"Feels wonderful. I didn't realise my shoulders were so tight."

Not one to miss an opportunity, he stepped right up. "I'll give you a massage after dinner."

She stiffened beneath him.

"You don't have to, Rory. I wasn't fishing for anything."

"I know that, gorgeous, but I want to. It gives me a great excuse to run my hands all over you in the guise of easing your tight muscles. Totally works for me." He chuckled knowingly.

She laughed that tinkling laugh. But this time it was lower, sultrier. She was killing him slowly and he doubted she even realised it.

The ding of the microwave temporarily broke the spell as he moved to reset the timer to heat the containers through.

"Where can I find plates and glasses?"

"Glasses top right cupboard by the sink, and plates are in the bottom cupboard to the left of the sink."

He moved around, organising drinks and plates, and then spooned the food from the containers when it was done.

They ate in silence for a few moments.

"Mmm, this is good. Your aunt is a great cook. But there's something a bit different about this lasagne. It tastes a little different than I've had before. Don't get me wrong—it's good but different."

"That's because the white sauce and the cheese are made from goat's milk, not cow's milk. All my dad's side of the family are allergic to cow's milk. And it seems that all of us kids inherited the gene as well. Mum's fine with cow's milk. But Aunt Clara and Mum always cook with goat's milk because it's easier."

He nodded his understanding. They both took a few more mouthfuls before his curiosity got the better of him.

"So what about you?" When she looked at him, clearly confused, he went on. "Can you cook as well?"

Pixie swallowed what was in her mouth before speaking. Even the sight of her throat contracting to swallow was enough to just about drive him nuts.

"Um, I can cook pretty well. I wouldn't say I'm as good as Mum or Aunt Clara but I haven't had any complaints."

"Well, that sounds promising. Seems I scored a bonus."

She looked at him, confused. "Ah, what are you on about?"

"My girlfriend can cook. Every guy's dream—perfect."

She giggled at him, shaking her head in disbelief.

"Has anyone ever told you, you're a bit odd?"

At that, he threw his head back and laughed.

"No, I've been called many things but I can't ever recall being called odd. Why odd?"

"Well, you never seem to take anything seriously and everything seems to never be a problem. And then you have other weird talents, like dog charming, if there is such a thing, and you obviously have some great hearing or a sixth sense for interruptions because you were aware of Aunt Clara this afternoon before she'd even set foot on the verandah. That's a skill I could have used during high school."

A moment of panic struck before he laughed it off again in true style. *Fuck, she didn't know how close to the truth she was cutting.* He was also floored at how much she'd picked up. Wow, she was observant. He'd have to be careful. Now, to avoid and deflect her observations, without telling any lies.

He started on a light chuckle. "In the interests of disclosure and you being my girlfriend, I think I should give you a heads-up on a few things about me. First, I seem to have really heightened senses. A lot more than most people. So I do hear and smell things in particular that most would miss. Um, I also have a rather large appetite. So I'll go grocery shopping tomorrow or I'll eat you out of house and home in no time."

She looked at him expectantly. "That all? Nothing I'm too alarmed about. I've got a brother who likes to eat. Nothing new there for me."

"You say that now, but I'm the sort all-you-can-eat buffets hate. Because I can literally eat them clean."

She answered him with a giggle. Ha, she thought he was joking. It was the truth but he could see she thought he was exaggerating.

"Anything else staggering I need to know about you?"

"Mmm, that will probably do for now, although I should probably mention I do have incredible stamina." He caught her eyes with his and winked.

"I'm not at all sure what you mean or why I would need to know that?" Her face gave nothing away. If he didn't have an inkling of the passionate woman underneath, he'd swear she was the picture of innocence; she was playing the role to perfection.

"Okay, play the good little Catholic girl. I'm always up for a little role playing."

"Really. I got great marks for drama in high school."

"I can see how that would be. Bet you had your teachers wrapped around your little finger, with that goody-two-shoes act. It's always the good ones you have to watch." He smirked at her. "And you I'm going to have to watch very closely."

He watched a slow seductive smile slide across her face. *Game on, Pixie.*

"Boss, it's Rory," he said into the sleek cell phone. He'd gone out onto the front verandah of the house to make his call. He'd left Pixie in the bathroom with a garbage bag at the ready to wrap around the plastic cast. He needed to have a chat with Jazz about what could and couldn't happen with that thing. Maybe they could take it off for a bit?

"I expected a call a couple of hours ago, Mr Southall. What was the holdup?"

"Ah, no real holdup, Boss—just got busy with a few things." Shit, he knew better than to leave the boss waiting but he really wanted to get dinner over and Pixie settled at home before he made the call. Experience told him it was best to keep the boss focused on business, rather than chewing his ass. "We've had a few developments today, Boss."

"Oh? What's happened?"

Mmm, maybe it would work...

"Well, first off, the truck that Pixie normally drives has been targeted."

"Back up, Rory. I take by Pixie you mean Miss Walsh. Why you can't use people's names is beyond me."

"Yes, Boss."

"Okay. How was the truck targeted?"

"Pixie sent the truck interstate a couple of days back because one of the others had a fuel pump issue. Anyway, when she spoke with the driver as to why he was late, he reported that he'd blown all four inners on the prime mover and two inners on the trailer. You and I both know that just isn't possible. So I told her to get him to have the other four changed out and throw them into the trailer. I figured we could run some tests and see what we find."

There was silence on the phone for a second.

"Good move, Rory. There's more to this than meets the eye. I have a feeling the tainted milk is just the tip of the iceberg, and at the moment all indicators lead to Miss Walsh being smack-bang in the middle of this regardless whether she has a clue or not to what's going on."

Rory felt his temper start to rise. Was the boss suggesting that Pixie knew more than she was letting on?

"Boss, I don't think she knows what's going on. I think she's somehow become a target but I don't know why yet. I do know that she's got a pissed-off stepcousin who seems to think she should marry him. Can we get Rheeba to run a check on Kelvin Walsh, please? He was very insistent today and I didn't like the vibes he was giving off at all."

"Will do. Anything else you need at the moment?"

"I've been thinking about it and I think the best way to determine the source is via our sense of smell. Today I started trying to catalogue the different scents at the dairy we went to. I'm guessing that whoever is behind this is not going to have a sole herd of genetically modified cattle. That would make no sense and be too easy to identify. If it were me, I'd be putting a couple into various herds here and there. See what I could get through the system. So based on that, we're going to have to try to identify the source and the tainted product from potentially low levels of concentrate of the actual genetically modified milk. I'm not sure this is going to be a quick process; it could take a while."

"I thought as much, Rory. At least we're not dealing with an eminent threat here. We most definitely need to stop this thing because of the potential health implications and the illegality of the practice. However, as far as we know, we don't have an immediate deadly threat like we had with the Hendra virus recently. Those sorts of threats we could do without."

"No, I agree, Boss. But there just seems to be a whole heap of shit tangled up around Pixie and I'm confident that once we untangle it, we'll get to the bottom of the contaminated milk as well."

The line was quiet for a moment. Rory was used to this. The boss was always very deliberate in his communication and phone calls with him could often get a bit strange. He was regularly left wondering whether he was talking to himself.

The boss's voice broke back into the silence. "That's what I'm counting on. I'll have Quade and Jazz check out the dairies serviced by Q-Trans some more. So far they've come up with nothing but I think you're right. The only way to track this is via a scent profile."

"Boss, any chance we can get some samples of the tainted product? If Quade, I, and anyone else working on this can get a profile, then tracking the source or product that is contaminated is going to be so much easier."

"Agreed. I'll talk to the LizDern people and the food authorities and see if we can get some samples. As you know, I need to be careful how we obtain the samples. All hell would rain down if word got out about the Centre's abilities. It may take a couple of days."

Rory had an idea. He wondered whether the boss would be on board or not. *Only one way to find out.* "Ah, Boss, what if you ran the story that the Centre has a new medical laboratory or something and we want to do tests to determine the true threat. I'd think they'd buy it. None of these guys really know what we do except we carry a lot of clout and have deep resources. I'm sure you could convince them it's in their best interest."

There was silence on the phone for a few seconds. "I like the idea, Mr Southall. I'll speak to the director of the Food Authority. He'll come at that line, I'd think."

"So you'll send over someone to look at the tyres as well?" He had his suspicions that they'd hold clues to part of this puzzle.

"I'll organise something. When is the truck supposed to be arriving back at base?"

"I'd say it should be safely in by oh-nine-hundred."

"Anything else, Mr Southall?"

"No, Boss. Good night."

"Oh, and one other thing before you go, Mr Southall. Don't be late calling in again." The line disconnected. The boss didn't need to say more than that. He knew he'd delivered his message.

Chapter Seven

Rory walked back into the house after the call. He immediately noticed the banging and crashing and huffing and puffing coming from Pixie's room. What on earth was going on?

The door was pulled closed but not caught on the lock.

He could hear what he'd swear were sobs.

"Pixie, are you okay? I'm coming in."

"Don't," was the feeble reply that came back to him.

Ignoring her request, which in his mind was not even that, he slowly pushed the door open and promptly burst out laughing at the sight of her on the bed.

My God, she was something to look at. Her white blonde hair was half falling from her ponytail. Her flushed cheeks were stained with tears of frustration and the right leg of her denim shorts seemed to be stuck over the hard plastic of her cast. Her left leg twisted at a funny angle. Somehow she'd managed to bind herself with her shorts. And she couldn't look sexier with her perfect, rounded little butt in the air. He was having a hard time dragging his eyes from the pale pink satin panties she wore to cover it.

"Ah, sweet thing—if you'd wanted to be bound, you only had to ask," he teased.

"Rory!" she yelled, frustration and disbelief streaming through.

Whoops! He winced. Sometimes he needed to filter better, and not everyone thought his attempts at humour were as funny as he did.

"Sorry, baby doll—I guess that wasn't as funny as it seemed."

"Not really, but now that you've barged in here could you at least see if you can get me untangled? I should never have put these rotten shorts on this morning. But a favourite is a favourite."

"Right—let me see what I can do," he replied stoically.

He moved to the bed and gently rolled her over until she was on her back. The problem was the right leg of the shorts was too tight to really fit over the cast. He knew he could get them off no problem at all but he didn't want to put force on the cast or her leg any more than necessary. That would hurt her for sure. And that was something he couldn't contemplate doing easily.

First off, he unhooked the fabric of the left leg from the cast. Somehow in her struggles, she must have got it caught, which had effectively tied her up. Then he placed his hand under her left knee and gently encouraged her to bend her leg for him. The shorts easily slid over her left leg. Now he just had to sort out the cast on her right leg, because the feel of his hand on her bare skin had already done wicked things to his libido.

He had images running through his head of sliding his hand upwards to run over her inner thighs. Of skirting the elastic on the legs of those pale pink panties that seemed to be calling his name, and delving his fingers inside.

This was some kind of torture. Having his hands on her body just did incredible things to his. He really wanted to caress and stroke, but he knew he'd better leave that for later when he managed to get her free of these shorts.

With a deep breath, he placed her left leg back on the cotton quilt of the bed, and then turned his attention to the right.

"Maybe we should just cut them. I'm over it," she suggested, obviously embarrassed and wanting this to end.

"Did you not just tell me these shorts were a favourite?"

"Well yeah, but I'm not that attached to them."

"Give me a sec and let me see what I can do."

He closed both strong hands around her thigh and slid his thumbs under the fabric of the shorts. He carefully managed to feed the fabric over the edge of the plastic cast and slowly worked it down over the boot. It took a couple of minutes and lots of careful sliding but he got it there in the end.

With the shorts finally free of the cast, he twirled them around his right index finger and let them fling across the room.

"Ah, escape from the killer shorts."

She giggled at his antics. "You don't know how close to the truth that felt. I was about to go searching for scissors."

"You only had to ask and I'd eagerly have offered to help." He waggled his eyebrows at her.

"Oh, I'm very sure you would have. But there are some things a girl likes to do for herself. Getting undressed is one of them."

"Well then, maybe you haven't been hanging out with anyone who knows how to do it for you better. I can't think of a thing I'd rather be doing than helping you out of your clothes." His voice was deeper than usual and a little husky. The sound portrayed every erotic thought he was having right now and she noticed. He sat on the edge of the bed and took her hand in his, gently stroking his thumb over the soft skin of the underside of her wrist.

The first thing that assaulted his senses was the fragrance of her increased arousal. She might be playing a little coy but she wanted him. There was something else there as well and that something else concerned him.

Her adrenalin was up and she started to become a little panicky. He could tell by the way her pulse had spiked. But to look at her face and body, she showed no signs of alarm at all. Outwardly, she seemed calm and into everything that was happening but inwardly there was something else going on.

He wanted to try something, to see whether his suspicions were right.

Rory moved his big frame up the bed and laid down on his back next to her on the queen-sized bed. He snaked his arm under her shoulders and urged her to move her body up and across his shoulders and chest.

The purple-blue of her eyes glinted at him with excitement and something else as she paused, not quite sure what he wanted. He could feel her heart pounding against his chest from the contact he'd initiated. He reached up and drew his hand through the silky strands of her hair, gently pulling the hair tie with it. A shower of the white blonde strands framed her face.

He cupped her jaw and cheek with his hand and traced the pad of his thumb over her plump lips. His eyes never left hers.

"Kiss me, sweet Pixie. I want to feel your lips on mine."

She drew in a breath. Her heartbeat increased to the point she could feel it smashing against her ribs. And even more anxiousness clawed at her belly. Logically, she knew she wanted him, his hands on her, his body close to hers. The dampness between her legs confirmed any confusion she may be feeling but still she momentarily hesitated.

All the things he could do to her she wanted so much, but she was scared at the same time. She would guarantee that he was a man who was used to getting what he wanted. Rory may be sweet and kind and funny but he was foremost an alpha male. There was an ever-present latent sexuality about him, but now he'd obviously decided to let it step to the forefront.

TJ had no doubt he was used to experienced women with advanced degrees in sexually satisfying a man. How could she compete? She'd barely even thrown the training wheels off when it came to sex, and for the last two and a half years there had been no one she'd even been remotely interested in.

He'd made it clear he was into her but how could she not disappoint him? She didn't want to hold back with him; she wanted to experience this attraction between them in its rawest, most primitive form.

Decision made—she'd do what she always did when fear raised its ugly head. Kick its ass and dive right in—or fake it till she could make it. They were two mottos she'd lived by for the last few years.

TJ inhaled deeply and plastered what she hoped was a siren's smile upon her lips. She lowered her head and joined her lips to his. Rory's lips felt soft and warm to hers but before she lost her nerve, she ground her mouth against his firmly and stabbed at his lips with her tongue. He opened his mouth for her slightly and she immediately thrust her tongue against his, sliding it furiously inside his mouth and taking firm control of the kiss.

Her hand slipped down between them, and she raked her nails lightly over his muscled belly and abs. The T-shirt he was wearing did nothing to disguise the definitions. His muscles rippled beneath her fingers. She found the waistband of his pants and slid her fingertips inside.

Her fingers found the coarser hairs of the trail that led like a map to her destination. She only needed to move her fingers a fraction of an inch farther and she found what she was looking for: the velvety smooth head of his very engorged cock.

Her mouth kept at his, furiously demanding something, but what she wasn't quite sure.

She wrapped her small hand around his iron length and stroked up and down, and was rewarded with a low groan from deep in his throat.

His hands came up and fisted in her hair, lightly tugging, but still she went on devouring his mouth like a starving woman, even though fear spiked through her.

He moved then, rolling her under him and trapping her beneath his hard body. She let out a little gasp and her heartbeat sped up even more to the point where all she could hear was the sound of her blood rushing through her veins as she tried to draw breaths that didn't seem to come.

To cover her surprise and almost overwhelming fear, she immediately locked her lips to his and resumed her campaign on his mouth. She tightened her grip around his hard length, her hand rendered immobile by his considerable weight on her much smaller frame.

Her breath was coming in short pants. She was climbing, reaching for something.

Rory planted his right hand on the bed beside her head and levered himself upwards away from her demanding mouth.

He knew her game.

The outwards signs she gave were saying one thing but his more than human senses were telling him something else. Yes, she wanted him, and if he had to guess, he'd say badly. But she was also frightened about something. Not just the usual anxiousness or curiosity about being with a new lover; she was frightened. Her fear had increased when he'd lightly tugged on her hair. The smell of her fear had increased even more when he'd trapped her beneath him. And her breathing was shallow and laboured to the point of hyperventilating.

He needed to take control of this now.

She was throwing herself at him, trying to convince him of something she wasn't comfortable giving yet. There was no way he'd accept anything from her but what she was willingly and comfortably able to give. He needed to protect her from herself. Something seemed to screw her judgement at times and she dived right in without thought for her own wellbeing.

That was going to stop now.

Rory shifted his body slightly to the right, resting his weight on his elbow. He kept one long leg thrown over hers to prevent her from moving away. They needed to talk and he didn't want her getting any ideas about running off.

He looked down into her confused eyes and stroked a lock of hair back from her face. He made certain to keep his touch light and soft.

"Want to tell me what that was about, sweetheart?"

She looked past him and uttered, "What do you mean?"

"I'm talking about the full onslaught I just got. I've got no problems with a woman taking control but, sweets, you weren't into it at all. You were going through some series of choreographed motions that I'm guessing you thought I'd like. That's not what I want between us."

Her eyes remained focused past his shoulder and he knew she was struggling to answer. He'd called her on the deception and she was totally off guard in how to proceed. So he went on, giving her more time.

"I want honesty and passion but only if it's mutual and real." He paused and then took a gamble. He was a lucky bastard and he was willing to bet the universe wouldn't change that now. "I know you're terrified for some reason and I just experienced your attempt at being worldly, wanton. The fear I can handle. I'll work through that with you till it's gone, but only if you really want to. If you're not into me, or this relationship we're trying, then we can call it all off now. No pressure. I'll still do everything I said I would but I won't touch you anymore. It'll be totally platonic. Two work colleagues—nothing more."

He felt and heard her gasp beside him. He'd hit her very bluntly with the options but he needed to establish a baseline of trust between them before things went any further.

Rory had no doubt he could have pushed her to the very edge, taken her over, and she would have given him everything. Something told him it would have cost her deeply, emotionally, but she would have still willingly paid the price.

The woman had no sense of self-preservation.

He knew then with absolute clarity that he'd have to look out for both of them.

His hand cupped her chin gently and he stroked her cheek with his thumb.

"Talk to me. We can get through this but you need to talk to me."

He watched emotions roll across her face. Her bottom lip trembled, and then she pulled her unfocused eyes back to his.

"I am into you, more than you can possibly know but I'm scared. Something happened to me a long time ago and I struggle to get past it."

He nodded his understanding, waiting to see if she'd give him anything else. When she didn't, he decided to take the initiative.

"Were you raped?" The question hung in the air—ugly, sinister and in polar opposite to the freshness and vibrancy of the woman in his arms.

He held his breath, hoping the answer to this question was in the negative. She turned her head into his chest. A whispered "no" squeezed up between them. Rory moved his hand to her head and stroked through the strands, trying to soothe and reassure. Then he let out some of the air he'd trapped in his lungs. Some semblance of relief washed through him.

There was something further he needed to know. He was in uncharted waters here and he needed a few landmarks to plot his course by.

"Are you a virgin?"

Another whispered "no" floated up.

"Do you want to tell me what happened?"

Pixie slowly shook her head from side to side.

"Okay, I won't push you to tell me yet. But know this, if things go as I hope, I'll want to know everything about you. That includes what happened. And in return, I'll give you all of me. We all have our secrets, things that we think we can't or shouldn't share. Some of these are harmless and some of them can burn a hole clear through you, eating you from the inside out. I'll make you a deal." At his words, she moved her head back from the security of his chest and looked at him, curiosity in her eyes. "When the time's right, we'll exorcise our demons and our secrets together. How's that sound?"

She didn't answer, just nodded her acceptance and agreement.

"Okay—so we go on with this, but how about you let me take control? But I'll promise you this, I won't push you any faster than you feel comfortable going."

Finally her eyes met his and she whispered, "Yes."

She was much calmer now. Her pulse almost back to normal and the scent of fear had almost completely diminished. All these signs pleased him immensely. He chuckled softly, which had her looking at him strangely.

"Just thought of something else I should have mentioned to you earlier. I hope you don't mind but I'm naturally a very affectionate type of guy. I know a lot of guys don't think it's cool but I like to touch, caress, and anything else that comes to mind. I like to be tactilely close to people who mean something to me. Do you think you can handle that?"

She giggled then and nodded. "I'm sure I can get used to it."

He looked at her again. His eyes were full of seriousness. "I need you to promise me that if you start to feel uncertain or afraid at any time, you tell me. If this is going to work between us, I want and need to be there for you in every way. That means in and out of the bedroom. It also means that I want you to feel free to be yourself around me. I don't want the Pixie that you think I'd prefer. I want the real one. If you want to touch me, kiss me, yell at me, whatever, do it. Don't think, don't wonder, do it!"

Before he could say anything further, she reached up and slid her hand around the back of his head and pulled him towards her. Her lips met his—soft, sweet, and a little unsure, in total contrast to what he'd experienced a few minutes before. This was the real Pixie. She was pure and honest and he knew without doubt he was already a little bit in love with her.

"I promise."

Chapter Eight

TJ woke to her internal alarm clock. She knew without looking at her bedside table that the numerals would read either a couple of minutes before or a couple of minutes after five. She needed to be at the depot by six. She moved slightly and noticed the clock read four fifty-seven. There were a few spare minutes she could savour.

And yes, she was savouring. Savouring the feel of Rory's long hard body pressed tightly to her back, his left arm draped over her ribs just under her breasts. His fingers entwined with hers.

They'd slept this way ever since they'd both fallen asleep late in the evening.

He'd been incredible. Understanding, caring, and considerate. She never would have thought she could be so lucky. Perhaps she wasn't as good of an actress as she thought. He'd obviously seen right through her seductress routine. They both knew he could have taken advantage but he didn't; that meant so much to her. She was into him but not ready to go further, but she would have regardless, if he'd wanted to.

For the first time in a very long while, she felt hope. Hope that things would turn out all right. Hope that life had something good and beautiful for her as well. And it was all due to Rory. He gave her this hope. He gave her something that she felt for the first time in what seemed like forever she could anchor to. Hold steady to, as the challenges her life threw at her blew past.

She knew he was going to make her face her fears but he was going to do it with honesty and with caring and consideration.

The conversations and events of last night scrolled through her memory. After they'd had "the discussion," as she thought of it, she'd kissed him.

She'd been nervous, not terrified but nervous. She'd also felt a little embarrassed by her previous actions. It wasn't her and he'd called her on it. It still floored her that he could read her so well.

Their first kiss post "the discussion" was so different. It was sweet, sensual, and honest. She'd pressed her lips to his hesitantly, shyly, not knowing quite what to do. And he'd caught her.

Rory had gently taken control as he said he would. He teased and tasted her mouth, slowly exploring. Building, coaxing, encouraging her to play with him, join with him.

Then he'd slowly started to use his hands. First he'd been content to stroke them softly through her hair, down the side of her face, across her collarbone.

For the first time in for what seemed like forever, she'd wanted more with a man. She let him set the pace but she felt content, excited, and needy. Not anxious, scared, and nearly terrified.

And just when she'd thought he'd press for more, he'd surprised her again. He'd slowly slid her T-shirt up and over her head. His hands had lightly traced over the slope of her shoulder and down her rib cage, tantalisingly skirting her nipples, which had been pebbled tightly in the cups of her bra. His fingertips had ignited all sorts of tiny fires over her skin.

All the while his eyes had held hers, promising, asking for trust, calling for her. Finally she'd moved towards him, wanting to feel her body pressed against his. He drew her close and held her in an embrace that promised everything. It promised understanding, caring, consideration, and passion.

The passion was well reined in, but it was unmistakable.

His hard erection had been nestled between them as a constant reminder of just how much he wanted her. It also reminded her of just how much he was giving her without taking, without pressing for more.

And for the final surprise of the evening, he'd rolled her onto her stomach and straddled her hips and butt. He'd placed his hands on her shoulders. He'd promised her a massage earlier and he'd delivered. His hands had been firm but caressing. Sometimes kneading, sometimes skimming lightly over the planes of her back and shoulders. His fingertips had slid under and around the straps of her bra that hid her breasts from him, teasing and suggesting but not pressing for more.

It had gone on for what seemed like hours. And just as when he was kissing her, she knew he was mapping her. Learning her body, studying, memorising, and cataloguing her responses for later. Finally he had undone the clasp of the bra and slid the straps up her arms in a long stroke. He'd then placed her hands through the armholes of the discarded T-shirt and drawn it slowly over her arms, head, and then body.

Finally he'd lie down beside her and rolled her into him. He'd dropped featherlike kisses over her ear, neck, and cheek, before he'd settled down to draw her even closer, spooning her back to his front.

"Sweet dreams, my beautiful Pixie," he'd whispered in her ear before the mist of sleep had taken her.

And that brought her to now—the morning after "the discussion."

She glanced at the clock again. It was now five past five and all she'd managed to do was get her all hot and bothered. His long, hard length was undeniable down her spine. She felt safe, content, and very turned on. She thought for a moment, considered. He'd said to go with what she wanted. She'd promised him.

Without further thought, she wriggled back into the solid body behind her. The cleft of her butt immediately found the hard rod of his morning erection.

His arm tightened around her middle, and he whispered in her ear in a very sexy, sleep rough voice.

"I can see you've taken to heart what I said last night, Pixie. I like it."

She giggled lightly in response.

He moved the arm he had around her waist and splayed his palm across her flat belly. Slowly, his hand crept under the soft cotton of her T-shirt that had moved up to her waist during the night. He started to trace a slow circular pattern on her stomach. Soft slow circles that did nothing but make her more needy.

Then his head moved slightly and he tucked his face into her neck, inhaling her scent. She felt his cock jolt against her butt. And she wriggled back in answer.

"Pixie, do you have any idea how much of a temptress you are and you're not even trying?"

She giggled lightly, relishing in his words.

"How much time do we have?"

"About ten minutes. I need to grab a shower and something to eat before I head to the yard."

"Okay, then let me play for a few minutes. Then we'll get up. But first let me drive myself to the point of insanity before I even start the day."

She nodded hazily. All the time his hand had not stopped its slow caress of her stomach, slowly but surely, inching up closer and closer to her breasts.

They felt heavy, with her nipples pebbled tight, longing for some attention. But did she dare push it? His thumb lightly flicked the full under curve of her breasts as he continued the circle. She waited impatiently for his hand to return to the under curve of her breasts, hoping he might be a bit more daring. The next caress mirrored the previous.

He'd mentioned something about the point of insanity. She was fast approaching it as well. The core of her ached for his touch; she could feel the wetness between her thighs— wet and wanting. But still he continued with the slow circles of insanity.

When finally she could stand it no more, she laid her hand over his and moved it upwards over her breast, encouraging him to take the fullness of her breast in his hand.

He lightly brushed the hard peak of her nipple as he murmured in her ear, "Are you sure?"

Her response was a low groan full of pleasure.

At the sound, he traced his tongue around the shell of her ear and she shivered at the delicious feeling. Prickles of pleasure raced down her neck and engulfed her. Her senses were starting to overload on need.

But before she could get used to the twin assault on her body, he upped the ante and lightly pinched the peaked nipple, causing a jolt of white-hot need to her feminine core. She tensed, absorbing the feeling, trying to centre herself with all the need floating around.

She felt her earlobe disappear into his mouth and he sucked and lightly pulled on it in time to the massaging, rolling, and light pinching of his fingers on her nipple.

She groaned again, wanting more, needing to turn in to him and press further. Just as she was about to act on the impulse, the impatient bleat of the alarm shattered the moment. TJ reached out and slammed her hand down on the alarm clock to silence its intrusion.

Rory stilled his glorious fingers, instead cupping her breast, weighing and massaging.

"I guess we need to get up, sweet Pixie."

"I guess we do." She scooted back again and wriggled firmly into him again.

"Oh, sweets, that's not playing fair. I'm hanging on by a thread here. Give me a little leniency."

"And you think I'm any different?"

He licked her earlobe again and blew lightly across it. It sent shivers all through her.

"Good to know. Now we need to get out of bed before this goes faster than you're ready for."

"I think I'm ready to go faster," she urged.

He moved his hand from her breast and gave her a light slap where her butt met her thigh.

"I said I was taking control. And I Am. Now up. Don't worry. I won't forget where I was up to."

TJ turned to face him and caught the devilish grin on his face. She moved to sit up and clambered from the bed.

It was just after seven when TJ settled back into her chair behind the desk. The morning rush was over. She'd gotten the guys out on the road and earning money. Albeit, with a lot of help from Rory.

This was the first time most of her staff had gotten to meet him. And to say they were curious was an understatement. In all the years that some of them had known her, she'd never had a boyfriend around.

He'd been lounging on the edge of her big desk, a friendly but protective presence as the guys had filed in, mostly in groups, looking for their morning runs.

The first couple of drivers had moved in, looking at her expectantly to introduce them. When she'd said nothing, Rory had cleared his throat and tilted his head at her, the chocolate brown pools of his eyes asking her the silent question *are you going to or am I?*

She'd blushed and then quickly introduced them. "Ah, guys, this is Rory, my boyfriend. Rory, this is Chris and Gavin." They shook hands and passed nods.

She'd been passing over paperwork for them when the curiosity obviously got the better of Chris. "I didn't think you dated, TJ?"

"Why would you think that" she'd replied, a little surprised.

"Well, I guess because we've never seen you with a guy and well, you know, you never show any interest, plus the, ah, whole Catholic thing."

TJ knew that by putting him on the spot she had made him nervous. Well, he'd asked; now he'd get his answer.

"Chris, not that it's any of your business, but I don't like to mix my personal and private lives."

At this point, Gavin had chimed in, slapping Chris on the shoulder. "See mate, wouldn't have made any difference if you knew she would date. She just said she wouldn't date you because you work for her."

Rory had remained silent throughout the exchange and she could see the amusement on his face. Chris had taken his paperwork and stomped out the door.

Similar scenes had replayed over the next half an hour as all the drivers doing local runs got their schedules for the day. Only difference was Rory took it upon himself to do the introductions first up and keep the drivers busy chatting, giving her a chance to sort out the paperwork and avoid more awkward questions.

TJ realised even more how powerful his laidback easy charm was. People immediately warmed to him, and he had that innate ability to put people at ease. He was the sort who made friends easily.

Her thoughts were on that as she drained the last of the coffee he'd made for her when they'd arrived at the office. It was her third for the morning. But who was counting? Coffee was a necessity given the hours she kept.

Rory came back through the door, a concerned look on his face.

"What's up?" she asked, immediately worried.

"I can smell gas. Have you got any gas cylinders around here that may be leaking?"

"No, nothing like that down here. Just diesel and some unleaded petroleum. I don't think we even have the gas BBQ down here anymore." She thought for a moment. "Yeah, it's back at Mum's place."

He still looked agitated; clearly concerned at what he thought he could smell. He turned to head back out the door when a loud *Boom* split the air. The noise caused her to flinch and then adrenalin immediately flooded her system. There was no mistaking that something close by had just exploded.

She saw Rory disappear through the door.

Fear clawed upwards, tightening around her throat as she tried to rush around the desk, hampered all the way by her cast. Before she made it to the door, he was coming back through.

"Call triple zero—the explosion was at your mum's place. I'm going to see what I can do." Before she could say another word, he streaked back out through the door.

It hit her then. Her mum, Aunt Clara, Marcus, and Katie. Oh God, they'd have been having breakfast. Getting ready for the day.

TJ felt her body start to crumble. Rory had yelled for her to do something—*what was it?* Her brain felt like cotton wool.

Think, TJ.

Her hand reached behind her for the portable phone on the desk as she slumped down in front of it.

Her shaking fingers somehow managed to dial the three zeros.

She placed the phone to her ear and tried to calm her ragged breathing.

"What's your emergency?" the operator asked.

"Gas explosion."

"Address please."

She gave the address, on auto pilot.

"Were there any people involved?"

"I think so…my…family," she sobbed.

"I've dispatched ambulances and the fire brigade. They'll be with you very soon. Are you located somewhere safe?"

"Yes," she whispered. The phone fell from her hand. She needed to get there. Needed to see for herself what was going on. TJ crawled the few feet to the door and used the frame to drag herself upwards. Her hand brushed the crutches leaning beside the door so she grabbed them and shoved them under her arms. Somehow she managed to get down the two steps and over to the golf cart without falling.

It seemed to take an eternity.

She slumped into the seat, pushed the crutches to the passenger's side and grabbed hold of the wheel, glad to have something solid to cling to.

TJ immediately went to stomp her right foot on the accelerator and realised her mistake. Angrily, she jerked her right leg aside and stomped on the accelerator with her left foot, sending the little cart lurching forward at full acceleration.

The three-quarters of a kilometre never seemed longer as she raced down the gravel driveway. She could hear the faint wail of sirens, getting closer and closer, louder and louder.

Then she did something she rarely did. She prayed.

Please God, let them be okay. You can't have them, too.

Her relationship with God had been strained since her father and her brother's deaths. How could he have taken them both?

The truth was she no longer thought she believed. But right now, she didn't know what else to do, so she fell back on habit.

She needed hope.

It soon became a chant in her mind. Over and over, she recited the words silently, begging for no more heartbreak, begging for no more tragedy. Surely there had to be a limit to what was her share?

TJ was torn. Not for the first time, she wished the cart went quicker to get her there sooner. But at the same time not wanting to know—not having to face the heartbreak.

She knew firsthand just how cruel life could be.

The death of her father and brother had hammered home that lesson.

As she rounded the final bend, TJ saw the red and blue lights flashing above the tall cane. Help was almost here.

Her senses were assaulted in the worst possible way as she drew closer to the house.

All the loss and grief she'd felt with the passing of her father and Alan gurgled back up, threatening to choke her.

Lying on the ground in a neat row were her younger brother, sister, aunt, and mother. Their lifeless forms, broken, twisted, covered in soot and debris.

Numbness overtook her.

The world stopped for a few seconds while she took it all in.

The breath ripped from her lungs, her vision obscured to everything but the horror in front of her.

Then she looked closer—really looked.

TJ saw what was there all the time for her too-foggy mind to comprehend.

Rory was on his knees beside her mother, his hands firmly at her chest, doing compressions. His mouth covered her mother's, trying to breathe life back into her frail body.

Somehow she managed to stop the cart and stumble closer.

She fell and felt pain radiate up her right side. It was enough to jolt her from the vortex of fear and numbness she'd descended into.

She made it a few metres from her family and collapsed to the ground; looking but not seeing, absorbing, but not believing.

Activity suddenly flooded the scene. Men and women yelled and shouted. She heard but didn't understand. They were gone, weren't they?

Taken from her again. Just like her father and Alan.

Arms closed around her and dragged her back, away from them.

A scream ripped from her throat. "No. Leave me with them," she wailed.

She closed her eyes and let the darkness engulf her.

Chapter Nine

"Pixie, wake up! Come on, Pixie, come back to me." The words were prodding at her consciousness but not making any sense. Was she dreaming? Did they want her? She just wanted to float back under the warm darkness that held her, the nothingness that was so peaceful. She was tired, so very tired and the darkness felt good, as if she were cuddled in a warm cocoon.

Something cool and wet wiped at her face. She resented the sensation as it dragged her further from the darkness she'd been resting in.

"Come on, Pixie, open those gorgeous purple-blue eyes I love. I want to see them now." At the command, she forced her eyelids upwards. They felt like lead weights. She blinked a few times in deference to the daylight.

"There you go, sweetheart. Come back to me now. Good girl." The cloth wiped at her face some more and she struggled to move, to sit up. She desperately tried to make sense of what was going on. His arms closed around her and held her tight.

When her focus returned, she looked up to see the warmth radiating from Rory's eyes. He was holding her, stroking her face with the cloth.

"What's going on?"

"You fainted. You've only been out for a couple of minutes."

It seemed longer. It was almost as if she'd woken from a really long sleep. The world seemed different. Not quite like she remembered.

He leant down and brushed his lips across her forehead in a very tender kiss.

"You gave me a scare, sweet Pixie. Are you feeling okay?"

"Yeah, just really tired."

"Okay. Do you feel up to heading to hospital?"

"What f—" She never finished the sentence. It all came flooding back. The horror of seeing her family laid out on the ground. Burnt, broken, gone.

She gulped in air, unable to form words. Silent tears gushed from her eyes.

He cradled her closer to him, feeding the strength of his body into hers.

"It's okay, baby girl. I've got you. We'll go see them when you're feeling a bit better." He stroked his hand over her hair, comforting her, stilling her hacking sobs. "It'll be a little while before they're up to visitors anyway."

At his words, hope flooded her veins. *Were they not gone?*

"Tell me, I need to know," she pleaded.

"They're on their way to hospital now. I'm not going to lie to you, Pixie. It's not good. Your mum and aunt are in a bad way. They both have some pretty serious burns."

She tried to absorb this, tried to make sense of his words.

Were they really alive?

"What about Marcus and Katie?"

"They should be fine in a few days. I think they may have a few broken bones but they were coming around by the time the ambulances left."

Relief swamped her when she realised she wasn't alone.

"Would you like some water?"

She nodded her head in acceptance. He held the glass to her lips for her while she took a couple of small sips.

"What happened?"

"Well, you know about the first part. I was with you when we heard the explosion. I took off across the paddock and got to the house as fast as I could. It was already on fire but I knew that they were in there so I got your brother and sister out first. They were in the lounge room closest to the entry. I checked to make sure they were breathing and went back in for your aunt and mother."

She glanced up at his face some more and for the first time noticed the soot stains on his cheeks as well. His clothes also carried the acrid smell of fire.

"I found your aunt in the dining room and your mother at the back of the kitchen. Your mother has some pretty bad burns and she was unconscious and not breathing when I got her out of there. I was doing CPR when I noticed you pull up in the cart. That was about the same time as the ambos and the firies arrived. Fortunately, they sent two ambulances so they transported your mum and aunt almost immediately; a couple of minutes later, another couple arrived and took your brother and sister."

It was so much to take in.

TJ tried to sit up once again and this time he helped her. He moved a few pillows and settled her back against the headboard of the bed.

"Why don't you finish that glass of water and rest for a couple of minutes while I jump in the shower and get rid of this smell of smoke?"

"Okay."

"Do you mind if I use your bathroom? I don't want to be too far from you in case you need anything."

She shook her head absently. She liked the thought of him being close. It somehow made all this craziness bearable.

True to his word, he was finished and dressed in fresh jeans and polo shirt. TJ didn't fail to notice how a few stray droplets of water hung desperately to the close cropped prickles of his darkish blonde hair.

She could relate to those droplets. It was exactly how she felt right now. Desperately clinging to Rory, trying not to fall.

He walked to the bed.

"Come on, Pixie, I'll help you get cleaned up then we'll head to the hospital."

Fifteen minutes later, they were on the road to hospital.

"Tom Anderson," the boss answered on the second ring. He'd left Pixie briefly in the waiting room. He should have called in to the boss immediately, but Pixie had needed him more. He'd take the heat gladly if it made her feel better.

"Rory, Boss. I've got a problem. Pixie's mum's place has just gone up in a gas explosion. I got her mum, aunt, and younger brother and sister out but we're at the hospital now and it's not looking good for the mum or aunt."

"Slow down, Rory. Start at the beginning. Tell me what happened."

Rory took a deep breath to calm the frustration and gather his thoughts as he recounted the events of the morning for the boss.

"Fuck, someone wants to screw with these people badly. What have we walked into here?"

"I wish I knew but it just seems to get deeper and deeper. As I said, I smelt the gas just a few moments before the explosion but I had no idea."

"Did you notice anything else off?"

Rory thought back. "Actually, I did. When we got back last night, I noticed a different scent. Someone who hadn't been there before but I didn't think much of it. I've only been involved for a few days. It's not as if I've been exposed to all the people who may or may not have business with the Walshs." Rory kicked himself. He should have been more attentive, but he'd been more concerned about getting Pixie back into the house and fed.

"Fuck. I should have checked it out more."

"Don't beat yourself up about things that you should have done, Rory. As you said, there was no way you could identify all the scents of people who should or shouldn't have been there."

The line went quite for a few seconds.

"I'll send Jazz and Quade over to hospital. She should be able to get some better answers out of the medicos, particularly now that she carries Centre ID. I'll brief Quade and tell him to keep watch for anything strange. We have to assume the whole family has become targets. For what reason, I have no fucking idea, and I don't like it. I'll also see who's available to assist. I have Dylan heading your way to take care of those tyres anyway. He can hang around and make himself useful. At the very least, he can help relieve Quade. More than ever, you need to stay glued to Miss Walsh. "

The boss didn't speak what they both knew. Pixie was a massive target and whomever this was seemed to be systematically picking off people or things close to her.

"Thanks Boss."

"Bloody hell, I could really use Brayden right now. Rheeba's up to her eyeballs running things here and just about everybody else is involved in that environmental spill in Victoria. Doesn't bloody rain, it pours around here. Anything further?"

"Ah, not at the moment, Boss."

"Okay, go do what you need to. And Rory, stay alert. I don't like it when we start getting suspicious gas explosions happening around my people. How the hell did genetically modified cattle morph into this?" he heard the boss say as the line went dead.

Rory walked back into the hospital waiting room and found Pixie, standing near the window and resting her hand against the wall for support. She was being hovered over by Kelvin and another middle-aged man. His temper immediately started to rise. He could smell the anxiousness and fear coming off her in waves and he was still fifty feet from her.

Just what they didn't need, a visit from cousin Kelvin.

He walked up behind her and looped his arms around her waist and drew her back into him protectively. He noted the surprise that was quickly covered on the face of the older man. The rage coming off the cousin was impossible to miss as well.

In the interests of being polite, he thrust his hand forward to the older man and introduced himself.

"Rory Southall, Teresa's boyfriend." The older man gripped his hand tightly. Rory laughed inwardly and increased the pressure himself. Two could play at this game and there'd only be one winner: him.

"Max Walsh," the older man gritted out as he dropped the contact with Rory's hand.

Something about these two alarmed Pixie to the point of fear. Just like last night, she looked outwardly calm but her pulse was racing and the smell of fear was flowing from her pores. Now that he was used to the smell, it was a cinch for his nose to detect.

He subtly pressed his front against her back, attempting to let her know he'd keep her safe.

"Any news?" he asked, trying to break the tension.

"Not as yet," Max replied. His eyes were cold and dead. Rory had seen it before; they were the eyes of a predator. Someone who took pleasure from others' weaknesses and misfortunes.

"Okay, Pixie, why don't we head down to the cafeteria and get a coffee? We could be in for a long wait and I'm starving."

She nodded her agreement but said nothing. He moved slightly back from her but kept his arm firmly around her shoulders, protecting her with his body. But also providing the support she needed to move more easily with the restrictions of the cast.

He moved her to the elevators and a brief glance at the map on the wall allowed him to locate the hospital café.

Inside the café, he found a quiet booth against the window. The tall backs of the benches provided a level of privacy that he liked. He helped her into the bench seat and then slid in beside her rather than across from her.

A waitress appeared a moment later and he placed their order.

"How're you feeling, sweetheart?"

She said nothing but nudged her shoulder towards his. He interpreted that to mean she wanted to snuggle so he put his arm around her shoulders, drawing her close, almost to the point she was sitting on his lap. That seemed to be what she wanted as she leant her head on his shoulder.

"So it seems you don't like that side of the family very much."

"Why do you say that?" she asked quietly.

"Well, I just got the impression that you weren't very comfortable around them. That's why I suggested we come down here. " He left it at that, didn't say any more about her family.

She tensed up a little and then relaxed, wriggling closer into him.

"They make me feel uneasy. I never feel comfortable. I know it's probably crazy but I always feel like a bug under a microscope with Uncle Max and Kelvin." There was more, he could tell, but she'd answer him when she was ready. He took her hand in his, lacing his fingers with hers.

"Has something specific happened or is it just a general feeling?" he asked quietly. He knew she felt safe snuggled into his shoulder and he wasn't directly staring at her. That's why he'd chosen to sit beside her rather than opposite her. Opposite would have been too intimidating.

"I don't really want to talk about it. I've never liked Uncle Max much. He even scared me as a child. Kelvin was okay until he became a teenager. Then we kind of had a falling out when I was about eighteen. Since then, I've been polite for the sake of the family and all that but I don't like spending time with them."

He noticed that her heartbeat accelerated whenever she mentioned them. Pixie also started to excrete fear from her pores. He could smell it, plain and simple. Something had happened to trigger that fear and he'd get to the bottom of it eventually.

At least she seemed to feel more comfortable around him. He was going to take it slow and steady, build her trust and her need. He was a patient man, and some things were worth waiting for. Pixie, he'd decided, was one of them.

Their food and coffees arrived. He devoured an omelette, bacon, sausages, and toast in double quick time. Pixie moved a croissant around her plate, picking at pieces.

"Wow, you were really hungry!"

She looked astonished as he placed his knife and fork together.

"I did warn you I'd eat you out of house and home. I have a very quick metabolism so I seem to be able to chow through food with little effect."

"Mmm, lucky you. Why is it always the guys who get the fast metabolisms?"

He tipped her face up to his and briefly brushed his lips across hers. The kiss was fleeting, playful and it helped lighten the gloom of the day. He intended to give her lots of them. Now was not the time for anything hot and heavy.

"That's easy, sweets. We wouldn't have the energy to chase after hot women like you if we had sluggish metabolisms. We need all our fast twitch fibres for the merry dance you fair lot lead us on. I'm just lucky I have an advantage at the moment with you being a little less than speedy!"

She giggled at his playfulness. Then her expression turned earnest.

"Are you ever serious?"

"Not if I can help it." He thought a moment and then went on. "Actually, I can be serious, but I like being playful, cracking jokes. The world is normally staid and serious enough without adding more to it. So I guess I go the other way. Sometimes a little too far, but I hate the atmosphere being tense for too long. So I change it. And besides, I see jokes and teasing in most everything. Most people just give me too much material and I can't help myself but to use it."

She nodded and drained the last of her coffee.

"Thank you, Rory. You've made a very bad situation bearable. I don't know what's going to happen today but I feel like I can at least face it with you beside me."

"And you wonder why I call you my sweet Pixie? What you just said explains it all. But know this: whatever happens, I'll be here. If you need me to make you laugh, I'll try. If you need to cry, I'll hold you till it passes. If you need to yell—that's okay, too. I meant what I said last night. I know I'm repeating myself but I think it warrants repeating and I don't think you've had a lot of support over the last couple of years. That all changed a few days ago."

She threw her arms around his neck and buried her face into the curve of his neck and shoulder. Her soft breath tickled and teased him. *Ohhhhh, did she just run her tongue over the hollow of his throat?* A twitch ran all the way down his spine. *Oh, have mercy Pixie; trying to be a gentleman was torture.*

He tightened his arms around her and just absorbed the feeling of her body against his. He tuned out the world and focused totally on the feeling of having her in his arms for a moment.

A throat cleared and he looked up. He'd scented them coming in but hadn't bothered to move. He was comfortable with Pixie in his arms. It was Quade and Jazz. Quade smirked at the sight they must have presented. Rory also knew categorically that Quade could scent the unspoken need between himself and Pixie. It wasn't strong at the moment but it was there nonetheless.

"Hey guys, how're you going?" Jazz asked as she slipped into the bench seat opposite them. Quade slid in beside her.

Pixie moved back, a little embarrassed by being caught in Rory's arms.

Jazz picked up on her embarrassment.

"Oh, honey, don't be embarrassed. If I was having as crappy few days as you are, I'd want a cuddle from Rory, too. It wasn't long ago that the bottom fell out of my world and Rory held me tight for a few hours while I cried my eyes out. I can vouch for his awesomeness at cuddles. But something tells me that your cuddles aren't quite as platonic as mine were."

Rory chuckled. "Sprung. Never can get anything past you, Jazz. And you say you don't have super senses. Well, you've definitely got something going, girl." He turned his attention slightly to Pixie. "I should warn you now, Pixie, Jazz will just wear you down till she gets everything from you. My suggestion is fess up quick. It's the most painless way to go. Wait till you meet Rihanna; then you might be able to get something on her. Until then, just prepare to hand it over immediately—it's the easiest way."

Jazz laughed that musical sound, which caught everyone's attention.

"Rory's right. I am insistent and I do mostly get what I want. You see, I have this thing for puzzles. I have to know the answers and why things happen. Can't help it and it will keep me awake at night if I don't get the answer. It drives this one beside me nuts."

"Never a truer word spoken, honey nose." Quade slid into the conversation after finally venturing in.

"So spill the beans, Rory—what's happening here?" Jazz asked, her eyes boring into him.

"Ah, we're having a second breakfast in the hospital café, waiting on some news from emergency." He knew his response was deadpan. He'd done it purposely to get a rise out of Jazz.

True to form, she came through.

"Yeah, very funny, Surfer Boy—you don't fool me for a second. You two are together and I want the gos," she threw back at him with interest.

Rory threw a look to Quade. Quade shook his head.

"You're on your own, man. You know how she is."

"Thanks a lot, brother." Rory fully intended to tell Jazz what was going on. He just wanted to prolong it to take Pixie's mind off why they were really here and to make Jazz work for it just a little bit.

"So—come on, Rory—details. What's going on?" Jazz prodded further.

Rory looked directly at Quade. Ooooo, this one was going to set the cat among the pigeons.

"Can't you control your woman any better?" he drawled.

Quade just smirked and shook his head. *Direct hit.*

Jazz outwardly protested.

"What the fuck are you talking about, Rory?"

He turned his expression innocent again. "Oh, my mistake. I thought there was something going on with you guys."

Jazz turned to Quade, fury written all over her face.

"What did you say to him, dickhead?"

"Not me, honey nose. You must have done something," Quade corrected.

"Of course I haven't. It was you growling the other night on the verandah. What was that about anyway?" she fumed.

Quade's eyes turned murderous.

"You really are the most frustrating woman ever to be put on this earth."

"Really?" Jazz spat at him.

"Yep—you are just so full of yourself."

"Ha—hardly—more like the pot calling the kettle black, Mr SUHAHAM."

Rory inwardly laughed. He shouldn't have done it but it was just too easy. These two enjoyed sparring at each other more than anything.

He leaned over and whispered to Pixie, "Ready to go, sweet?"

She nodded her head in agreement.

Unnoticed by the arguing pair, he helped her from the bench.

He went to move to the counter to pay the bill. Then he decided he'd have mercy on them.

"Oh, by the way, guys—Pixie is my girlfriend."

He said nothing more, just continued to the counter, Pixie tight at his side.

Rory could feel the stunned glances of both Jazz and Quade boring into his back. His news had rendered their conversation mute.

"Are they always like that?" Pixie asked him quietly as she hobbled along beside him.

"Yes, sweet cheeks, they are. Can I let you in on a little secret?"

She nodded immediately, obviously keen to be a co-conspirator.

"I think the problem is they both have the hots for each other something bad, but both are too stubborn to do anything about it. Until then, they just keep giving me too many opportunities to rib them."

She laughed quietly by his side.

"Ah, thanks for deflecting Jazz's queries—she can be a bit intense. What's with Mr Su...something?"

Rory laughed.

"She can be. The Mr SUHAHAM is Jazz's very derogatory nickname for him. Stands for stick up his arse high and mighty. You might say those two didn't hit it off all that well when they met." Pixie looked a bit shocked and slightly appalled. Rory went on, "But I should also say in Jazz's defence, she's incredibly loyal and an all-round great girl. You could do a lot worse than have her for a friend. I should also mention that in addition to being our team doctor, she's also a very highly qualified psychiatrist. At the risk of offending you, I'm going to say this: if you feel like you want to have a chat to somebody—other than me, of course—Jazz is a good option. The boss has put the resources of the Centre on the line for this thing happening to your family. That includes Jazz. She won't judge, just help the best way she can. And believe me—she loves nothing more than to feel useful."

He felt her nod against his side again, taking in the underwritten meaning in his words.

"Okay. I'll keep that in mind," she accepted graciously.

He really hoped he didn't offend her.

"Let's go up and see if they have any news on your family."

Chapter Ten

Max watched the scene unfold in the emergency reception area. He'd been on his way to visit with Rosemary when the ambulances had gone rushing the other way, leaving the house, so he'd diverted to hospital.

Rory and TJ had returned a few minutes ago from the café. He'd been pissed that Rory had taken her away but smart enough to let it slide. Now they'd returned with a very attractive redhead and a giant of a man in tow.

His skin prickled with alarm.

He wandered over to the edge of the scene, keen to find out exactly what was going on and who he was dealing with.

"Any word?" he asked at the group in general.

Rory immediately turned around, subtly blocking TJ with his body. The big man looked up, his eyes boring through him, and the redhead barely acknowledged his presence as she continued talking.

"Max, these are a couple of friends of ours—Quade Roston and Dr Jazz Carter."

Max offered his hand to Quade but didn't make the mistake of squeezing a little too hard this time. Something told him the giant would turn the tables in spades and take immense pleasure in doing so. The redhead nodded her head in acknowledgement but continued her conversation.

Ah, another uppity bitch who didn't know her place.

All the while, TJ had remained tucked tight to Rory's side, her attention focused on the conversation the redhead was having with the doctor in green scrubs.

His temper was rising. He took a deep breath to steady himself. He couldn't afford to show any emotion to these people. Never show your hand when you didn't know your enemy. It was a motto he lived by and it had served him well.

A few moments later, the doctor in the scrubs retreated behind the heavy doors and Jazz turned her attention to the group.

"Okay, here's the latest. Marcus has a broken arm and three fractured ribs. Katie has a broken collarbone and a sprained wrist. Both have a small degree of smoke inhalation. So they will be staying here for a couple of days. Clara is currently having some treatment for burns; they're still in the process of cleaning and assessing the extent but it is significant. They're estimating about twenty per cent of her body. So given her age and her solid health, she should be okay but she will be in here for a long stay."

Max noticed Jazz subtly looked at Rory before continuing on. He also noticed Rory tightened his hold on TJ.

"Rosemary is not so good. As you know, the chemo she's been going through has significantly compromised her immune and other major body systems. The last thing someone in her situation needs is this sort of trauma. They're giving her a lot of pain medication and antibiotics at the moment because of the significant infection risk due to her reduced white cell count. She is on oxygen and a series of IV drips. They're estimating her burns to be around thirty per cent of her body. Seems she copped the blast mainly on her left side. The doctors are also concerned about her lungs so they're monitoring her very carefully, particularly her oxygen saturation levels. Just so you know, normal is around ninety-seven or ninety-eight per cent. She's currently sitting at ninety-four. If the level drops below ninety, we've got significant problems. It's going to be a few hours before they can tell us much more."

He saw TJ crumple against Rory. His temper rose even higher. It should have been Kelvin or him providing the support she needed. Not a bunch of strangers. They were family.

Bloody hell, where was Kelvin anyway?

He watched as Rory eased TJ over to a vacant lounge and sat down, cuddling her close on his lap.

The man and the redhead closely flanked them.

Max could stand the tension no longer.

"So when can we see them?"

The redhead turned to face him and narrowed a superior stare at him.

"Not at the moment. It will be several hours before any visitors are allowed. Even then, it will be immediate family first and depending upon how bad things are, it may only be one or two visitors at a time."

Max fumed. He knew the line the redhead was pushing and he wasn't going to stand for it. *Patience*, he told himself as he plastered his most congenial smile on his face.

"Thanks for the update. Just a point of clarification—how is it that you are across the cases?"

He saw her bristle and felt a moment of satisfaction.

"I have privileges at this hospital—that means I'm endorsed to treat patients here. Additionally, I was also asked by TJ to assist with translating the medical speak."

The giant moved in close to the redhead and openly glared at him. The man didn't even make an attempt to hide his hostility.

Rory continued whispering to TJ and stroking her hair.

Kelvin chose that moment to return from the bathroom or wherever the hell he'd been.

Max noted he'd squared his shoulders and puffed out his chest in preparation for meeting the newcomers.

The introductions were short and Max knew tensions were drifting just a fraction too high for his liking. *Patience*.

He put his hand on his son's shoulder.

"Come on, son, I think we could both use a coffee," he decreed.

Kelvin meekly turned and they headed to the elevators.

"Who was that new guy?" Kelvin sniped.

"A friend of Rory's, apparently."

"You see what I mean, Dad? There's something about these guys. They're not quite like other blokes we know."

Max studied his son, somewhat impressed that he was astute enough to recognise what they were now dealing with.

He had learnt something riding shotgun to him all these years, but he still had a long way to go.

"What we're dealing with here, Kelvin, are a breed you haven't come across before. These aren't your average street thugs or standover men. These men are trained, hardened. Our normal rules don't apply."

Kelvin spun around and faced him, mouth a little slack in surprise.

"The big guy, he doesn't even bother to hide his true identity. He's highly dangerous. He's the sort who would think nothing about taking a shot. At least with him, you know where you stand. Where he's coming from. The other one, Rory. He's the worst type."

Max trailed off. He'd only met one other man like him in all his years in the military and business.

"What do you mean, Dad?"

Max watched his son go stonily quiet.

"He's the sort who you never can tell what he's thinking or what he's going to do. He's a chameleon of the highest order. He can blend in with any surrounds and seem like he's part of it. Don't let the laidback, easy going demeanour fool you. He's the coldest and most calculating of killers underneath. I've only met one other like him and we use to call him the smiling assassin."

He watched the blood drain from his son's face.

Good. It was exactly what he'd been wanting. Kelvin wasn't up to tangling with this crew without very specific instructions. He didn't want him getting any ideas about going it alone on this one.

Max knew what the outcome would be before they even started. He also knew he needed to play his cards very carefully.

Later in the afternoon, TJ looked up and noticed Jazz returned to the private room Katie and Marcus were sharing. Jazz had organised for them to be put in the same room to make things easier and to also give them some company.

The kids were doing fine. Both were taking a nap now after they'd eaten, but all in all they were going to be fine. The doctors wanted to keep them in for a few days just to make sure they had no ill effects from smoke inhalation and also to make sure they were comfortable through the early stages of recovery from their various breaks.

Her aunt was having some further treatment for her burns and was apparently quite heavily sedated but they should be able to see her tomorrow.

TJ was once again sharing the single lounge chair with Rory. He'd pulled her down into his lap a few moments ago when she'd made a move to sit on the straight-backed chair.

"I've just spoken with Dr Holden and you can go and see your mother now," Jazz informed her, giving nothing away with her expression.

"Is she going to be okay?"

TJ watched Jazz frown a little and then glance across at the kids. TJ knew she was checking to see whether they were asleep. Her stomach dropped; whatever Jazz had to say wasn't going to be good.

Jazz grabbed the nearby chair and pulled it over, bringing herself to the level of TJ and Rory.

"TJ, I figure you're the type who wants to know what you're dealing with. I also figure you've seen enough of hospitals and medicos to know the drill, so I'm not going to sugar-coat it for you or give you false hopes," she spoke quietly, obviously not wanting to disturb the kids.

TJ felt Rory stiffen beneath her and she thought she caught a glimpse of a warning glare he shared with Jazz.

Regardless, Jazz carried on. "Your mother is very ill and the prognosis is very uncertain at this stage. I need to explain something to you about burns." Jazz paused, making sure they understood what she was going to say was important. "We have a rule with burns and percentages. It goes like this. If you are fifty and you have fifty per cent of your body effected by burns, then that adds up to almost certainly a one hundred per cent chance of you not making it."

TJ sucked in a breath and felt the tears start to stream

down her face. Rory pressed a tissue into her hand and squeezed her tighter.

"Your mother is fifty-one. She's also been going through chemo and she has burns to thirty per cent of her body. She does have a chance of survival here but the odds are stacked against her. They're doing everything they can but the next couple of days are going to be crucial. If she doesn't deteriorate any further and we don't have any major infections, then the odds improve."

Jazz took her hand and squeezed it gently. "I really wish I had better news."

Her throat felt constricted and she could barely swallow, but she had to be strong. She had to get through this. She raised her head and pushed a grateful smile onto her face and squeezed Jazz's hand in return.

"Thanks so much, Jazz, for helping me out. It means a lot."

Jazz smiled at her warmly. "My pleasure, TJ. I'm more than happy to help you out with anything I can. This is likely going to be a long process, getting everyone well again. You'll need lots of support, in fact, probably just as much as they will."

"So can I go see her now?"

"Yep—you sure can."

TJ started to move up from Rory's lap. Jazz reached out a hand to steady her as Rory gently pushed her up to a standing position. She hadn't brought her crutches, which was probably stupid but they really hurt and she felt so awkward using them. Besides, being tight to Rory somehow felt right on so many levels.

They followed Jazz steadily down to the intensive care ward. Jazz paused and spoke briefly to a nurse standing outside a glass panel that gave them a clear view of her mother. The left side of her body was covered in dressings. The right side of her body was awash with IV tubes and other monitors.

The steady beep, beep, beep of monitors audibly reinforced the seriousness of the situation.

Her stomach rolled. She felt sick. The fear had been numbed to the point she just felt sick to her stomach.

Not at what she was seeing. But at what she and her brother and sister stood to lose.

TJ took yet another cleansing breath, willing herself to hold it together. If she wasn't relying so heavily on Rory for support, she knew categorically that she'd be on the floor.

She looked at Jazz and motioned to her, silently asking if she could go in.

Jazz moved closer to her.

"Yes, you can but you need to keep it brief. She's exhausted. I'm sorry; it seems that Max somehow managed to wangle his way in and that is going to cut into a bit of the time you can spend with her."

She felt Rory and Jazz exchange glances. They were communicating something in the unspoken language that friends use.

TJ was past the point of feeling. She knew she should be furious and probably was, but she just couldn't muster the energy right now.

Rory gently guided her into the room and helped support her by the bed. The nearby chair was low and her mother wouldn't be able to see her from the taller bed.

"Hey, sweet Pixie, do you want me to stay?" he whispered in her ear.

"Yes," she whispered back without hesitating. She needed his strength. He was her security blanket.

Her mother's eyes were closed but slowly opened at the sound of their low voices. Her face was red and swollen. The skin was shiny and looked as if it had been covered in some sort of gel.

"Hey Mum, how're you feeling?" TJ knew how dumb it sounded. It was obvious, but what else did you say? The words didn't even come close to what she was feeling.

She reached for her mother's right hand and gave it what she hoped was a comforting squeeze.

"Not so good," her mother croaked out in a harsh whisper.

"Is there anything I can get for you?" She really didn't know what else to say.

TJ watched her mother tense, as if gathering her strength to say what she needed to say.

"No, but there is something you can do for me." The words came out on a wheeze. There was more silence before her mother groaned out a harsh sounding cough.

TJ was becoming more desperate. The sound tore at her stomach. Jazz had tried to prepare her but she could never have imagined her mother was this bad. The pain and suffering were etched into the face she knew so well.

"What, Mum? Anything—you know that." Her voice sounded like a plea, even to her own ears. Rory remained motionless behind her. His arm tightened around her, trying to ease her pain.

Another strangled cough erupted from her mother and a little light red coloured spittle clung to her mouth.

TJ immediately reached out for a tissue from the trolley beside the bed and wiped it away. Her mother would be further upset at something like that. She took her dignity very seriously.

Finally, she went on. "It's too much, Teresa. I can't fight this and the cancer. Your father's calling me. It's nearly time for me to go."

TJ felt a fresh waterfall of tears cascade down her face.

Her mother had just admitted she was dying.

There was no fight left.

She tried to speak, but the words wouldn't move past the boulder that had lodged in her throat.

Her mother was struggling again, wanting to say more.

She felt her mother's hand weakly squeeze hers. Her mother's eyes bored into hers and held. Whatever it was that she wanted, it was important.

"I want you to marry. I need to know you're married before I can go." Her mother's words were punctuated with more coughing and more of the red spittle stained her chin. TJ diligently wiped it away.

Her mother's words had reduced her to all but robotic motion.

Her brain refused to function. TJ said nothing, not able to make sense of the request thrust upon her.

"I need to know that you and Marcus and Katie will be looked after. Your Uncle Max and I think you should marry Kelvin immediately."

Horror, dread, fear, and every other emotion imaginable assaulted her all at once. *How could her mother ask this of her?*

She couldn't do it.

But she'd have to.

She couldn't let her mother down. Couldn't deny her dying wish.

It was her job to be responsible and look after the family now.

There was no one else.

Her mind was blank to everything but what was asked of her.

Her mother continued to cough more and more. The sound was chilling. The volume of red spittle had increased and now there were specs of black material coming up as well. Something was wrong. Very wrong.

Before she could comprehend anything further, Jazz and the nurse rushed in.

Her mother's eyes sought hers and she squeezed her hand in answer.

TJ snatched a breath and held it tight to stave off the fear that threatened to consume her.

"Yes—I'll do it," she said in a voice far steadier than she felt.

Chapter Eleven

Rory watched the horror unfold before him. He'd seen a lot of things in his time but nothing as chilling or as emotionally gutting as what he'd just experienced.

The room was palpable with emotion as doctors bustled into the room.

He moved Pixie away from the bed and out into the hall. There was nothing more they could do at the moment.

As he moved down the hall, he scouted for a quiet place he could take Pixie. No person should ever have to go through what she'd just had levelled on her.

It was difficult enough controlling his own emotions; he could only imagine the pit of despair Pixie must currently be in.

Rory found a room that looked like some sort of small private lounge. Nobody was currently in there, so he decided to make use of it.

He guided them down to the lounge and hugged her close.

He let her sob for a few minutes, just diligently passing her tissues from the coffee table and stroking her hair. He noticed a water cooler off to the side and briefly broke contact with her to retrieve a couple of plastic cups of water before pulling her onto his lap again.

He held the cup to her lips and encouraged her to sip.

"That's it. See if you can finish it. You'll feel better, baby doll," he soothed.

Finally she looked up. Her beautiful purple-blue eyes seemed almost iridescent against the now bloodshot whites. Her nose was now swollen and red.

She still looked beautiful to him.

"I guess I'd better go find Kelvin."

Rory felt himself stiffen. The urge to get up and stalk around was overwhelming. The animal genes in him had been pushed to their breaking point.

He checked it back hard. Pixie needed him to be strong and he would be.

"Pixie, there is no way you are going to marry Kelvin." His voice had a hard edge to it, a tone that sounded even a bit foreign to his own ears.

She stiffened, preparing to argue.

"I have to. I promised Mum. I don't have any choice."

Rory forced himself to relax.

He continued to stroke her hair, desperately trying to send calming energy her way.

"You don't love him, you said so yourself, and you admitted to me earlier they both terrify you. Sorry, my beautiful girl, but there is no way I'm going to let you marry him."

Her eyes flashed daggers at him.

"You don't understand. Mum is terribly old-fashioned and she thinks she's doing the right thing by all of us, by me marrying him. I can't deny her dying wish. What sort of daughter would that make me? I'm sorry, Rory, but I couldn't live with that eating me alive." She let out a resigned breath. "I'll just have to learn to live with the fear."

So that was what this was all about—paying homage through some twisted sense of loyalty to her mother's antiquated ideas of a woman's place in the world.

He could understand her need to please her mother. He doubted there was a stronger bond than that between a child and its mother. On some level, he could also understand her mother's request based on her system of beliefs.

It didn't make it right and it placed Pixie in an untenable position.

Pixie was terrified of Kelvin. His senses told him so. Something had happened a long time ago and if his guess was right, cousin Kelvin was at the centre of the fear she'd relived last night.

Rory had learnt enough about Pixie over the last few days

to know that whenever she felt fear, she took a deep breath and dived in regardless how dangerous the current.

She was going to do it again.

Only this time, he'd be there to throw the life preserver.

The thought of her married to another man caused a primal reaction in his gut. It was a feeling he'd never experienced before. Possession, jealousy, and every protective instinct he had, screamed for him not to let her do this.

Never before had he ever felt like this about a woman.

Logic told him that could mean only one thing.

She was his.

He knew it was probably wrong but he couldn't let her go through with marrying Kelvin.

Rory realised he'd been silent for too long. With his hand, he reached up and cupped her chin gently, drawing her eyes to his. He needed to see into her soul.

He was about to manipulate her fear in order to protect her.

Would she ever forgive him?

"Are you absolutely, one hundred per cent committed to marrying in order to accommodate your mother's wish?"

"Yes," she whispered without hesitation, her eyes conveying the absolute conviction he anticipated.

He breathed in her scent and did the only thing that he could rationalise.

He took her hand in his.

"Teresa Jane Walsh, would you do me the incredible honour of becoming my wife?"

TJ looked at him, stunned. Her jaw felt like it had fallen far enough to hit the plastic boot that encased her ankle.

Did she hear him right?

Was she hallucinating?

She felt a spark of hope emerge from the darkness, but before she clung to it, she had to know.

"Did you just ask me to marry you?"

His chocolate eyes mesmerised hers as he answered her question.

"Yes, I did." His face was the picture of seriousness and conviction.

No, it was the truth. There was none of his usual joking here.

She was floored. Why would he do this?

"You can't be serious, surely?"

This time it was his answer that came back quick and confidently. "I've never been more serious about anything. You'll notice I haven't even made a joke," he said earnestly.

She felt the side of her mouth slightly curl in a weak attempt at a smile.

His offer was so tempting but she couldn't saddle him with her problems. She was a big girl and she'd sort it out. What other choice was there?

"I can't ask you to do this. You shouldn't be trying to make my problems yours."

"If I recall correctly, I'm the one who asked you to marry me."

"But why do you want to go through with it?"

She watched the emotions play back and forth across his face. Looking for something, all she saw was honesty and sincerity.

"I'm going to tell you the honest to goodness truth. It's something that I only realised a few moments ago myself." He paused, obviously trying to gather his thoughts. "I realised that the thought of you with any other man made me feel all sorts of possessive, jealous, and protective feelings all rolled into one. That has never happened to me before. I can't watch you throw your life away with someone who I'm certain will not love, respect, or care for you the way I know I can and will. I know we've only known each other for a few days but to me it seems much longer. I know I'm already a little bit in love with you. And maybe in time, you can feel the same way about me. If not, then there are always options."

His words floored her. *He loved her?*

How could that be?

Her mind was numb. Too many emotions were circling around, trying to swallow her. She couldn't rationalise it anymore. She needed something positive to cling to.

She needed Rory.

"I need you to understand that I may no longer be a truly practising Catholic but I was brought up to be one. The topic of divorce doesn't sit well with me. If we did this, I would be committed to making it work. I don't like failing at anything and I would see divorce as that."

He nodded his understanding.

"I've never failed at anything yet, my sweet. I don't intend to start now. There is a lot we both don't know about each other but if we're committed and we keep talking, I know we can make it work."

"I hope so," she agreed.

"Is that a yes?"

She nodded her head as a small smile crept across her face.

"Yes."

He squeezed her tightly and popped her his thousand-watt smile.

It was like a beacon guiding her to him.

He lowered his mouth to hers and replaced the fear and uncertainty with a kiss that spoke of light and the potential of love.

Chapter Twelve

Rory stepped out into the hallway—Jazz was in there talking quietly with Pixie. The news she'd just delivered to them both was overwhelming.

They'd had to put Rosemary on a ventilator.

It seemed that Rosemary had suffered respiratory burns during the explosion. The insides of her lungs had become burnt due to the intense heat she had inhaled.

As a result, her lungs were slowly filling with fluid and eventually pulmonary failure would result. The oxygen saturation levels in her blood were now hovering around the ninety per cent mark and it had been decided to put her on a ventilator to make breathing more comfortable for her.

There wasn't much more they could do.

Jazz had then given them the final piece of news that was the double-edged sword.

Rosemary was only expected to be with them for another twenty-four to forty-eight hours at best. Which, in many ways, was a blessing. Nobody deserved to suffer a slow and agonising death. However, the kicker was she would likely slip into delirium well before the end, due to her dropping oxygen saturation levels and the high doses of drugs to manage her pain.

If Rosemary was to witness the marriage—they had to move fast.

Rory found Quade waiting outside the door, just as he'd known he would be.

"Walk with me, mate. I've got a lot to talk to you about." Rory was all business and Quade immediately fell into step.

"First off—how are the kids?"

"All good. Both were sleeping when I left them. The floor is closed to visitors until morning but I'll keep an eye out, you know that."

Rory nodded his understanding.

"Make sure you stay on alert. We've got enough on our plate without any more targeting. Clara's still in ICU, so that should be okay for the moment."

They made it down to the cafeteria and both quickly grabbed a coffee before settling in a booth. The café was deserted, which suited Rory just fine. Dinner was hours ago but strangely even Rory didn't feel hungry tonight.

"I've got something to tell you that is going to shock the ass off you. I don't want to argue about it. I just want you to help me sort it out."

Rory read the alarm all over Quade's face.

"I'm getting married tomorrow."

He watched Quade shake his head as if trying to reconcile the idea. Before he could speak, Rory clarified it for him.

"It's Rosemary's dying wish to see her daughter married. I'm going to marry Pixie tomorrow."

Quade finally found his voice.

"Have you lost your fucking mind?"

"Nope, I haven't."

He sat and waited quietly while Quade wrestled with the news.

"Why would you do that?"

"Because I can't stand to see her married to that twat Kelvin and I actually think she's the one for me."

Quade closed his eyes and leant his head back against the high padded back of the booth. Long moments passed.

Finally he opened his eyes.

"I know you're serious because you're not joking. But is there absolutely no other way? You've known this girl for what—four or five days?"

"She's going to marry either Kelvin or I. No way I'm going to let her marry him. She's shit fucking scared of him and there is something evil about the little fucker."

"I can't disagree with either of those observations, mate. I've picked up the same vibes."

They both took long sips from their coffee.

"So do you love her?"

Rory thought for a moment. *How does one describe love, particularly to someone like Quade?*

"Well, I know I've never felt like this about anyone before. I've been in lust before but this feels different. It's new but it's there. I noticed it last night before all this craziness happened."

Quade nodded.

"Rory, you're probably the clearest thinker of the lot of us. I'm trying to keep that in mind as I reconcile this. But shit, bro, it's a lot to lay on a mate."

Rory chuckled lightly. One thing he knew about Quade was that he'd be on board with what was happening as soon as he got his head around it. Quade was many things, and loyal to a fault with his friends was one of them.

"Have you told Jazz yet?"

"Yeah, we told her a little while back. That's probably why you didn't hear. You would have been out of range on the kid's floor." The kids were on a ward five floors down. Their enhanced hearing was good but through all the concrete and steel, plus the hundreds of monitors and voices—nope. Even they would struggle to make sense of a conversation with that amount of white noise.

"And?"

"Surprisingly, she didn't say much at all. Just asked us the same sort of pointed questions you did, then turned her attention to Pixie. She's probably trying to see if she's of sound mind."

"Yeah, I'm sure that has crossed her mind. Knowing Jazz, she's probably in there now trying to talk her out of it."

"Well, if she does somehow manage it, I'm happy to wait for her. But if not—and I really think that will be the case, knowing how determined Pixie can be—then I guess I'm getting married tomorrow."

Quade flexed his shoulders and rolled his head from side to side, almost as if he were preparing for battle.

"Okay, what do you need me to do?"

ℯ◟ℯ◟ℯ◟ℯ◟

Rory sat in the living room of the studio apartment he'd managed to check them in to opposite the hospital. He'd sent Quade and Jazz back to Pixie's place to grab some sleep and come back early in the morning with what he needed. He'd had Dylan come over to the hospital to keep an eye on things during the night. Dylan was the most rested of all of them at this stage.

Pixie was in the bedroom, exhausted but finally asleep. Jazz had given her a light sleeping pill, finally convincing her that she needed a few hours' sleep.

As Rory had expected, Jazz had tried without success to convince Pixie to hold off on the wedding plans.

At the sharp rap on the door, Rory immediately jumped to open it. He knew exactly who was on the other side and to say he wasn't looking forward to this meeting was an understatement. But it needed to be done.

The sooner it was over, the sooner he could go and slide his body next to Pixie's in that big bed in the next room and hold her tight.

The boss nodded at him briefly as he strode through the door and immediately took a seat on the sofa. Rory chose the only other option, the single lounge chair adjacent.

"What's this about, Rory?"

The boss was pissed. Not at the lateness of the hour but because Rory had insisted he come here. But this was something he couldn't do over the phone.

"I need to talk to you about what's happened today, Boss. There've been a few escalations."

The boss nodded. "I think I'm aware of most of them. Jazz has been keeping me informed about the medical conditions of the four Walsh family members. It doesn't look good for Mrs Walsh, as I understand it."

For the first time in forever, Rory actually felt nervous about having a conversation. This must have been how Brayden felt a few months ago. What he wouldn't have given to have had a few minutes with Brayden before this but there was no way he'd interrupt his honeymoon because he felt anxious at having a conversation with the boss.

When Rory still said nothing, the boss raised his eyebrow and looked at him coolly. "I'm gathering you didn't drag me up from the Gold Coast to tell me what I already knew or what you could have told me on the phone. Out with it, Southall. I'd like to get to bed for at least three or four hours tonight. I need a little more sleep than you lot."

It was time.

"I'm marrying Pixie tomorrow."

The words dropped like marbles on a polished timber floor. Each bounced and punctuated as it landed.

The eye contact they'd been maintaining was dropped as the boss looked away. Rory saw him take a deep breath and fill his lungs with air. The news had shocked him. Of that, he was certain but the question was how was he going to react? This sort of situation just never came up. The closest frame of reference he had was the conversation Brayden had gone through a few months back. Brayden had stood firm and the boss had come around. He'd try the same approach.

What he got unsettled him even more.

"I guess you're looking for me to be shocked, outraged, something like that?"

Rory felt the urge to shift in his chair but checked it. He needed to appear solid, full of conviction.

"Well, to be honest, I didn't really know how you'd react. The only similar baseline is what happened with Brayden and Rihanna."

"I think you'd better tell me what happened today, Mr Southall, before we go any further."

Rory nodded his head and recounted the story for the third time in less than that many hours.

When he finished, the boss scrubbed his hand through his short-cropped hair. The salt and pepper spikes bent and then stood military straight again.

"Fuck. Nothing like playing emotional blackmail with your kids," was the boss's only comment.

"It's definitely up there with the all-time most fucked

things to do but regardless, Pixie's going through with it. So that means I am, too."

"I know I expect a lot from you guys but I don't expect this, Rory. Don't go marrying this girl through some misguided sense of loyalty to the Centre."

Rory nodded. He appreciated the sentiments from the boss. The boss was many things but deep down, he knew the man had their best interests at heart.

"I'm not marrying her because of that, Boss. I'm marrying her because I actually think I've found the one for me and I won't sit back and let Kelvin Walsh get his hands on something that should be mine because I'm not man enough to do what needs to be done."

The boss nodded his understanding.

"Rory, what I'm going to say stays between you and me. But this is so far from a normal circumstance, I'm sure the occasion warrants it." Rory sat up a little straighter. The boss could be a very peculiar man at times and to date this conversation had gone nowhere near how he'd expected it to go. Rory braced himself for the kicker as the boss went on. "If it was any other of your teammates, I'd probably be having a shit fit right about now. But son, you are the exception. Of all my team, I know you are the one who will have considered all the angles, all the options, calculated the risk, and made your decision based on those. I also have no doubt you know your own mind when it comes to Teresa. I had an inkling the other day, when we met, at the office. If you tell me it's real, then I will believe you."

Rory felt exhausted. He had been prepared for a fight, not this. It was so far from what he expected, and the boss had actually given him a compliment into the bargain.

That never happened.

Could somebody please tell him what they'd done with the real director of the Centre?

He'd better move on before the boss changed his mind or this bubble burst.

"Thanks, Boss, that means a lot to me." The boss said nothing, just nodded and held him with those intense eyes.

"It's as real for me as it can be with the time we've had. I know Pixie is also committed to making it work."

"Does she know yet?"

He shook his head in the negative.

"I've skirted the truth about how I have better senses than most people. I just haven't told her about my altered DNA. I think she's had enough to deal with at the moment. I'm not happy about keeping it from her and I will tell her as soon as the time is right. But for now, I just think it's too much."

"You're probably right and I'll let you be the best judge of when that time is. I don't need to remind you about the paperwork she'll need to sign."

"No, Boss. I'll make sure it's taken care of when the time comes. Speaking of paperwork, I was hoping you could help out with some."

"What do you need?"

"Well, after doing a quick Internet search, it seems we need to have applied for a marriage licence a month before the big event. That's not going to be possible. Apparently there is some clause in the marriage act that allows for extenuating circumstances or something along those lines. Any chance you can sort through that?"

"I'll get Rheeba on it now. I'm guessing you're doing this at Rosemary's bedside tomorrow?"

"That's the plan."

"Anyone else know about it?"

"No, just the team."

"Keep it that way if you can. We've been doing some more checks on Max Walsh. I don't have anything concrete yet but I do not like where the trail is going. It's hidden very deep and it's taking longer than normal to piece the puzzle together, but there's something there. I'm also going to send up Selena. She can keep an eye on things at the hospital. I need you, Quade, and Dylan on this. I am right in assuming there's not going to be a prolonged honeymoon, aren't I?"

Rory laughed at the final comment. *Honeymoon.* Shit, that had been the last thing from his mind. Although, now that the thought had been planted in his mind, it would be something to look forward to in the future.

The boss rose and headed to the door.

"I'll see you tomorrow, Rory. What time are the proceedings happening?"

Rory was a bit stunned. *Did the boss intend to be there?*

It must have shone through on his face.

"I'm gathering your parents aren't here to witness this, given that they live in Europe. And there's no way I'm going to let one of my team get hitched without me being there to see that the job gets done properly. I'll be there."

Rory was too shocked to mutter anything more than the time. Without a doubt, it was the craziest day of his life.

Chapter Thirteen

Rory woke early, just after dawn. Pixie was in his arms and the first thought that punched at him was this is what his life would be like every day from now on. He thought on that a moment and realised he was pretty damn happy about that. Having Pixie in his arms felt right.

Jazz would be here any minute. She'd promised she'd get an update from the hospital and be back here by six a.m. She wouldn't let him down. There were a couple of things he wanted to do, but he needed someone to keep an eye on Pixie while he did them. It would only take a couple of hours.

He hit the shower and dressed quickly, trying to be as quiet as he could. He wanted Pixie to sleep for as long as possible. She needed it.

He grabbed his phone from the bedside table as he noticed the text come in. Jazz was outside in the hall. He closed the door to the bedroom and quietly made his way to the front door.

As he opened the door, Jazz launched herself at him and he held her tight. He saw Quade behind her just raise his eyebrows and shrug, as if to say *I don't know what's gotten into her, mate.*

Rory accepted the hug and waited for Jazz to explain.

Finally, she released him and touched her hand to his cheek.

"I'm happy for you. I really am. I hope you'll be very happy together."

Rory looked at her sceptically.

"What?" she asked innocently.

"What's the catch, Jazz? That was way too easy."

"There is no catch. I'm just looking forward to all the drama that's still got to unfold. I'll have so much to tell Rihanna when she gets back. Plus, I think I'm going to start finally earning my keep around here doing doctor stuff rather than playing commando with him." She motioned her head towards Quade.

"Anything to get off training, honey nose. I didn't tell you, but now's as good a time as any. Boss sent me a note. He wants you to work out a bit with Dylan while he's around."

Rory watched the confusion spread across Jazz's face.

"Dylan's our resident martial arts expert. We're all good. That boy is in a whole other league of his own."

Jazz just rolled her eyes. "Whatever."

Rory decided it was time to bring matters back to the business at hand. He had a lot to do before eleven.

"How's Rosemary this morning?"

"Her condition is steady. She's not getting any better but she's not declining at an alarming rate yet either. Eleven should still be fine but I wouldn't be delaying much longer than that if you want to make sure she actually witnesses the service."

Rory nodded. "Is she awake at the moment?"

"She was a few moments ago." Jazz looked at him, curious as to what he was up to.

"I want to go and have a quick word with her."

"Do you think that's wise?"

"I need to do this, Jazz."

She nodded and said nothing further.

"Can you guys stay here and keep an eye on Pixie? She's been out since about fifteen minutes after you gave her the sleeper last night. I want her to get as much sleep as she can. Today's going to be very tough on her."

Talk about understatements. Tough didn't even begin to describe what he knew they'd face today.

The hospital was just starting to really wake up for the day as he made his way up to the ICU floor. He'd stopped briefly and spoken with Dylan. All had been quiet overnight, which was good news.

A different nurse was standing by the console, monitoring Rosemary's condition, as he walked in. He introduced himself and asked whether he could see her.

The nurse agreed but only if he kept it short.

Rory walked to the bed and stood beside it, not wanting to startle her in any way.

"Rosemary, can you hear me?" he asked softly as he lightly touched her hand to let her know he was there.

Slowly, her eyelids rose up and he was confronted with the same purple-blue colour that he saw every time he looked at Pixie. He hadn't noticed before but yesterday wasn't exactly normal.

The tube of the ventilator prevented her from speaking but he knew she was with him.

"I'm not sure if you remember but we met a few days ago. I'm Rory Southall."

Rosemary nodded her head slightly in recognition.

"I've been taking care of Teresa and I wanted to talk to you about something." He looked into her eyes and could see that she was still with him, so he carried on. "I was here yesterday when you asked Teresa to marry. She's going to go through with it, only she won't be marrying Kelvin. She'll be marrying me."

He could see the surprise and confusion register on the older woman's scarred face.

"I know it's sudden, but Teresa and I have something special between us. I care very deeply for her. In fact, I love her and given time, I know we could have a very good life together. I know I can make her happy."

She squeezed his hand and he knew she was anxious about something.

He looked around and noticed a little page-size whiteboard on the trolley beside the bed. He unclipped the pen and handed it to her, holding the board steady for her while she laboriously made three strokes on the board.

It was a *K*.

She wanted to know about Kelvin.

"Rosemary, I'm not sure if you know this or not but Teresa has been rebuking marriage proposals every week from Kelvin for the last six months. Teresa is also terrified of him. Something happened between them a few years ago that has her very spooked. She really doesn't want to marry him." He saw shock in her eyes. He was about to bend the truth a bit but under the circumstances he figured the universe would forgive him. "Teresa and I met a few months back. There's something between us, and I'm confident we can make it into a good marriage. I won't say that this time frame is what either of us had in mind. But we're on board with it.

"I just also want to say this. I know you don't know me, but I want to promise you this. Family means everything to me. I have a lot of brothers and sisters and they mean the world to me. I promise you I will love, protect, and support yours because very soon they will be mine as well."

He saw tears start to pool at the corner of her eyes. Like Pixie had done yesterday, he took a tissue and very gently wiped them away.

He raised her right hand to his lips and kissed the soft skin on the back of it before he gave her the biggest, warmest smile he could manage.

Her eyes softened and he thought she tried to return the smile.

"Rest now, Rosemary. I'll be back very soon with Teresa and Father Paul."

She squeezed his hand one final time before he left her to rest.

Rory was making his way back to the apartments when he passed Max in the corridor. He nodded his head at Max in order to be polite but he wasn't looking to engage him in a conversation.

Max grabbed his arm to stop him.

"Where's TJ?"

Rory's senses immediately went on high alert; something didn't seem right.

He slowly hauled his arm back towards his body, making a show of breaking the contact.

"Why, do you need her for something?"

Rory was good at reading people and what he read was Max searching. Searching for a plausible reason without revealing why he really wanted her.

"I just think it's time we spoke as a family."

It was code for *I need to get her to the altar to marry Kelvin.*

Well, sorry, old mate, not going to happen, Rory thought to himself.

"I'll let her know when she wakes up. Doc gave her a sleeping pill last night. She was pretty upset." He tried to use his best evasive tactics.

"Of course." Max smiled weakly and Rory felt the animosity radiate from the man. He wouldn't trust him as far as he could toss him.

Rory nodded again and moved on.

They needed to get this ceremony over and done with as fast as they could. He didn't have a good feeling about Max and his intentions.

TJ woke from a groggy sleep. Her eyes stung and her lids felt as if they had been lined with sandpaper. *Why did they hurt so much?*

Then she remembered.

Yesterday, her world fell apart.

The time she had left with her mother could now be measured in hours, minutes, and seconds. Death was such a ubiquitous, unknown concept until it was eminent or until it occurred out of the blue.

Now it was a ticking clock—every second pulling closer to the inevitable end. A finite time period; no longer something intangible and unquantifiable.

But there was something else she was waking with today.

A faint glimmer of hope through all the grey.

It was a thousand-watt smile, warm chocolate eyes, a body women's dreams were made of and a soul that was beautiful.

It was Rory and in a few short hours, he would be hers and she would be his.

Torn between despair and hope, darkness and light, TJ greeted the day.

She drew in a sharp breath and lurched from the bed quickly, somehow trying to outrun her own emotions. Shutting them off hadn't worked; maybe running from them could?

Gravity grabbed her plastic cast and sent it crashing to the floor. A sharp pain ripped through her leg and she let out a startled yelp.

TJ embraced the pain, wrapped herself around it and willed it to continue.

Its fierceness was strong enough to override the weight of the avalanche of emotions weighing on her soul.

The door to the bedroom flew open and Jazz charged in.

The spell of the pain was broken; the emotions began to rise again.

"TJ, are you okay?"

She nodded her head slowly.

"What happened? I heard a thud then you yelped."

She struggled to sit straighter and tugged the loose T-shirt into place.

"I just got up too quickly and the cast got away on me and crashed to the floor. It kind of hurt."

"Any pain now?"

"A little but it's getting less and less all the time."

She knew what she must look like. TJ saw the appraisal in Jazz's eyes both from her position as a doctor and from her place as a fellow woman.

"Okay, stay put for a few seconds. Let me go get a few things."

With that, Jazz retreated to the other room.

Where was Rory?

Before she could think on that much more, Jazz returned.

"Right. Start with these." Jazz passed her the pills she was carrying and a bottle of water. TJ realised that she must have looked concerned at what she was taking. "They're just some paracetamol. I'd give you something stronger but I don't think you'd be too happy with me at the moment."

TJ felt her head nodding on its own accord.

"Right. Well, if that's the case, then it's only fair I let you in on my new mission."

TJ looked at her curiously.

A warm smile broke across Jazz's face.

"My mission is to make you gorgeous for your wedding."

Jazz looked at her watch. "Right. We've got about two hours and we're going to make the most of it. You're going to be beautiful when I deliver you to Rory."

TJ could almost feel the infectious excitement that Jazz radiated.

But there was something she had to know.

"My mum—how is she?"

Jazz took her hand. "I saw her myself a couple of hours ago and she was comfortable and stable. I checked in a few minutes ago and the nurse advised she's sleeping. I know it's impossibly tough for you today but let's try to focus on the one amazing thing that's going to happen today. You're going to get the man of every girl's dreams. You lucky thing."

She didn't feel so lucky right about now but she did appreciate Jazz's efforts.

"Okay, missy moo, get this into you." She passed her a large cup filled to the brim with a thick-looking pink liquid. "It's a strawberry protein shake made with soy. Rory mentioned your allergy. You've got a couple of minutes while I run your bath. I want to see it all gone."

Jazz looked at her with mock sternness. A smile broke her face. She was starting to see what Rory liked so much about her.

TJ moved the straw to her lips and slowly sucked. Mmm, it was better than she thought. It was also a blessing that she didn't have to put anything in her mouth and chew. That whole process just seemed foreign and too complicated at the moment.

The smell of fragrant water wafted through from the bathroom.

Jazz reappeared and surveyed the glass.

"Good. Just a couple more sips and you're done. Come on."

TJ obliged and finished the drink. She took Jazz's extended hand as she helped her into the bathroom.

Somehow in the space of a couple of minutes, Jazz had transformed the bathroom into a veritable relaxation paradise.

The bath was almost filled with thick frothy bubbles. The light was dimmed and half a dozen tea lights flicked from strategic spaces around the tiled room. A thick stack of white towels were piled high beside the basin.

It was a little overwhelming. She didn't even know this woman and here she was doing all this for her.

After she'd stripped and wrapped a towel around herself, Jazz wrapped her leg in a large plastic garbage bag, and helped ease her body into the bath.

The warmth of the water assaulted all her senses and felt amazing.

"Lean forward for a second," Jazz urged her as she slid thick towels behind her head and neck. "There, that should be more comfortable."

The woman had thought of everything.

"Okay, I'm giving you a few minutes to soak in peace while I get everything else sorted. I'll be back in a little bit. If you want anything, just holler." Jazz clicked on some music on her way out. Jazz really had thought of everything.

What TJ wanted was not to have to think about anything for a very long time.

True to her word, Jazz came back a while later.

"Hope you haven't turned into a prune yet."

"Not quite."

"Okay, let's get your hair washed."

"I can do it myself," TJ protested, not wanting to be any more of a burden.

"Of course you can, sweetie, but I'm going to do it for you. You're a bride today, remember. I'm pampering you."

Jazz arranged everything and got to work. She competently washed and conditioned TJ's long hair and didn't even skimp on the scalp massage. It felt great.

Soon Jazz had her out of the bath, dried, slathered in rich moisturiser and had blow dried her hair. Now she was meticulously separating and rolling sections of her long hair onto hot rollers.

"Why are you doing all this?"

"Because it's what we do."

"I don't understand?"

"When Rory told us you were important to him, you became one of us. Has he mentioned much to you about the Centre?"

"Not really." She was curious now. The Centre was starting to sound more and more mysterious.

"Mmm. Okay, I'll give you a bit of a quick rundown. The Centre was established a number of years ago to investigate and eradicate environmental, biological, and agricultural threats and issues. You know that, right? From what we're doing with the milk."

TJ nodded slightly.

"The Centre is not government and it's not military. It kind of sits between the two. It's fully funded and sanctioned but it has a different agenda and operating protocols than either government or military. Rory and Quade are operators or operatives; we use the term interchangeably. There are another ten operatives at the moment. Plus Tom Anderson, myself, and Rihanna Mason or should I say James. I must ask her if she's going to take Brayden's name," she said, more to herself than TJ.

"Still with me?"

"Yes, so far."

"Okay, so the operatives are all very close. They've been through a lot together over the years. In fact, they are so close they often refer to each other as brother and sister. So just like when Brayden announced that he was with Rihanna, you immediately gained the status of a 'partner' to an operative. Therefore, that makes you family in everyone's eyes."

It was a lot to take in—she'd only met a couple of them. Sure, they seemed close but that wasn't unusual, was it?

"So how do you fit in? I mean, I know you're the team doctor but you kind of set yourself aside from them."

Jazz laughed; the musical sound floated between them. "Well, aren't you the perceptive one. Rory mentioned you were smart. I'm the team doctor, yes, and I've only just joined the Centre officially in the last week. I have been involved through Rihanna and Brayden for a few months now. And inadvertently I ended up involved in an assignment and I patched up Quade when the big lug decided to step in front of a bullet for me."

TJ drew in a breath at the mention of the shooting.

"Yeah, it was a bit full on."

"So what they do is dangerous?"

"It can be. But you need to understand they are all seriously good, each one of them special in their own way and incredibly well-trained. That Hendra assignment was an exception, not the rule to what they usually do."

TJ went quiet and reflected on Jazz's words. What did she really know about the man she was about to marry?

"You're thinking too much. Rihanna does this as well. Okay, spill the beans. What in particular have I said that's spooked you?"

Wow, Jazz could be to the point.

"Nothing in particular. I've just realised that I know next to nothing about him and what we're about to do seems extreme."

Jazz giggled knowingly.

"Oh, no two ways about it, TJ. It is extreme. But I also understand why you're doing it. At the end of the day, you need to be able to live with yourself and only you can determine what you can and can't emotionally bear. But let me assure you of this." Jazz wound the last section of hair onto the roller. "If ever there was somebody to be impulsive and irrational with, it's Rory. That guy is pure goodness. He is protective, caring, sensitive, funny, and just plain good to the core. And it doesn't hurt that he manages to be all that in a super-hot alpha male package as well. He won't let you fall and he'll work his butt off to make you happy. Girl, you've hit the jackpot!"

TJ let Jazz's words wash over her. He did seem to be almost too good to be true. But in a choice between Kelvin and Rory—there was none.

Rory was the only choice. It didn't escape her, either, what a commitment he was prepared to make to help her out. To have a choice made the decision a whole lot more bearable.

Oh God, please don't let her actions be sentencing them to an unhappy future.

She also realised what Jazz had just given her. She'd given her another family and she'd also given her peace of mind.

They had a fighting chance to make this work.

"Thank you, Jazz. You've helped a lot."

"My pleasure, sweetie. Rory has become a very close friend over the months I've known him. He matters to me. I need you to know how precious the man you're going to get truly is."

TJ just nodded, taking it all in.

She truly hoped she could make him happy.

Chapter Fourteen

A few minutes before eleven-hundred, they were gathering in the outer area of the ICU. The hospital was being generous and making some exceptions to the number of visitors, given the circumstances.

Beside Rosemary's bed there would be Father Paul, Jazz, and the boss, plus himself and Pixie, of course. At the door, would be Quade and Dylan. He'd given the guys a briefing. If Max or Kelvin came anywhere near the room, they were not to be given access under any circumstances.

Rory stood there waiting.

Quade had sent him a text a couple of minutes ago, letting him know they were on their way across. Jazz had taken it upon herself to try to give Pixie something special on her wedding day. For that he would never be able to thank her enough. She also just embedded herself a little more in his heart. That girl was so many things, thoughtful and giving just two of them.

The boss was talking quietly with the nurse.

Father Paul was dressed in his vestment, a Bible tucked under his arm, ready to perform the service.

He'd given the boss the rings earlier.

He pushed a finger between the skin of his neck and the collar of his dress shirt and tie. He hated wearing a suit but for Pixie he'd do it.

They were close; he could hear their voices move down the hall. He could smell her clearly now. Soon she'd be his.

Pixie walked through the double swinging doors to the ICU and Rory could have sworn his heart almost stopped.

Never had he seen a more beautiful sight. She was wearing a simple white dress that seemed to float around her body, held up by the finest of straps. A ballerina flat on one foot, a plastic cast on another.

The dress was incredible at short notice but it was her hair and face. Jazz had worked a miracle. Pixie was beautiful on any day but today she looked beyond beautiful, almost ethereal. Her white blonde hair was both up and down. Some of it was pinned up in a pile on her head; the rest draped the creamy porcelain skin of her shoulders, a curtain of heavy curls.

But it was her purple-blue eyes, searching, looking for his, that really mattered. They told the story. They told the truth.

He could see she was nervous and unsure; he could smell it. Not the intense fear he recognised when Max or Kelvin were around, but a lighter unease.

He smiled at her, trying to push across to her the message that everything would be okay.

She rewarded him with a shy smile.

It was enough for now.

They moved through into the room where Rosemary lay on the stark white hospital bed, tubes coming from everywhere.

Father Paul moved into the room first and gently stroked his hand over Rosemary's brow.

"Rosemary, can you hear me?" he asked softly.

Her eyes slowly opened and she looked around the room.

Rory took up position in front of Father Paul and the boss stood to his left.

Jazz moved over and stood to his right, allowing enough room for Pixie.

He turned and watched Pixie make the short walk on Quade's arm.

Somehow it was fitting that one of his brothers walked his bride to him.

Quade delivered her to him, placing her hand in his.

Her hand was cold, but her grip was sure.

Protocol be damned, he leant over and brushed his lips

across her forehead. She needed to know she was special to him, and he needed to do it.

Quade stepped back and filled the door with his frame, Dylan beside him. Two of his closest brothers. He wanted Brayden to be here but it just wasn't possible.

Father Paul cleared his throat.

"Let's get started, shall we?"

The service progressed in a blur. The words of Father Paul sounded in his ears and registered on a subconscious level but failed to really stir his soul. He kept his eyes on Pixie.

She needed him.

She needed the contact.

He knew he was the lifeline she was clinging tightly to.

He wouldn't fail her.

His thumbs stroked the backs of her hands—caressing, reassuring.

It was time to answer the questions and take the vows.

Father Paul drew their attention closer. He glanced at Rosemary and saw her eyes open, listening to every word.

"Rory Stephen Southall and Teresa Jane Walsh, have you come here freely and without reservation to give yourselves to each other in marriage?"

They both responded, "We have."

"Will you honour each other as man and wife for the rest of your lives?"

Again they responded, "We will."

"Will you accept children lovingly from God, and bring them up according to the law of Christ and his Church?"

They said a final "We will" in unison.

Children. The thought hit him like an arrow to the heart. Sure, he would love kids but they hadn't even discussed it, little alone done anything to even warrant worrying about them. Just another thing they had to learn about each other.

This was real.

Father Paul went on to the next part of the ceremony.

"Because it is your intention to enter into marriage, join your right hands, and declare your consent before God and his Church."

Rory closed his hand tighter around hers.

Father Paul looked directly at him, indicating he should follow.

"Please repeat after me. I, Rory Stephen Southall, take you, Teresa Jane Walsh, to be my wife. I promise to be true to you in good times and in bad, in sickness and in health. I will love and honour you all the days of my life."

His words were clear and strong, exactly as he felt. He meant every one of them.

It was Pixie's turn.

She turned briefly to look at Father Paul, taking her cue. Then she looked back at him and his stomach did a little flip. This was it.

"I, Teresa Jane Walsh, take you, Rory Stephen Southall, to be my husband. I promise to be true to you in good times and in bad, in sickness and in health. I will love and honour you all the days of my life."

No words could ever be sweeter. She was all but his.

"What God has joined, man must not divide."

His senses flared momentarily and he glanced out of the corner of his eye. Dylan was stalking forward, herding Max and Kelvin from the ICU centre.

There was something very satisfying to see them retreating back, their intentions foiled.

Father Paul asked for the rings and the boss placed them on the open Bible for the blessing. He then motioned for Rory to take Pixie's ring.

He slid the ring he'd managed to organise this morning onto her finger and looked into her eyes. Speaking only to her, he said, "Teresa Jane, take this ring as a sign of my love and fidelity. In the name of the Father, and of the Son, and of the Holy Spirit."

She blushed and smiled a tiny smile. It was enough to curl the corner of her mouth and to him, she couldn't have looked more beautiful or desirable.

It was Pixie's turn. She took the heavy platinum ring from the Bible and slid it onto the ring finger of his left hand.

"Rory Stephen, take this ring as a sign of my love and fidelity. In the name of the Father, and of the Son, and of the Holy Spirit."

Her voice was clear and precise. Her eyes were more. They spoke of the turmoil, the sadness, the duty, and the hope.

He silently vowed to take that hope and turn it into a lifetime of love.

Their rings in place, the vows done: it was almost finished.

"By the power vested in me, I now pronounce you husband and wife. You may kiss the bride."

Her eyes had not left Rory's for the last couple of minutes.

He was her strength. The reason she could get through this without being overcome with the mind-numbing fear. She felt anxious, excited, but not the fear she knew she would have been paralysed with had she not been here with Rory.

For the first time, she really studied his face. The tan skin framed the incredible pools of his eyes. They were deep chocolaty pools—overflowing with warmth and humour. His lips, full and sensual, promised sinful things. The cleft of his chin teased as if to add that little exclamation mark to the next line he'd deliver.

Jazz was right; he was gorgeous and now as unbelievable as it was—he was hers.

Rory's hand came out and cupped her jaw. His head lowered and his lips joined with hers. His lips were soft and warm against hers. Confident but still sensual. The tip of his tongue flicked out momentarily and touched her lower lip.

It was a reminder.

A promise.

He rolled them against her one last time before he gently broke from her and stroked his thumb across her cheek.

Then he smiled.

The big one—the thousand-watter—and for just a moment, she felt like the luckiest woman on earth.

The room and the reason they were here all receded. It was only her and Rory.

For a fleeting moment, it was perfect.

He pulled her towards him, further tucking her against his side.

They turned to her mother.

Tears of happiness leaked from the eyes identical in colour to her own. Rory passed her a tissue and she carefully dabbed at her mother's eyes.

She took her hand and squeezed it gently.

Her mother nodded slightly—TJ knew what it meant. It was a thank-you.

At that moment, whatever may come, she knew she'd done the right thing.

TJ leant close to her mother and whispered in her ear. "I can be happy with him, Mum."

Her mother let her eyelids fall and nodded slightly.

It was enough.

She had the approval she needed.

She'd done the right thing.

She could breathe easy—no regrets.

Father Paul, Jazz, and the boss had filed out of the ICU room, leaving them here with Rosemary.

She was sleeping now—exhaustion had taken her.

He leant forward and placed his lips against her forehead.

"Come on, my sweet Pixie. Let's go and have a little celebration. We'll come back in a couple of hours when she's had a chance to rest."

Pixie nodded her agreement and then buried her face into Rory's suit-covered chest.

It had to be hard on her.

He spoke to the nurse on the way out, asking that she advise them when Rosemary woke the next time.

He kept his arm wrapped firmly around her as he led her to the elevator. She still wasn't using her crutches and he guessed that wasn't about to change. He just hoped she wasn't doing more damage to her ankle or some other part of her by doing this half hobble, half shuffle thing that she had going.

The doors to the elevator opened and they walked in; he drew her to him and pressed his body down the length of hers.

His hand tangled in her hair and he tilted her head back and fit his mouth to hers. He took shallow, teasing little tastes, enough to inflame them both but not enough to get too out of control. As much as he'd like to, he needed to take his time. Pixie had to be his priority.

It was going to be an incredibly rough couple of days for her and he would not ask for more from her at the moment than she could give.

He drew his head back and just held her. There was something very soothing having her in his arms. He felt content, whole.

Rory stroked her hair from her face. "You look beautiful today, Pixie. I don't know how it's possible but somehow you look even more beautiful than normal. Thank you for becoming my wife."

He saw the blush heat her pale cheeks.

"It's me who should be thanking you, Rory. You've done so much."

He let out a low chuckle.

"How about we call it even and focus on the future."

"Sounds good," she agreed.

Chapter Fifteen

"So do you feel any different?" Quade asked.

They were sitting in the living room of the apartment. Pixie and Jazz were over visiting her brother and sister. Dylan had accompanied them. He could breathe easy. He knew Dylan wouldn't let anything happen to them. The guy was a weapon in so many ways.

They'd shared a light lunch with the boss and the members of his team who were around. Champagne had been opened and a brief toast exchanged but none of them really felt like celebrating. He vowed he'd change that when this was all over.

"Nope, can't say I do. But then I'd hardly say this is the normal sort of wedding most people go through."

"Well, mate, you never have been much good with sticking to the norm."

Rory chuckled at Quade's words. He was right. Normal and boring were not descriptors that Rory embraced.

A knock at the door sounded and Quade jumped up to let the boss in. They'd been waiting on him.

The boss immediately walked in and took a seat.

"Everything okay with Teresa?"

"Yeah, Boss, she's gone to hospital to spend some time with the kids. Jazz and Dylan went with her. I'd appreciate if we can make this quick. I realise that this is hardly a typical wedding day but I did at least expect to spend some time with my wife." The word wife rolled off his tongue. He liked the way it sounded and felt.

The boss nodded. "I think it's safe to say the threat from Max just escalated."

"What are you talking about?"

"Well, I'm not sure if you clocked it, but during the ceremony—you had a couple of visitors." Rory nodded. He'd not missed it.

"Dylan chased them out. I've pulled the security tapes from the hospital and they were two seriously pissed-off rellies. Good thing you bypassed the bit about anyone having any objections to the union. I think that would have caused a problem. It was also the right thing to do to post Dylan and Quade on the door."

Rory nodded resignedly but not before having a little chuckle at the boss's words. He really did have a sense of humour on occasion. It was dry and it rarely surfaced but sometimes.

"But it got me thinking. So I've had Rheeba pull a bit more paperwork and do some further digging. Namely Rosemary's will. It seems, Rory, you're about to inherit a trucking company and a property." Rheeba was a genius when it came to this deep digging stuff. What she couldn't manage with technology was not worth knowing but that didn't lessen the shock Rory felt.

"You mean Pixie is?"

"Well, sort of. It seems the property and business is specifically willed to Teresa and her husband. There are a few clauses that allow for the provision of the kids but fundamentally you're going to inherit. There was also a clause that if Teresa was not married, that the business and property would be put in trust for Teresa and the kids until she married. But that's not the kicker. The kicker is that Max was to be the trustee."

Rory thought through all the options.

Quade responded. "Well, that actually seems par for the course with this thing. It's been fucked up from the start. Why would it be different come will time?"

Rory chuckled. If he wasn't so close to Quade, he could have easily taken offence to his words.

"Can't disagree with you, mate. This family certainly seems to have done things a bit differently."

"Well, you were the one—"

The boss cut in again before they got a head of steam up with the teasing. "So the way I see it, Max thought he had his bases covered whichever way things went. You've come in and changed the play, Rory. Now we need to figure out why he wants the business so damn much and what else he's prepared to do."

Rory thought some more.

"I'm still not seeing the link with the genetically modified dairy cattle. What are we missing here?"

The boss nodded. "There may not be one. But regardless, we finish this thing with Max. You know how we operate. He's made an enemy of you and Teresa. Therefore, he's made an enemy of the Centre. The guy's slimy. We'll find something to pin him with."

"So what's the plan, boss?"

"Things are going to get a lot worse around here before they get better." It was a sobering thought. But correct as always with the boss. "But I don't think I need to tell you that. Rosemary will only be with us for a little longer. There will be a funeral to organise but there are also the kids to think about. They're going to need somewhere safe to stay. They can't go home. Plus we still need to work through the Max issue and the genetically modified product.

"I've been giving it some thought and I think the best thing to do would be to see if we can use Brayden's place for a bit for the kids to recover. It's the most secure we've got at the moment. I've spoken to Jazz and they're going to need at least a few weeks of R and R, not to mention the emotional state they'll be in."

Rory could see the merit in the idea but for Christ's sake, the guy was still on his honeymoon. He doubted Brayden and Rihanna would want to come home to having their house invaded. Shit, he knew how much Brayden valued his privacy. Before he could express that, the boss went on.

"We can put Jazz there with them and Quade, you, and Dylan can back each other up covering her and them until Brayden gets back. Rory, I figure you and Teresa will need to keep the business operating and I dare say Max is going to up his threats and antics. We just need to catch him in the act.

But you need to be careful. I haven't got the manpower to give you more coverage at the moment."

The boss walked to the small fridge in the kitchenette and grabbed a bottle of water; taking a long swallow, he continued on. "Things are wrapping up down south. We need to try to progress this the best we can until I can divert more people here. Another week on the GM stuff is probably not going to make that big of a difference; however, there has been more tainted product coming through. Food authorities briefed me late yesterday."

Shit. Rory and Quade both sighed. All the team hated when they were failing to make progress on neutralising a threat.

"What we need to do immediately is be on our guard to protect what we are aware of. Once the kids leave the hospital, there would be no reason to target Clara. She doesn't seem to add any leverage to the situation unless we've missed something. Max is not without significant resources. He has the money to achieve a lot of things."

Quade looked confused. "Then why get a hard-on for a business that's on the bones of its ass?"

"Because it's not about business; it's personal. It's about pride and ego and probably a hundred other things. And Pixie and I have just slighted him in the biggest of ways," Rory answered for him.

The boss nodded his agreement. "Absolutely, I would concur one hundred per cent with that appraisal, Mr Southall. Max wants the business for some reason and seems set to do whatever is necessary. I'm waiting on the forensic report from the explosion."

Rage shot through Rory's spine. He hadn't thought too much on the possibility but it made more and more sense now. "Fuck, it wasn't him, though that was there the day before."

"As I said, Rory, the man has very deep resources. He doesn't strike me as the type to get his hands dirty unless he really needs to."

"Yeah, I'm sure you're right. More's the pity. It just makes it that bit tougher to pin it on him."

"I'm trying to free up Rheeba as well. We could really use her doing some more techo digging."

"Shit, boss, the way we're going, you're going to need more operators," Quade chimed in.

The boss chuckled knowingly. "The thought has crossed my mind more than once, Mr Roston. Right. Anything further? Because we've all got plenty to do."

"Boss, have you contacted Brayden yet?"

"I haven't spoken to him but I sent a text a little while ago."

"If it's all the same to you, I'd like to speak to him about using his place. He's doing a favour for my family—I need to be the one who asks."

"Fair enough, Mr Southall, but I don't think he'll feel that way."

"That may be, Boss, but I need to do it."

"All yours then, Rory."

Rory hadn't even made it across to the hospital when his phone beeped.

WTF mate—you're married? Call me now!

He winced; guess the boss put more into the text than he thought.

Truth was he'd been resisting calling Bray for the last couple of days. Brayden had the most experience with relationships and he could have used his ear. But fuck, Bray was on his honeymoon.

He dialled anyway.

Brayden picked it up on the first ring.

"Start talking, Surfer Boy."

"Howdy, Stud. Glad you're well and everything's right with you too." He laughed sarcastically.

"The boss said you've got married—what the fuck's that about?"

"Mmm, I took a bit of a leaf from your book and got mixed up in an assignment that's gotten a bit complicated."

"There's complicated and there's married, mate."

"True but I know she's the one for me."

"Okay, if you say so, but I think you need to start talking."

And Rory did. He filled the stud in on everything.

Ten minutes later, Brayden laughed in disbelief.

"Fuck me, that's epic. I go away for a week and this is what happens. No way are we staying another week."

Rory could hear Brayden yell in the background, "*Minky, start packing, babe.*"

"Brayden, you can't do that. You're on your honeymoon, for fuck's sake."

"Bullshit. No way would either of us be happy sitting here on our asses while you've got serious issues. I'll get onto the airlines now. We'll be home as soon as we can. I'll text you with the details. Rihanna was missing Jazz anyway."

Rory thought about objecting, but he knew Brayden better. There was no way Brayden would change his mind.

"Thanks, mate. You don't know how much this means to me but I need to ask you another favour."

"Name it."

"Can we take the kids to your place to recuperate? It could be several weeks. Boss thinks it's the safest place. We're thinking we'll leave Jazz with them. Quade and Dylan can rotate in providing backup."

"Of course you can. You know how much Rihanna will love having an excuse to have Jazz with her again."

"You absolutely sure? I know you're on your honeymoon and everything. And I know people descending on you doesn't sit well."

"I'm learning to live with the privacy thing. And as for the honeymoon, if you think a few people in the house is going to slow us down, then you obviously don't have a very good memory of the time you shared with us about three months ago."

Rory just laughed. "I think we'd better put the kids in the bedrooms furthest from yours."

"Probably a good plan. The way things seem to be going at the moment, I was thinking I might build a guesthouse. It's not like I don't have the room." Rory chuckled again. "Got to go, mate. Give Rih a hug for me. Catch you soon." He ended the call.

It was a huge inconvenience but Brayden and Rihanna were going to drop everything for him, just as he'd do for them.

Fuck, he loved his family. He only hoped his new one liked them as much.

Max slammed his fist into the dash of the high-end BMW. *How dare she? How dare they?* This was not supposed to happen. Kelvin was supposed to marry TJ.

Didn't these people understand anything?

Kelvin sat there sullenly beside him.

"I can't believe she's done this, Dad."

The kid was still in shock. Max was beyond shock; his temper was white-hot with bubbling rage.

How could that stupid bitch Rosemary let this happen?

How could everything get so fucked up in a matter of hours?

It was time to kick things into overdrive.

No way would he be bested by a bunch of dick-swinging commandos.

He'd done his time and moved on. What he was now was smart.

It was time to get smarter.

"Well, she has. Now I'm just going to have to deal with the fallout."

"I still don't understand where these guys have appeared from. I can't understand why she'd choose him over me?"

Max just looked at him, appalled. "You can't be seriously saying that?"

Kelvin turned to Max, his face a portrait of rage, disbelief, and confusion.

For once, Max didn't check his temper.

"Well, take a look at yourself, son. You look like a slob. You've put on weight. Your hair's greasy and needs to be cut. Your clothes are all wrinkled. I raised you to have more respect for yourself. Maybe it's time you stood on your own two feet more."

Kelvin's face fell. Max rarely criticised anything he did. But fuck, when was the kid going to grow up? The world didn't revolve around him.

Kelvin turned and looked out the window.

Moody little bastard would sulk for the next hour. Fuck, he was worse than a woman. As if he didn't have enough on his mind.

Something had been bothering him for the last couple of hours. As if getting ejected from the ICU wasn't enough. That was a burn he'd carry for a long while and he was counting on returning the favour tenfold. But it was the ice blue eyes of the older man standing at the bedside with TJ and Rory that had really been gnawing at him.

He'd only seen eyes that cold and blue once. It had been a long time ago. Just the thought of it sent chills down his spine.

His unit had been pinned down in a hellhole so classified he'd purposely forgotten it. Battle had raged everywhere.

He'd been one of the few to walk out with his life.

The owner of those eyes wasn't so lucky.

The owner of those eyes was dead.

He'd stood over him while the life drained from him.

There were only two explanations.

So either the man who stood beside Rory today was his twin, or the man was a ghost.

If he was a ghost, Max didn't relish the thought of being haunted by him again. He'd created enough nightmares for Max a long time ago.

Chapter Sixteen

"Come on, my sweet Pixie, time for bed."

It was getting late and TJ felt exhausted. Their wedding ceremony seemed like days ago, not just mere hours. So much had happened; so much emotion.

The kids were physically beginning to recover and fortunately it seemed that they'd not have any lasting effects from the explosion other than the breaks. Which was great news. However, the emotional grief of what was happening was starting to set in.

She'd told them about her quickie marriage to Rory but not why. As she'd expected, they'd taken to him immediately. He just had that way about him. And they'd made it sound as if they'd been dating for a lot longer in secret and then decided to marry so that their mother could witness it.

And that was the elephant in the room. Their mother was dying. And now they knew.

The three of them had spent some time with her late this afternoon. Few words had been spoken as the enormity of what was happening unfolded.

Then, shortly after dinner, Jazz had urged them to come back to the hospital.

Rosemary was slipping into delirium triggered by the lowered oxygen levels in her blood. Even with the ventilator, the doctors couldn't keep the oxygen levels high enough for her to maintain any real conscious thought. She'd slipped past the magic ninety per cent mark and was now hovering around the eighty-seven mark.

She was with them in form, but not with them in mind.

They'd said their goodbyes. In a day of emotional ups and downs, they'd faced the biggest one any family would ever go through. Watching a loved one die and knowing it was just a matter of hours before the inevitable occurred.

There'd been tears and tantrums, despair and rage. Death triggered different emotions in everyone. Some felt it straight away, others took longer to comprehend and understand.

The kids had been shattered. Still in shock from what had happened at the house and then to learn that their mother was dying was very tough for them both to take.

TJ and Rory had spent the last couple of hours with them, trying to console and support them as they came to terms with the enormity of it. Finally, Jazz had quietly organised for them both to have a light sleeping pill to help them settle for the night. Regardless of the situation with their mother, they also needed to rest in order to heal from their own injuries.

There was nothing more to do or say—just the gut-wrenching waiting till the end.

Rory finished at his laptop and urged her up from the lounge. He swung her easily into his arms and carried her into the bedroom.

It was so foreign, so strange.

This was her wedding night and she felt so disconnected.

She wasn't sure what she should have felt. But one thing was for sure; she knew it wasn't supposed to be what she felt now.

Rory must have picked up on her uncertainty.

He leant forward and kissed her lightly on the forehead.

"I've got a couple of calls to make quickly. Why don't you get ready for bed, my sweet?"

She nodded weakly and then thought of what that meant. Arousal and the dormant, ever-present fear pressed back at her.

It was their wedding night—that came with expectations.

Expectations she had no idea how she could meet or enjoy.

"Stop thinking, baby doll. Just because we're married, nothing changes." He stroked her hair back from her forehead and looked into her eyes. "We'll take this as slow as you want. Give us both some time to get comfortable with each other."

Relief flooded her. He couldn't possibly know how much those few simple words helped, allayed her fears.

She smiled up at him, wanting him to have some idea. "Thank you."

He chuckled lightly. "No need to thank me."

With that, he turned and left.

TJ sorted through the bag Jazz had delivered earlier in the day. She hadn't a clue what to wear to bed. Her options were a baggy T-shirt or a short satin nightie with shoestring straps. She didn't know. The T-shirt spoke of comfort and the nightie suggested other things.

She wanted the other things, she wanted Rory against her, deep inside her but she couldn't cope just yet.

The ridiculousness of the situation struck her. She grabbed the nightie and hobbled to the bathroom, rushing through her night-time routine and making the journey back to the bed.

She crawled under the covers, glad for the warmth and protection they offered. The room was a little cold with the air-conditioning on, a little too stuffy and warm with it off.

A few minutes later, Rory emerged from the bathroom and slid into the massive bed.

He didn't hesitate; he rolled her right into him and spooned down her back.

She could feel the steady thud of his heart beating against her back. It was reassuring, comforting.

His right arm slipped over her rib cage, around her waist and pulled her close. Her mind immediately slipped back to where they had been a couple of days ago. How they'd greeted the day just like this.

It was comfortable, secure but it was also something more.

She could feel her awareness of his body breaking through the emotional quicksand she'd been living in for the past thirty-six hours.

It was something real, something positive, something pleasurable.

His citrusy scent filled her nostrils and she wanted to bury her head in his shoulder and forget.

She rolled in his arms, throwing her left leg over his strong thighs.

He'd come to bed clothed. He had some sort of loose shorts on and a T-shirt.

She wanted his skin against her cheek.

Her hand closed over the hem of the shirt and she urged it upwards.

"Hey, sweet thing, want to let me in on what you want?" he whispered into her hair.

Before she could feel embarrassed or overthink it, she asked for it. She pulled away from him a little. "I want to feel your chest beneath my cheek. I want to feel your skin against me."

He didn't say anything, just immediately moved to rid himself of the shirt.

Shirt gone, he pulled her back into his arms.

She snuggled into his chest like a cat looking for somewhere to curl up. His skin felt just like she'd imagined, only better. It was warm, smooth with just a smattering of hair and laying here with him like this, inhaling his essence, made her feel so much better. She felt connected to him— almost whole.

She was exhausted but not tired, if that made sense. Sleep was what she needed but not what she wanted. She was scared of what might come during the night if she let her mind wander into the land of dreams.

Rory felt so good against her. The longer she lay here with him wrapped around her, the more she needed something more.

No sooner than she admitted that to herself than he asked her, "What're you thinking, baby doll?"

"I'm not really thinking. In fact, I'm trying to avoid it. I'm going with the feeling bit right now."

He pulled her tighter to him and started to stroke her back. His fingers brushed the silky material against her back. It sent tingles up and down her spine and a shot of delicious heat to her core. Being with him like this was starting to become overwhelming in the best kind of way.

"Mmmm," she groaned. It felt so good.

"Like that, do you, baby?"

She didn't answer, just pushed herself harder against him.

His hand moved lower to her bare thigh. He drew it up and over her butt, stroking up and down a few times. The heat of his palm seeped through the satin of her panties. TJ shivered from how good it felt. His hand travelled higher under the nightie, following the curve of her spine, moving to the side to learn the feel of the tender skin on her waist.

She wanted to be closer to him. She wanted nothing between them.

Again she moved in his arms, drawing back and tugging at her nightie.

He picked up on her need and circled her hands with his.

"Let me do it. I've lived this fantasy for months. Let me have it."

She nodded into his throat and pressed her lips to the warm skin. She rained kisses over his flesh. He smelt so good, she wanted to nip and taste.

He drew back from her, pressing her body gently into the mattress. The blinds were slightly open, letting in a yellow glow from the street lights, storeys below.

His hand drew back to her thighs and stroked up and down in slow, lazy lengths. The light from below provided enough illumination for her to see the desire heavy in his eyes. She reached up and brushed her fingertips across his cheek, following the planes of his jaw round to his chin. On a whim, she pressed her thumb lightly into the cleft of his chin.

He let out a long breath and she raised her thumb and drew it across his bottom lip, enjoying the soft fullness beneath the pad of her thumb. His tongue snaked out and licked the tip of her thumb, suggesting other things.

She drew back a little, momentarily surprised where her mind took her.

The feel of his hand working the silky fabric up over her hips brought her back from her thoughts.

His hands stilled just below her breasts. Her nipples had stiffened long ago and were now starting to throb. She needed more but was she brave enough to ask for it?

"Are you still with me, my sweet?" he whispered into her neck and lightly nipped at the flesh before running his tongue over the little pain to soothe.

"Yes." Her answered pant sounded foreign to her ears.

Permission given, he slipped the nightie the remainder of the way up and over her head.

She sucked in a breath as the cooler air tickled her erect nipples. They throbbed more. She closed her eyes, letting the feeling wash over her. She was all but bare to him. She waited for the fear to come and felt nothing but the need to have him against her, closer, tighter to her.

Her hand reached up and circled his neck, urging him down to her. He resisted, using the strength in his left arm and shoulder to resist.

She let her fingers trail over his heavily muscled shoulders and biceps. She'd known he was built and very strong but she didn't realise he was this big. She immediately wished for more light. Light to see the man who was her husband.

He let out a long groan and lowered himself gently to the mattress. His hand came up and with a feather soft touch, he brushed his index finger across her right nipple. Her back arched off the bed in subconscious response to the fire that blazed hotter.

"Mmm, my sweet, sweet Pixie, you're so beautiful. Soon I want to look at you in the light of day but for now this is more than I could have hoped for."

His words warmed her through. He was leaving it all up to her. She was torn, wanting more but not sure how far to go.

He flicked her nipple playfully again and she gasped and let out a little sound of pleasure from her throat.

"I think my girl has very sensitive nipples. I love it. But I think I need to confirm it. How do you think you'd feel about having my tongue there? My mouth around you, sucking, nipping?"

He was asking and suggesting at the same time. He painted the most exquisitely erotic picture; there was no way she could refuse but he was also giving her the opportunity to consider what he wanted to do before she agreed.

"Mmm, please," she groaned and moved to get closer.

He moved his hand to her shoulder, lightly holding her in place. A low, sexy chuckle gurgled up from his throat as he lowered his head to her chest.

As promised, his tongue slipped out from behind his sensuous lips, and lightly lapped at her nipple. A slow, strong stroke sent her senses to high alert. Again, she subconsciously raised her body to meet his touch, silently begging for more.

Rory didn't disappoint. Somehow he knew what she wanted, what she needed and closed his teeth lightly around the pebbled flesh.

The feeling was exquisite and she immediately felt the seep of wetness between her legs. He growled deep in this throat and lightly sucked her nipple in, engulfing her with a hot fiery pleasure.

Before she could form coherent thought, a ragged "please" escaped her lips.

"You want some more, baby doll?"

He didn't wait for her answer but slowly slipped his hand down over the satiny skin of her flat belly and over the soft rise of her hip. He skimmed the curve where her leg and body meet, slowly easing his hand towards the centre of her that was almost begging for his touch.

She pressed her head back against the pillow, lightly panting. She wanted him so much.

His fingers edged along the elastic waist of her panties. He was teasing, taunting her—pushing her higher without really doing anything but suggesting what he wanted.

The tantalising feel of his lips at her breast continued.

He kissed a path across her chest to learn the swell and nipple of her other breast. And just like before, it was so incredibly exquisite.

He cupped his palm over her mound, trapping her heat within the confines of her panties.

"Mmm, sweetheart, I'm thinking I'd really like to feel the heat of your pussy against my fingers. Run my fingers over you, tease you. Would you like that?" To emphasise his question, he lightly nibbled on her nipple, causing another shot of electricity to shoot south to her core.

She wanted to feel his fingers against her bare flesh.

"Rory, touch me, please," she gasped out, her breath coming quicker, shallower.

His response was to suckle her breast firmer into his mouth. She only had to wait a few moments before his fingers found their way around the leg of her panties and into her delicate folds.

The thought of being touched intimately like this would normally have just about brought her to her knees with fear but with Rory it was different.

It felt right.

He made her feel special, cared for, treasured.

She wriggled beneath his fingers as he more boldly traced her outer lips and finally slid his finger down the centre, parting them. She could feel her wetness immediately coat his fingertips, but his movements were hampered, reduced by the constriction of her underwear. She wriggled her right hip at him in silent suggestion.

His hand broke from the centre of her and slid to the side, inching the fabric downwards. She brought her hand down to help with the other side. Together they slid the flimsy fabric down her legs and over the cast.

Finally she was rid of the constriction. She wanted to feel him stroking her, taking her to the edge and over. His fingers immediately returned to her centre and explored this time without the restrictions of the fabric binding her.

He moved his head up and joined his mouth to her lips. His fingers fanned a low groan of pleasure from her and he sucked it into his mouth—capturing and savouring. His tongue licked along her bottom lip and then slid into her mouth and wrapped around hers, stroking back and forth, in time to his questing fingers.

"Open your legs wider for me, baby doll. I need more room to explore," he breathed into her mouth, his voice hungry with need. It pleased her in a deep feminine way to know that he was as affected by this as she was.

He pressed the hard length of his erection against her right thigh, confirming just how much she aroused him.

His index finger circled the entrance to her channel. She could feel her muscles tighten and contract, aching for his touch.

At last, he slowly slipped his finger inside her throbbing channel. The muscles immediately clamped down, making it harder for him to progress further.

"Mmm, relax, gorgeous—let me feel you this way," he whispered into her ear, trailing his tongue over the shell of her ear before he slipped her earlobe into his mouth for a tantalising suckle. The feeling of his mouth at her neck sent delicious little fingers of shivering sensation playing over her skin.

Oh God, she was so close to the edge. He was building her desire with consummate ease. Teasing, touching, encouraging, letting her grow comfortable with everything and then offering her a glimpse at more.

He'd manage to seat his finger as far as it would go and now he was stroking, caressing her inside and out.

Her hips reached up to meet the slow thrusts of his finger buried deep within her. Then he slipped his thumb over her clit and her whole body went rigid, bracing for the end.

"Go with it, baby, come apart for me. I need to see you, need to know I can do this to you."

His words were enough; the tension was too much to bear. She tumbled headlong into the most mind-numbing orgasm of her life. The first she'd experienced with a man.

A ragged scream of passion ripped from her throat as her body convulsed under his, and all the time he didn't cease with his ministrations; he kept the waves of pleasure coming, rolling over her and taking her deeper, not letting her up.

Finally she managed to grip his forearm and beg, "Enough, please. I can't take anymore." She panted on a choppy giggle.

He tightened his arms around her and pulled her close, letting her come down in the shelter of his arms.

"That was beautiful, baby girl. I hope you'll let me do that to you often."

TJ giggled at his words and felt another rush of desire flood her core.

She felt safe and cherished. There was nowhere she'd rather be.

Long moments passed as she buried her head into the crook of his neck, simply languishing in the feeling of his arms around hers.

This was hers now. Whenever she wanted it. For the first time in a long while, she felt that maybe there would be a happy ending to all this turmoil.

Chapter Seventeen

The next few days had passed in an emotional haze. Her mother's broken body finally gave out late the day after their wedding. TJ felt torn at her passing. Hurt and alone beyond belief to have her gone, leaving her with the responsibility of raising her brother and sister—but relieved at not having to watch her suffer further. She'd watched her battle with cancer off and on for eight years and then for this to happen, it was just too much.

Her mother was with her father and eldest brother.

She had to believe it.

It was the only thing that gave her any sense of comfort at her passing.

Through it all, Rory had become more and more her rock. He was her safe haven from the emotional storms that churned through her. When she was with the kids, she tried to be strong, to give them some sense of comfort and grounding. Alone with Rory was a different story altogether. She fell apart with startling regularity. Each and every time, he picked her up and sheltered her in his arms until the emotional storm passed. She'd cried buckets. She'd cried for her loss and for the loss to her brother and sister.

The funeral had been the worst. She had to be strong for the kids, when all she wanted to do was fall to the ground and sob at her loss.

Max and Kelvin had been there to pay their respects, but the animosity between them was now undeniable. Her marriage to Rory was taken as a monumental insult and personal affront to them both.

TJ really didn't care about that so much. And there was a part of her that was incredibly relieved to not be living in fear. As Rory had mentioned more than once, it was Max and Kelvin's problem to overcome. Not theirs. Simple and accurate logic, but why did it seem like she'd just committed some major felony by marrying the man she wanted to? The man she at least hoped she'd have a chance of being happy with.

It was time to move on. The kids were being released from hospital and she needed to get back to work and sort out what was happening with the business. Somehow Rory seemed to have been managing to keep the wheels turning while she had been falling apart.

God knew what would await her when she returned tomorrow.

But first she had to get the kids settled at Brayden and Rihanna's.

TJ signed the last of the discharge papers and put her credit card back in her wallet. She had no idea how big her credit card bill was going to be—huge came to mind. Tomorrow she'd worry about how to pay it.

The kids were up ahead, being pushed in wheelchairs—hospital policy, apparently.

Rory had the SUV at the entrance and was helping the kids into the car when she reached them. She hopped in with a little help from Rory and they headed off. It struck her then that her role had changed. As well as being a big sister, she was now also a mother to her fifteen-year-old brother and twelve-year-old sister. They had a lot to work out.

Rory flicked on the stereo and one of Nickelback's latest songs came blaring out. He immediately started tapping his fingers against the steering wheel.

"Cool tunes," Marcus piped up from the back.

"One of my favourite bands, right behind Steel."

"Yeah, Steel is so awesome. I begged Mum to let me go to their concert in Brisvegas a couple of months ago but she wouldn't let me. I was so bummed."

TJ held her breath at the mention of her mother. She waited for the reaction, anything.

Rory laughed. "Well, mate, I think I can amend that situation."

"What d'ya mean?" Marcus asked, curious.

Now TJ was curious as well. What exactly did he mean? They hadn't spoken about how they were going to parent the kids. *Oh my God, this was overwhelming.* She hoped he wasn't about to go promising something she'd have to overrule.

"Did Jazz mention anything about the place you're staying?"

"Nuh, just that it's with her best friend and her husband. Apparently they have a big house and a games room and everything."

"Yep, all that's true. Did she happen to mention anything about Brayden?"

"No, just that he was a really close friend of yours and Quade's as well."

"Well, that's certainly true. He also works with me. But he has a bit of a side job. You see, Brayden writes most of the music for Steel and also fills in as lead guitar sometimes."

A high-pitched squeal and a lower roar filled the car and what sounded like a riot broke out in the back seat. TJ looked across at Rory, her eyes wide in disbelief.

"Oh man, that is so cool. And we're staying at his place. I can't believe it. Wait till I tell my mates. They're so not going to believe me."

"He's so hot. I saw his Byron performance on YouTube," Kate squealed. *God help me*, TJ thought. *She's twelve.*

TJ looked at Rory, his face the picture of amusement.

"Umm, do you think it might have been a good idea to let me in on this?" she asked him quietly.

He just chuckled. "To be honest, it didn't even cross my mind. He's just Brayden to me. One of my best friends."

"Are you sure it's a good idea for the kids to be in that sort of environment?"

He looked at her, a bit puzzled.

"You know, rock and roll, partying. That sort of thing," she said in a hushed whisper.

"Pixie, Brayden's not into any of that. He's a real homebody. The guys from Steel are all pretty much the same. Sure, they'll sit around throwing back a few beers and BBQing some meat but that's about as much as you'll ever see them partying down. I'm not even sure if they're around at the moment. They might be overseas touring."

Relief flooded through her. She wasn't looking forward to the prospect of having to change the plans if Brayden and Rihanna's place was in fact party central. She didn't want the kids exposed to that when they were so young and impressionable.

It wasn't long before Rory turned off the narrowing country road and stopped in front of a set of solid gates. A second later, they slowly opened and then closed immediately upon them passing through.

TJ's eyes looked everywhere at once. This place was amazing. The house sat up on a hill, looking imposing. A creek ran through the front paddock and they had to cross a shallow causeway to wind their way up the driveway to the house. The driveway was lined with a perfectly trimmed hedge. It screamed quality but not distance.

As Rory pulled the SUV to a stop, Jazz and another tall, willowy brunette emerged from the house. They were laughing and joking with each other. TJ envied the lightness of their hearts. Hopefully one day soon she would be laughing and joking again. There hadn't been much of it lately.

A few seconds later, Jazz introduced her to the brunette. "TJ, I'd like you to meet my best friend, Rihanna Mason." Rihanna immediately stretched her hand forward and TJ took it. She was beautiful in an understated way.

"Hey TJ, congratulations on your marriage to Rory, and I'm very sorry to hear about your mother."

TJ felt her throat constrict and she sucked in a breath, hoping to control the tears that threatened every time her mother's passing was mentioned.

Jazz noticed her discomfort. "Right. Let's get these kids settled. I'm sure they must be starving; they haven't eaten in a couple of hours."

Rihanna giggled. "Then they'll fit right in. I'm sure it wouldn't take much persuading for Brayden to fire up the BBQ."

And just like that, Jazz mustered them all inside and carried out the introductions. Rory had already moved the kid's meagre bags into their rooms. The house was beautiful from the outside but inside it was something else. Warm, homey, but still elegant and modern. The kids would be recuperating in the equivalent of a five-star resort. She hoped they'd be well behaved and respectful. They'd been raised to be but with everything that was going on, it was difficult to know how they'd react.

TJ checked out their rooms and quickly hobbled around, unpacking the few things that they'd brought from the hospital. She needed to organise more clothes and things for them. Their house was all but ruined. Their clothes and things had been either smoke or water damaged. That was just another thing she'd have to deal with—the insurance on the family home.

She opened the closet of the room Katie would be using and gasped. There, neatly hung up, were at least a dozen outfits in all the latest trends that would be enough to make any young girl squeal with delight and beside the hanging outfits were shelves filled with underwear, T-shirts, shorts, and even shoes lined neatly up below.

Who had done all this?

She felt the tears trailing down her face. Someone had been thoughtful enough to make sure the kids had everything they needed plus more. She was ever so grateful.

TJ felt familiar arms close around her waist and Rory's head rested on her shoulder.

"Are those tears I see?"

She nodded, unable to speak.

He looked at the open closet doors.

"Who did all this?"

"I asked Jazz and Quade to go do some shopping for me the other day. I knew the kids would need some new things."

She turned in his arms and buried her face into his chest, right over his heart. The strong beat always drew her in.

"They're only clothes, sweet pea. The kids needed them."

"I know but it was so thoughtful. I never got that far. I need to do better. I'm all they have and I couldn't even remember to get them clothes."

He stroked a hand through her hair.

The tears came harder and she sobbed a little.

"Sweet Pixie, I thought you realised, you're not in this alone. You're my wife. They're your family. Therefore they're my family. I'm not going to let anything happen to them or you. They needed clothes. I organised it. End of story."

He hugged her closer to him, and she drew on his strength.

"But I forgot to consider that. I should have—"

"Pix, will you just stop? You've had so much to deal with. This was the least I could do. We're a team now."

She nodded and sniffed.

"Why don't you go wash your face, then I'll introduce you to Brayden. Marcus and Katie may have lost some of their awestruck looks by now." He chuckled.

"Oh no, I hope they weren't too bad."

"Nah, nothing he can't handle. They'll soon realise he's just like every other guy. He just happens to be able to play a mean guitar."

"Well, I'll have a word to them anyway. I don't want them being a nuisance."

"Pixie, leave it, the kids will be fine. Brayden will let them know if they get too much but I think a little distraction at this stage might be a good thing to help take their minds off everything."

She nodded; he was right. She wanted them to move on but they were so young and a part of her was terrified the memories of their parents would fade to nothing for the kids.

Rory pointed her towards the en-suite bathroom and she made use of the facilities. He'd waited for her out in the bedroom. He rapped her in a hug and whispered into her hair, "Relax, Pix, everything will be fine."

She nodded against him, desperately wanting to believe him.

They found the kids, Jazz, Quade, Rihanna and Brayden all out on the verandah overlooking the pool.

He'd felt Pixie stand a little straighter and pull herself together a little more as they went outside.

"Pixie, I think the only one you haven't met now is Brayden. Brayden, this is my wife Pixie."

Pixie immediately stuck out her hand as Brayden stood. The epitome of Miss Manners.

Brayden took one look at her hand and then his eyes rose to Rory's and a devilish smile crossed his face. He leant forward and swept Pixie up in a huge hug, lifting her slender frame completely from the ground. She let out a high-pitched squeal of surprise.

"Welcome to the family," he said, gently releasing her back to the ground. Jazz and Rihanna just laughed; even Quade managed an amused smirk.

Pixie's head whipped around, searching for Rory. He just laughed at her unease.

"Like he said, welcome to the family. Come on, Pix, take a seat."

He guided her to the large outdoor table that Rihanna, Jazz, and Quade were seated at. The kids were off to the side, looking at some sort of electronic game that had morphed from somewhere.

Brayden appeared with a six-pack of stubbies and a bottle of wine and a couple of glasses. He dumped the lot in front of Rory. "Make yourself useful, mate."

Brayden disappeared and Rory made quick work of removing the top off the wine bottle and pouring a couple of glasses. He passed one to Jazz and placed the other in front of Pixie. She looked at him curiously and inclined her head towards Rihanna, indicating he'd missed giving a glass to her.

Rory laughed. "Ah, Rihanna's not drinking at the moment. She's busy growing a little Brayden."

He felt the heat rush to Pixie's cheeks.

"Why does everyone assume that the baby's going to be a boy?" Rihanna asked.

"Because it's easier to get our head around than having to figure out another woman," Quade answered for him.

"Well, in that case, I really hope you can deliver on a boy, Rih, because God knows we wouldn't want to tax poor Quade's little mind any further," Jazz threw in for a few laughs around the table.

At this point, Brayden returned with a tall glass of pineapple juice for Rihanna.

Rory laughed. "You still swigging that stuff down? I thought pregnant ladies were supposed to go off things. What's it been, three or four months?"

"About that and I still love the stuff. Or more to the point, junior loves it," Rihanna confirmed.

"So for real—am I getting a niece or nephew?" Rory asked.

"Yes, Rih, what are we getting?"

Brayden looked and Rihanna and she looked back at him. The table went very quiet for a second.

"Nope, out with it—you guys have a secret and we want it now," Jazz demanded playfully.

Rihanna turned to her and just grinned.

Jazz sat there, stony silent for a second. She'd gone absolutely still. "You're joking?"

Another conspiratorial look passed between Brayden and Rihanna. They didn't say a word.

"What? I don't get it?" Quade asked, confused.

Jazz spun around. "Oh derh—they're having twins. That's why they look so damned pleased with themselves. I should have known it was never going to be enough for Miss Overachiever to just have one baby. Of course she'd have to have two."

With that, Jazz squealed with delight and half dragged Rihanna into her arms for a hug. "I can't believe that you kept that from me."

"Um, Jazz, we only found out yesterday."

"And you think that's an excuse?"

Brayden turned to Rihanna. "Clearly we were mistaken, babe, in thinking that our babies might have been our business."

Rory turned to Pixie. "Sweets, I'd better warn you now there are no secrets among this group. Best to just fess up quickly. They'll get it out of you one way or another. Jazz in particular."

"And you still wonder why I call her honey nose. The woman's relentless," Quade added more to himself.

"Oh, shut up, Mr SUHAHAM, nobody asked you."

"Maybe not, but that's never stopped you."

"I was calling best friend privileges."

"What the fuck?"

Pixie sat up a little straighter and Quade immediately realised what he'd done.

"Oh sorry, completely forgot about the kids," he added sheepishly, glancing in their direction. They both still seemed occupied.

"It's okay, it's not like they haven't heard the word before. I'm just kind of new at this parenting thing, and I think I'm supposed to react to stuff like that."

They all sobered momentarily. The mood made Rory feel uncomfortable.

"So you still haven't told me whether I'm getting a niece and a nephew or two of each."

Brayden smiled. "Actually, we haven't told you anything. There's a lot of assuming been happening for the last few minutes."

"But you said babies," Jazz confirmed.

"Yeah, I did and you just assumed two," Brayden smirked.

"What? There's more?" Jazz's eyes had bugged out to the size of saucers.

Rihanna nodded, obviously amused at all the carrying on. It was easy to see the bond between Brayden and her. It was strong. They were a team.

"Oh, just tell her, Bray. She's going to pester us until we do. You know that."

"Yeah, I do. But how much should we tell?"

"Mmm, I don't know." Rihanna tipped her head up and looked at Brayden. They were purposely dragging out the suspense, just about driving Jazz out of her ever-loving mind.

Quade cut in, "Oh, for Christ's sake—would you just tell us, Brayden? The woman's about to internally combust from excitement. Geez, you'd swear they were *her* babies."

"Well, they are, dipshit. They're my nieces. I probably won't ever get around to having my own kids."

"That's because no man would ever be crazy enough to put up with you."

"Speak for yourself. I don't exactly see a path of women beating at your door."

"That's because you're always around. When do I have a chance for the door to be open?"

"That is such—"

"It's triplets," Brayden piped up, cutting Jazz off.

He turned and looked at Rih. "Sorry, baby, I couldn't stand them arguing any longer."

"It's okay; I was about to do the same thing." She giggled.

"Oh wow, that's great," Rory added.

"I'm not sure about that. I was still getting used to the idea of having just one baby. When the doctor told us it was three yesterday, I don't think I said anything for five minutes. I was so shocked."

"Three gorgeous little babies all in one go. Girl, I keep telling you, you are one lucky thing," Jazz added.

Rihanna giggled. "Ah, maybe, not sure that I'll feel that way in the middle of the night in about five months' time." Rihanna patted her little bump affectionately.

"You'll have plenty of help," Jazz confirmed, and started to talk to Rihanna.

Rory thought for a moment. "Ah, Brayden, you know that guest house you mentioned to me the other day? I think now would be a good time to call the architect."

Brayden just chuckled. "One step ahead of you, bro. Plans are already at the certifier."

Pixie seemed a bit confused by it all. "But this place is huge already."

"Yeah, I guess it is but it seems we have a lot of visitors now and I don't see that stopping any time soon."

"Umm, I'm really sorry about that. I can make other arrangements for the kids," Pixie threw in.

"Stop right there. That's not what I meant at all. Rory asked and I offered. It's what families do. The kids are welcome here as long as they need to be."

"But I don't want them getting in the way or you know, you're just newlyweds yourselves." She blushed again.

"Don't worry about any of that. As you mentioned before the house is large enough. I'm sure our privacy won't be imposed on too much."

"Well, only if you're sure, and I want you to let me know immediately if they're any problem."

"I will but there won't be any problems. Besides, we'll have Jazz here and I'm sure you guys will be over every few days. It'll be just like a few months ago," he said confidently. Rory just laughed.

"So Stud, you still haven't told us what sort of brood you're having."

"No, I haven't, have I?"

"Well, mate, if it's a state secret, I guess I can wait a few more months." Rory shrugged.

"Nah, it was just fun watching Jazz work herself into a frenzy."

"Woman's nothing but a pain in all our butts," Quade muttered.

A knowing look passed between Rory and Brayden. They could both smell the subtle arousal between Quade and Jazz. "That so, mate?" Rory asked.

"Don't you start."

Rory just laughed. "Well, if everything's okay here, I think we might make a move, baby doll. What do you think?"

"Sure. I hate to think what we're going home to. I guess the sooner we get started sorting it out, the sooner it's finished," Pixie added, obviously dreading what she would find.

"Oh, it won't be so bad," Rory reassured her.

They rose from the table and said their goodbyes.

Brayden walked them out. As they were in the SUV and about to drive away, Brayden poked his head in.

"Two boys and a girl," he said with a proud look on his face.

"You're the man!" Rory cheered. "Way to go, bro. You're going to be one busy guy."

"You're going to be on uncle duties. It'll be good practice for when your turn comes."

"Yep. Can't wait."

They drove for a while in silence. Rory was taking in Brayden and Rihanna's news. *Wow, fancy going from nothing to three newborns in the space of a few months.* Brayden's life had really changed. But so had his. It'd all been a bit of a whirlwind and he'd not really thought about all the aspects. He was now a substitute father figure to a fifteen-year-old boy and twelve-year-old girl. What did he know about doing that?

He could see the topics of the day were weighing heavily on Pixie as well. Being a mother figure to those two, plus looking at the reality of Brayden and Rihanna's impending parenthood, hammered home the home and family message.

"Hey, sweet pea, whatcha thinking?" he finally asked. Best to talk about this stuff. He had a feeling it could brew and become poisonous.

She sighed. "Just how so ill equipped I feel about this whole role of stand-in parent. What's even more to the point, you've now been placed in the role as well. I didn't really think that through before the whole marriage thing took place. I guess I was much more focused on pleasing Mum than really thinking about the reality of what we've done."

Pixie sounded resigned, even regretful. Her need to please her mum was obviously weighing very heavily on her now that she had time to process what it really meant.

"Pix, maybe if you looked at it another way." He had her attention and she looked across at him, waiting for him to go on.

"Well, the way I see it, you were going to step up as a mother figure to both the kids regardless of whether you married or not. I can't see that there would be any way you would desert those kids. Am I right?"

"Of course," she immediately confirmed.

"So your concerns about additional pressures the marriage part applies to parenting is really irrelevant, wouldn't you say? The question seems more about figuring out how to give the kids what they need and somehow try to accommodate our own at the same time."

"But Rory, they're my responsibility. I'm their sister and I'm all they have left now."

"Sure, but when I married you, Pixie, I did it knowing full well what the responsibilities were that I was taking on. Your family became mine. I'm more than happy to step up and do what I can for those kids. I'm just not sure what my role should be. I don't know if I should be more of a father figure, an older brother, or a friend. And I don't know the kids well enough to be able to figure this one out."

For the first time in a very long time he felt vulnerable, unsure. It wasn't an emotion that sat well with him. He was much more about decisive action. Having a plan and working towards it. This whole parenting thing felt decidedly rudderless. He wondered whether all parents felt like this. More to the point, they were picking up where others had already started. The foundations had already been set in place. Pixie and he were merely guiding the final construction as the kids grew to adulthood. But where were the blueprints to follow on with?

"I don't know the answer to that one either, Rory. I guess it's going to depend on how they accept you. We're going to need to have a discussion on boundaries and what we jointly agree is appropriate. I think the most important thing is consistency."

"I agree but we don't have to tie ourselves in knots trying to decide it all tonight. Given the circumstances, we'll probably have a bit of a 'grace' period before we need to really sort it all out. I think the most important thing we can do is present a united front and a solid relationship between us. If we have that, they should pick up on the vibes. Jazz says kids need stability and certainty. Let's work on giving them that."

"Okay, I think I can live with that." She turned to him and flashed him a smile.

"Pixie, there's something else. I fully respect that Marcus and Katie are a product of your mum and dad and they have started the process of raising them to their moral and value code. But I think it's important to realise their code may not be exactly the same as ours. We need to figure out our own position on things."

Rory could see his words hit her hard. Having to scrutinise her parent's morals and values this close to their passing had to be tough. In his opinion, the moral code of her parents had placed Pixie in an untenable position. He was smart enough not to raise that now. She'd married because she felt she had to in order to fulfil her mother's wishes. Not only was this probably an outdated concept, it also reeked of emotional blackmail.

He was party to this too now. For his own reasons, he'd presented Pixie with an opportunity to escape her fears and potentially live a more fulfilled life. At least that's what he hoped and what he'd manoeuvred for. He was the lesser of the evils that Pixie was presented with and he'd worked that angle.

Rory loved her already and he knew that his feelings for her would only grow every day. But she still had a lot of sorting out to do in her head. She may never love him as much as he knew he would love her. But it was a gamble he'd been prepared to take, because deep down he knew she belonged to him.

"Okay, I can see your point but I'm so scared they're going to forget Mum and Dad. I don't want that to happen. Their memories of Dad are already fading because they don't have as many as me. I'd hate them to lose what little they've had."

"Well, we'll come up with a plan to help them remember. It's probably a conversation you should have with Jazz. Maybe she has some ideas on how to help them remember while also letting go enough for them to move on."

Pixie was quiet for a long moment. It was obvious she was stewing over something.

"Just say it, Pixie. It's not getting any easier thinking about it."

"Do you really think Jazz has a clue about any of this stuff?"

He chuckled at her question and raised his eyebrows. It was the same one everyone asked if they hadn't seen Jazz in a professional capacity. "Yeah, I think she really does. In fact, I think it's her quirkiness that actually helps her relate better to people. She doesn't seem so distant or something. You get the feeling she really does understand and know what you're feeling."

"Well, if you trust her then I'll give her the benefit of the doubt. I must admit she was great to me on the day of our wedding. But I just don't get all that stuff between her and Quade. It seems so immature or something."

"It's certainly that, but what I think you're seeing is some primitive form of mating dance, for want of a better description. They're both attracted to each other but are equally stubborn and too prideful to actually do anything about it."

She nodded, vaguely considering his insight. "So what do you think will happen?"

"I think one day the attraction will overcome everything else and they'll end up doing the business. What happens after that is anyone's guess."

"By doing the 'business' you mean sleeping with each other?" she asked shyly.

"You got it in one." He smiled.

She shifted in her seat and looked uncomfortable again.

"Just say it, Pix."

He heard her take a deep breath. "So when are we going to do the business?"

Chapter Eighteen

Rory pulled the SUV into the driveway of Pixie's cottage. It was going to be his home as well now. It felt strange. He'd never really had his own home. The work he'd done for the Centre had meant that he'd moved around a lot. He kept an apartment on the northern beaches of Sydney, mainly because it was close to a good wave. But there were equally good waves here on the Gold Coast. He needed to talk to the boss about his plans to relocate here.

He also needed to answer Pixie's question.

Rory took her hand in his across the console.

"Truthfully, I don't know. I've said it before and I mean it. It'll happen when you're ready. When you can come to me with no fear. Until then, we'll get to know each other better, work our way towards it."

He saw the blush rise on her cheeks again. She really was quite shy and so far from the seductress she'd originally made herself out to be.

"But you haven't touched me in days, other than to hold me at night." He read the concern in her eyes. Intimacy between them was obviously playing on her mind.

"Sweetheart, it's not from not wanting you. Absolutely the opposite, to be exact." He moved their joined hands over and placed her palm against the hard bulge in his shorts. She wriggled her fingers slightly and he held his breath, trying to control his response to the simple touch. Pixie had no idea how potent she was to him.

"I've been trying to give you the space and the consideration that you need to get through all you've had to deal with. But this is the state I spend most of my days in. So don't doubt the me wanting you part."

"Thank you," she said, barely above a whisper. "But I want to move on. It's time for me to start resurrecting my life and you're now a central part of that."

He knew what she was asking and he wouldn't make her say the words just yet. She wanted intimacy with him; she needed to establish the connection that only making love could forge. Pixie was subtly telling him to step it up.

He was so on board with that plan.

Rather than using more words, he decided it was time to let his body do the talking. He leant forward and slid his left hand into her hair, cupping the back of her head. The light pressure of his hand urged her head forward, connecting her lips with his. Her lips were slightly ajar and he used the tip of his tongue to lick across the seam, asking for entry. She obliged with a sexy sigh, encouraging his exploration of her mouth.

Her tongue eagerly twined with his. Sliding, tasting, caressing his. He moved his torso across, trying to get closer to her. He needed to feel her body against his. A frustrated growl crawled from his throat when the console proved too much of a barrier for what he had in mind.

Rory pulled back, ending the kiss with a light puckered peck.

Pixie looked at him, confused, still caught up in the passion that was starting to really flare between them.

"Come on, this console is definitely going to be a problem. I think there's a bed in there with our name on it."

She ducked her head, nodding slightly.

"Don't go getting shy on me now, Pix. I had a feeling we were just about to get to something good," he joked with her.

She smiled. "You think so?"

"Well, I know what I had in mind and I think you'll be on board with it."

That sparked her curiosity. But before she could ask the question, he was out of the vehicle and had scooped her out of the passenger side and was carrying her up the couple of steps at the front verandah.

He shifted her in his arms. "Wrap your legs around my waist; I need to open the door."

Somehow he managed to extract the keys from his front pocket and open the door. It was far from easy with an armful of delicious woman and a raging hard-on that was stretching his shorts to a dangerous point. He kicked the door closed behind him and took her straight into the bedroom.

"What about our stuff?"

"What about it? It'll still be there when we're ready for it. Or was there something you needed?"

"Not really…just thinking about it."

He placed her gently on the bed. The bags were playing on her mind. "At the risk of using the most outdated of clichés, why don't you slip into something more comfortable while I go get our bags," he said with a flourish.

She giggled at his antics as he disappeared from the room.

A minute or two later, he returned, carrying their bags. He dumped them unceremoniously by the door of the bedroom and retreated again. He grabbed a couple of bottles of water from the fridge and went back to find her lounging on the bed, still dressed in what she'd had on. She'd turned on the bedside lamps so he took the opportunity and killed the harsher central light as he passed through the door.

"Didn't want to get changed?"

"Umm, more like it's still really difficult to get changed with this thing on my leg."

He put the picture together. She'd decided to do nothing rather than be half dressed or undressed when he'd come in.

"I spoke to Jazz today. She said you can leave the cast off at night in bed now but no moving around without it. In a week or two, they'll want you to start exercising it, apparently."

A huge smile settled over Pixie's face. "Really?"

"Yep, really. Want me to help you get it off?"

"Absolutely."

He laughed and started to undo the fastenings on the boot. She lay back and let him, the smile not leaving her face. A few seconds later, he was easing the boot off and Pixie sighed with what sounded like relief. She raised her leg up off the bed, testing the weight without the cast.

"You have no idea how heavenly that feels not to have that monstrosity hanging off the end of my leg." She moaned, the sound only heightening his need for her.

"I can only imagine, but I guess that means I'm going to have to help you out of your clothes given that you're not allowed to put any weight on that ankle."

"I didn't think of that," she mentioned sheepishly.

"I did." He smiled and winked at her. A nervous giggle slipped from her lips.

He placed his hand on her calf, just above where the bandage on her ankle stopped. Rory slowly ran his hand upwards. Her flesh goose pimpled at his touch and she shivered.

This caused him to chuckle. "Good or bad shivering?"

"Oh, definitely good."

"I thought I'd better check." He slid his hand under the hem of her loose shorts. After the first day with the cast, she'd taken to wearing looser shorts. Her favourite denim ones that hugged her butt so deliciously would just have to wait.

He eased his hands up and slipped his fingers under the elastic of the waistband. In a smooth motion, he slid the shorts down off her hips and over her legs to land on the floor. The satiny skin of her lightly tanned thighs was teasing him. He couldn't resist. Rory lowered his face to her thighs and placed light, feathery kisses on the soft skin. He drew the tip of his tongue across her flesh, sending off a fresh bout of shivers through her body.

"Mmm, somebody has sensitive skin."

He could smell her increasing arousal. There was a hint of fear there, as well, but nothing too shocking at the moment.

Rory dragged his fingertips up and down her thigh, teasing, purposely making her skin all prickly and sensitive. He wanted her feeling everything. He wanted her to understand just how much pleasure he could give her.

The long, slow strokes of his hand changed to light circles

with his index finger. The circles grew larger and larger, until they met the satiny fabric of her panties at her groin. He slid his finger underneath the elastic and pulled it away from her skin before letting the elastic snap back into place, causing her to jump a little from the surprise. He repeated the process, only this time his eyes held hers. Her pupils almost swallowed the purple-blue irises and her face had softened in pleasure.

This was how he wanted her. Relaxed, aroused, and willing.

He dropped his head to her mound and the scent of her arousal was enough to have him inhaling deeply, his senses demanding more of her essence. His lips brushed the silky material lightly before lifting again.

"I want to taste you. I want your juices all over my tongue. How would you feel about that?"

He heard her pulse increase to an even stronger hammering. She sucked in a breath and nodded her head in agreement.

"I want the words, my sweet. Not just a nod."

Her heavy eyelids flew up and she looked directly into his gaze.

"Please," she whimpered. But her body told him a different story. Her fear had also shot up. The scent of it assaulted his nostrils. She was torn, wanting more and wanting to please him but still fearful.

Rather than move straight to the sweet bounty he knew he'd find beneath the satin covering her from him, he moved upwards, sliding his hands under the fitted fabric of her T-shirt.

He wanted it gone.

He needed the shirt gone.

He needed her bare to him.

"This shirt has been teasing me all day, my wicked little temptress. I want it gone." His voice was heavy with desire and need. He did nothing to disguise it; he wanted her to hear just what effect she had on him.

TJ felt herself nodding her agreement to the shirt being removed. She wanted it gone as well. His hands felt so good against her skin. She moved her hands to the bottom hem of the shirt. He brushed them away.

"Let me do this."

His eyes held hers as she nodded once in agreement. She raised her body up off the bed as he drew the shirt over her head. His hands caught her under the arms and he raised her up the bed, slightly plumping some pillows up behind her back and head.

"Mmm, that's better. Now gravity is helping, not hindering, these beauties." His attention was firmly riveted on her rounded breasts encased in the plain white satin of her bra. Her pebbled nipples were undisguisable from his view.

He swooped down and closed his mouth over her distended right nipple. The satiny covering only served to heighten the sensation as he sucked and licked at her flesh through its sheer covering.

She let out a small start that turned into a throaty moan as he increased the suction on her nipple.

Rory caressed her waist and moved upwards to her breasts. His hand closed over her left breast, massaging and caressing the globe, before his fingers sought the peaked cap of her nipple.

The ache shot straight to her feminine core as he lightly pinched and rolled one nipple while hungrily sucking on the other. The sensation was so intense. The feeling of every nerve ending constricting, tensing, waiting for further stimulation and to finally be set free.

Her breath was coming in short pants and her heartbeat was racing. All she could think about was the focus points of pleasure he was creating on her body.

His hands slipped from her breasts and reached behind her, seeking the clasp of her bra. His mouth felt incredible on her breasts even through the fabric of her bra but the thought of his mouth directly on her flesh created an even more desperate craving.

Rory slowly slid the straps of the bra down her arms, making a total production out of the unveiling of her breasts.

"Mmm, I don't think I'll ever be able to get enough of these beauties. God, you're gorgeous."

She giggled lightly at his words. Nobody had ever said things like that to her before.

"How did I get so lucky?" he growled more to himself than her.

"I don't know that you're that lucky. I'm thinking you're more like a glutton for punishment with all the dramas you've taken on with me."

"Well, if this is punishment, I'm about to get a lot more wicked."

Before she could answer, he took her lips with his again. There was no hesitation or gentle asking this time. He wanted in and he let her know immediately.

There was no way she could deny him anything.

His tongue slipped, slid, and explored her mouth before he broke the intensity and began kissing a trail down her neck. His hand cupped her behind the head before he entwined his fingers into her hair and firmly pulled her head back to give him better access to her neck.

TJ instantaneously felt a surge of fear rush through her body. Her heart began beating uncontrollably; she sucked in a breath to try to control it.

Rory immediately moved his hand and pulled back from her, giving her space. He reached for her hands and gently cradled them in his.

"What happened? Was the trigger for your fear me pulling your hair or kissing your neck?"

She looked at him incredulously, his words blurring in her brain. She was still trying to control the fear that she knew was unfounded on this occasion.

"The hair—you pulled a lot harder than normal," she managed to blurt out a second later.

He opened his arms and she immediately moved into them, accepting the hug of comfort he was offering.

"Want to tell me about it?" he whispered.

She shook her head. *Nope, she didn't want to talk to him*

about it yet. She just wanted to soak up his strength and get back to where they were. Anger flashed through her as well. *Would she ever get back to normal?*

She hated them for what they had done to her.

His hand moved to her head again, almost hesitantly, and he stroked over her hair lightly.

"Is this okay?"

She nodded and croaked out a "yes."

He continued stroking her hair and she buried her nose closer into his chest. She felt safe and protected in his arms and wanted to go back to where they were before but knew she'd have to make the first move.

TJ slid her hands around his waist and under the hem of his T-shirt. She rubbed her hands up and down his back and enjoyed the feel of the muscles contracting under her touch. Feeling bolder, she lightly raked her nails down his back and was rewarded with a throaty groan. His hips shot forward and collided with hers. She couldn't miss the hard length of his erection pressing into her.

"Ahhh, that feels so good. I love having my back scratched."

She giggled, pleased that something so simple could affect him so much. She dug her nails in just a little harder.

"Oh yeah, even harder still." He almost sounded as if he were begging.

"How's that?"

"Incredibly good, too good," he said as he slightly rolled her away from him while he removed his shirt.

TJ decided then and there that the man shouldn't be allowed to wear a shirt; he was just too sexy for words. His shoulders and arms were sculptured to within an inch of their lives. It must be hell keeping that shape.

"So how many hours a week do you put in to keep these?" she asked, rubbing her hands down over his shoulders and chest.

"Not many, maybe one or two workouts a week. Surfing helps but it's more about genetics than anything else. It's not the end of the world if I miss a few."

"Mmm, now I'm thinking I'm the lucky one," she murmured as she pulled herself closer to him again. She slipped her hands down over his washboard abs and toyed with the waistband of his shorts. Her fingers played with the button for a few seconds before she mustered the courage to slip the cool metal through the denim.

Before she thought too much about it, she grasped the tab of the zipper and slid that down as well. She couldn't miss the feeling of the hard ridge beneath her knuckles as she did so.

What would it feel like bare against her skin, inside her?

She reached for the waistband on both sides of his hips and tugged downwards. Rory helped dispense with the shorts and rolled her back onto the bed. Back to where she was before fear had interrupted them.

TJ reached for him and he followed her down, laying his body along the righthand side of hers. His hand rested on her stomach and his mouth immediately latched on to her nipple. He fanned the fires within her again with long, slow intoxicating sucks and nibbles.

The hand at her stomach inched lower and moved to cover her mound. His index finger lightly traced the slit between her feminine lips over the fabric of her panties. The sensation sent a ripple of shivers through her body. She wanted him to touch her. The barrier between her flesh and his fingers needed to go.

She moaned her frustration at the teasing.

"Mmm, time to lose these panties, I think?"

Ah, the man was a mind reader!

Rory moved from beside her to shimmy down the bed and off the end. He reached up and slid the offending garment down the length of her skin.

For the first time, she was completely exposed to him in the muted lamp light. It threw shadows around the room but there was no way he could miss the sight of her naked body laid out in front of him.

Her gaze focused on the ridge throbbing beneath the black fabric of his boxer briefs. Somehow it seemed safer to focus her attention there than on his face. Too revealing—too intimate, perhaps.

Eventually, she had to know and looked up. The warm chocolate of his eyes had heated to the colour of rich chocolate fudge. Attraction and desire for her radiated from their centres.

It was a heady feeling as he stared at her body.

"I can't believe how beautiful you are. All soft curves and silky skin. You're a feast for my senses."

He carefully lifted her right leg to the side. She instinctively turned her hips to hide her feminine centre from him. He gently grasped her behind her knee and parted her legs, completely exposing him to his view.

She felt vulnerable and exposed, but worshipped at the same time. Was that possible?

Rory placed his knees between her thighs and knelt on the bed between them. It was a little awkward for him but he'd manage. His preference would have been to drag her down to the end of the bed and throw her legs over his shoulders so he could tease and torment his fill, but something told him that would be too much for his first time between her thighs.

He lowered his head towards her mound and looked up at her from under hooded eyes.

"I'm going to taste you now, my sweet Pixie. Relax and let me rock your world."

She squirmed beneath him and thrust her hips towards his face. He knew she was both a little shocked and equally turned on by his words. He wanted her to know what was coming. He didn't want a repeat of her fear resurfacing.

When he said he'd work through her demons with her, he meant it.

All he could smell was arousal.

His nose was just about overloaded on it now—he needed it on his tongue as well.

He could wait no longer. The first swipe of his tongue along the slit of her feminine lips was enough to have him groaning.

It was even better than he'd thought possible. Pixie was just as sweet as he knew she'd be, but she was so much more.

She was soft, velvety, and tangy all at the same time. He wanted nothing more than to get a good taste of her and then thrust his cock, which seemed as if it had turned to forged steel, into her soft centre.

But he wouldn't. This was about Pixie.

His turn would come and he had no doubt it would be wonderful.

He flicked his tongue out and dipped it into her channel, where her feminine dew was most concentrated. The taste on his tongue exploded like sherbet.

Pixie moaned but held her body still. He knew she was bursting to move her hips but she was still a little unsure.

He ran his tongue up the centre fold of her femininity and then flicked his tongue, once, twice, three times across her over-sensitised clit before drawing the bundle of nerves completely into his mouth and lightly sucking.

She let out a long, throaty moan and pushed at his head.

He looked up at her questioningly.

"Ahhh, it's so intense," she panted out.

"Good, then I'm doing it right. That's how it's supposed to feel." He grinned and winked at her from his position at her mound. He wanted sex hot and passionate but he also wanted it to be fun. He wanted her completely relaxed and confident with him.

An amused smile crossed her face before she flopped back down on the bed.

His mouth dropped to her clit once more and he began to trace her delicate folds with his fingers.

He could hear her breaths coming in even more ragged pants than before. She was nearly there.

Mmmm, what to do? He could tease and torment her a bit more, take her to the edge and then pull her back or help her soar.

The feel of all her muscles tightening beneath his touch answered his question. He couldn't do it to her this time. So instead, he edged one long finger into her wet channel, giving her body something to cling to and then he flicked the tip of his tongue over her clit at a rapid fire pace. The change in sensation was enough.

She lasted but a second before the sweetest sound of her release met his ears.

Her body tensed, frozen in ecstasy, before dropping and then tensing again.

"Ohhh, Rory, that's so good," she managed to pant out between waves.

He chuckled to himself and lightly tweaked her clit every second or two to draw out the most of her orgasm.

When she'd finally quieted, he moved up the bed and drew her into his arms. It felt special to be able to hold close somebody who truly meant something to him.

Chapter Nineteen

Sleeping in her own bed did something about returning her time clock to business. She woke at two minutes to five and reached out and shut off the alarm clock before it chimed five and woke Rory.

As much as it would have been nice to linger in bed, she needed to get moving. There was a lot to do today. TJ eased herself up and began to swing her legs to the side to move from the bed. That's when she realised she needed the cast. It was on the floor at the base of the bed. She turned and crawled up the bed. She eased her hips to the end and could just reach the cast with the tips of her fingers to drag it back.

But before she could hook it all the way back to her, strong arms closed around her waist, dragging her back from the edge.

"What are you doing, princess?" Rory mumbled sleepily.

"Mmm, getting my cast. I have to get moving," she protested, struggling to move from his arms and back to the cast.

"Just stop. You'll bump your leg and hurt yourself. I'll get it for you." She watched him lever himself from the bed. He was all toned and tanned muscle. The only thing covering him was the black boxer briefs. Somehow she'd married an Adonis and didn't even know it.

He'd retrieved the cast and was moving to place it back on her ankle when he stopped and looked at her.

"What?" he asked obviously curious at why she was staring at him.

"Umm, I'm just having a female moment."

He shook his head, not understanding.

"Should I be worried?"

"Nope, just admiring the view." It was then that he realised what she was going on about.

He dropped the cast to the floor and crawled up the bed like a big jungle cat on the prowl.

Somehow her stare had stirred him and she knew he was coming for her now. She put up her hands in a defensive mode.

"We can't. I have to get to the office and get things sorted out."

He stopped momentarily and drew his finger under her chin, raising her eyes to look at him. "Okay, I'll let you off this once but tonight you're mine."

She let out a nervous giggle.

"Mmm, I can tell you don't know whether to be anxious or expectant. Looks like I've got my work cut out for me today." A devilish grin split his face. It was nearly as good as the thousand-watter she loved so much.

She dipped her head, a little embarrassed by his carry-on.

"Umm, do you think you could help me with this cast? I really need to get going."

He laughed at her businesslike attitude.

"Yep, definitely going to have my work cut out for me today and I do recall having more than one discussion with you about the you-and-I team thing. So I'd say that means *we* need to get going. Let's get this thing back on you. I'll be glad when the six or eight weeks are up and I don't have to watch you hobble everywhere. As cute as it is, I live in constant fear you're about to go base over apex and break your other ankle."

She sat up a little straighter, pretending to be offended by his comments.

"I'll have you know I'm not clumsy and I've never broken or sprained anything in the past. You can hardly blame me for this. It's not like I stepped from the truck. I was dragged and came to a rather sudden stop."

"I know. I witnessed it and it was the longest second of my life, watching you fall." He covered his sentence with a teasing voice but she knew him well enough now to know that it upset him to watch her attack.

"Oh well, you'll just have to keep me safe from more threats," she jokingly said. Unexpectedly, his mood sobered.

"I intend to, sweet pea. I'd like even more if they no longer existed but until we figure all this out, I need you to be really careful and don't go doing impulsive, reckless things."

She started to object but he shook his head slightly and the look on his face told her whatever he was telling her was very important to him.

"I'd feel much better if you were within arm's reach of me all the time but I realise that's hardly practical and you're not likely to agree to it, but that's just how I feel. So for my sake—please just be really careful and if anything feels, sounds, or even smells off for that matter, I want to know about it immediately. And if for some reason, you can't reach me, I want you to check in or call one of the guys. I've programmed their numbers into your phone. I know this sounds extreme but I need you to promise me you'll do this."

She nodded her head. "Okay, I'll try to do this."

"Don't try—make sure you do it."

That flared her temper. "Rory, I'm not eight, nor am I stupid."

"I know that, Pix, but you have a tendency to jump right in when threatened or challenged. Sometimes you take things to the extreme." He tried to soothe while still making his point.

"Name something that I've done that's lacked judgement."

"I don't want to end up in an argument with you over this. Just try to think through the consequences before you jump in, for my sake, please."

"You still haven't given me any examples of how I've been reckless." Her temper was still flaring, but obviously he wasn't about to back down either.

"How about trying to get the truck off the trailer at the sale? It's not generally considered smart to go messing around removing a prime mover when the trailer's engulfed in flames. Nor is it advisable to try to drive a monster rig with a broken ankle. And I'm not even going to discuss that little introduction to seduction you gave me. Do I need to go on?"

She shook her head quickly. She could feel the tightness in her face. TJ didn't want him to go on, because she knew what the next reckless thing on the list would be. Somehow, if he didn't say it—it wouldn't be true.

"I had my reasons for doing all the things I did," she said quietly.

"I know and they were good ones. But did it ever cross your mind to ask for help rather than just dive in?"

"And if I recall correctly, you helped me in all those cases," she spat back at him.

"Yes I did and I'd willingly help you with anything you wanted but I don't want you putting yourself in danger first, before you come to me for help."

"Just because I'm little doesn't mean I'm helpless, Rory."

"Don't even start pulling that little chestnut, Pixie. Your size has nothing to do with it and you know it. You're so far from helpless it's not funny. But you still refuse to ask for help. Why is that? Is it because you think that people won't help? Or is it because you haven't had help in the past when you've asked for it? Or is it something else completely, like the fear that drives you? I'd really like to know, then maybe I can work on convincing you that whatever it is, it's nothing but bullshit and we can move on."

She felt tears start to fall from her eyes and her throat started to constrict.

He looked at her and all the frustration she'd seen on his face crumpled like a sandcastle smashed by a wave.

He didn't say anything more; he just drew her into his arms and held her tightly. She held herself rigid for a second and then succumbed to the warmth and all the delicious things she always felt in his arms.

"God, I'm such a thoughtless shit. I'm sorry, Pixie, you didn't deserve for me to go unloading like that," he crooned into her hair.

She sobbed once more. "It's okay—you're right. I do everything you said. I know I do and I admit it consciously."

He didn't say anything, just let her gather herself again in his arms. It was a place that she'd become very used to over the last couple of weeks. A place that she now thought of as her safe haven.

Rory deserved an explanation.

"When I feel fear, I have a tendency to face it to the extreme rather than do what's probably smart." Her voice sounded small and fragile even to her own ears. He said nothing, just waited for her to continue. "So to tackle the fear, I tend to try to overwhelm it by doing something large. It's how I've learned to cope, particularly over the last few years."

He nodded his head against hers and then brushed his lips across her forehead.

"Well, let's see if we can do something about reducing the fears in your life. Maybe then we won't have to deal with your reactions to it. The last thing I want is for you to feel fear about anything."

She nodded her agreement. That sounded really good.

Rory helped her in and out of the shower and through her morning routine in double quick time. He would have loved to linger and turn something quite innocent into something totally erotic but it hadn't been the time for it. Pixie needed love and caring, not him hound dogging her after he'd emotionally ambushed her.

They had been running late thanks to his ill thought through emotional ambush. He still couldn't fathom what drove him to head down the path he did. He knew he was normally more conscious of people's feelings but he just couldn't seem to stop himself.

But he'd also learnt something. Reading between the lines, her recklessness, or fear fighting for want of better words, probably escalated after whatever happened to her a few years ago. He had mentally catalogued it as an attack but the truth was he didn't know. Just another mystery he had yet to solve when it came to his wife.

What's more of a mystery was he couldn't believe she hadn't banished him to the dog house with Zeus and Thor, who he was now feeding. He'd already helped load up half a dozen trucks and fuel up three others and it was barely eight o'clock. Was it always this busy around here in the mornings? He considered it briefly before he dragged his mind back to the problem at hand. Sure, he'd wanted to know the answers to the questions but he hadn't finessed it at all.

Talk about clomping in with steel-capped boots.

Fuck, he must have spent too much time of late around Quade!

He scratched behind Zeus's ear and knelt to give the big dog a fierce hug and wrestle. He knew they were both enjoying having him around.

As he went to rise again, Zeus moved and the smell assaulted him. It was faint but it was there nonetheless. Maybe a couple of days old.

Whoever had been around her mother's house before the explosion had been here recently as well. That got his senses going and his hackles on alert.

He headed over to the office. Maybe he could take Pixie out for a bit of a late breakfast now that the rush was over.

She was hunched over the computer when he walked in. Her leg propped up on another chair caused the strange angle of her body. Just looking at her made his back hurt from the thought of how it must feel to be sitting like that.

"Sweet pea, you can't possibly be comfortable like that."

"I'm not," she replied absently, without taking her eyes from the screen.

"Then why are you sitting like that?"

"Because my leg feels better when it's up like this."

He stood and processed that for a second.

"So what you're saying is that your back hurts less than your leg."

That got a giggle from her and she looked up from her computer.

"Yep, something like that."

He shook his head, struggling with the logic.

"Have you got much to do?"

"Not as much as I thought. I've just got to get these last few entries done then send this off to the accountant so he can lodge it with the tax department. That's pretty well it. The place seems to have run surprisingly well while I've been gone," she said the last bit almost in disbelief.

He just nodded, knowingly.

"What did you do?"

"Me? Nothing really."

"I know you came over a few mornings and sorted everything out. So you must have done something to get it running so smoothly. You'd hardly know I've been gone except for these damn tax statements."

"Well, that's good then. You'll have time to head down the coast with your husband before the afternoon milk run. I assume we're picking that up again?" He shot her a smile and a wink.

"Yeah, I want to do that. I've always done it for the last two and a half years and it wouldn't seem right somehow if I left it for someone else to do. Why do we need to head down the coast?"

"Well, first off, I thought we could stop for a late breakfast and secondly, the boss has called a meeting. Seems Rheeba has found some stuff and he wants to go through it with us."

"Can't he just talk to us on the phone?"

"Ah, Pixie, I do recall you being with me the last few times I've met with the boss. Does he strike you as the sort of guy you argue with about having the meeting over the phone when he politely tells you to get your butt into the office?"

She huffed out a long breath. "No, I guess not. I was just expecting to spend the day in the office."

"And do what?"

"I don't know—stuff." She threw her hands up in frustration.

"Well, you just got through telling me that the 'stuff' had already been done. Let's blow this popsicle stand. I want to have a late breakfast down at Sanctuary Cove with my wife."

He chuckled to himself before she could respond. "I do like the sound of that wife bit."

Rory looked back to Pixie and she was just smiling, shaking her head in response.

"You know you're a complete clown, don't you?"

"Yep, I've worked really hard to hone this level of clowniness."

She laughed at his antics. "That's not even a word, is it?"

"Probably not but it should be. It's a good word. I like it—clowniness."

"Okay, we'll go. But I just need another ten minutes before we head out."

"Done. I need to make a couple of calls anyway. But first I need to do this."

Before she had a chance to resist, he leant forward over her desk and planted a scorching kiss on her lips. It was hot and playful all at the same time. This was the first step in his all-day seduction plan. He was setting himself his own personal challenge.

How badly could he make her want him in one day?

"Hey, D. How's it going?" Rory said when Dylan picked up the call.

"Good, mate, and you?"

"Yeah, not too bad. I do have something that I wouldn't mind you checking out, though."

"Sure, what's up?"

"Well, not sure if I mentioned it to you but the night before the explosion, I noticed a new scent around the place. Something strange. Someone I hadn't met here before. Anyway, I noticed it again this morning. Not as pronounced, more like whoever it was, was here a couple of days ago. You know what I mean."

"That I do. Any ideas about who it is?"

"Nope but it's not a relative. I'm not picking up any sort of blood tie in the scent. It's also not Kelvin, in case you're wondering."

"Who do you think then? Hired help?"

"I don't know but I let it go once and a few hours later we had an explosion. This time I'm not letting it go. I'm just about to take Pixie out for breakfast and head down the coast to catch up with the boss. Any chance you can swing by and take a whiff?"

"Sure, I'll bring Quade and Brayden as well. Boss has called us in for a meeting at thirteen hundred."

"We'll be there."

"So what scent am I looking for and where's it concentrated?"

Rory went about explaining what to look out for and where to best scent the smell.

"Oh, just so you know, the dogs' names are Zeus and Thor. They're friendly enough but probably not so much with Quade."

The sound of Dylan's laughter came through the phone. They all had funny stories to relay about Quade and his misadventures with the canines of the four-legged type. Cats and canines didn't mix so well, it seemed.

"No problem—you can count on me to forget to mention it."

Rory chuckled. "Knew I could, mate. See you this arvo."

Rory ended the connection. That was just another thing he had to broach with Pixie and the sooner the better. She needed to know he was a little more than just the man he presented.

Good thing she seemed to be an animal lover. At least he hoped she was. Otherwise, maybe he would be living in the dog house for real.

Chapter Twenty

Max leafed through the papers on his desk as he searched for what he was looking for. It was the yield results for the latest studies he'd commissioned on his genetically modified dairy cattle herd. He'd done it through one of his offshore shelf companies and he was carrying out the research across a couple of Asian countries.

He could never hope to achieve here what he could there for a fraction of the cost. It was almost carte blanche. Coin was king and bureaucracy could be bought off easily. One thing he had was plenty of coin, and this was something he'd set his mind to almost fifteen years ago.

He not only wanted to produce a higher-yielding cow, he also wanted to develop one that produced milk that wasn't an issue for lactose-intolerant people. Why should they miss out on all those great products when technology could solve the problem? He'd been lactose-intolerant most of his life. He missed dairy products. Missed the rich creamy taste.

But what he really wanted was the big fat "cash cow" the discovery was sure to make.

A chuckle escaped his lips at his own little private joke. The ultimate cow and it would make him even richer. It was a rainbow he'd been chasing for years but the pot of gold was almost within his reach—he could taste it. The sweet rich taste of cream. Oooo weeee.

First things first though, he had to get the Centre off his back. It'd taken him a few days but now the he knew who they were, he could figure out a way around them. It's what he liked to do—study his opponent and then make his move.

It'd taken some doing and pulling in a few favours but now he'd started to have a handle on the Centre. Money talks and lips get looser. Max was a firm believer no secret could withstand the siren's song of money.

He'd just pull the genetically modified cows from the herds for a little bit. He'd only put them into the commercial herds in the first place as a test to see how good the surveillance really was.

Given the fact that it had brought the Centre crawling around things, the surveillance was better than he'd thought. And that was exactly why he ran these little "tests" to see who was really watching. To determine how good his opponents really were.

And now he knew what he was up against.

Now he knew what he had to do.

One thing about "agencies" was that if they thought the threat was over or they corralled an "infringement," they were happy—case closed.

Too easy—he'd give them one. Even wrap it all up with a bow for them.

Then he could get down to the real business.

The Teresa matter was a whole other story. He needed to talk to Kelvin about that.

And now he had the questions over Tom Anderson—wouldn't it be good if he could tidy up the loose ends in his life in one fell swoop?

He could rest a fulfilled man.

TJ took a sip of her soy cappuccino. It was heavenly. Whoever was working the espresso machine was a genius to behold. It seemed so peaceful, so normal sitting out here on the deck at Sanctuary Cove eating breakfast at a little café overlooking the marina with her husband. That bit she was still getting used to. It felt strange to be somebody's wife. Probably because she had only a few hours to comprehend that it was going to happen. She guessed she'd get used to it soon.

"You look, dare I say it, happy." Rory smiled at her, his eyes twinkling.

"I do feel a bit lighter. I have to say I was pleasantly surprised by how little I had to do to sort out the business side of things." She paused to make sure she had his full attention. TJ wanted to let him know just how much his help meant to her. "Thank you for everything you've done." She hoped the sincerity she felt at her words was expressed in her face.

"You're very welcome, my sweet." He smiled the big one.

TJ felt her blood start to race and heartbeat pick up. Her girly bits contracted and she felt want for him again. She smiled shyly and wriggled in her seat.

"What?" he said, obviously curious at her behaviour.

She felt herself blushing but what the hell. "When you smile like that, it makes me go all tingly."

He laughed a deep, low chuckle that sounded sexy to her ears.

"Good to know it's that easy to get you going."

"I think you've discovered I'm pretty easy when it comes to you."

"I haven't discovered anywhere near enough about you, but I intend to change that in good time."

She knew he'd added the "in good time" so she didn't feel pressured. Right about now the only pressure she was feeling was the type that was due to wanting him. Nothing else.

He sipped his coffee, still lightly holding her eyes with his. It was intimate without feeling weird or uncomfortable.

She reached out and took his hand, wanting to feel some sort of physical connection to him. TJ was immediately rewarded when he took her hand and slowly started to stroke the inside of her wrist with his thumb. *Oh wow.* She didn't know it could be such an erogenous zone.

She looked away from him briefly, trying to pull herself together. If she wasn't careful, she'd expire on the spot.

Finally she returned her focus to him. The louse. He knew exactly what he was doing, what she was feeling. The satisfied smirk on his face told her so.

"I'd suggest going for a walk but probably not the best of ideas."

"Ah, no. I'll be so glad to get this damned thing off and get back to normal."

"Oh, I don't know. At least while you've got this on your leg, I have a legitimate excuse to pick you up and carry you places." He looked away momentarily as if thinking about something. "Plus I also have a good excuse to help you dress and the part I like better—the undressing."

She burst out laughing. "You're incorrigible."

"Mmm, maybe. But only where you're concerned and I have a feeling that you just might like it."

Before she could temper her thoughts, a little whispered "I do" slipped out. TJ slapped her hand to her face in horror— she couldn't believe she'd just said that out loud.

Rory threw his head back and laughed. "It's okay, sweet pea—your secret's safe with me. I'd also pegged that you might like to get a little naughty, given enough encouragement."

TJ's head spun around, looking to see whether anyone was listening. Fortunately the nearest occupied table was several tables away and the couple of guys there looked totally engrossed in whatever documents they were reviewing.

"Rory!" she shrieked through a clenched teeth whisper. "You can't say that here."

"Why not? It's just you and me."

"But…" She trailed off, nothing immediately coming to mind. Then she looked down and saw the delicate gold band around the ring finger on her left hand. Her protest seemed silly all of the sudden.

Rory reached over and traced his finger around the band. "I need to get you an engagement ring to go with this one."

She felt heat rising to her face again. Another ring wasn't necessary. She hadn't even expected this one, given how quickly things had happened. "Don't worry about it. This one is more than enough. Besides, you could hardly call the few hours we had together an engagement."

He chuckled at her words. "True but I want the world to know you're mine and nothing says that more than a big sparkler."

She looked at him a little sheepishly. "Rory, it's really not necessary."

"I know, but I want to. And I will soon."

She left the conversation at that. She had a feeling this was not an argument she could easily win. TJ drained the last of the coffee from her cup.

"Do you want another or should we get going?"

"As tempting as another sounds, I try to limit my caffeine intake to no more than three cups a day and I'm already at that. I'll never sleep otherwise and five a.m. rolls around quickly."

Rory smiled at her with a grin that couldn't be described as anything other than wicked. "I don't think you'll have trouble sleeping tonight, my sweet Pixie."

She wasn't exactly sure what he had in mind but she could guess and a whole new wave of want washed over her.

He signalled for the waitress to bring the bill. TJ automatically reached for her handbag below the table. He shook his head and reached for his wallet and put a few notes in the folder.

"But Rory, it's only fair I pay my way." She thought about all the clothes that he'd had Jazz and Quade buy. She needed to fix that up as well.

"Pixie, we're a team and you're my wife. Where I come from, the guy pays the bills."

She could understand that. That was the way she'd grown up but she knew it wasn't the norm anymore. Or at least in some cases. Plus, she'd got used to paying all the bills over the last couple of years. Finances were another thing they needed to have a chat about, it seemed.

"We can talk about money another day. We don't need to sort out everything today or even this week. We've got a lot of ground to make up as a couple but it doesn't all have to be sorted out straight away." He squeezed her hand, letting her know it was going to be alright.

She nodded her agreement.

"Come on, let's get out of here," he said, drawing her up to him as he got up from the table.

The heat was back in his eyes.

Rory nearly left Pixie on a seat at the edge of the carpark while he went to get the SUV. Then he thought better of it and swung her up into his arms. Carrying her gave him just another opportunity to have his hands all over her. She didn't need to be walking or hobbling any farther than necessary.

Before they'd left home, she'd changed into a loose skirt that mostly covered the cast and a delicate-looking tank top. She looked absolutely gorgeous and completely unaware of it.

His hard cock had definitely noticed and was more than happy to step up the action when the occasion arose. It seemed he'd been sporting wood for days. It was uncomfortable but it wouldn't kill him. He knew Pixie was worth it. Initially he'd done his best to hide it and he doubted she even noticed, given all the other things that were pressing for her attention.

Today was different; he wasn't hiding anything from her anymore.

He'd helped her into the SUV. The vehicle was really too high for her to get into without help while she had the cast on. He hadn't missed the opportunity to give her rounded butt a lingering squeeze, and he dropped a feathery kiss on her neck and trailed his tongue around the rim of her delicate little ear before he'd got in the SUV himself.

Just as he'd hoped, she'd shivered and was wriggling in her seat. The musky smell of her arousal was the first thing he'd noted when he'd opened his door and hopped in. The enclosed space of the vehicle only served to intensify the scent. It had been there during their breakfast—he'd worked to make sure of it.

Fuck, he could overload on it.

Now they were travelling down the old Pacific Highway, heading to the office. The traffic was light but the traffic lights were a pain in the butt.

He knew he shouldn't, but damn it, he wanted to.

Fuck it.

Rory reached over and dragged her loose skirt up until his hand could rest on her silky thigh. Pixie immediately stiffened and looked over at him in question, but he said nothing, just kept his focus on the road.

Slowly he started to move his hand in slow circles, inching up. Pixie had relaxed, becoming more accustomed to the sensation. She'd pulled her skirt around his hand. It was an attempt at modesty but he'd let her have it. There was no way anyone could see in. The windows were darker than legal tint, a little side benefit of the SUV being a Centre vehicle, and the extra height cocooned them from any prying eyes.

He wouldn't have even considered doing this if he thought someone might get to see her. This was for him and him alone.

Rory flicked the elastic of leg of her panties, and continued to burrow his fingers underneath. He retreated momentarily and urged her thighs apart with his hand.

"I need some more room, sweetness."

She said nothing, just did as he asked, making a hot little sigh that had his cock clenching and then surprised him by tilting her hips forward, giving him better access than he expected.

He flicked on the car stereo from a button on the steering wheel; it was Bluetooth-connected to his phone. Thinking ahead, he'd set his phone to shuffle through Pink's latest album *The Truth About Love*.

He knew Pixie loved this album. He didn't mind Pink; she was a kick-ass chick and that he could respect.

His fingers went questing again and were rewarded with the feel of her slick, hot pussy just begging for his touch. He slid his fingers through her folds, painting her with the wetness he found.

"Oh, baby doll, you're so wet for me. I wish I could taste you, lick you until you come right now…"

Pixie's breathing hitched and a whole new batch of wetness flowed over his fingers. *Ah, his little Pixie liked him talking dirty to her.*

He trailed off, glancing sideways at her from behind his shades. He'd love nothing more to have his mouth on her hot wet centre right now but this would have to do.

Rory dragged his attention back to the front, forcing himself to concentrate on the road.

Her breath was coming in little tight pants and he knew she was close.

He changed the pressure on her clit and slipped his middle finger into her channel.

Just as he'd guessed—it was enough.

The panting became a long, throaty moan as she dragged out his name across her lips. Her wet centre clamped around his hand and her thighs slammed shut against his hand, holding him to her.

He hazarded a glance at her and saw her with her head thrown back. The throes of passion were written across her face. She was so beautiful like this. He'd never get enough of seeing her like this.

TJ couldn't believe she'd just done that with Rory. They'd been driving down a public road! She'd had a release but, geez, that was intense! She cast a glance over at Rory.

He had that satisfied male look on his face. She glanced down further and saw the very noticeable bulge at the front of his jeans.

Without thinking further, she snaked her hand across and stroked him through the thick denim fabric. His erection jerked and pulsed into her hand in response.

Rory let out a low growl from the back of his throat and covered her hand with his, lifting it from him.

"Not now, sweetheart, you'll have me coming in my jeans."

TJ took her hand back.

"So let me get this straight. You can tease me mercilessly but I can't touch you?"

Rory swung into the driveway of the nondescript office block and stopped at the card reader.

He hunted through the console for the card, hit the button to lower the window and swiped the card.

While the heavy door was rising, he turned to her.

"Something like that. You can touch me whenever you want, just not now. We've got a couple of meetings to get through and I'm on a hair trigger at the moment. As it is, I'm going to head straight to the bathroom and take care of this before I head upstairs."

TJ was a little shocked by just how up front he'd been with her. "Umm, I could take care of it for you," she offered shyly.

He headed the vehicle down into the underground carpark and pulled into a spot beside a large pylon. Rory shut off the engine and turned to her, grabbing her hands in his.

"Thanks for the offer, baby doll, but I don't want my first time with you to be a quick hand job in the car. It's not that it wouldn't be great but, I had something else and another setting in mind. Nor do I want to be pressed for time and by my watch, we've got nine minutes. I want to be able to enjoy what you do to me without worrying about time pressures and pissing the boss off any more. And it seriously sucks to keep the boss waiting or piss him off."

TJ didn't know what to say. She kind of felt at a bit of a loss.

Rory was out of the car and opening her door. He lifted her from the car and pulled her into his arms and then lowered his mouth to hers for a scorching kiss.

It was heady and overwhelming. TJ wrapped her arms around his neck and hung on to keep upright. She was so turned on again. It was insane what he could do to her.

Rory finally broke the contact and handed her the crutches from the car. It wasn't feasible for him to be there all the time.

He beeped them through the ground floor door with his card. It was a long, boring looking corridor with a few doors heading off each way. About halfway along, they came to the bathrooms. He slipped inside the mens' room and she took the opportunity to freshen up in the ladies' room.

For some reason, it seemed to turn her on even more, thinking of him taking his long length into his hand and jacking off.

TJ thought on that for a few moments as she washed her hands and face. They needed to finish this thing between them so they could move on comfortably. But first she had to get through today. That in itself was going to be difficult. Just being near him or thinking about him had her in a constant state of arousal. It was easier to focus on them than everything else. She needed some time away from the responsibility and the mental processing of her loss. It'd been eating her from the inside out for days. Now she just wanted to feel alive again, to really start living.

She headed to the elevator and waited for him. A few moments later, he walked up and she couldn't help but glance down looking for the bulge, which seemed to have abated for the moment.

"More comfortable?" she asked a little saucily, not being able to resist the opportunity to tease.

"Slightly. But only for about five minutes, I'm predicting."

She burst out with a laugh. "You can't be serious?"

"As a heart attack. If you have any mercy at all, you'll try not to be so damned attractive and gorgeous for the next few hours until I can do something about it."

"You really are a clown."

"Maybe, but I'm feeling like a very horny clown today. So watch out." He made a mock lunge at her and she shrieked and giggled as he wrapped her in his arms and pulled her into the   elevator.

He pulled her tight and made sure he managed to rub his hands over her breasts and butt in the process. Quickly, he stepped back.

"Damn."

"What?" She looked at him in surprise.

He raised his eyebrows and she followed his eyes. "Cameras. Stop looking, Rheeba," he called at the round darkly shaded bulb in the corner.

A voice came over the intercom. "It's not Rheeba, but me, Surfer Boy." A low sultry laugh came through the speaker.

"You know better, Selena."

"Oh, but having something on you is chips in the bank. It happens so rarely."

"And nothing happened this time. It's hardly a stretch to think I'm not going to take the opportunity to feel up my delectable wife. I'm a newly married man, for crying out loud. It's what we do. You have seen Brayden and Rih, I'm taking it?"

The sexy laugh came back through. "Oh yeah, more than once. If that girl wasn't already pregnant, I'd swear he was hellbent on knocking her up. He's definitely a stud servicing his mare. You should probably remind him that we're all really happy for him but if he could keep the PDAs to a minimum or at least to an M rating, it would be appreciated. I think my eyeballs are permanently scarred."

The doors opened and Rory chuckled. "Noted. Catch you soon, Slinky."

Rory steadied her as she got the crutches sorted out again. "Are you guys always like that?"

"Yeah, probably worse, to be honest."

It was difficult to believe. They all just seemed so comfortable around each other. Like family but even slightly different from that.

They headed down to the boardroom where they would meet the boss. Rory picked two chairs at the table facing the river. He helped TJ into her chair before taking the other one himself.

Something Selena had said sat strangely with her.

"Something's bothering you—out with it."

"Um, what did she mean when she said he's definitely a stud servicing his mare?"

Rory sighed and TJ knew she'd stumbled onto something.

"I should have guessed you would have picked up on that."

She looked at him expectantly.

"I'll tell you the whole story later but for now just know that Brayden's nickname within the Centre is Stud."

TJ nodded.

The boss chose that moment to walk in and their attention turned to him.

As expected, he took the seat at the head of the long board table and placed his notebook and a couple of document wallets neatly in front of him.

"How are you both?"

"Well, Boss."

TJ didn't feel the need to answer; Rory had done it for her.

"So I thought it would be best if I called you both in here to go through a few things rather than over the phone. As you know, I've had Rheeba doing some digging to try to figure out why you and your business have been targeted." The boss opened one of the document wallets and passed a sheet of paper to both of them.

TJ quickly read the information on the page but could barely take it in. It just didn't make sense. The words began to swim before her eyes.

Rory must have noticed her flagging and reached across the table and poured a glass of water from the pitcher in the centre of the table for her.

"Here, Pixie, drink this, sweetheart," he urged.

Somehow she choked down the water, but she still couldn't believe the words swimming in front of her eyes.

Finally she composed herself enough to ask, "Is it true?"

Tom answered, "We believe so, from what we can ascertain."

Tears started to pool in her eyes and she felt the telltale constriction of her throat. She gulped another mouthful of water and nearly swallowed it the wrong way but somehow manage to keep herself in check.

Never had she felt so betrayed.

"How could he?"

"Only he can answer that question but that's what Rheeba's investigations have turned up."

"He's family. Why would he do this to me? To us? What have we done to deserve this?"

"I can't answer that, Teresa, but the facts are Max acquired a fifty per cent stake in Q-Trans a little over two years ago. As you can see, it's been done through a trail of companies both on and offshore but it looks like Rheeba has got to the bottom of this one."

She nodded her understanding.

TJ took a deep breath and asked the question, "Do you think he's behind what's been going on for the last few months?"

She saw Rory look to the boss and then he reached for her hand.

Tom looked directly at her. She understood why these guys all respected him so much. He just oozed something that made you sit up straighter and become more alert to what he wanted.

"Well, before I answer that question, let me ask you one, Teresa. Does Max know about the issues that you've been having for the last few months?"

A cold sick feeling stabbed at her gut. Uncle Max knew. In fact, he'd been urging her to get out. To marry Kelvin and let him run the business.

"Yes," she finally whispered. TJ squeezed Rory's hand tighter and she wanted nothing more than to bury her face in his chest and have him hold her tight.

"Fuck. There's no doubt then," Rory spat.

"It would seem so," Tom said simply.

"So what do we do now, Boss?"

"We need to gather what evidence we can. I'll get onto the lab and see what the damned holdup is on the results of those tyres. They've had them well over a week. Rheeba has finished down south now. I've told her I want everything she can dig up on Max and Kelvin, and I mean everything. If they've so much as stepped off a crossing and jaywalked, I want to know."

TJ sat there, stunned. Uncle Max knew about the attacks on her, probably even ordered them. Well, he certainly didn't do anything to stop them. Plus the pushing to marry Kelvin. Where did it stop?

Her stomach lurched and her breakfast threatened to return. She took another big gulp of water in defence.

Both men looked at her in concern. Rory reached over to her and looked as if he were about to scoop her into his arms.

"I'm okay," she rushed out. "He's going to keep terrorising us, isn't he?"

Rory just nodded but Tom answered. "Yes, Teresa, I'm afraid he is. For some reason, Max wants control of Walsh Haulage. Do you have any idea why that is?"

"Not really."

The room went quiet for a second as Tom leafed through his notebook.

"Something's been bothering me for a few days. Tell me what you know about Max from a career perspective. I'm particularly interested in why he didn't go into the business when he was a young man like your father."

TJ thought back. What she knew was probably patchy and irrelevant. "Umm, from what I recall, Dad said that Pop and Uncle Max didn't really get on, so when the time came for Uncle Max to leave school, he went into the army or something. Then apparently he started renovating houses when he got out and the property development stuff came from there."

"So when your pop died, was there ever any talk of your uncle coming into the business?" Tom asked.

"Not that I recall. The will specifically stated that Dad was to inherit the business. Dad and Uncle Max might have had some conversations but I guess everyone figured Uncle Max was more than busy with his own companies. I mean, they're worth squillions more than Walsh Haulage. Why would he even be interested?" She looked at Rory and immediately saw the concern and comfort in his eyes. He was trying to be there from her.

"Teresa, people do things for a lot of reasons. Given that money doesn't seem to be an obvious driver for Max in this case, I'd guess it's one of two things. Either Walsh Haulage has or could have something Max wants or there's some type of emotional motivation. From my experience, they're the toughest ones to figure out because there's often very flawed logic behind the thinking and the actions. You've met the man, Rory. What do you think?"

Rory was still for a second and TJ could see him considering Tom's question.

"I think it's most likely some sort of emotional pull but I wouldn't rule out there being some sort of side benefit. The guy strikes me as someone who's always looking to maximise the 'return on investment' so to speak."

Tom considered that for a moment and then nodded. "I'd agree with that thinking." TJ watched him very precisely close the folders and his notebook. His actions clearly said he was looking to wrap up the meeting.

Tom looked off into the distance for a second and she knew he was contemplating something. This man was direct; something obviously was playing on his mind.

Finally he looked at her. "Teresa, I didn't really want to bring this up but in light of the circumstances, I think you should know." TJ braced herself; she knew it was going to be a body blow before it was even delivered. "I've assigned some people to investigate the deaths of your father and brother. I've gone over the files and too many questions are unanswered for my liking."

Was it possible to be flooded with multiple emotions at once? Because that's how she felt. She felt pain at the loss of her father and brother but she also felt hope that someone else actually felt the same way about this that she did.

"Thank you, sir. You have no idea how it makes me feel to know that someone else thinks that there was something off about the accident. But it also haunts me to think that my uncle, Dad's brother, could in some way be involved. That's what you left unsaid, wasn't it? What sort of monster would do that?"

"You're right, that's what I left unspoken. I'm very sorry you're having to go through all this, Ms Walsh—or are you going by Mrs Southall?" TJ watched Tom's lip quirk in amusement as he contemplated it. Mrs Southall sounded strange to her ears as well, but that was who she was now. "But this situation needs to be solved once and for all, and from everything we've got here, it seems Max isn't going to go away without some sort of showdown."

TJ watched Rory nod. It was obvious both men thought it was inevitable but that didn't make it seem or feel any better.

This was her family they were talking about.

The picture was very clear to her now. None of this really surprised her that much. Hurt her, yes, but surprised her, no. From firsthand experience, she knew just how cruel and twisted Kelvin could be and she feared it was a skill he'd learnt from his father. The gap between them had been widening for the last few years.

Her options were simple. She either worked with the Centre to rid herself of Uncle Max and she assumed Kelvin, or she'd be living in fear of what they planned next.

There was no choice to consider now. She'd made that decision the day Rory asked her to marry him.

Chapter Twenty-One

An hour or so later, Rory found himself back in the boardroom. This time he was surrounded by his teammates. Seems the Boss had called in whoever was around. At last count that was Brayden, Quade, Dylan, Selena, and Rheeba.

It was good to be around his teammates. He really did enjoy spending time with them.

"So who's up for taking the Jet Skis out this weekend?" Brayden asked the group in general.

There was a chorus of "yeah's" around the table.

"How about we grab the skis and the bay cruiser and head over to Straddie or somewhere near there for a morning, or a day if we can afford the time? If we take the boat as well then we can take the kids. They're not up to hanging on the back and if TJ's not up to riding the ski, then she can hitch a ride as well."

There was another chorus of "cool, sounds good."

"Slinky, how do you feel about being in charge of catering and would you mind piloting the boat?" Brayden asked.

"Sure, no problem. I can dial the number for Subway catering as well as any of you. How does vegetarian sound, Rat Brat?" Her point was not lost on the guys.

"Fine with me." Rheeba giggled.

"Oh babe, you wouldn't. Don't even think it. We need our meat, you know that," Dylan whined.

"How about I just bring over a bucket of protein powder?" Selena teased, making a jab at his incredibly cut form. All the guys were incredibly fit and cut. Dylan just liked to take it to a whole new level. Total body is a temple regime.

"Well, that would work as well but I'd prefer cold cuts, I think. I'll need to keep up my strength. I want a rematch, Rheeba." Dylan gave her his best sad puppy dog eye face to Selena and then turned and smiled in challenge to Rheeba.

"You're on, hotshot. Bring your best game. Last time must have sucked to be you." Both Rheeba and Dylan eyed each other like prize fighters about to spring from the bell.

"Let's just hope we don't get shot at this time. The last time we all went out as a group, we nearly got our asses filled with holes," Quade said philosophically, referring to their recent run-in with a group of Chinese extremists.

"Yeah, I'm in support of the no additional holes in asses approach. Quade, mate, you're a big enough asshole without adding another one to your hide," Dylan threw in. Everyone just laughed. Quade just shook his head, growled, and glared.

Jazz, who had slipped in a few seconds ago, piped up. "See, it's not just me who thinks you're an asshole. Must be something to it then." She smiled sweetly at him, purposely taking another swipe.

Quade flashed his azure eyes directly at Jazz. "Anyone ever tell you what happens when you grab a tiger by its tail?"

"Not much, from what I've seen so far," she shot back like lightning, her emerald eyes flaring in challenge.

Low giggles and chuckles came from around the room. Everyone was settling in to watch another match of Quade and Jazz. It was such a great fun spectator sport. It beat daytime television hands down.

Rory half got out of his chair, and put his hands up in a time out symbol to stop them. "Just hold fire for a sec, guys. I need to go throw some popcorn in the microwave. This looks like it's going to be fun but I really need something to munch on while we watch."

Brayden threw his head back and laughed. "Yeah, Surfer Boy. Popcorn does sound good."

A deep throat cleared. And they all spun around to face the door. Even with their animal senses, they'd been too preoccupied with the floor show to notice the boss entering the room.

Whoops!

"What's this about popcorn?"

All eyes and heads turned to Rory.

"Ah, nothing, Boss, just mentioning that I was starting to feel a little hungry and some popcorn would go down well."

Yeah, they were no better than school kids. The boss gave him a wry smile and Rory matched it back. Message delivered—he didn't fool the boss in the least.

"Well, if you're all ready, let's get started." The boss brought everyone up to speed on what had happened with Q-Trans. He also mentioned that it seemed that no genetically modified product had been moved through that transport company. So that meant that the cows responsible for the product had to be located on the twenty or so farms that Walsh Haulage serviced.

"I think we need to go take a closer look at those cattle. Brayden, I think we could use Rihanna and Peter's help." Brayden's wife Rihanna was a vet, as was her father Peter. Both had worked closely with the Centre on the recent Hendra virus case.

"I'm thinking we concoct some sort of Department of Agriculture herd sampling process or something similar. Rheeba, I'll leave you to sort out the cover story."

"Sure, Boss," Rheeba acknowledged.

"I'd like to start as soon as possible. The sooner we get this done, the sooner we move onto something else. Anything else, people?"

"Boss, if Rihanna's going to be in the field then I want to be assigned to be with her."

The boss looked directly at Brayden with a glare that told him his comment was totally unnecessary. "I wouldn't have it any other way."

Rory now knew exactly how Brayden felt. There was no way he could stand being apart from Pixie at the moment, given the threat to her. He was uncomfortable with her just being a few rooms away, while she hung out with Rihanna and the kids.

The boss wrapped things up and he was first out the door.

TJ wandered into the kitchen area to make herself a tea. The kids were sprawled out, watching a movie in the "down" room. Whatever the devil that was. It looked more like a man's dream recreation room to her. Full of plush leather lounges, the biggest flat-screen TV she'd ever seen, and a vast array of electronic gadgetry that had Marcus "ohing" and "ahhing" but was way over her head.

Jazz picked that moment to walk into the kitchen as well.

"Can I get you one?" TJ asked politely.

"No thanks, I'm going to grab a juice."

Jazz plonked herself down at the table and pulled out a chair for TJ. TJ laughed inwardly. *Guess she was sitting down.*

Tea in hand, she managed to hobble through the manoeuvre.

"I'm guessing Rory mentioned to you that you can have the cast off now as long as you don't put any weight on the leg."

"Yeah, it was heaven last night getting to sleep without the rotten thing."

Jazz laughed the musical tinkling sound TJ now associated with her. "I'm figuring Rory also appreciated being able to get close to you without clocking himself with that thing. They hurt like nothing else if you run into them."

"Ah yeah, he didn't mention it but I think he was happy enough not to have to contend with it." TJ felt the colour rise in her cheeks. Suddenly, she remembered Rory's words. Jazz would get out of her what she wanted.

"So you two are settling in together okay?"

"Are you asking as a friend or a doctor?" TJ asked suspiciously.

Jazz just giggled again. "A little of both, I guess. I'd prefer to be your friend but I can also be a doctor if that's what's needed. I'd like to think Rory is a good friend of mine, and I hope that you can be soon as well."

TJ thought about that for a moment. "I'd like that. I guess I don't have many friends. I kind of lost track of a lot of people, given what's happened to me over the last two or three years. I have a very different life to all my school and uni friends."

Jazz nodded. "You'll find that you'll probably end up socialising a lot with the Centre team. They're all very close. Well, I guess it's now we tend to socialise together because there's that common bond."

There it was again. The hint of something secret. Something more than what you would consider normal. Walsh Haulage was essentially a family business. Many of the staff had worked for the company for several years. The bond between the staff was strong but nothing like this.

"What am I missing here, Jazz? These guys are all super close, strangely close."

Jazz looked at her, deadpan. "I'm not sure what you're talking about."

TJ knew immediately it was a lie. She'd seen enough of Jazz to know she was always animated and probing. She was the sort of person who grabbed life by the throat. Deadpan wasn't in her repertoire.

Two could play at this game. TJ smiled knowingly. "Try again, Jazz."

Jazz smiled and TJ immediately realised she'd hit the target. "You're very good. You know. But it's not my secret to tell. You need to ask Rory about it."

TJ contemplated that. She wasn't really sure how to answer; she didn't want to give Jazz too much insight into their relationship.

"He mentioned something about wanting to have a chat to me about a few things but not wanting to stress me any further given the circumstances."

Jazz gave her a genuine smile. "That's totally Rory. He'll tell you when he's ready and when he thinks you're in the right frame of mind. You've had an awful lot to deal with in the last couple of weeks without even mentioning what you've been dealing with for the last few months."

TJ nodded; it was all true.

Jazz took a sip from her juice. "There was something else I wanted to talk to you about."

"Sure," TJ said a little more confidently than she felt.

"It's about the kids. Have you contacted the school to advise them what's happened?"

"Ah darn. It completely slipped my mind." TJ shook her head, mentally chastising herself. She needed to get her act together. "I'll call them in a minute."

Jazz nodded. "Rihanna and I were just discussing their schooling this morning and if the school can provide their curriculum, she'll make sure they do their work. Rih did a lot of tutoring in uni, so she said she'd be happy to help out and supervise. I'll do the same, of course."

TJ was touched. It was a job she should be doing. But she also knew there was no way she could do it. In fact, she wasn't even sure she should have much contact with the kids given what she'd learnt about Uncle Max earlier.

"Thank you. It means a lot to me that you and Rihanna are prepared to do all you are for the kids."

Jazz laughed and waved her hand. "Think nothing of it. They're great. We've been having lots of fun."

"I hope they haven't been causing any problems."

"Not at all. They've only been there for a day but I'm sure we're all going to get along just fine. Marcus has already conned Brayden into giving him guitar lessons."

TJ felt her jaw drop. She hoped Marcus wasn't being a nuisance. "That's not necessary. I'm sure Brayden's got better things to do than teach Marcus to play the guitar."

"I wouldn't worry about it too much. Brayden seemed pretty chuffed to me. Besides, I got the inside story from Rih. Apparently, Brayden's looking forward to it. He says it's good practice for when he tries to teach their kids."

"They're sure going to have their hands full with triplets."

"Isn't that the truth. It'll be fun. A lot's happened in a short few months for them. But I think you and Rory even beat them in the speedy stakes."

"We won't be having a bundle of newborns in a few months, though," TJ reassured her.

"I agree you probably could use some time for things to settle down. But no contraception is ever one hundred per cent sure. That shot I gave you last week should be fully effective by now. I'm sure Rory will be glad to know he can ditch the condoms. So you shouldn't need to worry just yet about surprise pregnancies."

TJ stiffened and felt her face grow warmer. She was fast learning for herself, Jazz left nothing on the table. They hadn't even properly consummated their marriage yet. She wasn't sure she wanted Jazz to know that.

Jazz reached for her hand. "Oh my God, I've made you really uncomfortable. I just assumed, which I absolutely know better than to do. I guess because I'm a woman and I have eyes and I know what I'd want to do if I was in your shoes." Jazz must have seen the look on her face. "And I should seriously shut up now because I'm making this worse."

TJ couldn't help but giggle and nod.

"Well, let me just say then, I'm sure you'll sort it out at your own pace and it will be earth shattering." Jazz threw up her hands to emphasis the earth shattering and the funny face she pulled let TJ know she was trying to make light of the situation to erase her unease.

Before she realised what she was doing, TJ just blurted it out. "Something happened to me a few years back." She looked away, not able to look at the concern written on Jazz's face. "I wasn't raped but it wasn't far from it."

Jazz didn't say anything. She waited, letting TJ come back to her. When TJ finally raised her eyes to Jazz's again, she went on softly, "Do you want to talk about it?"

After what seemed like a really long time, TJ answered. "Yes, I think I do."

The guys pulled him aside after the meeting in the boardroom.

"We checked out the scent you were talking about," Dylan confirmed.

"Yeah, what do you think?" Rory asked, curious.

"I agree—not a relative."

"Those the only couple of times you've smelt it?" Brayden asked.

"Yeah, so I'm guessing whoever it is has come and gone for whatever reason. I'm pretty sure I know the reason the first time with the explosion. I'm just not sure about the second time and that's what worries me."

"You think the trucks are going to be targeted next?" Quade asked, lounging against the wall of the team room.

Rory nodded. "That would be my guess. Either the trucks or the yard."

"Fuck, what do you want to do?" Brayden asked, frustration and fury in his voice at the thought of all this bullshit.

"Well, I'm open to suggestions right about now, fellas. Pixie's being targeted in a big way and I'm nervous about being more than twenty feet away from her at the moment. But at the same time, I'm trying to let her get her life sorted out. What she's had to deal with over the last few years is fucking monumental. I'm not about to tell you all of it, so don't ask. Just know it makes what we've dealt with look like a Sunday picnic."

Rory looked over at Dylan for a moment. He'd gone unusually quiet.

"What?"

Dylan shrugged his massive shoulders. "I was just thinking. Have you actually bothered to ask Max what his problem is?"

Rory felt his jaw drop.

Fuck, it was obvious.

It was the sort of logic he'd ordinarily come up with. This whole being personally involved thing was seriously messing with his head. All he could think about was making sure Pixie was safe. He looked across at Brayden and Quade. They held similar slack jaw expressions.

"It was just a thought but maybe it would give you a bit more insight. What've you got to lose?"

Now that he put it like that, probably nothing.

"It's so obvious and simple it'll probably work. I'll call him and see if I can set up a meet." They all nodded their acceptance of the plan except Quade.

"No fucking way are you going alone, mate."

"If I show up with a posse, he might get spooked. I think this is something I need to do by myself."

Quade pushed off the wall. "Maybe, but I think at least D and I need to be close by in case the shit hits the fan. One thing we do know about this fucker is that he's determined and he has an ego."

"Okay, I can live with that. Why don't I try to set it up for some place like a café or something? Then you guys can take a table a few away."

They all nodded.

Brayden turned to head off. "Make the call, mate. Drop Pixie over at my place and I'll keep an eye on the kids and the girls."

Quade lightly chuckled, which sounded more like a snigger. "You've been doing lots of that lately, mate. If my memory serves correctly, Surfer Boy and I ended up in a knife fight while you were kicking back looking after the girls."

"Let me think for a second." Brayden made a big show of considering something. "Knife fight...looking after the girls. Nope, not a hardship or a competition. You're just jealous I get the girls and not you. If you weren't such an asshole most of the time, you might find it can actually be kind of fun. Never ceases to amaze me what they chat about."

"Nothing would surprise me if honey nose was involved," Quade muttered.

"So when are you going to just admit you have a boner for the lady and do something about it?" This time it was Dylan who nailed him between the eyes. "You guys are starting to let off some serious pheromones."

Rory couldn't help but laugh. "See, mate, I did tell you the other day you needed to do something about it."

"When fucking hell freezes over," Quade spat.

"Wait...Stud, D—is it getting chilly in here? I swear I could use a jumper; must be a cold snap coming on."

"Ha, ha, very funny," Quade snarled, stalking off.

"I thought so." Rory chuckled.

Chapter Twenty-Two

Rory pulled the golf cart into the depot yard. Pixie was beside him. He daren't leave her anywhere on the property by herself. Not when he was so unsure of who was potentially prowling around.

Dylan was going to bunk in the caravan that was left onsite in case any drivers needed to crash out for a few hours. There was simply too much distance between the house and the depot for Rory to be able to effectively use his senses. He needed to be closer and there was no way he was dragging Pixie down here to camp in the caravan. D had come to his rescue.

"Hey there, what's happening?" Dylan called, rising from his chair outside the caravan, the epitome of casual.

"Not much, just thought we'd come check on you before we hit the sack. Anything interesting going on?" Rory could smell the unknown scent was fresh and strong and he had no doubt Dylan had been out prowling around, checking things out prior to their arrival. They all knew how to play a part and Dylan was playing his.

"Mmm, just getting sorted out for the night." It seemed like an innocent comment but Rory knew categorically that Dylan's idea of sorted and most people's would be vastly different.

"There's clean linen and towels in the top cupboards. And if the water's not hot in the shower, the switch for the hot water cylinder is in the console under the sink," Pixie called from the cart.

"Thanks, Pixie, I found everything."

The dogs charged up to the cart and shoved their heads in, wanting a pat from Pixie.

"The dogs aren't a problem for you either?" she asked, obviously confused.

"Nope, we're best of friends all ready. Hey, fellas." Dylan dropped to a crouch and the dogs loped over for a pat and a scratch.

Had whoever was the owner of the scent been trying to befriend the dogs or did he already know them?

"So you're all set for the night?" Rory asked, giving Dylan a knowing look.

"Yep, all set," Dylan confirmed.

Rory took a glance around and then subtly moved a couple of steps away. A reasonable wind was blowing across the flats tonight and the scent was strong. The guy had been there this afternoon. Nothing surer.

"What can you smell?" Pixie asked.

Both Rory and Dylan looked at her, stunned. Rory forced his face to relax and hoped Dylan was doing the same. He didn't dare glance sideways to check.

"What do you mean, sweetheart?"

"Well, I figured you must have been able to smell something. You had that exact same look on your face as when you came charging in just before the explosion."

He could hear the concern in her voice.

"It's probably nothing. Nothing I can identify, anyway." There, a great use of the Centre motto. Always stick as close to the truth as possible.

Dylan cleared his throat. "Don't worry, I've got it covered. You two go back and enjoy being newlyweds."

Rory turned to Dylan and didn't miss the wicked gleam in his eyes. Dylan loved nothing more than a good close-contact battle. He was itching to use his animal strength and speed in battle. If someone was bold enough to come looking for trouble tonight, they were in for a very nasty surprise. Dylan was definitely the type you wanted fighting at your back, not coming at your front.

Rory hadn't seen anyone come close to besting him in hand-to-hand combat. He'd studied martial arts since he was four and no one really knew how many styles he knew. There wasn't a move he couldn't counter or better. Add to that his animal strength, speed, and endurance and he was quite probably the "ultimate fighter."

The boss brought in lots of different martial arts specialist to keep all their skills honed. It was hardly necessary when Dylan could have more than adequately performed the task.

"Well, if you're sure. I'll keep my phone on or whistle if you need me."

"I won't, but thanks." Dylan grinned at him.

"Okay, Pixie, if the man says he's fine, he's fine. I believe the man said also said something about being newlyweds. I'm totally on board with the plan. How about you, sweet pea?" Rory asked as he got into the cart beside her.

"Rory!" she shrieked, lightly flicking him on the arm.

He just chuckled. "Want to play a little rough, do you, sweets?"

"Oh, stop it. You're incorrigible."

TJ was nervous and excited all at once. It wasn't the paralysing fear she'd become accustomed to. This was more along the lines of the butterflies in your stomach type. Tonight he was going to make love to her. She just knew it. He'd been hinting at it all day.

Subtle touches, hot kisses, and the whole pussy plundering session he pulled in the SUV. Wow! He knew what he'd been doing to her and tonight she wanted the main event with him.

She was relaxing in the bath, her head propped up on a thick towel. Rory had sent her here while he finished up some calls to his teammates and the Centre.

Her mind wandered back to the strange meeting they'd had with Dylan not thirty minutes ago. Something was very strange about these Centre guys. She was positive he'd smelt something. Yet nothing seemed out of the ordinary to her. He'd also smelt the gas and she hadn't noticed it at all. Plus there were the strange comments that had been made. And something certainly passed unsaid between Rory and Dylan. There was also that time Aunt Clara had come over. He'd heard or sensed her or something.

He had mentioned he had very sensitive hearing and smell—but really?

She knew he had something to tell her and she wondered now even more whether it had something to do with it.

A light knock and then the door opening a little brought her thoughts back to the here and now.

"Is that a water nymph I see or my wife? On second thought, maybe both."

She giggled at his teasing and gave him a coy smile.

"Need some help getting out?" He waggled his eyebrows at her.

The butterflies were back stronger than ever but she managed to push them aside. She needed to if she wanted this to go forward.

"I wouldn't say no to an offer like that. It's not easy to manoeuvre with this ankle."

He chuckled. "I'll be glad when the cast is gone and your ankle's healed. Then I can snuggle in tighter to you without bashing my leg. I swear my shins have got lumps and bumps all over them."

She ducked her head and pulled a pained face in sympathy. It really did hurt when it smashed into you. TJ had managed to bash it into her other leg enough times to know this as fact.

The bubble bath she'd put into the water was fast vanishing. TJ's thoughts flew to how she could get out of the bath with some modicum of dignity. Sure, he'd seen her naked before but their relationship was so new and she was a long way from being comfortable parading naked for him.

Before she had further time to think about it, Rory moved past the bath to the shower and turned it on. He turned around and grinned at her.

"You mind if I take a shower? I figured we could multitask." The grin turned into the sexy sort of smile that made her remember exactly why she was a woman.

TJ's heart raced—no, it pounded—in her chest.

His hands dropped to the hem of his shirt and drew it slowly over his head and let it fall to the floor.

Inch after inch of glorious tanned skin was exposed. Her hands itched to touch him.

He tilted his head and gave her a little one-sided grin. His eyes spoke to her. Rory wanted to move things along too but he wanted to do it in a way that was relaxed and fun.

His hands dropped to the waistband of his jeans and he stood still for a moment. Teasing her, asking her. Her eyes were drawn to the pronounced V shape of muscle flowing from his hips. The darker line of hair directed her eyes to the place she'd yet to see.

She nodded her head in encouragement and he lowered the zipper and hooked his thumbs under the fabric before sliding the denim down over his butt and thighs.

The denim puddled at the floor around his bare feet and he kicked them aside, leaving him standing before her in nothing but his navy boxer briefs.

This was it—a turning point. They both knew it.

His hands moved to the waistband of his underwear.

"Are you ready for this?" His voice was husky and low. The sound of it sent a shock of the most delicious tingles down her spine.

TJ swallowed hard. Her mouth went dry. She needed to answer.

Was she ready?

Oh yeah!

She wanted him. The incredibly desirable man standing in front of her was her husband. She'd gotten to know him as a true friend over the last few weeks. He'd treated her with the utmost respect, understanding, and tenderness.

Now she wanted to know him as her husband.

She was calling dibs on his butt right now.

"Yes." The strength and conviction in her voice surprised even her.

And before she could form another thought, he gave her the big one, the thousand-watter, and lowered the boxer briefs.

Her eyes travelled slowly south. Words didn't really come close to describing the sight in front of her. It was an image she knew she'd carry for the rest of her days. Rory standing naked in front of her for the very first time, a cloud of steam rising from the forgotten running water. The epitome of masculinity, all hard sculptured planes of muscles with a liberal sprinkling of darker hair in all the right places. There was nothing metrosexual about this guy. He was totally as Mother Nature had intended. And oh, had she got things right.

Finally her eyes dipped to the spot she'd avoided looking at. She was torn, wanting to look but not wanting to seem to stare. His hard cock stood at full attention. Looking at Rory, she understood for the first time the fascination with phallic symbols. She was looking at a living, breathing one and rather than making her nervous as she feared, it did the opposite.

Want, longing, desire—whatever you called it—screamed through her, demanding to get out.

"I promise you can look as much as you like in a minute, because I know I'm going to take my time staring at you tonight, oh gorgeous one." He softened the intensity of his words with a playful sound in his voice. "But I really would prefer to take this shower before the water goes cold. Not that I think it would have any effect on my friend here. I'd suggest you join me but I think shower play is just a bit too risky with a broken ankle." She must have looked a little disappointed. "But I'm definitely putting it on my to-do list."

He turned and moved into the shower, closing the glass door behind him.

TJ took a deep breath and fanned her face. Between the steam and Rory, the temperature had certainly risen in here.

A few minutes later, Rory had finished showering and shaving. He'd helped her out of the bath and very sensually rubbed her dry with one of the plush towels she loved.

Unable to resist any longer, she put her hand on his face and rubbed her palm and fingers over the smooth skin, now devoid of any stubble. TJ had always thought there was something incredibly sexy about watching a man shave and watching Rory had been off the charts sexy. What made it even sexier was that she knew he was doing it for her.

He'd asked her whether she wanted stubble or smooth. Stubble could look hot but TJ loved the feel of his smooth masculine skin. It was no contest.

Rory growled low in his throat at her touch and swivelled his head to plant a kiss on the inside of her wrist. Taking her a little by surprise, he swept her into his arms and padded through to the bedroom, placing her gently in the centre of the bed.

He followed her down and captured her in his arms for a hug. TJ immediately rolled and pressed her body against him. He'd been taunting her for the last twenty minutes. Now she just wanted to be close to him.

It was so good just to feel his naked body along the length of hers. Her face was pressed into the place where his chest and shoulder met. She loved his clean citrusy scent. It was heady and gave her all sorts of urges.

His hand ran down the length of her back, continuing down over her rounded butt. He pulled her hips in tightly to his, pressing his very aroused flesh against her. She felt her feminine core contract at the sensory overload she was feeling.

"Mmm, I love having you in my arms like this. It feels so good," he whispered into her hair in a low husky voice. His hand trailed down over her butt again but this time retracted via her hip and ribs.

She wriggled and giggled lightly at the tickling sensation. "Whoops, sorry," she mumbled.

"What are you sorry for?"

"I laughed."

He rolled onto his back and pulled her on top of him.

"And you're sorry for that?"

"Well, it just doesn't seem right somehow."

This time he laughed and TJ felt her body rising and falling as his abdomen expanded and lifted her up and down.

"Baby doll—there are no rules between us. If you want to laugh, laugh. Making love doesn't have to be serious all the time. It can be anything we want. I just want you to be happy."

She felt as if she could drown in the tenderness he expressed with his eyes. He really did mean it.

"And fulfilled and I want to see you come apart in my arms again...and again...and again." He reached up with his head to peck her on the lips to emphasis each "again."

TJ wriggled on top of him, eager to move on but not really sure where to start.

"I'd say you have ants in your pants but you don't have any on." He chuckled at her wriggles.

She planted her hands beside his head and pushed back. Her nipples swayed dangerously close to his mouth.

Never one to miss an opportunity, Rory reached up and latched his mouth around the tight bud, drawing it firmly into his greedy mouth.

The feeling of his mouth locked onto her breast had her thrusting her hips into his. She felt his fingers trail down over her butt and trace up the crack between them, only to return lower to the wetness of her pussy.

He lightly traced her outside lips before burrowing his fingers in deeper, searching for the true centre of her. He applied a light pressure to both her inner thighs, silently suggesting she plant her knees on either side of his hips. She complied without conscious thought.

TJ lifted her head and shuddered in the response to the feel of his suckling at her nipples while his hands returned to tormenting her very needy pussy.

His fingers stroked and teased and explored. Sometimes his tongue lapped at her nipples; other times he nibbled and then the best of all, when he sucked her nipple in deep, each time it caused a bolt of need to run through her at warp speed.

Her breath was coming in ragged pants and her arms were starting to shake from the strain of holding her body like this. The tension in her muscles only seemed to heighten the sensations running through her.

A questing finger settled deep within her channel as he found a spot on her front wall to lovingly stroke.

She felt the need bubbling within her; she was almost to the point of overflowing with it. There was no further room for it to grow or spread.

He bit down sharply on her nipple and it was enough to burst the fragile hold. The ecstasy flowed from her in wave after wave. Her hips slammed into his, his hold on her never waning.

Finally, she could no longer hold her weight and collapsed against him, her skin moist with perspiration.

Rory took her lips in a slow, scorching kiss. His tongue slid into her mouth and tangled with hers. It mimicked what he wanted to do with her. He broke the kiss and hugged her to him tightly, not able to get close enough.

He loved having the weight of her against him. His fingertips stroked up and down her back, enjoying the feel of her skin beneath them.

Her breathing was slowly returning to normal and he felt his cock flex between them, almost as if to say *don't forget about me*. He smirked slightly at his own thoughts.

Finally she raised her head and looked into his eyes. The purple-blue irises were nothing but a thin band around her very dark pupils. She looked satisfied and well loved. That alone made him feel good.

Maybe he should just leave it at that?

Pixie was happy and looked content.

It was enough.

Then she leant forward and kissed him. He let her lead, let her take control, and he knew immediately she wasn't done for the night.

Her lips nibbled and teased along his. Her hands moved to his head and her fingers massaged his scalp. He could tell she was enjoying the feel that the different textures his hair provided. The sides being a little shorter were quite bristly, whereas the top being a little longer, was thick and silky.

Every time she touched him, another shower of sparks ignited in his blood.

Unable to hold it in any longer, he growled low in his throat. That was how he felt, all pent-up sexual need. He wanted her so badly. Needed her with an intensity he'd never felt before.

Pixie raised her mouth from his. The amusement from his growl was very clear in her eyes.

"Sounds like someone's turned on."

"Like you wouldn't believe, sweetheart," he managed to croak out.

She slid off the left side of his body and laid her head on his chest. Her delicate hand immediately started to trace the muscles of his pecs.

At the feel of her touch, he couldn't help but flex the muscles of his abdomen, which created even more ridges and hollows for her to trace and she seemed determined to learn every one of them. Now he understood the true meaning of torture.

It was sweet, erotic torture.

The promise and suggestion was far more powerful than the act.

She was slaying him and she didn't have a clue.

And he'd gladly lay here and take every touch until she'd had her fill.

His erect cock bounced against his stomach.

She giggled and then he realised maybe he'd misjudged the situation. Maybe she knew only too well what this was doing to him.

She lifted her head to look into his eyes and then dropped hers to his steely length.

Immediately, he realised Pixie was silently asking him for permission to proceed.

Oh God, yes please!

For once, he didn't have a witty line or a quick comeback. His brain refused to function—the blood was somewhere else.

He managed a nod and she rewarded him with a shy smile.

She dropped her head to his chest again and let her hand

wander lower. The first tentative touch of her fingers nearly undid him.

A long hiss escaped through his teeth and his breath came on a ragged pant.

Her hand flew back as if burnt and her head shot up off his chest.

"What did I do?" she rushed.

"Nothing. It just felt incredible. And I'm so turned on, it nearly undid me."

"Do you want me to keep going?"

Was the Pope a Catholic?

"Oh yeah."

Her hand settled on him again, this time gripping. It felt great, not quite as teasing.

Pixie tentatively stroked him and he immediately knew he'd only last a few strokes if she kept this up.

"I'm guessing I've got another thirty seconds tops if you keep doing that."

A surprised "Oh" came from her on an amused laugh.

Her hand stilled and she raised her head again to look at him.

He felt and heard her draw in a deep breath.

"Are we going to make love?" Her voice was timid, almost a whisper. And he was so damned proud of her. He knew how scared she'd been and here she was trusting him enough to take the next step. Her true fear was gone. Just their first time together nervousness remained.

He could understand that. Hell, he felt a little bit like that himself. He wanted to make it special for her.

"I'd love nothing more," he whispered back to her, his voice full of the sincerity he felt.

A slow smile spread across her lovely face.

He wasn't going to wait any longer.

Taking her in his arms, he rolled her to her back and settled himself between her thighs. His hand cupped her jaw and his thumb caressed her cheek. The other slipped between them, seeking her feminine heat.

A shudder rippled through her when his fingers found her lush centre.

He stroked her a couple of times before sliding first one and then two fingers deep inside her. She was so tight. He knew it had been a very long time for her and he also knew that somehow he was going to have to go slow.

Unsure how, he just knew he would.

He moved slightly, reaching for the condom he'd placed under one of the pillows earlier. Pixie noticed and shook her head.

"Jazz gave me a contraceptive injection last week so you don't need those. And I don't have any other nasties."

The thought of entering her bare nearly ended it right there for him.

"I'm clean, too. The Centre's regularly testing us for all sorts of things."

She nodded and closed her hands around his shoulders.

He inhaled deeply one last time, checking for fear that was no longer there, before centring himself against her wet channel.

With a long, steady stroke, he pushed into her.

TJ let out the breath she'd been holding as she felt him push into her. He was filling her from her needy feminine core up—breathing somehow seemed superfluous. Her channel burnt and pulsed with want all at the same time. She was being stretched and filled to the limit but somehow it felt so right. Any concerns or fears she'd had were gone.

All that was left was a molten pleasure so hot she felt it burning everywhere. *So incredible.*

Finally he was fully seated within her and he paused for a moment, pressing a lingering kiss to her lips.

"How're you feeling, sweetheart?" he whispered to her in a husky voice.

She just moaned back. She couldn't form words. There were so many emotions rushing through her, how did she name them all?

The word, "Complete," came rushing from her mouth without conscious thought. For a second, she was stunned at what she'd said.

Rory gently brushed the hair back from her forehead and captured her eyes with his.

"You don't know what you just gave me."

Her hands tightened on his shoulders and she urged him to move within her. She wanted to feel the slide and pleasure their bodies could bring to one another.

It was incredible. The feeling of him so deep inside her, filling every corner of her, with either his flesh or his presence.

Her body was climbing again.

Her hands gripped tight to his shoulders, needing the grounding comfort. She knew she was going to explode in overwhelming pleasure but somehow being connected to him would keep her together, safe.

She raised her thighs higher around his hips and somehow he seemed to slip even deeper into her centre, showering her with even more pleasure.

"Are you with me, baby doll?" he ground out through gritted teeth.

She nodded and shrieked her release as his hips slammed forward into her one final time before he joined her sailing over the edge. Both of them gasped for breath like sprinters breaking the tape after a hundred-metre dash.

They lay together in boneless exhaustion. Contentment settled like a blanket over both of them.

TJ knew then and there what she needed to say. She hoped it wasn't clichéd but it felt right to her in this moment and she knew it was the truth.

"I love you," she whispered against his ear.

He pulled her tighter to him and kissed her neck. "I love you, too, my beautiful Pixie."

They were perhaps the sweetest words she'd ever heard.

Chapter Twenty-Three

Rory woke with a start from a sound sleep. His animal senses were on full alert and screamed danger.

He felt Pixie's delicate weight tucked into his side, half sprawled across his chest. He quickly slid out from under her and reached for his phone. Before he could dial, the sharp ping of a text came through.

Three bogies down here—two headed your way.

He gently shook Pixie.

"Wake up, sweetheart."

Her eyelids immediately flew open. "What's the matter?" she asked groggily.

"Trouble headed this way. I need you awake and with me, sweetheart." He placed a quick kiss to her lips and reached for the jeans he'd left beside the bed.

He dropped a pair of his loose shorts, his T-shirt, and her ankle brace beside her.

"Come on, baby, I need you to move now."

His hand slipped to the top drawer of the nightstand and his fingers curled around the grip of his weapon. He automatically checked the safety and slid it into the waistband of his jeans.

Rory moved quickly to the bedroom window he'd purposely left open a couple of inches. He inhaled deeply, pushed the curtains back a fraction and listened.

Yeah, he had them. Two of them coming in slowly from the southeast towards the back of the house.

Pixie reached for the bedside lamp.

"No lights, Pix."

Her hand drew back and she fumbled into the clothes and brace he'd left for her. "Who's out there?"

"I don't know yet but I guarantee you I'll find out very soon."

He eased the curtain back again. They were at about a hundred and fifty metres and closing.

A second later, Rory scooped Pixie into his arms and carried her into the kitchen, placing her butt on the edge of the table. He figured it was faster this way. He could feel and smell the fear radiating from her. They didn't need her stumbling around in the dark.

"Hey, don't worry, sweet pea. Nothing I can't handle."

"Shouldn't we just call the police?" Her voice was full of concern.

"Probably but I want to find out what the go is with these guys first." He moved to one of the drawers and grabbed a handful of the cable ties he'd noticed there the other day and shoved them in his pocket.

"Okay, Pixie, here's how this is going to go. I'm going to slip out the side door in a second. I need you to stay in the laundry. You'll be totally safe there. This should only take me a minute or two to sort out."

"But you could get hurt."

"Pix, this is what I'm trained to do. I've got more combat skills than most Special Forces operators. I'll be fine. But I need to know you're safe."

She nodded reluctantly and started to move to the laundry.

"But what if there's more than two?"

"There's only two."

"How can you be sure?"

His patience was just about out. "I just know, okay? Stop worrying and let me do my job." With that parting comment, he slid out through the side door. He immediately regretted being short with her. She was only concerned and being logical, after all. It wasn't Pixie's fault that she didn't know that his senses told him there were only two close enough to worry   about.

He used the shadows of the house and slipped over to the

nearby garden shed. From there, he cut through a strand of melaleuca trees and circled around behind them.

Both seemed to be unarmed but he had a fair idea what was in the backpacks both men carried.

Rory moved silently in closer until he was a mere arm's length from the smaller man at the back. He reached out and tapped him on the shoulder. Just as he expected, the guy spun around in alarm and Rory clocked him with a vicious right hook. He shot his hands out and cupped the guy behind the head and drove his right knee into his solar plexus.

He released his hands and let the mute form drop to the ground. It all happened in just over a second. The other man spun around in surprise at the impact of Rory's first punch. He came charging in with a haymaker that Rory easily blocked and then spun his hand and caught the man in a painful wrist lock and arm bar.

Without wasting a second, Rory used the pain associated with the move to encourage the guy to the ground. He didn't fail to drop his knee into his kidney as he pulled both of his hands behind his back and secured them with a couple of cables ties. He quickly slipped down and did the same with his feet. Twenty seconds later and he'd trussed up the first guy as well.

It felt good to finally let off a bit of steam with these assholes. He'd been wanting to hit one of these fuckers for days.

Rory unzipped one of the backpacks and as he'd expected, it contained a couple of crude looking pipe bombs. Yep, his temper was really starting to run thin now.

Was it too much for a man to ask for a quiet night in with his wife?

Now these fuckers could answer his questions, starting with who the fuck they worked for.

"Pixie, honey, could you turn on the outside floodies, please?"

She reached over from her vantage point at the small laundry window and flicked the light switch. The back of the house was immediately illuminated for a thirty-metre radius with the strong light.

Rory was dragging the two men towards the back verandah as if they were nothing but small sacks of grain. She'd watched it all from her vantage point at the windows. The moonlit night had provided plenty of light for her to see the action.

She'd never seen anything like it.

He'd moved so quickly, his body was almost a blur and the ease with which he'd taken the two of them down was incredibly impressive and a little bit frightening at the same time. The sound of Rory's fist crashing into the first man was so clear she could have sworn she was standing a metre away from it all, not nearly forty.

She hobbled to the back door and waited just inside.

Rory dropped the two guys to the ground just below the couple of steps and called out for her to come out.

She moved across the verandah and stood beside him. Her eyes never left his face. For the first time ever, it was devoid of emotion. A steely intensity had veiled his normally light-hearted personality. She'd never seen him like this.

He turned and looked at her. His eyes immediately softened slightly.

"Do you have any idea who these guys are?"

Her eyes shot to the men on the ground. For the first time, she really looked.

A short gasp escaped her throat and she felt Rory stiffen beside her. Suddenly her legs felt like jelly and she felt even more unsteady—she didn't have her full cast on, just a softer brace, and was trying desperately not to put any weight on the ankle.

His hand shot out to steady her and she turned her body into his, looking for support.

"What is it, Pixie? Who are they?"

Fear gurgled up in her throat till it felt like it was going to choke her.

His arm came around her waist and he swung her up into his arms and placed her on the outdoor settee.

He bent down and looked at her in concern, stroking the hair from her face.

"Who are they, sweetheart?"

It was the Rory she knew asking, not the fierce warrior she'd watched only a couple of minutes before. She knew she could trust him to keep her safe. TJ sucked in a deep breath.

"It's them…" She took a deep breath. "Some of the guys who attacked me."

Pixie's breath was coming in laboured pants. He knew she was moments away from descending into an all-out panic attack. The fear radiating from her was like a wall that hit him stronger than any punch or kick ever could.

"Breathe, sweetheart. In and out—just breathe for me." He kept his voice to its most soothing and rubbed his hand over her back in circles.

Slowly she started to respond to his presence and the comfort he provided.

The rage in him was near blinding. If it wasn't for her need for him to remain in control at the moment, Rory feared once and for all he might just let his temper rule.

He pulled his phone from his pocket and placed a quick call to Dylan to confirm what had happened and to check on what he'd managed to hunt down.

His night suddenly felt a whole lot better when Dylan gave him the news. Dylan had his three tangos neatly trussed up and taking a nap in one of the machinery sheds away from the yard. Rory asked him to come up and collect his trash as well.

The next call was to Quade. He was going to need some help for what he had in mind. And the big cat was just the man to bring him what he wanted.

His final call was to the boss. There'd be hell to pay if he didn't let him know what was about to go down.

Now he needed to see whether Pixie was up for a chat.

Chapter Twenty-Four

Rory carried her into the bedroom and returned a couple of minutes later with a mug of hot tea. The temperature was cool but nowhere near cold, but TJ felt frozen to the bone.

He propped himself up against the head of the bed and drew her into the shelter of his arms. Her face nestled into the warm skin of his chest and she was immediately grateful he hadn't put on a shirt.

His left arm tucked round her back and held her protectively against his body and his right one linked with her left hand, completing the connection.

When he held her like this, the fear was gone. If only she could stay like this forever.

Finally he spoke. "Remember the first night we spent in this bed together we had a chat about sharing some secrets when the time was right?"

She nodded her understanding.

"Well, sweetheart, I think tonight is the night we exorcise those demons as well."

Her heart rate began to race again and she took a deep, calming breath in a hope of bringing it under control. She knew he deserved to know the truth but she hated thinking about what had happened; she hated thinking about that night.

"Those guys out there were part of whatever bad happened to you, weren't they?"

Flashes of their faces paraded before her eyes and just like she'd felt that night, she felt powerless to stop the intrusion.

She didn't want to remember.

Didn't want to think about it.

But she knew she had to tell him and then maybe she could put this behind her. It's what she'd discussed with Jazz earlier in the day. It's what had to happen. But still, it was killing her inside.

"Yes," she pushed out.

"Tell me what happened to you, sweetheart, please. I need to know." She'd never heard his voice sound so pained.

She nodded her head and steadied her breathing.

"It was the summer of my graduation from high school. I was dating Geoff, a boy who I'd gone to school with. We'd been hanging out together for most of the summer, getting closer and closer. We'd shared a few kisses and those kisses had turned to more. Neither of us had any experience with sex but I guess we'd both got to the stage where we were curious.

"Anyway, my folks weren't happy about me spending too much time with him because they didn't know him or his parents. And like most teenagers, the more they tried to keep us apart, the more we were determined to be together.

"The weekend of my eighteenth birthday rolled around and we had a big party here on Friday night. Everyone was here, including family and a lot of my friends. Kelvin and Uncle Max were here as well." She paused, collecting her thoughts before she pushed on.

"Geoff was a good friend of Kelvin's, even though we didn't go to the same school. Kelvin and Geoff had played some sport together. I can't for the life of me remember what that was. But it's not important.

"What is important was that Geoff had a word with Kelvin about needing to organise some alone time with me.

"Kelvin being Kelvin, he organised for Geoff and I, plus four other friends of theirs, to go out the next night. He said he was having a few friends over for a BBQ but really we were all going clubbing.

"I guess I'll never know how he did it but somehow he got Mum and Dad to agree to allow me to go out with them. Mum and Dad only ever saw what they wanted to see when it came to Kelvin. And I guess that never changed." Her voice trailed off. They'd never got to see just how evil he could be. TJ steadied her thoughts and went on.

"All the next day, I was so excited. The thought of going out with them was all I could think about. I even went and bought a new dress. How stupid was I?

"So we went to a few clubs and we danced and had a couple of drinks. The night wore on and Geoff was all over me. I'd be lying if I said I was repelling his advances. I wasn't. I'm pretty sure I was encouraging him. I really liked him and I wanted him to like me, I guess." She shook her head in annoyance at her own stupidity.

"Around one, we headed back to Uncle Max's place. He wasn't supposed to be home for the weekend or something like that. I can't remember where he was but he wasn't there. So we played some pool and drank a few more beers when finally Geoff asked me to go upstairs with him.

"I knew what was going to happen. I knew what he was asking me and I agreed to go."

She sucked in a breath and steeled herself against the emotions that ran through her. Just thinking about it made her feel sick to her stomach.

"We went up to one of the guest bedrooms and things got pretty hot and heavy quickly. It was all over in a few minutes and I guess it was okay. It's not like I had anything to compare it to." She chuckled sardonically at herself.

Rory squeezed her tighter to him, trying to give her comfort.

The fear returned in great waves. Tears flowed over her bottom lashes and her throat felt like it had completely closed up.

"Take a break, sweet pea, if it's too much." His voice was steady, no more than a whisper. He pressed his lips to her forehead and rocked her gently.

How she wanted to bottle the memory away and never have to face it again. But it hadn't worked. It still haunted her, every damned day.

It was time to try something different.

She could do this.

On a long breath, she went on.

"We were lying there, trying to comprehend what had happened, in a lot of ways, I guess, when the door sprung open and Kelvin and the other boys came in. He was drunk and roughhousing with the other guys. I think it started out as a bit of a prank. I don't know, but the next thing I know, Kelvin was on top of me, fumbling with his pants and thanking Geoff for warming me up, as he put it."

Tears were again running down her face, this time at the vivid memories she'd worked so hard to bury. "I started to struggle and cry out so Kelvin told the guys to grab me and hold me down. I remember so clearly how he grabbed my hair in a big hand full and dragged my head back. It hurt so much. I felt so trapped and helpless. I didn't stand a chance against all of them. By this time, Geoff had caught the gang mentality and he was telling me to be still and let them have their turns. I felt so betrayed. How could he do this to me?"

Rory's body had gone as stiff as a board at her words. She felt him struggling to get his anger and emotions under control. Slowly the seconds passed and he relaxed again in fractions. The little break helped her, too. She needed to finish this story and never retell it again.

"Kelvin eventually managed to get his pants down and was just about to..." She couldn't say it. It hurt too much. The memory flooded her with feelings she needed to let go of. She knew she had to let them go in order to fully move on. They'd always be there to some extent but she had to take away their power and by telling the story she'd never told anyone, she was taking back that power.

Rory stroked her hip and squeezed her fingers tightly.

"Take a minute, baby, if you need to."

She shook her head; she just wanted to get through it. Finish it.

"Rape me. Just as he was about to rape me, Uncle Max came storming up the stairs and flung open the door. He yelled at them all and told them to get downstairs and clean up their mess. He didn't even acknowledge me. He just turned and left.

"I'd never felt so grateful for being saved and so alone all in the space of a minute. I don't know how long I laid there crying. It could have been half an hour or four. I just don't know. Eventually I got myself together enough and found my way into another bedroom. I locked the door and stayed there until early morning.

"Just after dawn, I snuck out and drove myself home. I came here first. At the time, this house was vacant. Mum and Dad had a foreman who used to live here. So I came in here and had a shower and scrubbed myself clean. I just felt so dirty and it was as if my skin crawled at the thought of their hands."

She shuddered involuntarily at the memory. He hugged her tighter, somehow seeming to push more reassurance into her.

"I never told anyone. Nobody's ever spoken about it. But it did happen. I lived it. I've been haunted by it. I'm done with it."

She let out a massive sigh and collapsed against him. All the tension she'd felt recounting the attack just seemed to dissipate. She wouldn't give it power anymore. Somebody else knew now.

Rory knew.

Rory pulled her tighter to him. He was doing his damnedest to relax. All he wanted to do was kill them, a slow and agonising death, preferably. What the fuck was wrong with people like that? How could they possibly think what they did was okay? And Max, what sort of man let his son get away with that?

That was a question he was going to have answered in the morning. Even if he had to beat it out of him.

Right now, Pixie was his priority and in a couple of hours, a few people were going to start wishing they'd never been born.

He leashed his temper; he'd let it loose later.

"Are you okay, baby doll? That had to be tough."

She nodded beside him, her face still buried in his chest.

He could tell the tears had stopped. There was no telltale dampness against his skin anymore.

His lips found her forehead again and he rained down kisses there.

She seemed content to lay there in his arms and he wasn't going to change that until she was ready.

Finally she broke the silence.

"Rory."

"Yeah, Pix."

"You mentioned to me that you had some secrets as well. I think now that I've bared my soul that it's only fair you should return the favour. I know there's something you're not telling me but I can't quite figure out what."

His pulse accelerated and he concentrated on keeping his breathing even. He'd never told his secret to anyone before. He'd never had to. Everyone he was close to was either the same as him or knew. How did you explain it?

Maybe from the beginning?

"Umm, sweetheart, are you sure you want to hear this tonight? I mean, you've been through a lot." *How much more could this woman take emotionally?* kept running through his head.

She pushed away from him and turned her head to look at him. Her beautiful purple-blue eyes were all swollen and red and he couldn't have loved her more.

"Don't think you're getting out of this that easily, buster." Her voice sounded even a little bit pissed.

"Well, if you want to know, I'll tell you. I just hope you'll still talk to me at the end."

"Why would you be worried about that?"

"I haven't told you my secret yet."

She relaxed back down onto his chest.

"Whenever you're ready."

Oh God. Where did he start?

Then it came to him.

"Well, you know how I mentioned I've got extra sensitive hearing and smell. Well, there's a reason for it."

"Oh, what's that?"

Here it comes. Should he relax his arms now in preparation for when she wanted to get away from him?

"My DNA was altered and spliced with animal DNA." He heard the sharp intake of breath.

Her head came up again and she looked directly at him. "How?"

"It happened before I was born. I was one of the first IVF babies, but it seems the scientists had a little more fun with a few of us. They put in a mix of different animal DNA."

"Wow, that's out there." She looked at him laid out on the bed. He could feel her eyes assessing him, cataloguing every inch of him. For the first time ever, he felt self-conscious about his body. *Would she find him lacking in some way? Repulsive?*

Finally her eyes met his again.

"Well, now I understand why you're too good to be true."

He shook his head, trying to make sense of her words. His stomach was in knots. What was she getting at?

"I don't understand."

She dropped her chin a little coyly.

"Rory, in the few weeks that you've known me, you've been amazing. You've been kind, compassionate, considerate, thoughtful, loving, friendly, funny, and that's leaving out all the more X-rated parts and I've not even started on how incredible you look. You're so much more than the total package. You've put every other man I ever met so far behind and I wondered why. Now I know. You're perfect because that was what you were made to be."

Rory was gobsmacked. *She thought he was perfect!* Of all the responses for her to have come back with, this was not the one he was expecting.

"Pixie, I'm not perfect."

"To me you are," she said defiantly.

"Well, I guess that's all that matters." Now he was curious. "So how come you're not shocked or irate or running from me screaming?"

She was quiet for a few long seconds and Rory kicked himself for putting thoughts into her head.

"Well, unless you're suddenly going to change into someone who I don't know, then I can honestly say I fell in love with the man you've been with me. I don't have anything else to go on. So I can only judge on what I've seen and how you've made me feel."

His heart leapt and he couldn't resist any longer. He drew her head up and kissed her passionately. He poured all his relief and hope and love into that one kiss.

Finally she broke away, a sweet smile on her lips.

"Now I know why you could smell the gas. You also smelt something tonight, didn't you?"

"I did. There's a scent around here that I can't attach to anyone that I've met."

Now she looked intrigued.

"Tell me how it works."

"Well, all my senses are heightened to the range of animals. Each of us at the Centre has animal DNA from the twelve animal signs of the Chinese zodiac. Apparently that was supposed to be the ultimate balance or something. None of us really know, although we've speculated a whole lot."

He searched her face again and this time he was seeing her fascination.

"My dominant DNA is canine."

Pixie gasped and his heart leapt to his throat again.

"That's why you get on so well with Zeus and Thor! That had been bugging me for days." He saw the smile on her face. She seemed happy that a piece of a mental jig-saw puzzle had fallen into place.

"Yeah, they immediately recognise me as the alpha."

She thought on that for a moment. Then the expression on her face changed to what he guessed was suspicion. Once again his stomach dropped. *What had her concerned now?*

"You don't turn into a dog or anything else, do you? I read a book once and the hero was a shifter. I'm not sure I could cope with that."

He laughed. Sure, he had some canine DNA but he didn't have that much!

"Nope, nothing as exciting as that. In addition to my heightened senses, I'm just faster, stronger, and I have much greater endurance than a normal man. I also need to eat a lot more and I can comfortably survive on about three hours' sleep a day. If I have to miss a few days' sleep—no biggy.

But I'd definitely prefer to have six or eight a day if it means I get to snuggle up to you, not that I need them."

He could see her mind racing again.

"You partly told me all this in the beginning, didn't you?"

"I did. I couldn't tell you then, but I didn't want to lie to you or mislead you. So I told you part of the truth. Just not the extent."

She nodded her head in acceptance of his answer. And he asked himself for at least the hundredth time how on earth he'd gotten so lucky to have married this woman.

"So all the operators at the Centre are like you, aren't they?"

"Yeah, that's right. There're twelve of us."

"Who else knows about your altered DNA?"

"Nobody outside the Centre and a few high-ranking government officials. Let's just say it wouldn't be in their best interest to disclose our secret. There would be too many difficult questions for them to answer regarding how we came to be in the first place."

He could see Pixie thinking again.

"So Jazz and Rihanna know, right?"

He nodded his confirmation.

Her luscious mouth then moved into a perfect *O* shape and her hand covered it a fraction later.

"What?"

"I just thought about Rihanna being pregnant. Does that mean the babies will have altered DNA as well?"

"We expect so. From all accounts, they're apparently developing as you would expect normal babies, maybe just a little bit bigger. I don't think there's anything to worry about. We were all born normally. The universe wouldn't do that to us."

She laughed at his quip and then became more serious again.

"We've never talked about it, Rory, but do you want children?"

He knew the answer to that question but he wondered what he should say. *How would she feel about it?*

"I'd love children someday." It was the truth. "I haven't mentioned much about my family but I was an only child because my folks had fertility problems." He waved his arm down his length. "Hence the exhibit you see here before you, my love. I would have loved to have had brothers or sisters growing up. I didn't really get that true family feel till I met my brothers and sisters at the Centre."

"Where are your parents now?"

"They live in Europe. Mum's Italian and she got homesick for Italy. So when I left for university, they left for Italy."

"Do you see them much?"

"Not as much as I'd like. Maybe once every couple of years. More often if I'm lucky. It's much better now that we have web-based communications but still, it's not quite the same thing."

She hugged him tighter and he knew she was trying to make up for the loss he felt at not having his family around all the time.

"Well, I guess whether you wanted it or not, I came complete with a strange but albeit ready-made family."

"Oh, I wanted it all right."

He stroked the hair back from her face and lightly brushed his lips across hers. She promptly followed it up with a big yawn. The night had been an emotional rollercoaster. Pixie needed some more sleep. He had a date in the machinery shed.

"So are we good?"

She didn't hesitate. "We're great."

He chuckled lightly. "Go to sleep, my love."

"Mmm, I like that my love part. Will you be here when I wake up?"

"What makes you think I'm going anywhere?"

"Well, I know you've got those guys who attacked me down in the machinery shed and something tells me you're not going to go down there for a friendly chat over a beer."

"Knowing little thing, aren't you?"

"Just don't kill them. I don't think I'd like having to visit you in jail. I like you in bed beside me," she trailed off sleepily.

"Duly noted." He dropped a kiss on her forehead. She was already asleep.

Chapter Twenty-Five

The five men were all propped up against oil drums lining the wall of the old machinery shed. The whites of their eyes shone out in the semi-darkness. And the smell of fear was wafting off them in hefty doses.

The shed was basically empty except for a large tool bench and a heap of equipment that would come in handy if you wanted to fix or maintain anything mechanical. Its presence gave Rory some other more exotic ideas as well. Revenge and payback were running hard through his veins. These fuckers were going to pay.

Rory walked to Dylan, who was lounging against the bench, looking incredibly menacing. Rory had a laugh to himself at how D had set the stage. He'd purposely left his shirt off to show off his massive chest and shoulders covered in a variety of martial arts and other tats. There was no doubt about it: D was a lady killer but to these guys, he'd look just like your worst sort of nightmare badass killer.

"Quade's about five out."

Rory nodded.

He raised his voice slightly to make sure the men all heard.

"Which one of these fuckers is Geoff?"

None of them needed to respond; the body language and facial expressions told him. Geoff was the lanky-looking guy with the brown hair second from the left. His eyes mirrored his fear at being singled out.

None of the men were gagged because there was no need: no one would hear them out here.

Rory took a look around the room. Finally he found what he was looking for. He walked to the wall and spotted what looked like a wooden engine crate.

He moved over and picked it up as if it were nothing and plonked it in the middle of the shed floor. A fire burned through his veins as he'd never felt before.

He needed to be careful. If he let the beast out, then there was a good chance these men would die. He called on an image of Pixie lying peacefully in bed to calm the beast. She was a double-edged sword in this case. He was avenging her but she was also the siren who would keep him from slipping over the edge.

Rory grabbed the hem of his shirt and slipped it over his head. If D wanted some theatrics, they might as well make it a good show. Besides, he didn't want to get too much blood on him. Pixie might freak.

He made a show of rolling his shoulders and didn't fail to drop an evil smile to the bastards on the ground.

Finally, he stalked over to Geoff and grabbed him by the arm in a punishing grip. For once, Rory didn't try to disguise his natural strength and jerked him clean off the floor in one easy motion. Three strides and he planted Geoff's sorry ass on the crate.

"Today's not looking so hot for you, Geoff. You see, last night when you morons were fuckin' dumb enough to come wandering onto private property with a shit load of pipe bombs, Teresa told me what you fuckers did to her a few years back. I was pissed before that you thought to come over uninvited and interrupt my night with my wife. Now I'm fucking beyond furious about what you bunch of lowlife motherfucking scumbags did to an innocent girl."

Quade chose that moment to wander in with Kelvin in tow. His hands and feet were bound just like the others. Quade pushed him down to the ground on the far end.

"Hey, bro, looks like we're just in time for the floor show. Wouldn't want Kelvin to miss any of that. You see, it seems old mate Kelvin here has a thing for beatings, particularly whips."

Rory turned his head and looked at Quade in surprise for half a second before he transformed the look to sadistic.

"Well, isn't that interesting? Do tell, bro."

"Found the greasy little fucker in a BDSM club beating the hell out of a little blonde thing that looked uncannily like Pixie."

Dylan chose that moment to push back from the bench and stroll over to the centre where the action was.

"Hey, Surfer Boy, do you reckon he's as good at taking a beating as he is at giving them out?"

"Don't know, D, but I'm all for finding out."

"What's this all about? You can't do this." Kelvin's voice was filled with hollow outrage. Rory and his brothers could both hear and smell the fear.

Rory spun around and glared at Kelvin. The man visibly shrunk before his eyes.

"Well, why don't you enlighten me on why five of your best mates came calling tonight with a bunch of pipe bombs? And while you're at it, you might want to explain what the fuck you thought you were doing that night these very same mates of yours held Teresa down while you tried to rape her."

Kelvin's face paled and he started to backpeddle.

"You're fucking kidding me, man," Quade spat and glared at Kelvin. Rory could feel the rage now seething from Quade as well.

"Unfortunately not. She's been traumatised by that night for six fucking years. And you lot have felt nothing. That changes today. The scales will balance again by the time I'm finished with you."

"It wasn't like that," Kelvin stammered. "We were just all having some fun. Maybe it went a bit too far but it was just fun."

"That's not how Teresa recounts the night, and you know what else? I'm inclined to believe her. Because ever since I first laid eyes on you, I knew you were a perverted little fucker who takes great pleasure in terrorising smaller, weaker people. How does it feel to be the smaller, weaker one tonight, asshole?"

Rory saw the terror in his eyes and decided to capitalise on it.

"Can't we just talk about it?"

An evil smile crossed Rory's face.

"Grab another crate, D. Old mate here wants to talk. Let's make him comfortable. Quade, if you wouldn't mind bringing Kelvin over here. Oh, and you might want to remove his bindings. We wouldn't want him to be uncomfortable, would we?"

Dylan returned with the crate and thumped it down beside Geoff. Quade plonked Kelvin on the crate and then whipped a cruel-looking hunting knife from his right boot. He threw it into the air and grabbed the blade open handed, flicked his wrist, dropping the handle into his palm, and sliced through both the bindings in a fraction of a second. The open handed thing was one of Quade's favourite party tricks.

It never failed to create a stir. In this case, the acidic stench of urine told them one of them had just lost control of his bladder.

"Ah fuck, now one of these pussies has just pissed his pants like a little girl." Dylan shook his head in disgust.

"So Kelvin, why don't you tell me how it really happened, then?"

He could see the fear in Kelvin's eyes slink back for a second. The little creep really thought he stood a chance of convincing him he had it wrong.

"We all went out clubbing that night and we all drank a lot. TJ was all over us. She wanted it, man. She was hot for cock that night. Begging for it. That's what happened. I swear it is."

"Watch your mouth, ass-wipe. That's my wife you're talking about," Rory fumed.

Rory looked between Quade and Dylan.

"What do you think, guys? Is he telling the truth?" His voice was filled with sarcasm.

Dylan chuckled. "I'm not confident of that, Surfer Boy."

"Me either."

"Let's see if anyone else has a different recollection of the night." Rory stalked over to the four men on the ground and stood imposingly over the one who had let his bladder go. It was the smaller man he'd hammered with a right hook earlier. His nose was splayed across the righthand side of his face. The only thing that would come close to fixing that mess was surgery.

"What about you? What do you remember?" Rory knew this guy would tell the truth. He'd give up his mates in a heartbeat if he thought he'd avoid another beating.

The smaller man looked up at him with terror in his eyes.

"Weeeee'd all had a lot to drink that night," he stammered. "But TJ was definitely Geoff's girl. They went upstairs and about half an hour later, Kelvin said we should go up and join them. He'd planned it with Geoff."

"I don't think you need to say anymore. What you've said correlates just fine with what I know." Rory spun to Kelvin. "So I guess that makes you the liar then, Kelvin."

Rory walked to him and viciously grabbed a handful of his hair and yanked his head back. "How does that feel, to have your head yanked back? That's what you did to Teresa and it still terrifies her. The only difference was that you did it while five of your mates held her down as you're fumbling around trying to dip your pathetic wick."

He shoved Kelvin's head forward with enough force the man fell from the crate to the floor and he went to stand in front of Geoff. He glanced down and noticed the wide gold band on the man's hand.

"So tell me about yourself, Geoff. How did you possibly go from being the sort of lowlife piece of shit who takes a girl's virginity then passes her to his mates—to being married?"

Geoff couldn't look him in the eye and didn't say anything.

Rory drew his hand back and swiped it across the man's face. The back of his hand connected with Geoff's cheek. Rory felt satisfaction flow through him.

"I'm waiting, asshole."

Geoff shook his head from the impact, no doubt seeing stars, and swung around as much as his binds would allow and hissed at Kelvin, "None of this was supposed to happen, Kelvin. You said the bitch was going to go to the cops and we needed to torch her house and the trucks to scare her. You didn't say anything about these maniacs."

"Shut up, Geoff," Kelvin muttered from his position on the ground.

"No, on the contrary—keep talking, Geoff. This is just starting to get interesting. But let me just make sure I've got this straight. You five go to do the dirty work and rich boy here stays home to go beat on some poor defenceless sub. Why would you morons do that?"

Rory knew there would be no answer to his question. Fear and the obvious stupidity of the situation prevented it.

"Well, I sure hope he paid you guys a lot. You're going to need it for the legal bills you're about to come up against."

"What do you mean?" Geoff foolishly interrupted.

Rory laughed inwardly. Here comes the kicker.

"Oh, I've arranged a nice cosy cell for you down at the watch house, soon as we finish our discussion here."

"But you can't hold us like this," Geoff protested.

Quade just grinned at him and ran the blade of the knife across his palm for effect—a thin trail of blood was left in the wake of the blade. Quade made sure they all saw it. "Mate, from where I'm standing, we can do just about anything we want. I'm up for a little pain—how about you lot? But I guaran-fucking-tee it's going to hurt you lot a hell of a lot more than us."

It was enough.

Geoff just about swallowed his tongue. Quade could be a completely sick bastard when he wanted to be. And this little show just proved it.

The message had been delivered.

Rory had had enough. He just wanted to get back to Pixie.

"So here's what's going to happen, fellas. You're going to forget anymore crazy-assed ideas about retribution against Teresa or any of her family. But you're going to remember every day of your miserable lives what you put an innocent girl through. You're going to remember her cries for help and you're going to remember that she trusted you all and you broke it in the worst way possible like the sorry excuse for men you are. And if I ever hear you're near us or that you've done something to another woman again, I swear to God I'll hunt each and every one of you down and extract a slow and painful death. I'd also advise that you find someplace else to live. The farther from here the better. I hear there're some good deals on ice in the Arctic at the moment. I suggest you check it out. This is no longer your home."

Rory moved past Geoff and struck out with a crushing elbow strike to the other side of his face. He felt the guy's cheekbone fracture underneath the force.

"That's for giving men a bad name and terrorising young women."

He strode over to Kelvin, who was still lying on the ground and put all his formidable strength behind a well-placed kick to the groin. The man immediately curled into a ball. His nuts probably now sat just below his tonsils.

"When you can use your junk again, you sick fuck, remember who put you out of commission and be thankful I didn't castrate you. Try fucking with me or mine again and you're a dead man—tenuous family ties or not."

He needed to get out of here and shower. He was a millimetre from losing all control. They made him sick.

He strode towards the door. Just before exiting, he stopped and turned, giving them all one more look laced with contempt.

"Oh, and if any of you want to get cute, I've got a couple of press releases ready to roll with some journalist friends. Let's see how well your careers go when you've got arrests for sexual assault plastered against your name on Google. Don't test me. Man up and take your medicine for a change. The only reason you're not dead now is because Teresa asked me not to kill you all. Why the fuck, I'll never know. You're nothing but a cancer on society. Quade, Dylan, call Jimmy down at the station. I've already spoken to him, and he's waiting for the pickup. I guess it sucks if they just happened to sustain a few more injuries while resisting arrest."

His exit was punctuated by Quade's deeply sinister chuckle.

Chapter Twenty-Six

TJ rolled over and snuggled closer into Rory. She was in that dozy state between sleep and awake. Her body seemed to have recognised when he'd returned to the bed and immediately sought him. She knew she had to get up soon, but she wanted to be close to him.

Her hand trailed up to his chest and she could smell the fresh scent of soap. He'd just showered.

"Hey, baby doll. You awake?"

She groaned in response and snuggled in tighter.

He chuckled at her actions.

"Want to fool around or do you want to sleep some more?"

There was no choice. Acting on autopilot, she slid her hand down to his very erect cock.

"I have to say, my love, I do like your choice."

She snuggled in again and felt his hand seek her wet heat, his fingers sliding up and down through her drenched flesh. The want she was feeling quickly multiplied.

"What were you dreaming about, Pix? You're so wet already."

"Mmm, you probably," she managed to form.

He chuckled. "Are you even awake or talking to me through a dream?"

"Sort of awake." Her body felt heavy and lazy.

"Why don't you roll back there and I'll wake you up nice and slow?" He gently pushed her onto her back.

"Mmm." She groaned her response.

His hands traced down over her chest, stopping to cup her breasts and massage the full curves. Then he flicked his thumbs over her nipples until they were two stiff peaks. It felt wonderful.

A few seconds later, his mouth closed over the right peak and he flicked his tongue back and forth across the nipple. The fire rocketed through her sleepy body and collected in her needy feminine core.

Her hand somehow managed to find his scalp and she wriggled her fingers in his hair, enjoying the feel of the texture. His lips shifted to her other breast and her eyelids flew open at the sensation as he sucked the nipple firmly into his mouth.

Mmm, definitely more awake now.

Rory licked and nibbled his way down over her stomach until he came to her mound. He placed wet kisses all over the top before dipping his tongue lower and taking one long, slow lick after another.

"Christ, you taste good."

She wriggled her hips a little, trying to encourage him to hit the part that needed his attention. After what seemed like an eternity, he obliged and licked and sucked at her clit.

Her body was awake and needy. Very needy.

"Ah, please," she whimpered.

"What do you want, baby doll?" he managed between licks and kisses.

"You inside me. Now," she managed to groan out.

"Now there's four words I'll always be happy to hear."

Rory didn't need to be asked twice. He slid up her body a little more and slowly pushed into her.

The feeling of him invading her was enough to chase away any last morsels of sleep.

Having him inside her was an experience she struggled to put into words. She felt so many things all at once. There was the obvious physical fulfilment of need but it was something more. Having him inside her and all around her felt good for her soul.

She'd been close before—now she was racing towards the edge.

"I can't hold on," she panted.

"Don't. I'll catch up in a sec."

The delicious pressure built until she had no option but to explode. Her body spun off in millions of tiny molecules of sensation as wave after wave of pleasure crashed through her in time to Rory's hips.

A few seconds later, his hips thrust even harder against her and she felt his body spasm all around her. Mmm, she had that lazy heavy feeling again, as she enjoyed the weight of him trapping her beneath him as he rode out his release.

"You awake now?"

"I was for a moment but I could be convinced to go back to sleep."

He laughed at her sleepy voice. "Why don't you stay in bed for a couple more hours? I can get the guys sorted this morning. I'll send Dylan up to hang out here for a bit."

"Mmm, sounds good..."

TJ woke up and looked at the clock. *Damn, it was nearly nine. How had she slept so long?* Mmm, pretty easy to answer that one. Her husband had worn her out. Plus, there'd been the few hours of interruption with her teenage attackers during the night.

Somehow thinking about the attack didn't seem as daunting or crippling. She knew emphatically that she'd always carry the emotional scars but they didn't seem as rugged today.

Maybe she should have told somebody a long time ago.

But who?

She could hear low voices in the kitchen and figured it was Rory and Dylan.

A few seconds later, the door to the bedroom opened and Rory poked his head in.

"Good morning, my sweet Pixie. Feel like some breakfast?"

At the mention of food, she realised she was hungry.

"Sounds good. Just give me a couple of minutes to go to the bathroom."

"Do you need some help?" He winked at her suggestively.

"Just with my cast."

"You sure? I'm happy to help."

"Oh, you've never left me in any doubt that you're happy to help. But I have a feeling we won't get out of here for quite a while."

"And the problem with that?"

"Isn't Dylan out there?"

"Yeah, so?"

"Rory, it'd be rude."

"Maybe to the normal world but he already knows we're talking about it. Nor can we disguise the scent of our joint arousal."

TJ felt her face burn. She hadn't yet thought about the logistics of them being "gifted."

"How far can you hear?"

"It depends on the conditions but if it's clear with few obstructions, probably about six or seven hundred metres. The depot is just on the edge of my range when I'm here."

She looked at him with an incredulous expression on her face.

"Are you serious?"

"Yes. Some of us have different ranges but we all have certain things we are particularly good at. Mine is smell, because of the canine genes. So my nose is about ten thousand times better than yours. Quade around eight thousand and Brayden around seven thousand."

She scrambled to the edge of the bed, trying not to bump her leg. Rory and the other team members fascinated her. She wanted to know more, to understand how it worked and felt.

"Steady, sweet pea. What's the hurry?"

"I want to learn all about your…gifts," she said, searching for an appropriate word.

"I'm not sure about gifts." He chuckled. "But certainly enhancements or abilities."

Rory helped her slide her leg back into the cast and she hobbled to the bathroom.

True to her word, it was only a couple of minutes before she'd attended to her bathroom needs and dressed.

She found Rory and Dylan sipping coffee around the kitchen table.

"Morning, Dylan."

"Hey Pixie, or is it TJ? I never know what to call you."

She giggled. "I've kind of got used to answering to both considering somebody here refuses to call me TJ."

"Well, I would if the name suited. But it just doesn't— sorry. I only call it as I see it." He shrugged with indifference. Rory put a mug of coffee in front of her and a couple of pieces of toast and marmalade.

"Thank you," she said distractedly to Rory.

"So, Surfer Boy, are you going to take my head off if I call her Pixie?"

"Do I seriously look stupid enough to try it? It's important to understand your limitations and taking on you is way beyond my skill set. Besides, it doesn't bother me at all," Rory joked.

Dylan laughed. "I think you're exaggerating."

TJ looked at them. "I don't get it."

"Dylan's our resident martial arts expert. Let's just say the whole team are exceptional at hand-to-hand combat but Dylan here, he takes even the title of master to another level," Rory explained.

"That's because I've trained since I was three or four and it certainly doesn't hurt to have some extra enhancements. We all tend to have one skill or speciality we really excel in."

TJ turned to Rory. "What's yours?"

"Firearms."

That shocked her. "Really?"

He nodded. "Yeah, really."

"Rory can shoot the eye out of a fly if he needs to. He seems to have the right mix of animal genes to be suited to it," Dylan confirmed.

"I noticed the pistol in your jeans last night. Have you got other guns here?"

He looked at her sheepishly. "A few."

"I haven't noticed. I haven't been looking but I haven't found anything," she said, still surprised at learning this about Rory.

"There's a locked box under the back seat in the SUV with a few of my favourites. I have another couple in a duffle in the bedroom and more than my fair share back at the Centre. The reality is I don't get much call to use them but if I need to, I can."

"Wow, I've learnt so much about you in the last twelve hours."

"Well, we haven't exactly had the typical start to a relationship, or marriage for that matter."

She giggled. "Well, I can see I won't be bored by a long stretch."

"I had no intention of letting you get bored, sweetheart." He gave her a very suggestive smile and it told her exactly what he was thinking.

TJ felt her cheeks heat. She still wasn't really comfortable talking about sex in front of other people. Particularly men.

Dylan decided to explain things. "One thing you'll learn about all of us, Pixie, is that there are no secrets among the team, because it's next to impossible to keep them or have them. If someone's having sex or aroused, we all know about it. If a female is menstruating, we all know. We can all smell it. Therefore we have a very different mentality about that sort of stuff, I guess. Same as conversations. If you don't want others to hear, you need to probably go about a kilometre away to be truly sure no one else on the team can hear. That's why we don't tend to keep secrets and why we're all very close. We know everything about one another. Whether we want to or not."

Now that was something to lay on her. They'd all acted so normal.

She looked at Rory for confirmation.

"That about sums it up, Pix. It will probably take you some getting used to but for us this is just normal."

What a different concept, never really having any privacy when they were around each other. But then she thought about it some more. Privacy was really a very human type of concept. Animals tended to live in packs or colonies and didn't really have a need for it because they were not self-conscious of their bodies like humans.

The Centre operators walked the line between both.

"Uh-oh Surfer Boy—she's gone really quiet and looks to be deep in thought. Should we be worried?" Dylan asked the question in a light-hearted manner but the underlying question remained.

"Nothing to worry about, Dylan. I'm just thinking it all through. You've got to remember Rory only let me in on your little secret a few hours ago."

"Wow, mate! And she's still talking to you today? You're the man. She must really love you. It took the Stud longer than that to bring Rihanna around."

"I don't think our situations were quite the same, Dylan," Rory pointed out.

"Maybe not but you both got the girl."

Rory's phone rang and he moved away from the table to answer it.

TJ hadn't asked but she needed to know.

"Was it bad?"

"You mean last night?"

She nodded her head in confirmation.

"Well, it would have sucked to have been one of them or Kelvin."

"Kelvin was there too?" she said in surprise.

"Yeah, Rory had Quade pick him up. Surfer Boy was as worked up as I've ever seen him but he kept it together. I would have gone further but Rory mentioned you didn't want them killed. They're all answering some questions for the boys in blue this morning about why they were caught trespassing with pipe bombs. Rory also mentioned to the chief of police that it was an attempt to silence you for an attack they'd all been involved in six years ago. Pinning the attack on them would be hard to prove but not hard to use as leverage," Dylan explained for her.

"So do you work with the police or something?" she asked.

"We work really closely with the military and the cops on most of our operations. Generally there's some sort of criminal element. So that kind of gives us certain authorities.

Most of the time we just hand 'em over to the feds or the local cops. Saves us the paperwork."

"I'm learning a lot today it seems." She grinned.

"Well, Pixie, I'd say you've kind of had a lot on your plate, but you did all right when you hitched up with Rory. He's about the best of us."

"That's a really nice thing to say about someone, Dylan."

"Only the truth."

"I know."

Rory returned and looked from one to the other. "Okay, what were you two chatting about?"

"I thought you could hear everything?"

"We can. It doesn't mean we choose to listen."

She turned to Dylan. "You see, I was warned about this. Once men get married, their hearing becomes selective."

"Ha, ha, very funny."

"You're going to have your hands full, mate. I think when you give her a few months to settle in, she's going to give you a run for your money."

"Don't I know it. She keeps me on my toes now."

They all had a little smile and chuckle at that.

"That was Brayden. He wanted to know if we could go over and spend some time with the kids today. They all have to go out on some herd sampling assignment the boss has dreamed up."

"Sure."

"When are you meeting with Max?" Dylan asked.

TJ looked at Rory. "What's this?"

Dylan cringed, realising he'd put his foot in it.

"Sorry, mate. Didn't realise Pixie didn't know."

Rory sighed. "It was actually Dylan's suggestion. He suggested I go and have a chat with Max and see what it is that's got him so hellbent on being upset about everything. Maybe we can work this out amicably."

"Maybe I should go along as well?"

His reply was immediate and emphatic. "You're not going anywhere near that maniac. Besides, the meeting is tomorrow and the kids have those appointments at the hospital and Jazz mentioned that you need to get that ankle x-rayed again.

Brayden, Rihanna, and Jazz will go with you. I thought you might want to go catch up with your aunt as well."

She would like to see Aunt Clara; it had been a few days since she'd managed to get to see her. The loss of her mother had to be hard on her aunt as well.

"Yes, that sounds like a good idea. I have no real desire to see Uncle Max now I know what he's really about."

"Okay, then, that's sorted. We'll meet up with Brayden tomorrow at ten and then Dylan and Quade will come with me to the meeting with Max."

"I wouldn't hold much hope for a successful outcome. Uncle Max doesn't exactly have a track record of being easily persuaded."

"I just want to know what his issue is and to see if we can sort it before this situation escalates into all-out war."

"Emasculating his son last night may not have been the best course of action there," Dylan offered.

"Probably not. But it was what he should have done six years ago and the little prick is just lucky I managed to keep my temper in check and not castrate him."

"You came damned close. I wouldn't want to be pissing let alone anything else out of his package for a long while." Dylan shuddered at the thought.

TJ turned to Rory. "What did you do to him?"

"I just delivered a very well-placed kick to his groin."

Part of TJ wanted to cheer. It was something she'd fantasised about doing hundreds of times. Another part of her dreaded what would come. Max and Kelvin were spiteful and deceitful at the best of times.

They were also ruthless and not known to follow the rules.

She really hoped Rory didn't underestimate them.

Chapter Twenty-Seven

Max sat outside in a secluded corner of a Tuscan-themed café in Surfers Paradise. Given that it was a weekday, the trade was busy, but not intensely so. This café was yet another of his secret little business ventures. An excellent cash business. The coffee trade was booming by day.

And by night the very same establishment morphed seamlessly into an upmarket wine and tapas bar.

He'd chosen the venue for today's meeting when he'd received the call from Rory. He liked doing business on his home turf; it gave him an advantage and a sense of comfort.

If he admitted the truth to himself, then he'd have to say the call took him by surprise. A call from Rory was the last thing he expected. Now his curiosity had been piqued.

Being the type who prided himself on being ready for anything, Max had posted a couple of his senior security people just inside the door. Only just out of earshot but well close enough if trouble came knocking. He didn't trust Rory or his band of commando mates one little bit. So far in the last month, they'd caused him a lot of grief. That was going to stop today.

Max sipped his coffee and waited. He noticed Quade and Dylan walk into the tabled area. Their eyes did a split-second surveillance of the café and shot him a challenging smile before they selected the table across from his men. He hadn't seen them since the funeral. They'd been on the outskirts of the proceedings, but there, nonetheless. His temper was still smarting from the ejection at the bedside wedding ceremony.

He took their presence and manner today to be both a challenge and a threat.

A couple of minutes later, Rory walked in, looking relaxed and casual but entirely too confident of his place in the world, Max thought.

Max noticed that Rory had immediately spotted him and made a direct line to him. He also noticed that Rory didn't once seem to glance around looking for Quade and Dylan. All this told him that Rory either didn't care or was very confident of what to expect from his friends.

As Rory approached the table, Max rose. He prided himself on his manners.

"Morning, Max." Rory extended his hand in greeting and Max accepted it.

"Rory," Max said in return greeting.

"Lovely weather we're having at the moment."

"Yes, it certainly is. Nothing better than the weather in Queensland."

A waitress hovered nearby. "Can I get you a coffee?"

"Thanks—a double-shot black would be great."

The waitress scurried away with the order.

There was another moment of silence where both men summed each other up. Finally Max broke the silence.

"So Rory, I have to say I was a little surprised to hear from you."

Rory nodded his head. "I can see why that would be, Max." He wasn't ready to give anything away just yet.

"So what is it that you wanted to discuss?"

Rory, who'd been lounging in his chair, looking relaxed and carefree, suddenly seemed so much more intense. Max noted that he hadn't moved. It was more like he changed his energy. It was a very strange phenomenon to observe and immediately Max felt his heart rate begin to climb.

"I want to know why you seem so hellbent on destroying Teresa, Walsh Haulage, and the family."

"Oh, I'm not sure exactly what you mean by any of that, Rory," Max brushed off. He knew he didn't fool the younger man for a second but the game had to play out a little further first.

"Look, Max, I didn't come here today looking to create more hostilities between us. Quite the opposite, in fact. I wanted to see if whatever it is that's bothering you can be resolved with some discussion so we can all move on peacefully before any more damage is done to the family."

Max just laughed. "So you've been part of the family a whole of what—ten days?—and you think you can come to me, looking to broker deals?"

"At this stage, Max, I'm just trying to understand why you're acting the way you are."

"I'm not sure I understand what you're driving at, son." Max purposely used the word "son" to get a rise out of Rory. Disappointingly, it didn't look as if he was going to take the bait.

"Okay, then, let's start from the beginning. Why are you so determined to get control of Walsh Haulage?" Rory's question was asked very calmly and in a tone that gave nothing away.

This guy was good.

"I have some expansion plans. Walsh Haulage would fit nicely into those," Max responded carefully.

"So why not just offer to buy the business?"

"Why should I purchase something that should rightfully be mine?"

Rory let the comment hang for a second before he picked it up again. "Maybe I've missed something but I thought the business was left to Teresa's father when your father passed."

"That's correct. Doesn't make it right, though." Max knew he hadn't managed to keep the edge from his voice.

"So if you were so unhappy about this situation, why have you let it go on so long? Why didn't you sort it out with your brother while he was alive? You had nearly eight or ten years, didn't you?"

"Rory, I find it quite presumptuous of you to come marching in here and think you have a right to go through all of this with me," Max said in a superior voice.

Rory just shrugged and grinned. "Yeah, I can see how you could think I was presumptuous. I call it looking out for my family."

"Your family!" Max felt his temper rise. Normally he

could manage to control it, but there was just something about this guy that rubbed him the wrong way.

"They became that the day I married Teresa," Rory clarified for him.

"Teresa was supposed to marry Kelvin. That had been planned for years. Until you waltzed in. You must be hell in the sack, mate. I can't figure out any other reason she'd want to marry a stranger." Max clenched his hands together and ground his teeth. He'd promised himself he wouldn't get angry but how dare this young buck sit there and think it was his God-given right to question or judge him.

Rory let out an amused laugh. "You seriously don't believe that pile of crap you just spewed out, surely? Do you not recall a certain night about six years ago when your son and five of his best buddies tried to rape an innocent girl? Well, she's still haunted by it at times."

"Innocent girl, my arse. All women are whores, just some are more practised at the art," Max muttered.

Rory flew forward in his chair and slammed his palms on the table. Every head in the place turned and looked, plus a few passers by on the street.

"How dare you speak about women in general like that? What sort of fucked-up perspective is that? I now understand why that pathetic piece of shit you call a son is the way he is. They say kids are a product of their environment and given that Kelvin is not your biological son, I can only conclude he's a product of his environment. That means it's all on you, mate." Rory paused and looked around briefly. "What sort of man turns his back on a woman who's lying on a bed crying because she's just been violated?"

"It wasn't like that; she wanted it," Max spat.

"And what led you to that conclusion, Max? The five fuckers holding her down?" Rory waited a split second. "Nope, there's just no getting around it. You ignored your son's actions because they're probably exactly like yours. Well, I gave him and his little friends a reminder to keep his dick in his pants and his hands off women unless they ask to be touched. Maybe you need the same reminder?"

"Just who the fuck do you think you are?" Max seethed.

"Oh, Max, I know exactly who I am and over the years, I learnt to control the beasts that live within me. You I've seen clearly now and I don't need a psych degree to tell me you're a sociopath. I'm only going to say this once. Stay the fuck away from Teresa and her family. Stay the fuck away from Walsh Haulage and we won't have any further problems. You only need to breathe in their direction and I promise you I will personally dance at your funeral."

"Big threats coming from a man who, when it's all said and done, is no more than an over-muscled thug. As you've no doubt determined, I'm a man not without substantial resources at his disposal. Do you seriously think you can stop me from doing anything if I put my mind and my resources to the cause?" Max's tone was condescending and cold.

"I wouldn't bother wasting any of your resources, Max. You're going to need every bit of coin you've got to dig you out of the stink-hole your ego and perverted tendencies have buried you in. You've hit Tom Anderson's radar and let me tell you, that's a place no smart man ever wants to be. So not only am I gunning for you, you now have Tom Anderson looking up your arse with a microscope. It's about to get real uncomfortable. I'll give you the same advice I gave Kelvin. Find someplace else to live. You're not welcome around here anymore."

With that, Rory spun on his heel and stalked from the restaurant. His two men leapt from their seat, about to give chase, but Dylan and Quade were quicker. They'd immobilised his two best men and left them slumped in their seats as if they weren't even a consideration.

Just who were these men?

A set of ice blue eyes flashed through his brain and a cold shiver ran up his spine. Who was Tom Anderson, really?

He needed this done. Time was becoming his enemy and he was bored with the resistance he was getting. It was time to change the play for good.

Max pulled his phone from his pocket and sent a quick text.

Do it!

Chapter Twenty-Eight

Katie was enjoying spending a few minutes visiting with Aunt Clara in her hospital room before they headed back to Brayden and Rihanna's. They were cool to hang out with but she missed her mum and her aunt. She hadn't said anything but her heart hurt and she really needed a big hug. She felt kinda bad she'd hardly seen Aunt Clara since the explosion.

"Hey Aunt Clara, how are you feeling?" She sat beside the bed and took her aunt's hand. Her arm was covered in different sorts of dressings and weird-looking plastic stuff.

"Getting there, Katie, very slowly," her aunt whispered. "Tell me about what's been going on."

Katie paused for only a second before she dove into the long, rambling narratives typical of kids. "Um, sure. Well, Marcus and I are living with Brayden and his wife Rihanna. Jazz is there, too." A quick glance to her aunt indicated that she had no idea who Katie was talking about. "Oh, sorry, I forgot you don't know them. Brayden and Rihanna are friends of Rory and TJ. Oh, I just realised you haven't met Jazz either. Wow, so much has happened. Anyway, they're all way cool. They make us do our homework but Jazz and Rihanna are super smart doctors or something so they know all about my science homework. And Jazz and Quade, oh, he's a friend of Rory and TJ's as well, bought us all these really awesome clothes. Wait till Madison sees my new wardrobe. She's gonna totally flip."

Katie was a little relieved that Aunt Clara wasn't feeling so good, because she knew that there was no way she'd normally be allowed to wear shorts and a singlet top out. Her mother and her aunt always insisted she wear some dorky dress. It was one thing being a brainiac but it totally sucked to be a brainiac with lame clothes. Now she was a brainiac with a wardrobe full of trendy clothes. All the cool labels.

"So Brayden is like totally amazing. He's the songwriter for Steel and he even plays with them sometimes. They are just the coolest. Brayden says he'll take me to a concert the next time they're playing around here and I can go backstage with him and everything. How cool is that?"

Worry was etched all over Aunt Clara's face and Katie regretted getting so caught up on Brayden and her new clothes.

"Is your sister here today?"

"Um, yeah, she's just down having an x-ray or something."

"Well, tell her I want to see her when she's through."

Uh-oh—they were in trouble now. Katie knew that disapproving look well.

"Sure. She might be a while, though."

Her aunt nodded slightly and Katie noticed that she kept swallowing. She helped her take a sip of water from the cup with the bendy straw on the nearby table. Aunt Clara really didn't look very good.

"Is there anything I can get you?" Katie asked, hoping to ease the tension that had now settled over them.

"I'd love some of those mint lollies from the hospital shop—you know the ones I like."

Katie squeezed her aunt's hand. Brayden and Jazz had told her specifically she needed to stay here and not move from her aunt's room because of security or something. She didn't want to let Aunt Clara down, nor did she want to mention Brayden or Jazz to her again. When she'd mentioned them before, she'd got very agitated.

Surely it would be alright if she just slipped downstairs and got the mints? She'd only be gone a couple of minutes and nobody would be any the wiser.

"I'll be back in a few minutes."

Katie walked out of the room and looked left and right, trying to get her bearings. The hospital was huge. She headed towards the lifts; partway along the corridor, she noticed the enclosed gantry bridge that adjoined the two hospitals on that floor. She'd been dying to walk across that bridge. It looked so awesome from the ground. Kind of space age, as if it belonged on the space station rather than here.

Unable to resist, she headed across the bridge. Halfway across, she stopped. *Wow, the view was incredible.* She could just about see the whole city from here. Farther across the bridge was another bank of elevators. She'd take those and head down to the shop.

She waited for the next car, moved in and pressed Ground. A couple of men were in the elevator but she paid no attention to them. It was rude to stare.

The bell dinged and the doors opened. She looked left and right, trying to figure out where she was. The corridor that went off this big open foyer area looked familiar.

Yeah, that was the way out onto the street. The little shop was just around the corner.

She headed slowly to the corridor. Her shoulder was starting to get sore and she was feeling really tired but she'd be ok. She headed down the corridor and turned right down another, looking for the sign to the shop. It should be just there.

Panic started to rise up in her chest. The sign wasn't there. She was lost. All the corridors looked the same.

Katie spun around and almost crashed directly into the two men who were in the elevator. One look at their eyes and her panic turned to cold, icy terror. She opened her mouth to scream and a hand covered by a cloth covered her mouth. It smelt funny and she suddenly felt weird. Her body began to sag and everything went black.

TJ relaxed back on the table, waiting for the radiographer to come in and take the x-ray on her ankle. She was so over this cast and really hoped it had healed enough that she could commence more intense physio and a little weight-bearing activity.

Rory had been great throughout it all but she was getting sick of being partially incapacitated. It didn't suit her at all. She was used to being very active and getting on with things.

Plus there were a few naughty things she'd like to try with her extremely hot husband if she could get rid of the damned cast. What was the fun of having all that willing male hotness at her fingertips if she couldn't put it to good use? And she was quickly learning she had some very good uses.

She hoped the kids were okay. Katie was off visiting with Aunt Clara. TJ really needed to call in and see her as well. She loved her aunt but sometimes she just got fed up with all the disapproving looks and claustrophobic ideas.

Jazz was with Marcus. The doctors had wanted to run some more tests on him and Jazz suggested that she should go and have a chat to them. It suited TJ just fine. Jazz would fill her in later.

Brayden was supposed to be watching them all—which in reality was impossible in this place. There were three different groups of doctors wanting to look at three different patients in three different areas. Plus, Rihanna was also having another scan.

Yep, relaxing in this dark room was definitely a nice place to be—away from all the craziness.

She closed her eyes and just let the time move past.

A few minutes later, the door opened and she heard the radiographer enter and sit beside her. She briefly opened her eyes and the doctor had his back to her.

"How are you this morning?"

"Well, thanks."

"Just relax there while I get this all setup," he said as he moved camera arms and other pieces of the machine around.

"Sure. I was nearly asleep," TJ admitted.

A hand moved across her face and pressed a cloth tightly over her mouth and nose.

"Well, in that case, have a little something more to make sure you're really asleep."

TJ struggled with everything she was worth but whatever was in the cloth was making her weak and she couldn't focus.

The world faded to black.

Jazz poked her head into the x-ray room she'd left TJ in. There was no one inside. That was strange. She headed to the desk a few doors down. Marcus moved behind her, a couple of paces back.

A harried-looking clerical assistant looked up at her.

"Have you seen Teresa Southall? She may have been registered as Teresa Walsh. I was supposed to meet her here after her x-ray."

The woman shuffled through her files and pulled out the one she was looking for.

"I've got the file but she didn't seem to show for the films. The radiographer's made a note that she was a no-show."

Jazz's heart started to pound in her chest. Something was wrong. She'd left TJ here not more than twenty minutes ago.

"Did you see her? She's about five two, very pretty with long white blonde hair."

"I'm sorry. I've just come down from another section; the normal receptionist has gone home sick."

Jazz's stomach dropped as well.

"Thanks for your help."

She looked up and down the corridor and saw what she was looking for. The bathrooms were located down the corridor and to the right. Jazz pulled out her phone and turned it on, hoping for a message of some kind.

"Marcus, have you got any messages from TJ?"

The young man immediately reached into his pocket for his phone and quickly checked. "Nope, nothing."

Jazz rushed off a text message to TJ and sent it.

"Shit—maybe she's in the bathroom?" Jazz had a really bad feeling about all this.

They hurried down to the bathrooms.

"Don't move. I'll just be a sec."

Jazz pushed through the outer and then the inner doors to

the bathroom and quickly moved from cubicle to cubicle. There was nobody here.

She needed to find Brayden, pronto.

Jazz hurried from the bathroom and headed to the OB/GYN floor, basically dragging Marcus behind her. *Why were hospitals always so bloody difficult to navigate and why did it take an eternity to get from one place to another in them?* She cursed for the hundredth time.

On the way, she decided to go with her gut.

She pulled her phone from her pocket again and flicked to Quade's number.

Thank God he answered on the second ring.

"What's up, honey nose?"

She ignored the jibe; she was just so glad to have him to talk to.

"We've lost TJ in the hospital. Quade, I have a really bad feeling about this."

"Slow down; tell me what's happened."

She quickly filled him in.

"Fuck. We'll head there right now." She heard him telling Dylan to change where they were headed.

"Is Rory with you?"

"No, he was going to head home then meet you later. He got a call from the truck depot. There was some kind of problem. I'll ring him."

Jazz didn't like the sound of it. Too many things were conveniently happening.

"We're about twenty minutes away. I'll call the boss as well. You get Brayden's ass on it now. He may be able to find a scent if we're lucky. If not, I'll take care of it when we get there. Where's Katie?"

Oh fuck. Jazz hadn't even thought about her; she'd been so concerned about TJ. *Maybe she went to do something with Katie?*

"I think she's up visiting Clara."

"Don't think about it; confirm it, babe. And for fuck's sake, find Brayden and stay with him. I don't want to be looking for you as well."

Something just occurred to Jazz. It was the first time Quade had actually demonstrated anything other than contempt for her. In fact, if she wasn't mistaken, he sounded concerned. Even his bossy attitude and the way he called her *babe* didn't annoy her.

What was that about?

Jazz and Marcus finally located Rihanna and Brayden coming out of the OB/GYN section of the hospital. They were all smiles and looking at yet another series of baby pictures.

Brayden looked up as he noticed Jazz coming up the corridor. He immediately straightened.

"What's up?"

She could hear the alarm in his voice. Her face must have betrayed her.

"I can't find TJ. I left her down at x-ray while I went with Marcus for some more tests and now I can't find her and apparently she didn't show for the x-ray."

"Could she be up with Clara?" he asked, obviously becoming more and more concerned.

"We need to check there. I've spoken with Quade. Dylan and he will be here in about ten minutes. He's calling Rory, too. Quade said we're not to leave you."

"What a fucking mess. Come on, we need to go find Katie." Rihanna started to object to Brayden's language.

"Minky, he's a teenage boy. He's heard the word fuck before now and I have no doubt he's used it and thought about doing it, if he hasn't already done it."

Marcus shot him a grin that Jazz didn't miss. It was one of those guy moments.

The four of them moved through the maze of corridors and found Clara's room.

"Marcus, can you go and talk to her, please? Find out if she's seen or knows where Katie is. It will only alarm her more if one of us goes in there. She hasn't met any of us."

"Okay." He turned and headed into the room.

"Where are Quade and Dylan meeting us?"

"How about I text them to come around to the outpatient entrance? X-ray is just down the corridor from there."

"Yeah, do it."

Jazz hastily pecked out a quick text.

Brayden looked like a thundercloud. Jazz had never seen him this agitated.

"Fuck, how could I be so stupid?" he muttered to himself.

Marcus came back through the door.

"She says that Katie was here and she asked her to go and get her some mints from the shop downstairs. She hasn't come back yet. Apparently that was about half an hour ago."

Jazz's stomach lurched again.

"I don't like it."

"I'm not keen on it, either. Give me a second and let me see if I can pick anything up." He moved a few metres away from them and subtly sniffed and tried to listen.

"What's he doing?" Marcus asked Jazz and Rihanna.

They both looked at each other, and then Jazz shrugged.

"He's trying to see if he can pick up her scent or hear her."

"How?" Marcus's face scrunched up, clearly confused.

"All the Centre operators have altered DNA. Their DNA has been spliced with animal DNA. As a result, they have heightened sense on equivalent to animals."

Marcus's eyes went wide.

"Oh wow—that is so cool!"

"Yeah, it might be, but you also can't tell anyone. Not a soul. It's not your secret and it's a national security breach if you do. Plus you're going to have to sign a heap of papers saying you won't tell anyone. Do you get how serious I am and how important this is? All their lives could be at risk if people knew. Your lives also, now that Rory is married to your sister. "

His face was solemn and he nodded. Then the boyish grin broke out.

"Rory's like this, too?"

"Yes, he is."

"And I'm now related to him. That's so awesome."

"Not a word, Marcus," Jazz reminded him.

"My lips are sealed." He motioned to his lips.

"Make sure they stay that way."

Brayden moved back to them.

"She went down past the lifts and onto the bridge." He looked at Marcus and Marcus grinned. "You'd better not forget that this is a secret, mate. If you do, I'll kick your ass. What Jazz didn't tell you is we have animal speed, strength, and endurance. It'll be a beating you won't forget. You want to know something, you come to Rory or me privately. Are we clear?"

"Crystal."

Brayden placed his hand on the kid's shoulder.

"Good. I really like you, kid—don't disappoint me."

Marcus grinned even wider.

Jazz knew then that Brayden had handled it perfectly. There was exactly the right balance of trust, fear, and respect.

They followed the path Katie had taken. It took her nowhere near the shop. She'd gone to the wrong building and then gone down and wound her way through a few back corridors.

Brayden abruptly stopped. He looked up and down, checking for any unwanted ears.

"She was here. Two men caught up with her here. I'm assuming she was taken. I can smell the scent of her fear lingering. It started slightly in the lift and then it got really pronounced just here. I have a feeling I know where this trail is going to end."

He headed off again and they all followed. After a few more twists and turns, he stopped just inside a side exit door to the carpark near the outpatient entrance.

Braden moved through the door and they all followed. He headed across the carpark and stopped at a spot off to the side behind a large concrete pillar.

"The scent stops here."

Quade and Dylan must have seen or tracked them and walked up.

Jazz noticed Quade and Dylan sniffed the air and Brayden stiffened with what she recognised as rage.

"They're both gone. Fuck, fuck, fuck," Brayden spat.

"Who's going to tell Rory?" Dylan asked quietly.

"I will. I fucked up and let his family get abducted. This is on me."

Rihanna looked to Jazz and Jazz looked back.

The women both knew they were in uncharted territory. Jazz had a feeling they were going to see a whole other side of these guys they hadn't seen before.

Chapter Twenty-Nine

They were all assembled in the Situation Room at the Centre. A large bank of sixty-five inch televisions occupied an entire wall. Rheeba and Selena sat behind a series of very impressive-looking computers and screens. The boss and the rest of them sat at the table in front of the televisions.

The exception to that was Rory. He had to stand. He needed to move.

At this very moment, he wanted to rip some fucker's throat out—ideally starting with Max.

His gut was churning equally with untold rage and icy fear. A rage so hot that all he wanted to do was kill. A fear so icy he knew he'd never warm up until Pixie was back safe and sound in his arms.

When Brayden had called him and told him what had happened, he just about lost it. He'd never felt pain like it. He could only assume Max had his wife, which probably meant that lowlife piece of shit son of his had access to her as well.

How could this have happened? How did Brayden let this happen?

Why did he go through with the stupid meeting and entice the fucker more?

Was the retribution he'd delivered to Kelvin really worth the pain that Pixie would feel at their hands?

It was all his fault.

His lack of judgement caused this.

The one thing he was supposed to have.

He'd let her down. The need for physical violence was strong.

"What do you think, Rory?"

His mind snapped back to the conversation that was going on around the table.

"About what?" he asked at no one in particular.

"About how this may play out," the boss stated.

"Sorry, Boss. I wasn't really listening. I'm so torn up over that bastard having them. All I know is that I need them both back yesterday and those fuckers out of our lives for good."

"We all understand that, Rory, but you need to keep it together. Given the circumstances, I think we can safely assume that Max has them. I also think that the cocky bastard will not be making any demands. This is not a hostage negotiation. This is a showdown. Winner takes all. He wants the business, Teresa, and whatever else his crazy-assed logic dictates. Plus, he wants to see you take a fall trying to get them back."

"I'd happily take the fall if it meant they could be safe," Rory said philosophically.

"Don't even talk like that. You're not going to take a fall and we will get them back and that's an order."

"Not military, Boss," Rory quipped. Rory hated anything that resembled military rules and regulations and his temper was running close to the wire.

"I'm the director of this Centre. You work for it. I am the boss and you will take that as an order. The military be damned. This is not helping, Rory. I need you to get your head straight. Teresa needs you to get your head straight."

That was the reminder he needed. Pixie needed him to find her.

Rory didn't answer. He just gave the boss a curt nod. He couldn't manage any more at the moment.

"Right. Rheeba, give me all the latest intel you've got on this. Let's see what we've got to work with. I'm looking for points of leverage. Anything we can pin on him. Also anything we might have on where he could be holding them."

"Right, Boss. Well, if we start with the herd samples that the guys took yesterday. Oh, by the way, Rihanna, good plan getting Brayden and Quade to sniff out the differences in the cattle so you and Peter could take the various samples."

"Thanks, Rheeb," Rihanna acknowledged.

"So from the tests that the lab have rushed through, it looks like we've got seven that have been genetically modified. I have a list here of the ear tag numbers and the result. Interestingly enough, the genetically modified cattle are not limited to one property of the ten that you sampled yesterday. Three properties had genetically modified cattle. I've also done some more digging around the ownership of those properties and you guessed it. The ownership is through an elaborate series of companies both on and offshore. If I had to lay money, I'd put it on the fact that Max will be the ultimate owner. I've got a few more layers to peel back yet but the trail is the same as I found for the trucking company. My guess is that whoever set up the trail of companies was the same person."

"Rheeba, who's Max's accountant and lawyer?" the boss asked before she could go on.

"Um, just a sec...okay, the accountant seems to be Mclaughins and the lawyers O'Donnell and Partners."

"Selena, find out Max's contacts in both. I want them picked up now. I'll make the calls for the warrants in a minute."

"What else have you got?"

"Well, the guys looking into the deaths of TJ's father and brother seem to think they're close to being able to give you something. Apparently they have some strange paperwork anomalies," Rheeba replied.

"Have you got anything else on where they might be keeping the girls?"

"I don't yet. I've got a search running right now for all the properties that are owned by any company Max seems to be involved with."

"Okay. Miss Carter, have you got any idea where a guy like this would keep the girls?"

Rory could see Jazz think over the question for a few seconds. *God, he hoped she had some sort of insight.* He felt so fucking useless. Those sick fuckers could be doing anything to them and here he was standing around shooting the breeze. This time, they were going to pay when he caught up to them.

"Tom, given what we know about this guy, I'd guess, and I'm saying guess because I might be a psychiatrist but I'm not a profiler, that he's going to want this to play out to some sort of audience. I don't think the audience will be his normal peers but more like the Centre because we've challenged him and taken what he thinks is rightfully his. I'd also say that I think he's got a point to prove to family—he'll be looking for some type of connection. It may not make sense to anyone but him. So Marcus, Clara, and any other family members who need to see him come out on top. He'll keep them somewhere remote until he sets the stage," Jazz concluded.

Rory's mind whirred with what Jazz had said. Where would he want this to play out? A farm, the depot, a road, the processing plant, somewhere else? The possibilities were endless.

"Do you think he's got both the girls together or holding them separately?" the boss asked.

"Hard to say. I could see the appeal of both options for different reasons. I don't think I can make a suggestion on that one."

"Marcus," Tom said in his normal commanding tone.

The young man sat up straight in his chair and looked as if he'd been caught by the principal, up to no good.

"Yes, sir."

"Where do you think Max would take them? Can you think of any family homes or holidays or something like that?"

Rory could see Marcus trying to rack his brain for an answer to this.

"We used to have a dairy farm that got left to Dad when Pops died. Is that the sort of thing you mean?" The kid twisted his face up, not sure whether he was giving the right answer.

"Good job, son. That's exactly the sort of thing I'm talking about. Tell me some more about it."

Marcus's face beamed under the praise of the boss.

"I was only little but I remember going there. Apparently it got left to Pops from his mother's side or something. I really don't know. I think Dad sold it to get the money to expand Walsh Haulage. I always got the feeling that Uncle Max liked it there."

"Can you remember where the property is?"

"Sure. I was about seven or eight the last time I went there but I used to play this game with my dad where I'd have to give him directions to places. If I got them right, he used to let me steer the truck from the main road up to the yard."

"Do you think you could take us there now?"

"Yeah, I reckon I could."

"Okay, Rory, Quade, and Dylan—you take Marcus and go find out where that property is. Brayden, I want you to round up the accountant and lawyer. I've sent Allison off to the hospital to watch out for Clara. Rheeba, you and Selena keep digging. Rihanna, I want you to go through the sampling reports and see if you can pick any further patterns. We need to wrap this GM thing up as well. Miss Carter, I need you to get organised for a full field operation. We're not sure the timing of this but let's get organised, team. Any questions?"

The boss looked from one to another of them.

"Keep a lid on it, Mr Southall. We'll get them back. Get busy, people."

Rory curtly nodded and strode from the room.

Less than an hour later, Quade pulled the SUV to the side of the dirt road where Marcus had led them. He'd purposely driven past the driveway and up over a ridge so that he could use the terrain to hide the vehicle.

"Okay, I'm going to go skirting around and see what I can find. Rory, why don't you come with me? I know you're not going to want to stay in the car. Quade, you stay with Marcus. He's not up to a hike through the paddocks just yet with his injuries." Dylan took charge before there was any discussion or negotiation.

"Let's go," Rory said, getting out of the SUV.

"We'll be back in about thirty," Dylan shot at Quade.

"Cool. I'll call in the GPS location so Rheeba can start

running traces. Stay out of trouble. I don't think I feel like rescuing you two."

Dylan just smiled and took off behind Rory.

Rory vaulted the barbed-wire fence and took off at a long lope along the gully side of the ridge, using it to hide their presence from any prying eyes. Dylan was a couple of paces off his left side, easily keeping pace. Fuck it, he felt like a run and upped the pace. He was probably covering a kilometre in around two minutes. The homestead and dairy sheds were located a long way from the road. He'd done a milk pickup from this place not more than two days ago. The irony was not lost on him.

At the end of the gully, he headed towards the creek that adjoined. It provided a bit more cover than the open paddocks. Quite a few trees had been left along the banks of the creek to provide shade for the cattle.

They ran in silence for another couple of minutes until the homestead and sheds came into view about three hundred metres away. Rory slowed for a few paces and then stopped, squatting down under a tree. Dylan followed.

"There's no cover between here and the buildings. Let's wait here a few minutes and see if we can pick up how many and where."

"Okay."

Both men rested on one knee in silence. Their eyes scanned the buildings, looking for movement.

Finally Dylan broke the silence. "I've got four guys and there's some sort of electronic beep."

"Yeah, that's what I've got. I'm thinking the beep is one of those handheld video games."

"Yeah, that's it."

"Have you got any scents? I've got three. The two that are over in the dairy shed and the guy who just walked between there and the house. I'm figuring I can't get a read on any others because the wind's blowing the other way."

Dylan sniffed the air again and nodded. "Yeah, I've got them."

"We need to get a look in that house. I'm wondering if they're trying to entertain a twelve-year-old girl with a video game."

"Could be. Either that or one of the guys hasn't moved up to anything more mature."

"Okay, you up for a sprint? Let's see if we can cover it in less than fifteen. We'll head for those tanks behind the house."

"Done."

Both men sprung from their positions on the ground like sprinters from the starting blocks—only much faster. The ground blurred beneath their feet and they very quickly arrived in the shadows of the tanks.

They both stood silent for a few seconds, neither of them breathing hard.

"I've got two in the house and I'm pretty sure it's Katie. I get a faint scent coming from that bathroom window, when the breeze blows this way," Rory whispered.

"Yep, I've got it as well."

"How about you go around to the south and I'll go to the north. Let's see if we can see her."

"Okay, mate."

They were about to split up when Rory reached out and put his hand on Dylan's arm, stilling him. Rory nodded at the house and then motioned with his hand that he could hear talking.

"She behaving?"

"Yeah, she's been playing that thing for hours. How long are we going to be holed up here?"

"Not sure. Max said he'd get back to me. He's got a few things to set up, apparently. I'd say we're going to be here for today and probably tomorrow."

"Okay," the man huffed out.

"What, you got a hot date or something?"

"Yeah, something like that."

"Well, don't fuck this up by thinking with your dick. Max will have your guts for garters."

"So where's TJ? I wouldn't mind helpin' myself to some of

that pussy. Had my eye on that little babe for the last coupla years."

"She's with Kelvin. I think he's got her stashed at that apartment he used to live in. And get that thought right out of your mind. Max and Kelvin are already fuckin' freaking out over her getting hitched to some guy. You don't want to buy into that cluster fuck."

Rory's head felt as if it were going to explode. The mother fucking, slimy shit for brains, perverted, ferret-faced asshole had his wife.

The man she was shit fucking scared to be near.

He wanted to kill—the need was so bad.

His fists clenched and he sucked in a huge breath, trying to calm the beast.

He had to keep it together.

They heard one of the men walk off and the door beside the bathroom window closed.

Dylan broke the silence. "He's taking a slash."

"Yeah, let's go."

They both moved to the building as quiet as shadows and almost became part of the brick wall as they skirted from window to window, peeking in.

Rory came to one of the back bedrooms and looked in. Katie was sitting on the bed, her back propped against the wall, her legs pulled up close to her chin. The video game rested on her knees and her nimble fingers flew over the controls.

She looked fine, unhurt.

Now he was torn. He wanted to go and grab her out of there, but terror filled him at what would happen to Pixie if they took Katie back. He'd made a mistake with Max once; he couldn't afford to do the same again.

He took one last look and skirted back to the tanks. Dylan joined him there a few seconds later.

"Katie's in there. In the back bedroom on the corner."

"Are we going to get her?" Dylan asked, confused.

"I really want to but she's okay. If we take her, I have no idea what they'll do to Pixie. The thought makes me fucking crazy." Rory was still struggling to keep his rage under control.

"Okay, that makes sense. Why don't we do this? I'll stay here and keep watch on Katie. You head back to the creek and see if you can get a phone signal, call the boss and let him know. I don't like leaving a kid with these assholes either." Dylan slipped his phone from his pocket. "I've got intermittent signal. I'll be able to text at least."

"You sure? It might be a while before we can get back out here to relieve you."

Dylan gave him a look that was the equivalent of "*Oh please.*"

"For fuck's sake, be careful," Rory growled, not liking leaving Dylan behind one bit, but liking the idea of leaving Katie unprotected and abandoned even less.

They glanced around, nodded silently to each other, and then Rory took off, using all the animal speed he contained.

Rory stopped briefly at the creek but the phone reception was non-existent. He ran back to the car and had the boss on the phone a few seconds later, and a few seconds after that, he'd explained the situation.

"I think it's the right call, Rory." The boss agreed with their actions. "I know it feels like hell but Max and his asshole son are not right in the head. Teresa doesn't need to have them further triggered. You know Dylan can take care of just about anything that comes his way. I'll get Rheeba working on a location for the apartment. Head back here. I'll see you soon." In typical fashion, the call dropped.

"Let's go, mate. At least we have a fair idea of where they are and you know Dylan won't let anything happen to her," Quade reassured him.

It was something to know where Pixie probably was, but it still felt like nothing.

He knew she'd be terrified, even more so being around Kelvin, and she'd do crazy things when she felt like that.

For the millionth time that day, he cursed his lack of judgement and what he'd done to Kelvin. He should have left it alone or finished it.

He'd done nothing except brought a boatload of trouble for Pixie.

Chapter Thirty

She'd woken a couple of hours ago in a strange bed and her head felt as if she were swimming through clouds. A few seconds later, her mind raced back to what had happened.

Kelvin had her.

She hadn't seen or heard anything—she just knew.

This was payback for marrying Rory, and all the other things that had happened over the years.

He'd made no secret of the fact he wanted her and now Kelvin seemed hellbent on carrying through. The fear she felt was totally numbing. She knew beyond doubt that Kelvin would be in an incredible rage over everything that had happened. TJ also knew he'd take it out on her. He might be a family member by blood or other—none of that mattered.

He was evil to the core. And this was all about her paying the piper.

As soon as her eyes had opened, TJ recognised the room. It was the spare room in Kelvin's old apartment. She'd visited here once before with her older brother. She'd never stayed but she had been in this place before. She'd also noticed the webcams pointed at the bed, both with their little lights blinking green. Was he planning to record something or was he just using them to keep an eye on her? Either way, the thought that he was watching her made her skin crawl.

She'd closed her eyes again and rolled over, feigning sleep. TJ didn't want to open her eyes but there was no way she could get away with pretending to be asleep forever. Sooner or later they would come in here. She also really needed to go to the bathroom.

Eventually the need to go to the bathroom won out and TJ rolled to the edge of the bed and hobbled into the adjoining en-suite bathroom. After quickly going about her business, she took a quick glance around. There was nothing in here she could realistically use as a weapon.

A little further investigation in the vanity revealed a toothbrush in a new packet and toothpaste, plus a little canister of breath spray. Without thinking too much more, she pocketed the breath spray and cleaned her teeth. Whatever they'd given her left a crappy taste in her mouth.

A few moments later, she heard someone out in the room she'd just been in. The fear almost overwhelmed her again.

She just had to hang on.

Rory would come for her.

This she knew with unending clarity.

He would come.

"Get out here, TJ. You can't hide in the bathroom forever," Kelvin called. His voice was laced with a smugness that turned her stomach.

TJ took one last look in the mirror and sucked in a deep breath to fight away the fear that was threatening to suffocate her. She closed her eyes and willed herself to be brave and sassy. There was no choice but to go with her usual approach. Attack her fears the best way she could. She could do this. She had to. Rory would need the time to come and find her.

When she opened her eyes, the face she saw reflected almost convinced her.

With a solid push, TJ opened the door and hobbled through as purposefully as possible.

"What the fuck is this about, Kelvin?" she fumed at him, on the attack. She'd try to use the fear to fuel the rage that she needed to feel.

Rory was right. There was something incredibly liberating about letting loose with a swear word every now and then.

"That's hardly any way to say good afternoon." He looked slightly shocked; she never swore. Her mother would have been horrified.

"Fuck good afternoon, Kelvin. You've abducted me. I'm beyond pissed. And I want out of here now. Take me home immediately," she demanded.

She stood beside the bed. He was closer to the door. She'd have to go through him first. Why couldn't she have been born a five-foot-ten Amazon—preferably without a cast on her ankle—rather than a five-foot-two Pixie who weighed fifty-five kilos wringing wet, on her heaviest day.

"I can see your language has deteriorated considerably since you've taken up with him. Oh well, nothing we can't fix, now that you're out of there."

Her temper shot into uncharted territory. It had never reached the nuclear range before.

"What bit don't you get about me being married to Rory?" She spat each word; it felt as if she were landing a blow.

His face turned red and he fumed.

"Do not utter his name again. His name will tarnish your lips no more."

Kelvin's words enraged her further. Rory was the nicest name she'd ever heard and Kelvin was the name of a lowlife, snivelling scumbag.

"Grow up, Kelvin. There was never anything between us but what you took. This is only going to end badly. Just let me pass and we'll call it a misunderstanding. You don't want to go up against Rory and his team. For this, I have no doubt they will kill you."

He lashed out at her with his hand and caught her across the cheek. It stung in the worst way and she had a hard time not reacting to the pain. He wasn't going to win at this.

"I told you not to utter his name."

She narrowed her eyes.

Hysterical laughter assaulted her ears.

"I don't think you understand, TJ. It's I who holds all the cards—not you."

Was the man delusional or something? He wasn't all there, surely?

"Yeah, I've no doubt you think so. But I know Rory and he'll find me. And when he does, you'll wish you'd never been born."

Kelvin lashed out with his hand once again. This time TJ anticipated it and stepped back, making him even more furious. He charged her and threw her to the bed. His body came down on top of hers and she felt the wind rush from her lungs.

The memory of having him on top of her again clicked in her head and she fought him with a blind terror that was totally foreign to her.

She thrust the knee up of her good leg and felt immense satisfaction when she connected squarely with his groin, still obviously very tender from Rory's efforts. He rolled into the foetal position and moaned. It was music to her ears.

"You're such an asshole, Kelvin."

TJ didn't waste any more time. She slid from the bed and headed for the door. She was nearly at the front door when a giant hand clasped her around the shoulder and yanked her backwards. With the cast on, she had next to no balance.

She felt herself falling. Then her head connected with something solid and horrendous pain radiated through her head. Her vision blurred and the blackness took her again.

"Got it," Rheeba shouted and thrust her fist in the air from behind her computer in the Situation Room.

"Way to go," Quade cheered from across the floor.

"Where?" Rory demanded.

"Surfers Palms Apartments. Apartment 32A. Top floor."

"Is that the place on Main Beach Parade?" Brayden called.

"Yeah. You know it?" Rheeba asked him.

"Yeah."

"Let's go." Rory leapt from his chair.

"Sit down for a second, Mr Southall. Let's think this through," the boss commanded. His words allowed no leeway.

Rory plonked his ass in the chair—right about now, he wanted to put his fist through the boss's face. He wanted— no, he needed—to have his wife in his arms.

He needed her to be safe and with him.

Nothing less would do.

"So we have a location on Teresa. That means we also need to have a team in place to extract Katie and Dylan, otherwise the danger they'll face will be extreme." The boss fell silent for a moment and everyone knew he was formalising the plan in his head. "Right. This is what we'll do. Rory, Brayden, and Angelo, you're the advance party for the extraction from the apartment. Quade and Miss Carter, I want you to take another SUV and wait below. Watch the entrances and exits. I'll take Aaron with me. We'll get Katie and Dylan out. Rheeba, Selena, and Rihanna—you keep working here. Dig deep and start feeding everything you've got on these assholes to the feds. Build the case—they're expecting it. Start with what we got from the accountant and the lawyer. Full field kits, people. Let's move. This ends today." The boss stood and moved along with everyone else.

A few minutes later, Rory was in the passenger seat of the SUV, Brayden was at the wheel, and Angelo was in the back seat. The tension between Rory and Brayden was palpable.

Finally, Brayden could stand it no longer.

"I let you down, mate. I was responsible for them and I fucked up. I got distracted with Rihanna and I should have been more aware of the dangers. I'm so sorry, mate. I don't know how I can make it up to you."

Rory said nothing, just let his anger roll around for a bit longer. He knew logically Brayden was both right and wrong. There was no way he could have effectively provided protection for Pixie, Katie, and Marcus when they were all heading off to different parts of the hospital. They'd been stupid to let them go to the hospital so under protected.

Brayden had also let his wife distract him but hey, they were having babies and he wondered whether he would have been any better if the positions were reversed. He got all of that, but it didn't help Pixie now.

Pixie had said to him don't underestimate them and she'd been exactly right. They were dealing with some very dangerous opponents.

"It's not totally your fault. Yes, you should have been more alert to the dangers. But you needed more of us to help you out. It's more on me. I should have either finished that fucker off when I had the chance or let it alone. All we can focus on now is getting them back."

"You're not a killer, Rory, regardless of what you think. There's no way you would have taken him out in cold blood and God knows you had justification. We'll get them back. Then we burn those fuckers to the ground." Rory noticed Brayden's knuckles turning white on the steering wheel.

"Don't be so sure of that, Stud. I seem to be the one in this outfit with blood on my hands. Sooner or later we all need to recognise the truth. I can and do kill without remorse." He trailed off and looked out the window.

"That's such shit and you know it. Every single life you've taken has been in either self-defence or defence of someone else. You've never had a case to answer because they've all been justified," Angelo pointed out from the back seat.

"I shot the last guy in the back, if you recall. That's about as cold as it gets. Particularly in the eyes of a jury," Rory said emphatically.

"Yeah and that very same scumbag had a pistol to Rihanna's head and was a hair's breadth away from ending her life. I'll never forget that moment as long as I live. And I'll be eternally grateful, otherwise I wouldn't have my wife or my unborn children. You gave me that family, Rory. Please don't take yourself away from me. You'll always be my brother. We'll get through this somehow and get Teresa back. Our kids will be playing together one day."

"God, I hope you're right," Rory murmured.

"The universe wouldn't do it to you. She owes you, brother."

Brayden was using his own line against him.

Jazz couldn't stand it any longer. This situation was making her crazy. They were driving along a car's length behind Brayden, Rory, and Angelo.

She turned to look at Quade. "You called me babe."

His eyes narrowed but didn't shift in his focus of the road.
"So?"

"What's that about?" she demanded.

"I don't know. I just dropped some word and you're
making some sort of huge deal about it."

"It's more than that. You even sounded concerned."

He shifted swiftly in the seat and bought his hand down in
a harsh slap on the wheel.

"For fuck's sake, you're part of the team. Of course I give
a shit about what happens to you."

She didn't say anything for a few seconds, just let his
words resonate within her. The day of the sale a few short
months ago flashed before her eyes. She'd been staring down
the barrel of a gun with a maniac holding it and he'd thought
nothing of diving in front of her to take the bullets meant for
her.

Who did that sort of shit? She knew the answer. Someone
who cared. How did she feel about that? The big lug actually
cared.

"I care, too, you know," she finally whispered.

"I know. I may have been in and out of consciousness that
day but I caught enough to know that I owe my life to you. If
you hadn't been there and taken charge, I might not have
made it to the operating theatre."

She laughed—it was so ironic.

"What?"

"You realise we're probably having our first civil
conversation and there's no one here to witness it."

He grinned and curled up his mouth in amusement. The
guy was seriously handsome in a dark and brooding kind of
way. Jazz knew she was lying to herself if she didn't
recognise just how much he affected her as a woman. The
warm fuzzy feeling raced through her body.

"It is kind of funny." He chuckled.

"Why do you think it is we can't have a conversation
without antagonising each other?"

"I don't know. Haven't really thought about it. I guess we
just like to torment and terrorise the shit out of each other."

He was lying. His eyes looked away and he fidgeted. She could tell the signs anywhere and she knew this guy.

"Yeah, maybe," she agreed, letting him have his way.

"Have you ever wondered?" He turned the question on her.

"Sure."

"And what's your answer, Freud?"

How did she answer this? The truth would be very revealing but then she knew he'd be able to smell the dampness in her panties that his little grin had created a few moments ago. How did she deny something he was more than capable of determining for himself? There wasn't anyway—she'd be lying herself.

"Do you really want the truth or are we going to dance some more?" she asked.

He flicked the indicator on and rolled his jaw. He was contemplating her question.

"The truth, although I think dancing will be less uncomfortable," he admitted.

She let out a low, sexy giggle. Well, at least that's what guys had told her it sounded like to them. To her, it was just the way she laughed.

She watched him closely—yeah, he was not immune.

"I think there's a level of attraction between us and we keep skirting it by arguing," Jazz finally admitted.

"Yeah, it's there," he agreed nonchalantly.

God, he was impossible! Was there any wonder they argued?

"So you're admitting you're attracted to me? It's a little hard for me to hide it from you, as I don't have the advantage of your super sniffer. You do realise how embarrassing that is for us 'human' girls, don't you? Knowing that men can smell your arousal?"

He chuckled.

"I don't know about embarrassing. Us Centre guys, at least, tend to think it's as sexy as it fucking gets. Kind of good for the ego knowing a female wants you."

She shook her head. *Unbelievable!*

"You guys have such an advantage. You know if your attention is wanted. And you're almost given a treasure map to navigate our bodies by."

He turned to her and grinned, not before giving her a very sexy wink.

"So why are you winking at me?"

"Just thought I'd try out a little flirting instead of bickering. See if that fits any better."

"And how exactly do you think that's working out for you, hotshot?"

He tilted his chin up towards her and gave her a cheeky smile.

"Pretty fuckin' well, by the smell of it."

Jazz didn't know whether she wanted to slap him silly or spread her legs for him. She was certain both would give her unending amounts of satisfaction and pleasure.

Chapter Thirty-One

"We've got a guard at the front door. We're going to need a diversion," Brayden announced into the speakerphone. He was using the phone out of politeness to Jazz. They'd pulled into the side street and placed the call to Quade, who had pulled up behind. "Any ideas?"

There was silence between the two vehicles.

"I've got it covered," Jazz said confidently.

"Whatcha thinking, Jazz?" Rory asked.

"She's not fucking thinking anything. She's staying here out of harm's way," Quade clarified for them all.

"Oh, shut up. I'm just going to walk up to him and ask him to come and help me loosen some nuts on a flat tyre. One of you macho men can gently encourage him into the land of nod and everyone can go on about their business."

"Plan works for me," Rory said.

"Fuck me. Must we put all our women in danger?" Quade spat. There were a few responding sniggers but no real words to be heard. It was a very telling outburst.

"You don't treat Rheeba and Selena like this," Jazz protested.

"Rheeba and Selena could stop five men with their hands tied behind their backs. They happen to have a few enhancements you don't," Quade pointed out for her.

"Well, if you're so damned worried—make sure I don't get hurt."

"Ah, guys, are you two quite finished? Rory's about to blow a gasket here," Brayden reminded them.

"Ah yeah, sorry about that," Jazz said.

They discussed a few more details and ended the call. Jazz undid another button on her shirt and reached into her handbag for some perfume, which she sprayed on her cleavage. She then fluffed her long, red hair out and slicked some more gloss over her lips.

"Are you fucking kidding me?" Quade asked her, a look of exasperation on his face.

"What?" She threw her hands up in question. "I'm just getting in character."

"Just hurry up and lure the poor sucker to his demise before I take you here on the front seat of the car."

"Just because my body seems to think you're something interesting doesn't mean I'm going to act on it."

"Bullshit. It's going to happen and soon. Before I go out of my fucking mind," he growled.

"Did you just growl at me? And must you swear all the time?"

"Where you're concerned, yes." He turned his head and glared out the window at Rory, Brayden, and Angelo, who were standing discreetly beside the SUV, smirking. They could hear every word.

"We're going to talk about this. This is not over." She flung the door open and slammed it shut.

He watched her shimmy around the corner and across the carpark. Her hips swayed and he was sure his cock pulsed in time to their movement. *God, she was killing him. Why did he have to be attracted to such a ball buster?*

Quade watched Rory and Brayden lounge against the hood of their SUV, apparently looking over some documents that they'd conveniently spread out over the hood. Occasionally one of them pointed at a building as if explaining something.

Angelo sauntered up to the window that Quade had rolled down.

"So you finally admitted it, did you?" There was an annoying grin a mile wide across Angelo's face.

"Just fucking shut up. I don't want to hear it."

"Oh, we heard it all, mate. I'm about to start a pool as to when. I reckon we should get some interesting odds."

"The woman drives me out of my fucking mind," Quade fumed.

"That may be so but she sure is a hottie and scary smart to boot."

"All of that and the most annoying woman I've ever met."

"Well, speaking of annoying women, here she comes now with a friend in tow."

Quade glanced up at the rearview mirror and saw Jazz walk the guy towards them. She was smiling and flirting with him. Seeing her cosying up to this guy made him wild with rage. The animal inside him wanted to rip the guy apart for going near her. The human side of him was pissed that he even felt this way.

Talk about being conflicted.

They walked towards Rory and Brayden. Angelo dropped in silently behind, a few paces back. As they passed Rory, he reached out and caught the guy between the neck and shoulder and squeezed a certain point. And right on cue, the front door guard was no longer a problem. Angelo caught his large body before he even crumpled to the ground and hefted him over his shoulder to quietly settle him in the shade behind a bank of shrubs.

Jazz walked back to the SUV and hopped in.

"See, I returned and not a hair out of place. Really, I don't know what you were so worried about," she jabbed at him.

"You got lucky. You're not trained for this sort of thing," he muttered.

"Well, who's to blame for that? I thought you were responsible for my training?"

"I am, but how much do you really think you can learn in just a few weeks?" His defences kicked into place at her questioning of his work ethic.

"You'd be surprised. I was always a dean's list student." She smiled sweetly. And his blood almost boiled. "So what do we do now?"

"We wait while they go in and get Pixie."

Jazz turned and pinned him with those emerald green eyes of hers.

"Well, what are we going to talk about?"

Fuck talking. A few more interesting things sprang to mind.

"Angelo, you take the lifts. We'll take the stairs. They won't have seen you anywhere before. They may notice Brayden and they certainly know me."

Angelo headed to the lifts, and Rory and Brayden slipped into the stairwell and started leaping up the stairs, taking them three at a time.

Rory opened the door a crack to the top floor and noticed Angelo standing there with a puzzled look on his face. The first thing he noticed was Pixie's perfume. He could smell her scent and Kelvin's, too.

"What's up?" Brayden asked as they slipped through.

"No guard on the door."

Rory's stomach dropped. They'd been had. He sniffed the air again. She'd been through here recently and he'd bet it was to move her somewhere else. The guard posted out front was nothing more than window dressing.

Frustration won out and he splintered the door to the apartment with a punishing front kick. He needed to be sure but he was almost positive she was no longer here.

A quick survey of the apartment told him he was correct. His eyes cut to the bedroom where she'd been held. The bed was crumpled and her scent was strongest here.

Relief flooded his system; there was no scent of sex in the room.

He turned and strode from the apartment, frustration rode his being.

Now what?

He placed a call to the boss.

"Tom Anderson," the boss answered on the first ring.

"They've moved her, Boss. What do you reckon?" He quickly explained what they'd found.

"Head back to the office. I've got a feeling we're going to get a call real soon. We'll meet you there in about forty minutes. I'll try reaching Dylan and see if he's got anything further for us."

"Roger that."

Rory slammed his palm into the dash. He just wanted her back. God help him, when that happened, he was never going to let her out of his sight again.

TJ woke up in yet another bedroom. Her head thumped as if there were a marching band practising in there. Never had she had such a headache. She gingerly reached up and placed her hand behind her head and immediately winced at the pain. Gently she moved her fingers over the back of her skull and she felt the massive egg.

Then she remembered—she'd almost been free. TJ tried to open her eyes again. The pain was intense—blinding, even.

"Are you awake, TJ?"

She opened her eyes again and turned her body towards the voice.

Katie? Was it Katie she heard?

Where was she?

"Is that you, Katie?" TJ finally managed to string together.

"Yeah, it's me."

"Where are we?" The agony seemed to get worse when she spoke or thought.

"I think we're somewhere in the country. I could hear cows mooing. And every now and then it really smells when the wind comes through the window."

"How long have you been here?" she croaked out.

"Since this morning. Those men out there grabbed me at the hospital." Before Katie spoke another word, she launched herself at TJ lying on the bed. Her smaller body crashed into TJ. TJ felt her stomach roll with nausea from the pain.

"I'm scared, TJ."

"I know, honey—it's going to be fine." Somehow TJ managed to sound reassuring. What she wouldn't give for some painkillers. TJ absently stroked her sister's hair and shoulders.

"Katie, can you tell me who's here?"

"Umm, Kelvin brought you in here, but I don't know any of these other men. Why are they doing this to us?" Katie asked in a small voice.

"I don't really know, sweetie. But I do know Uncle Max and Kelvin are not very nice and they're trying to hurt us because they want Walsh Haulage. They're also upset at me because I married Rory instead of Kelvin."

"Rory is much nicer than Kelvin and besides that, he's just plain yummy."

"Katie Walsh, I can't believe you said that. Not the part about Rory being nicer than Kelvin—that's a given. But you're not supposed to know about yummy men."

"TJ, I'm nearly thirteen, not five. I know what a hot guy looks like and you're married to one of the hottest I've ever seen."

"Ah, Katie, I'm not really sure I'm comfortable with you thinking about Rory like that. Remember he's your brother-in-law." She tried to gently chastise without crushing Katie.

"Oh, I don't mean anything by it, TJ. I just think you're so lucky to have him."

"I do, too. And I'll think we're even luckier when he comes to get us."

"Is he really coming to get us?" Katie asked, her voice full of hope.

"He is, sweetheart. I know he's trying to get to us." Her voice sounded confident and she knew he would be coming for her. It couldn't be soon enough. She just wanted to be back in his arms.

Katie went to say something else.

"Shhhh, I hear something," TJ urged.

They both lay there, silent, for a few seconds.

"It's Uncle Max and Kelvin out there," Katie whispered.

"It is. I can't tell what they're saying, though."

"Me either."

A couple of seconds later, the door sprung open and TJ's mind travelled back in time to a night six years ago. The pose and the mood of Max at the door almost seemed identical.

What had she ever done to displease this man so much?

"Get up. We need to have a little chat," Max demanded.

TJ's stomach turned and she fought back nausea. Maybe she had a concussion as well as being terrified.

Katie moved from the bed and headed to the door.

"Why are you being so mean to us, Uncle Max? I thought you loved us?" The pain in her voice nearly broke TJ's heart.

"I'm not being mean to you, Katie. I'm setting things straight and you women need to understand your proper place and role. Now get out to the lounge room. I'm not standing in here having this discussion."

TJ tried to move and she felt her stomach roll again.

"I'm going to throw up." She smashed her hand to her mouth and forced it back down.

"Get me a bucket," Max yelled.

A few seconds later, he thrust a bucket in her face and she emptied the contents of her stomach into it.

"Uncle Max, I don't think I can make it out there," she groaned.

He took the bucket from her and dragged her from the bed. Her whole body ached and her head felt as if it were about to split open. Max dragged her through the door of the bedroom and across the hall to the bathroom, where he dumped her.

"Get yourself together and cleaned up," he snapped before turning on his heel and marching off.

Slowly TJ managed to pull herself upright, using the counter for support. She splashed some water on her face and rinsed her mouth out. Finally her brain cleared enough for her to realise she was standing in front of a bathroom medicine cabinet.

Could she be lucky enough?

Gingerly, she opened the cabinet, trying not to be too hopeful. She reached up and moved a couple boxes and bottles aside. Just when she was about to give up the search, she spotted what she'd hoped for. A bottle of ibuprofen tablets.

She cautiously unscrewed the cap and shook out two and then thought about it briefly before shaking out another two. Right now she didn't care; she just wanted the pain to stop.

TJ quickly swallowed the pills with a little water she cupped in her hand. She replaced the bottle in the cupboard and wiped her hands on the towel folded on the counter.

Fear, nausea, and pain gripped at her. All she wanted was Rory. Tears pricked her eyes but she sucked them back and looked away—she had to be strong for Katie.

Slowly she made her way from the bathroom and out into what must be the lounge room. Max and Kelvin were seated at the dining room table of the combined lounge/dining room. Two other large men were standing over by the door. They looked familiar but TJ was struggling to place them just at the moment. Instinct told her they were employees of Q-Trans.

But it was Katie who really tugged at her heartstrings. She was sitting on the lounge, her hands clasped together in her lap, looking totally lost.

TJ could just imagine what was going through her head. She'd lost both her parents and now her uncle and cousin were behaving like this. What twelve-year-old girl needed this in her life?

TJ hobbled over and sat next to Katie. She took one of her hands and clasped it in hers, trying to instil a sense in Katie that she was not alone.

Please hurry, Rory! she silently prayed in her mind.

The minutes passed, the pain continued, and she felt as if she'd descended into some sick hell.

"Mike, get the ladies a drink. Where are your manners, man?" Max barked and one of the guys by the door immediately moved to the kitchen.

Max briefly looked at them before returning his eyes to the papers he was reading. TJ had no idea what he was thinking. Outwardly, she recognised the man sitting at the table but he was a monster in every other way.

Mike silently handed them each a glass of juice and moved to stand at the door.

TJ watched Max glance at his watch and then pick up his phone and dial a number. A few moments later, a smug grin emerged from his face and he said, "It's time to talk a little business, Tom."

Chapter Thirty-Two

The Centre team were back again in the Situation Room. Fingers flew over keyboards and the normal friendly conversation and teasing banter was absent—silence, brooding, and reflection in its place. Tom missed their normal team atmosphere but this was temporary. They were dealing with a crisis.

Everyone in the room felt Rory's pain. Rory was the barometer of the team in many ways. He was the light where there was darkness. The logic when there was confusion. But this was different. Today he was fighting his own beasts, his guts being torn apart by what was playing out with Teresa and Katie.

Tom's phone buzzed in his pocket. He reached for it and briefly glanced at the number. One he didn't know. His gut told him it was the call they were waiting for before he even pressed the connect button.

"Tom Anderson." He watched every head in the room turn to focus on him.

"It's time to talk a little business, Tom."

"With whom am I speaking?" he asked, already knowing the answer to the question.

The returning answer was a self-serving chuckle. "Oh, Tom…I'm disappointed. I thought you would have at least expected my call, given that I have something of yours. Oh, actually it's two somethings of yours that I'm assuming our young friend Rory wants back."

"Cut the crap, Max—we're both too old for schoolyard bullshit and you're now facing abduction charges among a myriad of other things. Wise up," Tom barked back.

Max chuckled again and Tom felt his anger rise.

Yeah, this fucker was going down.

"Oh, Tom, you have to catch me first and so far you haven't proved very proficient at that."

"This game you're playing ends today, Max. I'm done. We're done."

"Well, you see, that's the great thing. I haven't exactly decided yet how it's all going to end," Max said, chuckling again.

Tiring of playing this twisted, fucked-up game, Tom asked again, "So what is it you think you want?"

"I want you, Tom."

Tom flinched, a little surprised at that.

"Why do you want me?"

"That wounds me, Tom, to think that you've forgotten our past. You of all people I would have thought would remember our last meeting."

What the fuck was he talking about? The question raced through his mind and, as he looked around the table, the minds of all his operators. They were all eavesdropping because they could.

Max was stark raving mad if he thought they'd met before. Tom never forgot a face or a meeting, particularly if it involved an asshole like Max.

"I'm sorry, Max, it escapes me. Are you sure you've got the right person?"

"You forget? I watched you bleed. I watched those eerie, ice blue eyes of yours close and you forget?" The rage in Max's voice was now teetering again. "Don't push me, Tom. You don't get that privilege. This time, I'm in charge."

He was dealing with someone who was mentally unstable; negotiating wasn't going to be an option. They needed to get in and get the girls out.

"Okay, Max, you're in charge. Where do you want me?"

"Oh, Tom, it's not just you I want. I want Rory as well. The both of you are going to come to me, and we'll have a discussion about how things are going to be."

"Okay, we can do that. When suits you?" It pained him but Tom softened his usual commanding tone. He didn't want to risk infuriating Max any further when he was obviously mentally unstable.

"Tonight. Nine o'clock. The western carpark at the Nerang Mall Shopping Centre. My men will be waiting for you. You two come alone or they both die. I'm done with this interference, Tom, in my business and my family. You and Rory need to understand that."

"Like you said, Max, I'm sure a discussion will clear things up for us."

"Don't be late."

"Never."

"I've heard that before, Tom."

The call ended.

Tom looked round the room again. None of them spoke, but all eyes held questions.

"Oh, this just sucks and is hardly fair. You've all heard every word but Rihanna and I are left guessing. What's the go, Tom?" Jazz huffed.

"Max wants Rory and me to meet him tonight at nine o'clock at the Nerang Mall Shopping Centre carpark. He also seems to think we have met before, somehow," he confirmed for her.

"Do you know him, Boss?" Brayden asked.

"No, I don't know him."

"Well then, what's he on about?" Jazz questioned.

Tom sat and thought for a second. He'd never disclosed much about his life. It wasn't his style. But in this case, it didn't look as if he had much of an option but to disclose a bit about his past.

"I think he's confusing me with my twin brother. I had an identical twin. He died almost thirty years ago."

The atmosphere in the room had become incredibly tense. You could have heard a pin drop and all the operators would, in fact, have heard it. They were all waiting for him to go on.

"He led a black ops team. They got into some trouble and my brother was shot multiple times. None of the reports really confirmed or denied what happened." That was the easy part of the conversation. The next part would be more difficult. "Back then, there was a lot of highly secretive experimentation going on with genetics, cloning, and a whole range of things. It was kept highly classified. John, my brother, had signed a release, giving the military the right to use his body for experimentation if he ever sustained the level of injuries he did in combat."

Tom looked around the room. They were all captivated by the story. Somehow they knew that John's story was connected to theirs.

"He was almost dead when he arrived at the field hospital. From there, he was transferred to a secret facility and treated. The doctors tried something radical and highly experimental. They infused a number of fast, regenerating animal genes into him, the thinking being that this would enhance and create a more rapid recovery. The scientists were also keen to understand if animal material could be infused into humans after conception. John made a full recovery and yes, it was significantly faster than normal. He was put back out in the field in an individual black ops role. About two years later, he was killed on an assignment under questionable circumstances."

Several gasps around the table revealed their surprise.

"I'm guessing Max was there the night John was wounded. He obviously doesn't know that John was an identical twin. John wasn't the friendly sort and would have kept his own counsel, so I'm not surprised Max didn't know he was a twin," Tom completed the pieces of the puzzle for them.

"Wow, Boss, that's some story," Brayden said, shaking his head.

"Are there more people out there that have had their DNA altered after conception?" Rheeba spoke up from behind her bank of computers.

"I honestly can't say. I do know that the process worked at least once. And I also know that the government wouldn't be keen to let this become anything other than top-secret information."

All his people were mulling it over in their minds and considering the consequences and the outcomes.

"Tom, you may be able to use Max's confusion to your advantage, you know," Jazz suggested.

He looked over at Jazz and could see the wheels spinning in her mind. She was a dynamo even without genetic enhancements.

"What are you getting at, Miss Carter?" His voice gave nothing away.

"Well, if he thinks you're in fact your brother John, you may be able to play on that fact. It could rattle him. He's going to have to wonder about whatever happened that day and how you've come to be."

"Not a bad idea. Rheeba, have you finally got Max's military documentation out of those archives?" Tom almost barked.

"Yeah, it's just come through in the last few minutes. I've been riding those guys all day. Apparently they had to find the hard copies in archive then scan it...and you don't care about the rest. Yes, I've got it and for the rest of the black ops team as well," Rheeba explained.

"Great, flick it over to me."

"It's on the printer now."

Tom looked at his watch. It was seventeen hundred hours.

"Okay, people, we need to work through some scenarios and some planning. Let's run the options," Tom demanded of them.

They all sat up straighter. There was a huge amount of planning and preparation to do. The next four hours were not only going to be frantic, they were also going to be crucial.

Mike had brought them a bowl of soup each a couple of hours ago. TJ's head still throbbed and the nausea was still there. Katie was very quiet and seemed shell shocked, for want of a better word.

They'd heard the one-sided conversation between Max and Tom. TJ had watched the play of emotions across Max's face during that call and she was convinced he was no longer fully sane.

The reality was she had no idea the depths he was capable of and it terrified her. She knew Rory and Tom were coming. TJ also knew that Max would have something planned to create the maximum amount of emotional trauma for Rory and Tom, and no doubt Katie and she would play the pivotal role in that.

She just wanted it over. The thought of being able to fall asleep in Rory's arms and wake up with him still curled around her was her goal. That's what they'd diminished her to—the need to survive however she could. Getting out of here with their lives was the priority.

They were still sitting on the lounge where Max had demanded earlier. Mike walked over with a shopping bag.

"Max wants you and the girl in this stuff." He tossed the bag into her lap.

TJ looked inside and inwardly groaned. There was a flimsy-looking teddy, nightdress thingy that would barely cover her butt in white satin, lace, and gauze. It was something she'd never wear in a million years.

She knew without trying it on that it would leave her nipples visible through the gauzy fabric. In addition to the slutty number that was for her, there was a long, loose white cotton nightdress with three-quarter sleeves and a small pink bow at the throat.

The visual impression these garments were designed to have didn't evade her throbbing head. Max and Kelvin wanted her portrayed as the harlot. The slut who gave up her innocence to the wrong man and then failed to marry the "right" one when the opportunity arose. And poor Katie was to play the epitome of innocence, a young girl yet to reach womanhood and untouched by her impending sexuality.

The depravity of their minds stunned TJ. *Had they always been this sick?*

TJ finally looked up. Mike was still standing there with a wolfish grin on his face.

"Can't wait to see you in that little number, babe."

"You may see it, but you'll never touch it," she fumed back, unsure where the words had even come from.

He laughed in her face.

"Don't make promises you can't keep, TJ. Kelvin's always been generous with his women and I've had a hard-on for you for the last two years. I'm looking forward to enjoying my rewards." His voice was just above a whisper, no doubt to avoid Kelvin or Max hearing. The lecherous grin made TJ's stomach turn for real this time and she felt the bile and the contents of her last meal rise up in her throat.

Somehow she clamped her hand over her mouth and pushed from the lounge and staggered to the bathroom, barely managing to make the porcelain bowl of the toilet. As soon as she'd emptied the contents of her stomach for the second time today, she crumpled to the cold tile floor.

The coolness felt good under her cheek. And she didn't want to move.

A few seconds later, Katie appeared in the bathroom, with Mike trailing. He pushed her towards TJ.

"Get in there and get cleaned the fuck up, the pair of you. We don't want to be fucking bitches who smell like vomit," he growled at them and shut the door.

TJ watched Katie's eyes explode to the size of saucers, clearly terrified at what Mike had said. His words really sunk home with her that they were indeed in very deep shit.

"What's going to happen to us, TJ?" Katie sobbed in a very small voice.

"We're going to be fine and we're going to get out of here very soon." She tried to sound confident. It was all she had to give her sister. "Don't worry—it's me they're upset with, not you. Rory's going to be here soon—he won't let anything happen to us."

"Do you really think so?" Katie asked, almost pleaded, through her tears.

"I know so, but you need to play it really cool. Do you think you can do that? Don't give anything away?" TJ reassured her.

Katie nodded her head.

"Good girl. Rory will come for us but we need to be smart as well. Whatever happens tonight, whatever you see or hear, I don't want you to think about it. It probably won't be true. I want you to think of a really happy place and I want you to go there in your head. Can you do that for me?" TJ wanted to prepare her. She had a fair idea what it would be like later and she didn't want it to scar her young mind, if at all possible.

She pulled her sister into a hug. TJ sucked every bit of strength she could from the connection she had with her sister. She had to be tough; she could do this for Katie. There was no way she was going to let them screw with Katie while she drew breath.

"I love you, honey. Never forget it."

"I love you, too, TJ." Katie squeezed her tighter.

"I know—we'll be fine," she said confidently.

Katie nodded.

"Come on, we need to get cleaned up a bit. Just think of this like dressing up. It's just like doing a play. We're acting a part. You're going to be a good girl and I'm going to be a bit naughty. I want them to focus on me, Katie. You do everything you can to make them ignore you. Think invisible."

Katie nodded again.

TJ knew regardless of how terrible she felt today, tonight she had to give the performance of her life. Both her life and Katie's would likely depend on it and for the first time in a long time, TJ had something that she wanted to live for. She wanted her chance at a bright and colourful life with Rory and by God, she was prepared to fight for it—Max and Kelvin be damned to hell.

A couple of hours after the call from Max, Rory was prowling around the corridors. The wait was killing him. Thinking about Pixie and Katie being in the hands of those mongrels was driving him to distraction. He couldn't remember ever feeling this agitated.

Dylan had sent a text in earlier, giving them an update that Pixie was there and that all seemed to be reasonably quiet in the house. There was apparently some action over in the barn. He was trying to find out exactly what they were up to.

Jazz passed him in the corridor and concern registered across her expressive face. She paused and put a hand on his arm.

"Come and have a cuppa with me, will you?" she asked him, making it sound more as if she needed the help but he knew this was her way.

Maybe having a chat to Jazz would help. *What did he have to lose, anyway?*

"Sure." He turned and followed her to the kitchen.

She made them both a coffee and then she nodded for him to follow her out on to the balcony. The fresh air felt good on his face. The lights of the buildings around the area reflected onto the surface of the river in front of them. Ordinarily it would be pretty, romantic even with the right person; tonight it felt empty.

Jazz took a chair and Rory followed her lead and took the one opposite, a small table between them.

"Talk to me," she stated flatly.

"What do you mean?" he asked, a bit taken a back.

"I mean exactly that. Talk to me—I'm not going to do the shrink thing. I just want you to talk to me about anything you want to. I want to hear your voice."

He shrugged and shifted in his chair.

"I really need to burn some of this energy off. I feel as if I'm about to explode. All these animals want to get out and rip the hell out of those fuckers." His voice was harsh and tense.

"Yeah, I can only imagine what it feels like. I'd love to understand more about it. Can you recognise the individual animals inside you or are they more like a chorus?"

Rory almost chuckled despite his inner turmoil. Jazz was back in her notorious puzzle-solving mode.

"A chorus is a really good way to describe them. Most of the time they do sing in harmony but sometimes they argue and fight. Tonight they're all in agreement. They want Max and Kelvin dead. Only their deaths will satisfy the fire that's raging among them."

She nodded her head. "That must be really conflicting—

having your human side telling you not to kill and the more primal animals demanding it. Is that how you do it?"

"Do what?" he asked, a little confused and much more abruptly than normal.

"I heard you once refer to yourself as a cold-blooded killer and I know you took that shot at the stables a few months back. I was just wondering how you deal? You always seem so relaxed, logical, insightful even, but totally in control. I worked with a lot of soldiers while I was training and very few have the composure you do. Many get eaten away by what they have to do. How do you reconcile it?" She took a sip of her coffee and waited.

He thought about it for a moment. *How did he reconcile it?*

"I have to make a call—a judgement call, if you like. In a way, I have to play judge, jury, and executioner. In a split second, I have to decide who deserves to live more and who is the better person. Sometimes I get longer to decide but the decision always seems to come just as quick. I've killed a handful of times, Jazz, in the course of carrying out my duties for the Centre and never once have I felt remorse or guilt. Doesn't that make me a cold-blooded killer?" His eyes sought hers across the table. He needed to see how she felt about him now that she knew what he was really capable of.

"Have you ever killed when it wasn't justified?" she asked, letting him connect to her eyes.

"I don't believe I have," he answered immediately and her gaze didn't waver.

"Then there you go. You were doing your duty. It's not like you randomly went out and decided to pick someone to kill. From what you're telling me, all these people had a lot to be accountable for."

He nodded his head.

"Then there's your answer. You're not a cold-blooded killer—you're an operator carrying out your duties. I've had the misfortune of working with a few of what I would call cold-blooded killers and do you know what I think the difference is?"

That had him interested. Jazz was just full of surprises. He shook his head, indicating he didn't.

"Cold-blooded killers enjoy killing. You don't. You can do it but you don't get any emotional gratification out of it. It's just another facet of your job. Something that you might have to do from time to time. All it means is that you can do it when called upon."

What she said made sense.

How did that always seem to happen?

Someone who could seem to be so flighty could also be so astute.

Something had been nagging at him for a while.

"What if I get it wrong? What if I make the wrong call?"

She surprised him then and let out that light musical laugh.

"Well, there you go again. That is not the thought process of a cold-blooded killer. Whether you know it or not, subconsciously you're weighing your decisions very heavily before you decide. You've wondered about whether you'll make the right decisions. Sure, maybe you'll get it wrong—nobody can be perfect all the time. But you'll only know that at some time in the future. Not at the time the decision needs to be made. So I'm confident even if you feel confused, your moral compass will lead you true. As they say—whoever *they* are—go with your gut."

Rory took a long pull from his coffee.

"You're very confident in my moral compass, Jazz."

She nodded vigorously. "I am."

Jazz chugged back the rest of her coffee and he did the same.

"If anything happens to them tonight, Jazz, I don't know what I'll do. She's come to mean everything to me in such a short period of time. I worry constantly that I'm not good for her. If I hadn't gone and fucked with Kelvin, this wouldn't have happened. It's my fault they're both in danger."

"You don't know that, Rory. Kelvin and Max are not right upstairs. I doubt anything would have swayed them from their path."

The emotions he felt were bubbling higher and higher, drowning him. The need to move, the need to hurt was overwhelming. He stood and smashed his fist into the brickwork of the building. The pain in his hand and arm momentarily distracted him from the pain in his heart. He could lose her tonight and it would all be his fault.

The universe could not be that cruel to him, surely.

"Thanks for the pep talk, Jazz, but I'm still to blame." The edge in his voice had not diminished. He was being an asshole and he knew it but couldn't seem to do anything about it.

"You don't need me to tell you this, Rory, but smashing your hand against a wall is not going to help. I know you're hurting but you need to keep it together for Teresa. She needs you to be in control. To take charge and get her and Katie out of there safely. Her life depends on you making the right decisions. And you will—never doubt that or the fact that people only have respect for you."

He leant against the wall and wriggled his leg. He wanted to run and fight and brawl. He wanted her back. Logically, he knew Jazz was right but logic wasn't anywhere near as strong as the pain he felt right now.

He looked down at his watch. *Shit, he needed to go.*

"You need to go?"

"Yeah, I do."

"Just remember, Rory. Tonight, you'll make the right decision—you always do. Trust your judgement. Trust yourself. Pixie is counting on you to get it right. I know you won't let her down."

He wrapped his arms around her and gave her a quick hug.

"Thanks, Jazz. You're the best. Even if I seem like an ungrateful bastard tonight."

"Oh, I know. I know. And for Christ's sake, look after yourself," she called to his retreating frame.

He went back inside and headed to the Situation Room.

The worry about Pixie and Katie had never dissipated but at least his mind felt a little clearer. His knuckles were still smarting and he enjoyed the feel of focusing on some other pain. He did feel more focused, more in control, but still half out of his mind with worry.

Now the hardest part. The waiting.

Jazz passed Tom in the hall. He had his ever-present file under his arm and a stern look on his face.

She nodded at him as she passed.

"Miss Carter, can I have a word in my office, please?"

"Certainly." She stopped and followed along.

Tom held the door open for her and motioned with his head to take a seat. He moved around the big oak desk.

"How is he?"

She looked around the room, wondering how much to say. She knew they could all hear her if they chose to listen.

"You can speak frankly. This room is soundproofed."

"He's holding up well, considering, but I'm a bit surprised at how hard he is on himself."

"What do you mean?"

"He seems to think that because he's killed in the line of duty and has not felt remorse or guilt that somehow he's a cold-blooded killer. His words—not mine."

"And what do you think?"

"He's so far from that it's not funny. He's one of the most level-headed and rational people I think I've ever met. Maybe even too much that way. That's why he struggles to let himself just be. He's also feeling that he's responsible for Max and Kelvin abducting the girls. Hopefully I cleared that up for him, but in his current emotional state, I can't tell yet."

Tom nodded.

"So he'll be okay tonight?"

"I think so. Look, I can't predict what sort of show Max is going to put on but I think we all know it's going to be designed to inflict the optimum amount of emotional pain for them all. That's what he needs to feel better. I've spoken to Rory about keeping it together for Teresa, and I believe he will. I think there's a good chance neither Kelvin nor Max will see the morning, but if that's the way it has to be, then so be it."

Tom had remained silent while she spoke. His intelligent eyes had been fixed on her the whole time. It really felt as if he could hold you still with just his eyes.

"I'm going to need you out in the field tonight, Jazz. I'm not sure what state the women will be in when we get them nor am I sure exactly what's going to go down. I think you need to be prepared for some urgent evacuations to medical facilities."

"Yeah, I figured as much. I've already made the calls according to the field protocols I set up a couple of weeks back. I'll phone in the location of the farm now but tell them to be on standby to move if we need them to."

"I'd bank on it being at that farm. For some reason, that place means a lot to Max. Maybe tonight we'll find out exactly why." Tom trailed off.

"Something bothering you, Tom?" Jazz didn't miss the faraway look on Tom's face. This was very unusual for him.

"Oh, just trying to put all the pieces together about my brother is all."

"Max was involved in the shooting that night, wasn't he?"

Tom's head snapped up and he looked almost shocked.

"What makes you say that?"

"Just your mannerisms. I'd lay a solid bet that whatever Rheeba dug up on Max is in those files and that it somehow implicates Max."

A smirk slowly slid across Tom's handsome face.

"I didn't employ you to analyse me, Miss Carter."

"Who said anything about analysing, Tom? I'm just vocalising my observations," she smirked back at him.

"And Quade—you've been working with him for a few weeks now. Are you confident he's right to go into a situation like this?"

"Quade's fine. His problem isn't conflict or carrying out his job. It's more to do with dealing with rather a personal matter of control," Jazz trailed off evasively.

"You mean the fact that he's sniffing around your skirt?" Tom said bluntly.

Jazz shifted in her chair a little uncomfortably, but trying not to seem so.

"Yes, that would sum it up."

Tom laughed.

"So what are you going to do about that?"

"I'm sorry—I don't understand what you mean." Jazz responded as if she didn't have a clue what Tom was talking about.

"I mean is it mutual? Am I going to have yet another couple on my hands around here?"

"I'm not sure that would be professional," Jazz said, trying to avoid answering the question altogether.

"Professional in the sense of relationships seems to have taken on a new meaning around here of late. Why would you and Quade be any different?" Tom pinned her with another of his holding stares.

"There is no Quade and I," Jazz refuted, eyes blazing directly back at him.

"Just be sure the integrity of the missions is not affected— nor individual performance. I can't say I like it but I guess I'm learning to live with it."

Jazz nodded once, deciding it was better to leave any further discussion on the topic alone for the moment. She quickly carried on.

"Getting back to tonight's mission—are you all set? I've seen all the medical files on the team. So I know everything there I need to watch out for. But I've not seen anything on you. You're going into the field. Is there anything I should know about?" She looked him directly in the eye and he returned her stare.

"No, there's not."

She shrugged. "If you say so. No heart problems or anything like that?"

"I thought it was a prerequisite to have a heart in order to have issues. I've been frequently told I'm a heartless bastard."

"Then they don't know you too well, do they?"

Tom chuckled.

"Let's just keep it as our little secret, Miss Carter." He winked at her.

"I took the oath, Tom. Doctor-patient confidentiality and all that."

"I said before, I'm not your concern."

"Great, then don't get shot or anything like that. Then you definitely won't be my concern. You get wounded, I'll patch you up. It's all up to you, Tom. As I said—don't get wounded."

"Now I fully get why my team can't win an argument with you. That will be all, Miss Carter."

She smiled sweetly and rose. "As you wish, Tom."

As she walked from the office, Jazz would have sworn she heard Tom say, *Quade's doomed—that is far too much of a woman for that boy to handle.*

Chapter Thirty-Three

"Are you ready?" the boss asked Rory as they neared the Nerang meet.

"Yes. I want my family back," Rory stated, not checking the determination and anger in his voice. The knuckles of his hands on the wheel were starting to turn white.

"Okay, I get that, but I need you to keep it together. The girls need you to do the same."

"I got it, Boss. I can do this but don't ask me to go easy on those fuckers."

"I'm not, Rory, but you need to be in control. The greatest asset you have is your animal DNA. You need to keep that concealed. There will come a time tonight when we'll need it."

"Figured as much, Boss."

"Just as long as we're clear, Mr Southall."

"We're clear."

Rory pulled off the highway and made a couple of turns. A second later, he noticed two vehicles in the carpark.

That was their pick-up.

He pulled up about twenty metres from the other vehicles.

"You ready, Boss?"

"Everyone in place?" he asked of the call he'd placed on speakerphone.

"Roger, Boss," Rheeba confirmed for them over the call.

"Do it right, people." The boss pushed the End button.

"Let's go." The boss opened his door and Rory followed.

As they approached the vehicles, the doors opened and the guys from the café got out.

"Max has asked us to escort you to him."

They nodded.

"If you wouldn't mind putting your hands out—we need to cuff you. I'm sure you understand how these things work."

Both Rory and the boss held out their hands, and they were quickly fitted with flexicuffs. *Perfect. They'd be easy for him to break when the time came.*

"This way, gentlemen."

They were each patted down and searched for weapons and phones before being individually escorted into the back seat of one of the SUVs.

A few seconds later, they were heading towards the hinterland. It was a good sign, and somewhat of a relief. It seemed they were going to the farm Rory had been on earlier in the day. Dylan had let them know that Pixie was there, but there was always the possibility they might try to move them at the very last minute.

Selena had stitched tiny GPS granules into both of their clothes just in case. Rheeba was tracking them and relaying their route to the team. Aaron and Angelo were waiting for word from Rheeba to move into position and join Dylan at the dairy. Jazz, Quade, and Brayden were floating, waiting for further instructions.

The minutes ticked by and as they headed towards the dairy farm, Rory relaxed slightly. It was time to have some fun and see whether he could find anything useful.

"So, guys, any clues about what Max is planning tonight?" he asked the two guys in front casually.

"We wouldn't want to ruin the surprise," the big guy in the passenger seat replied.

"Oh come on, fellas, you're no fun. But I do love surprises. What's Max and old mate Kelvin up to?"

"Come on, mate, you know we can't tell you but let's just say we're all going to get an eyeful of that little honey."

Rory's blood turned to raging fire and his temper flared to just short of a nuclear reactor on a code red warning. But he knew he had to keep it together. Had to play the game. Anything he found out now could help.

"She sure is something," he agreed with enough edge in his voice to make it believable. The desire to break the cuffs now and choke each asshole to death was dancing front and centre in his mind.

"Well, you should know—she's your wife."

"That she is," he said aloud and to himself. *And for that, you'll pay dearly, fuckers.*

"So how did you manage to snag her? She might as well have had 'Property of Kelvin' stamped across her forehead," the guy driving asked.

"That, gentlemen, will be my secret," Rory responded nonchalantly. "So what's Max want with the young girl?"

The big guy shrugged. "Not much. I think he had us grab her just to make sure we didn't have any other problems. She's a sweet kid and going to be a looker, just like her sister, in a few years."

Rory hoped to God they didn't get any ideas about violating a twelve-year-old girl. That would be enough to send him totally over the edge. He hoped the team were close by; he wanted this thing over quick.

A few minutes later, they pulled into the long gravel driveway.

"Hey, mate, would you mind rolling down the window? I love the smell of the country," he asked.

The window silently retracted and Rory started sniffing the air subtly. As they moved closer to the lights of the buildings, he finally scented what he wanted. Dylan, Aaron, and Angelo—they were out there. He felt better. His brothers were close by.

The two SUVs pulled up just outside the large barn. The men got them out and started to march them to the door. He could hear another vehicle on the driveway. It was too faint for the totally human ear but he had no problem hearing it. He knew it was Quade and he'd be travelling without lights.

The boss looked at him, and he slightly tilted his head and slowly moved his eyes, indicating the direction he heard the vehicle. He also sniffed and wriggled his nose. The boss nodded ever so slightly.

They were on the same page. The team were in place.

Inside the barn, Max and Kelvin had done a little redecorating. Bales of hay were stacked up the length of the righthand side wall. The middle of the barn had been completely cleared of everything. At the far end of the barn was a high steel fenced area, with a series of doors and gates behind it. This was an area that the cattle could be brought into for the administration of medicine or other sorts of examination and attention. Rory knew from his previous reconnaissance of the property that there were cattle yards adjoining the barn and the dairy shed.

A desk was pushed up against the steel yards and a couple of straight-backed chairs had been set up directly in front of it. Another couple of chairs were off to the side and two more opposite, essentially flanking the central aisle of the barn.

The men who had escorted them here tonight walked them to the chairs on the left side of the aisle and sat them down there.

Rory casually took a look around the barn without making it too obvious. The central roof section of the barn had skylights. The only obvious open door was the one they'd entered through.

The barn was filled with all sorts of stuff. In addition to the hay, there were a few pallets of grain bags and about a dozen drums of what he recognised as molasses by the smell.

The rest of the barn was filled with bits and pieces of farm equipment. Everything from spray units to star pickets and fencing wire—all the sorts of stuff you'd expect to find on a farm. The lighting wasn't great and there were a lot of shadows—particularly along the side walls, as the only lights were the fluros down the centre aisle.

After checking out the barn, he took a cursory glance at the guys who had picked them up. All over six feet and powerfully built. They all carried the frames of bodybuilders rather than fighters and he guessed they were more about intimidation than anything much else. All wore side arms. The general impression he got was that these guys looked a little stiff and slow. He figured they'd find out soon enough.

Rory slightly flexed his wrists to get the feel of how much pressure he'd need to exert to break the flexicuffs. They were stock standard cuffs. He and the rest of his team played with these things for shits and giggles; even the girls had no trouble breaking them.

Quade held the record—he'd managed to break free with six sets around his wrists. Rory had managed five. His biggest worry tonight wasn't busting them open but rather not inadvertently flexing too much and breaking them open too soon.

Now that he'd surveyed his immediate surrounds, Rory focused his attentions farther afield. A herd of cattle was in the dairy next door, but he was more interested in people.

Yeah, he could hear they were just leaving the house. Unfortunately, the breeze was strong tonight and it was blowing the wrong way for him to catch a scent yet. They'd need to get closer for him to really be able to pick up their scents.

They were all walking in silence, but he could hear their footsteps. He counted eight sets. The boss passed a casual glance and Rory wriggled his fingers to catch the boss's attention. Then as casual as he could, he opened his hand and then flexed his thumb.

Yeah, the boss was on the ball; he got it.

Her scent hit him before he could see her. It floated across the moving air and tantalised his nostrils. Others surrounded her scent, but his brain wanted to focus on that smell. It both soothed his beasts but also enraged them further. As beautiful as the scent was, it was tainted with the fear he'd worked so hard to eradicate. That and the fact that Pixie was not by his side, safe, incited the rage in the beasts.

Max led the procession through the door, looking every bit the clichéd bad guy in a B-grade movie. Was it his imagination or did his eyes look just a bit more insane and vacant? Kelvin followed a couple of steps behind. He looked smug and very full of his own unimportance. The contempt Rory felt for both of them was beyond measure.

The thing that really concerned Rory, though, was that both men wore side arms.

Weapons within the reach of lunatics—never a good situation.

Pixie held Katie's hand as they slowly walked behind.

Both were dressed in virginal white. Katie was wearing a long cotton nightdress that was very proper whereas Pixie had been dressed in the epitome of slutty lingerie, a white one-piece nighty thing that rode high on her hips and left her legs bare. He couldn't think of what it was called but needless to say it was designed to tantalise. The satin, lace, and netting left nothing to the imagination.

He could clearly see the outlines of her nipples. Which meant so could every other man in the building and it made him crazy. It was a cool night and they were erect in response to the cold and the fear her body was radiating.

For that alone, they'd die tonight.

Max—or was it Kelvin?—was making a very obvious point.

What was wrong with these fuckers? How did people get this screwed up?

As she moved closer, Rory realised she was missing the cast.

Fuck!

She hadn't been cleared to have weight on that ankle without the brace yet. If this caused permanent damage, he'd have another reason to kill them all over again.

Yet another four clones of the four who were already standing watch flanked the girls. Maybe there was a sale on at "rent-a-thug"?

They were all so forgettable. Just your garden-variety tough guys was what he read. Probably a few low-level skills but he'd bet they were best at intimidation rather than really fighting if it came to that.

Max cast his eyes over them as he moved past. He was carrying a briefcase. He laid it on the desk and took out two document wallets and laid them out neatly.

He could feel and see every openly lecherous stare from the men who had escorted her here directed towards Pixie.

The two men behind Pixie and Katie, both also armed, stepped up and guided them to the vacant chairs on the opposite side of the aisle. He watched Pixie sit and keep her eyes cast downwards. She was scared beyond belief but he knew she felt relief at having him here. He could also tell she was in pain. Her ankle must be giving her hell. His fists clenched automatically in rage and he took a deep breath to release the tension.

Slowly, she lifted her head and gave him a shy smile.

The shadows before had concealed her face. Now he could see the black and blue bruise on her cheek. Someone had given her a hell of a backhander. The rage in his veins boiled just that little bit hotter.

He softened his mouth and tried to project with his eyes what he felt for her. He didn't want to give too much away to this lot. It was taking everything he had not to rip them to pieces now.

Maybe she nodded slightly, maybe he imagined it.

Time to get this show on the road.

Rory sensed the boss had had enough as well.

"Well, Max, you've got our undivided attention. What are we here for?" Even in restraints, the boss's voice lost none of its presence or authority.

Max moved over towards them slowly. His eyes never left the boss's and the boss held his glare every step of the way.

"Good evening, Tom, or is it John?" John was the boss's dead twin brother. The boss smiled ruefully.

"Long time, no see, I guess you could say, Max."

"The last time I saw you, you'd taken multiple rounds and you were bleeding to death. In fact, I swore you drew your last breath before my eyes." The man looked a little rattled. It was easy to see his mind wandered back and forth to that night.

"Well, I guess that makes me a ghost who walks then. You see, I was dead for ten minutes. But not before I saw you turn tail and leave Tony and me for dead. The official report says you lost contact with us. We both know that didn't happen. How does it feel to know you broke the cardinal rule of the teams? Nobody gets left behind." The boss paused, letting his words sink in. "Your actions then set the scene perfectly for the rest of your life, Max. You're the greedy sort who only thinks of yourself. You didn't know the meaning of the words loyalty and honour then—and from what I've seen over the last few weeks—you're no closer to finding it now."

"Shut the fuck up! You were dead." Max paced back and forth in front of the boss.

"Obviously not very dead, because here I sit." The boss let the morbid humour flow through into his tone.

"I said shut the fuck up. This time when I kill you, you'll stay dead," Max taunted.

"Fair enough. Thanks for clearing that up. I always figured it was you who shot me. I'd taken out all the enemy bogies. No wonder you hightailed it out of the army before the investigation was closed. Nothing like being caught shooting your own commanding officer to tarnish your record." The boss had narrowed his eyes and was boring them through Max.

A ripple went around the room. All of Max's men were justifiably concerned. And he could see a few of them where thinking they may not be getting paid enough for this. The boss was providing them with a little more insight into the maniac they worked for.

The boss went on, "But I figure you must have wanted us here for something more. Care to move on? Reminiscing is starting to bore me." The boss twisted and stretched his neck and seemed to be totally bored. Rory had never seen the boss like this. He was acting the part to perfection.

"Oh, we've got a lot to get through tonight before we say our final goodbyes," Max assured him.

Rory heard the audible gasp Pixie let out.

Max walked to her and ran his palm down her damaged cheek.

"Oh, not you, my precious Teresa. Tonight you'll return to your rightful place at Kelvin's side."

Fresh fear twisted the features on her face. Her purple-blue eyes were wild with fear and a fresh wave of rage wash through him.

No man in the barn missed her fear.

Most loved seeing the fear, fed on it.

He deplored men who could behave like this. Who could subject women to this sort of degradation and do nothing other than add to it—it was gang mentality of the lowest form.

How he wished he could burst free right now and take them all down. But he had to be smart. They needed to finish it tonight—all of it. These two would haunt their lives no longer.

TJ looked from Max to Rory to Tom to Max's men. He was insane. Nothing else explained it.

How could he be rational and be behaving like this?

The words he'd just said were still reverberating around her head, which still hurt like the bejeeezus.

Her eyes settled back on Rory. He was sitting there calmly but she knew him well enough now to know that he was seething. His face was blank. That wasn't right. There was normally so much expression and emotion crossing his face. This is the Rory she'd seen the night out on the back verandah when he'd taken down those two guys who had participated in her attack.

She wished she could read his mind. *What was he thinking?*

What did he have planned?

Max spun on his heel and moved back to the desk.

"Well, John, you did ask what else was on the agenda for tonight. I think it's time to move on to the more interesting components." He opened one of the document wallets and withdrew some papers.

"The first document I have here is the share transfers for Walsh Haulage, and the new shareholding agreement I've taken the liberty of having my lawyers draft. Tonight I'm taking back the business that should have been mine," he stated with a smug look on his face.

TJ felt rage rush through her. *How could he do this?*

Everything her father had worked so hard for. Everything she'd worked for over the last couple of years and now he wanted to effectively steal it?

"Uncle Max, why do you even want it? You already own half of Q-Trans and Walsh Haulage is worth nothing compared to your other businesses. Plus, we have a mountain of debt. Why would you want that?" TJ asked, completely mystified about why he'd want the ailing business.

Max propped his butt on the edge of the desk and crossed his arms over his chest.

"I'm glad you asked, Teresa. It's time you knew the truth. Let me tell you a little story about how it was growing up as the younger brother to your father." The spite and hatred in his voice was acidic.

"When I was about Marcus's age, my father pulled me aside and told me that I was nothing but a disappointment to him. I wasn't as smart or as good at sports as your father. You see, all I ever wanted to do was hang out at the yard and work on the trucks or drive them. I didn't want anything else. When your father left school, he immediately joined our father in the business. That's what I wanted, too." TJ could see the jealousy and hurt in his eyes even after all these years.

"But what hurt even more was that your father knew how much I wanted to work with him. We'd always been close. Or at least I thought we were. But no, he didn't want me either. I begged him to help me convince our father and he did nothing. I figured out a few years later that your father was nothing but a greedy, entitled prick." Max's final sentence was said with such venom that she flinched from the impact.

Pain sliced at her heart as Max continued on with his vicious attack on her father and grandfather. *This was not at all how these men were—they were kind and loving.*

"So I was left with nothing. Everything I wanted was stripped from me before I even got started. So with nothing left, I couldn't stand to be around them anymore. They didn't want me—their own flesh and blood. I went off and joined the military. It gave me a wage, some useful skills, and a means of getting out from under their clutches. No way could I have stayed at home and watched my brother live my dream." Max's lips turned up into an ugly sneer as he finished his sentence.

TJ could only imagine how difficult it was to carry all that angst, hate, and animosity around. She also knew she'd never know the full story. Both her father and her grandfather were dead, but she knew emphatically that Max must have some warped version of the truth running around in his head.

"So I joined the military but I made a promise to myself then. One day Walsh Haulage would be mine. I lived in hope for many years after that. Sure, I became wealthy and successful but it was never enough. Never good enough. Your father was always the golden child. I was nothing but chopped liver in the eyes of my father. But I never gave up hope that one day when he passed, he would leave half the business to me, and we could be working together as we should have been.

"That day came, and what did I get? Nothing. Fucking nothing!" Max's yelled words echoed from the walls. "I shouldn't have been surprised—that's what I got my whole life. Nothing. Everything for the golden boy. Not just the trucking business but this very dairy farm we stand on. Everything." Max hung his head for a second.

"I went and spoke to your father about coming in as a partner in some capacity. But again the answer was no. So that's when I decided I would have it all, take it all. Then we'd see who really was the smart one." A slow chuckle slipped from his lips and she watched Kelvin grin in support of his father. "And slowly but surely, I've been putting the foundations in place to do exactly that. Tonight is a culmination of all that. Tonight I take control of what should have been mine from the beginning. Tonight I set things straight."

A horrible feeling of foreboding came over her. She'd always had her suspicions about the accident that killed her father. Now she was almost certain she had the answer.

She couldn't keep quiet about it any longer.

"You did it, didn't you?" she screeched at him.

"What are you talking about, Teresa? What did I do?"

Max looked surprised by her outburst.

"You were behind the accident that killed my father and brother, weren't you?"

Max clapped his hands together a few times in a slow, mocking way.

"Oh, very good, Teresa—you finally figured it out. They had to go. They were foiling my plans. I needed them gone." Max clicked his fingers. "So poof—gone they are. Simple as that."

Her mind raced; she'd also bet that he'd somehow prevented the insurance company paying out.

"Why don't you tell her the rest, Max? Why don't you let her really know why she's been struggling to make ends meet for the last two and a half years—working her ass off seven days a week?" Tom antagonised.

Max chuckled evilly. "Oh that? Well, I needed to make sure the deck was stacked the right way. So I just paid a few people to adjust some findings. Quite simple, really."

It was too much—she wanted to kill him with her bare hands.

He was evil to the core. Yet again she asked herself how family could behave this way. This was preposterous. *This didn't happen—did it?*

"How could you? You left us almost destitute and struggling. I gave up school and worked my butt off these last two and a half years to make ends meet to support my family. And the whole time it was my own family who had put us in the predicament," TJ spat. She didn't recognise the voice that came from her throat. She'd never been so hurt and angry all at once. She was shaking from the rage, fear, and sorrow.

She felt their deaths all over again.

Tears streamed from her eyes.

"Such a shame. You could have stopped the pain at any time, Teresa. All you had to do was marry Kelvin," Max added philosophically.

"When will you get it through your thick skull that I don't love him? In fact, I don't even like him and there is no way I would ever marry him. You won't get away with this. I'll fight you both with every last breath in my body," she screamed at him, letting all her rage erupt.

A look passed between Max and Kelvin and they smiled to each other, before they looked lecherously at Katie. TJ's stomach turned to acid. She read their intent, as if it was the simplest sentence. If she fought, they'd start messing with Katie. There was no end to the depths of evil these two harnessed.

Her eyes flew to Katie, trying to assess how this was impacting her. A soft sound drifted across she hadn't noticed before. TJ then realised her little sister was very quietly humming to herself. Some tune she didn't recognise but if it worked, if it got her through, then that's all that mattered.

"Right, let's get on with it. Here are the documents that will facilitate the share transfer of Walsh Haulage to Kelvin and me. You both will sign them." Max waved his hand between Rory and TJ.

At this point, Rory rose his head a little and drew Max's attention.

"When we had our little chat earlier, Max, I asked you why you wanted Walsh Haulage. You said you had plans for it and you hinted at some sort of expansion. Call me curious, given that my breaths are numbered, but what are you really intending to do with it?"

TJ sucked in a breath. *Why was Rory taunting Max? Why was he admitting he was going to die soon? Surely he didn't believe it, did he?*

Her eyes frantically searched his face looking for a sign— something.

There was nothing, just the blank "warrior mode" stare she'd experienced that night.

She sent a silent prayer to the heavens—she really hoped he knew what he was doing.

Max threw back his head and laughed. The sound sent shivers of terror down her spine. The man was mad.

Totally and utterly insane.

"Oh Rory, if the circumstances were different, I really think I would have enjoyed getting to know you." Max clasped his hands together and rolled his wrists. A very self-satisfied smirk took up residence on his face. "You see, I'm just completing my little supply chain. I've been busy over the last few years."

Max looked to the ceiling and pondered. "Oh, where to start my story? Well, once I was very established in the property development arena, I needed some tax reliefs. One of my financial advisers suggested biotech research. It was just starting to get big about fifteen years ago. I gave it some thought and decided it was exactly the right thing to invest in and use as a deductible for my other ventures.

"I've always resented the fact that I developed dairy intolerance in my twenties. It was genetically passed on from my father; just another burden I've had to carry because of him. I used to love eating cream and drinking milk. So I thought what better area to carry out research? And I get to remove yet another of his shackles from my life. He'd never own me or control me again."

He nodded towards the dairy next door. "It's ironic, don't you think, that some of my earliest research was carried out in secret on this very property? That was yet another reason I was annoyed when your father sold it. I was in the middle of some very important findings and I had to move my whole operation offshore for a bit, until I could set up the company structure to purchase this property and the half dozen surrounding it. Most inconvenient." He shook his head, more to himself, but TJ didn't miss how much this had all contributed to making him the monster he was today.

TJ hazarded a glance over at Rory and Tom. They were both wearing stony-faced glares. Max was going to kill them if he got the chance.

She pushed the thought away—she wasn't going to let that happen.

"Well, early testing was a bit hit-or-miss, to be truthful, and we got some interesting results. And some unfortunate side effects." Max clenched his jaw and pulled his lips back. "Nasty stuff."

"What type of side effects are you talking about, Max?" Tom asked.

"Oh, just your normal birth defects, two-headed cows,

strange shaped tails, that sort of thing. Not that big a deal in the animals but we did have a few issues with people, unfortunately," Max trailed off.

TJ's blood ran ice cold. Her mind raced, putting it all together.

"Oh my God. Mum's cancer. She drank the milk from this dairy for years. Dad used to bring it home in a bucket with a lid because she liked the fresh milk, not the pasteurised and homogenised stuff. You killed her, too. How many others, Max?"

She was living a nightmare.

A nightmare that had all been orchestrated by her uncle.

He shrugged. "Three that I know of. You see, I was quite specific with my sample. I organised it so that the experimental cattle were only used to supply the milk to ten people who I knew." Max shrugged again. "Oh well, I guess they learnt the lesson the hard way—that nothing's free in this world."

Out of nowhere, TJ was almost deafened by the scream of pain beside her ear. *Katie.*

"You killed our mother, too? How could you, Uncle Max? You killed our whole family."

TJ pulled her into a hug and the young girl sobbed on her chest. TJ's tears would come later for her mother. Right now, she was teetering between incredible fear and incredible anger.

"Well, my dear, there is always a price to pay for progress and unfortunately Rosemary paid it. But you'll be pleased to know that her health issues weren't in vain. I managed to get all of her medical records and my people learnt a lot from that."

It was a nightmare. This couldn't possibly be real—could it? The extent of the evil and manipulation this monster had gone to was beyond belief. *Where would it end?*

"So where was I? Oh, yes. The research. Yes, we have been making tremendous progress in the last couple of years. So that's when I decided to start slowly shifting a little product through the processing supply chain. I wanted to test the surveillance before I put the rest of my plan into place, including the purchase of the processing plant." A collective gasp went up from the floor. "I take ownership of that next Monday. And that brings us to your involvement, John and Rory. You've been causing me a little grief, nothing more than an inconvenience really, but one I'd rather not experience any longer now that I'm almost ready to fully realise my plans. That meddling will stop tonight as well."

TJ noticed the look on Tom's face change. "I'm curious, Max—how do you propose to get away with it? Questions will be asked about our deaths. Difficult questions."

"Oh, that's easy. I've got a nice little herd of cattle just next door at the dairy—a rambunctious lot. I even had a couple of Mickey bulls shipped in from north Queensland, perfect for the job, really. They've been running wild since the day they were born, and even tore through a set of steel yards before we got them here. Unfortunately, you and Rory will be doing some sampling and the herd will get spooked and both of you will just happen to get crushed against the cattle rails. Hard to charge a herd of cattle with murder, don't you think?" He chuckled at his own genius. "Brad and Steve, would you mind sending them up?" It wasn't a question but rather a request. Two of the "rent-a-thugs" got up and moved from the barn.

"Well, Max, I'll have to give you an A for theatrics. You've certainly thought this all through." Tom nodded his approval.

"I have, haven't I?" he agreed smugly.

TJ wrapped her arms tighter around Katie, grateful to have something to cling to. They were all in the hands of a madman. She looked across at Rory, silently begging him to look at her. He glanced her way but his face was unreadable.

Come on, Rory—we need a miracle and fast, she silently prayed.

Chapter Thirty-Four

He'd just about had this little pantomime. Surely it must be time to move soon? He cast a sideways glance at the boss, hopeful for some indication it was time to move.

The boss twisted his bound wrists and looked at his watch. A move not lost on Max.

"Well, the night is getting on and I'm sure everyone is eager to wrap this up. I know Kelvin will be keen to take TJ from here. He's waited a long time for what's his."

Rory could contain his anger no longer. He let a long, low growl escape his throat but somehow managed to avoid ripping his hands apart.

"Oh, Rory, I do apologise if that's not to your taste but I promise you won't have to suffer much longer."

Max opened the second document wallet.

"Now for the other little surprise I have in here." Max pulled out the papers. "You see this quickie marriage you two have embarked upon hasn't set well with me. In fact, I'm sure Teresa was married under incredible duress, her mother on her deathbed and all. So I've had my lawyer draw up the necessary annulment papers. All I need is a signature from both of you." The smug look was back. Rory was going to take immense pleasure in wiping it from his face very soon.

"Joe, Marco, please bring Teresa up to the desk. Jason, Phil, if you'd escort John and Rory to the crush, we'll get this all sorted out."

Rory could feel the fear pouring out of Pixie. The two men grabbed her roughly by the shoulders and she struggled against their grasp. He knew he'd find bruises there later.

Just another mark to tally against their names.

Katie was screaming now between sobbing uncontrollably as her sister was pulled from her.

They finally managed to get Pixie seated on one of the chairs at the desk. Phil and Jason frog-marched him and Tom through into the steel yards. If he wasn't moving closer to Pixie, he'd have killed them right now. The boss had better step this up; he was almost at the point of making the call himself.

He took up his position at the fence and looked at her. He tried to portray his love for her through his eyes for a fleeting moment before his eyes bored holes into Max and then Kelvin.

He wanted them to feel his loathing—to taste it.

Max placed the papers in front of Pixie.

First the shares transfer.

She picked up the pen but before she signed her name, she raised her head and looked at him. Those gorgeous purple-blue pools were filled with tears and confusion. She was looking to him for guidance.

He wanted to tell her *no, don't sign*. But the boss was obviously waiting for something. For now, they needed to play along.

Rory nodded once and watched a single glassy tear roll from her eye and drop to the page as she completed her signature.

Max picked up the document and moved it over in front of him.

He could hear the cattle moving up and then there was a loud crash as they moved in just behind the thin corrugated iron sheeting that covered the steel frames of the cattle doors.

Pixie shrieked and he could feel and smell her fear rise even more.

Rory took one last look at the matching smug smiles between father and son before he picked up the pen. Now he understood why they'd bound his hands in front. Awkwardly, he managed to sign his name on the page.

Pixie was openly weeping now, tears coming down her face in little streams.

She'd just signed away her family heritage.

Max picked up the paper and kissed it before placing it back in the document wallet.

"I hope you choke on it," he spat.

Max's only response was a droll laugh.

Max moved to place the annulment papers in front of Pixie.

"I don't get it, Max. If you're about to kill me, then why bother with an annulment? She'll be free to marry anyway."

"You make an excellent point, Rory. But you see, an annulment is as close to wiping the slate clean in the eyes of God that we can manage. So that's why this sham of a marriage needs to end this way." The malice in his voice punctuated the words.

Rory was hit with a whole new round of fear and distress coming from Pixie. He decided then and there no one was going to annul his marriage, regardless of what some phony paperwork said. He'd had enough. These fuckers were about to go down big time and he was just the man to send them to hell.

He sent his senses scanning out one last time. His brothers were close, very close in fact. He'd noticed them edging in over the last few minutes. Dylan and Quade were in the barn and if he was to hazard a guess, he'd bet Angelo and Aaron were on the roof. Their ascent to the roof was being covered by the racket the cattle were now making against the back wall of the barn. He'd heard them immobilise Brad and Steve after they'd opened the gate to the cattle.

Max slammed his palm on the desk.

"Pick up the pen, you whore, and redeem yourself!" he shouted at her.

TJ slowly picked up the pen and looked up at him; tears streamed down her face. He nodded once more and she choked back a sob and signed her name.

Kelvin moved in behind her and stroked his hand through her hair. "Almost mine, you little slut. Very soon you'll learn what it means to redeem yourself."

Rory looked directly into Kelvin's eyes and signed the paper—letting him think he'd won.

He didn't need to look at Pixie to know he'd just broken her heart. He couldn't live with looking at the image of her loss and his betrayal on her face for the rest of his life.

First he had to get them out of here alive.

Then somehow he had to make it right.

Max nodded to one of his men and the mechanical sound of the doors being slid back punctured the air. He spun around and faced the door the cattle were about to spill through.

He heard Kelvin goad her. "Almost over, Teresa. Just a few minutes more and your precious Rory will be nothing but a memory."

She was hysterical now and fighting him with everything her small frame had, as the first of the cattle crashed through the doors, closely followed by another beast.

It was one of the Mickey bulls—the animal's eyes were wide with fear and its horns caught and scraped through the narrow opening, only slightly slowing its forward progress.

Katie's high-pitched scream assaulted his ears.

He knew what the scene would look like to them, the beast's horns only feet from his body.

Rory ripped his hands apart, breaking the flexicuffs as if they were no more than limp spaghetti and moved his body in front of the boss's.

He threw his arms wide, making him seem even bigger. Then Rory projected all his animal instincts forward, letting the beast know he was a bigger, badder predator than whatever lurked outside.

The animal screeched to a halt and snorted. Its eyes flashed wildly as it sniffed the air and no doubt smelt his animal make-up.

A moment passed between him and the beast.

Rory held his stance and then stepped forward aggressively.

The beast backed up hastily, crashing into the animal on its heels that was now halfway through the gate. The bull began to retreat along the path it had entered through. Rory still moved forward at full force to ensure it didn't have a change of heart.

"What the fuck?" he heard Max yell in confusion.

"Never work with kids or animals, Max." The boss laughed from his now safe position at the fence.

Then chaos erupted everywhere at once.

In a simultaneous macabre attack that was almost beautiful in the way it was executed, Quade emerged from the shadows and silently slit the throat of the guy at the cattle door with his favourite eight-inch hunting knife. The man slumped to the floor and Quade pushed the button retracting the door to the closed position before tossing his knife to Rory to allow him to slice the flexicuffs from the boss.

Dylan sprang from behind the molasses drums and ripped Kelvin clean off the ground as he wrapped his arm around the man's throat and hauled him from Pixie. Dylan's left hand came up behind Kelvin's skull, completing the chokehold and with a vicious twist of his hands, assured Kelvin would never draw breath again.

Angelo and Aaron came crashing through the skylights, dropping from the ceiling and disabled their targets within a fraction of a second. They moved to cover Pixie as Max started to move from his shocked paralysis.

He glanced up and held his breath.

Was she okay?

A split second later, he breathed again.

She was safe.

Angelo and Aaron had her protected and were holding her tightly as she tried to make her way to Katie.

Dylan moved in behind the man who was standing guard over Katie. He pulled him off Katie but unlike the others, this guy fancied he had a few skills. The guy stood and led with a quick jab, cross combination to Dylan's jaw, which he arrogantly didn't bother blocking. Dylan should have gone down from the blows; instead, he shook his head and grinned.

As Rory moved forward to the boss, he watched the moment of panic strike through the man and inwardly grinned. Very rarely did Dylan ever get a civilian opponent to fight back. The guy then made a poor tactical decision and threw a roundhouse kick aimed for Dylan's ribs.

It was too easy.

Dylan advanced and caught the kick against his hip and locked the guy's leg up with his left arm. With all the control and time in the world, Dylan took out the leg the guy was hopping on and followed him to the ground, breaking his cheekbone and sending him into unconscious oblivion with a striking elbow to the face.

One quick slice and the boss's hands were free again. Quade was finishing off the final rent-a-thug as Rory vaulted over the steeling railings and began to move towards Pixie.

He could breathe again.

The crack of a shot shattered his relief as it reverberated around the corrugated iron of the barn.

"Hands in the air. Nobody moves," Max yelled.

Rory eased around to see what was happening and slowly raised his hands.

In all the confusion, Max had somehow managed to get a gun to Katie's head.

But even worse—it looked like he'd totally flipped out this time.

Sweat was pouring from him and his breathing was erratic. Even from twenty feet away, Rory could see the shaking of Max's hand as he held the gun to Katie's head.

There was nothing more dangerous than a flipping out madman with a gun.

Rory chanced a sideways glance at Pixie. She was fine for the moment but terror was surging from her pores in rivers.

They needed to keep the attention away from her and Katie.

Angelo and Aaron stood still as statues in the middle of the aisle, their bodies protecting Pixie.

Dylan was on one knee beside the man he'd taken down.

"Well, well. Looks like we've got a few more for the cattle," Max said to no one in particular.

"Do you seriously think you're going to get away with killing six men here tonight? People are watching, Max, and there is no way you'll get away with it. At the very least, you'll face a life in prison." The boss calmly spoke from the railing.

"Oh, I don't know, John. I seem to recall getting away with it last time. But then, I guess I didn't really commit murder, did I? Why would now be any different?" Max drew his weapon and placed it at the base of Katie's skull.

Surely it had to be now or Katie was dead.

"No, Uncle Max—don't hurt her," Pixie wailed and fought against the hold Angelo and Aaron had her in.

The pain and anguish in her cry ripped him to the core. She was losing her family all over again and right before her eyes.

Max laughed; it was again the sound of the insane and mentally unstable.

"Oh Teresa, everyone dies—some young, some old. I guess her time is now."

The boss had stealthily moved from the yard and was now slowly making his way across the distance to where Max held Katie. He had one of the sheaves of papers in his hand.

"Max, stop right now." The boss's voice was as full of authority as Rory had ever heard it.

Max's head shot up on reflex to the boss's words. Rory figured that was the ingrained conditioning responding to authority. Everyone watched Max slightly shake his head.

"You don't give the orders here tonight, John—I do," Max retaliated.

"Is that right, Max? Do you seriously think you're going to walk out of here with your life? Think about it. There's me plus five of my operators. Where are all your boys? Take a look, Max." Rory watched Max's eyes flick from one crumpled figure to the next: all either dead or on the injured list for the foreseeable future. "This is a no-win situation for you—regardless of whether you take the shot or not. You've lost everything tonight."

Rory knew Max had no qualms about shooting anyone. He glanced quickly between Quade and Dylan, hoping to hell they were on the same page as him.

The boss moved his hand holding the papers behind his back and Rory clearly saw the thumbs-up.

He nodded and extended his right hand towards Dylan.

A split second later, he felt the grip of the pistol Dylan threw at him land firmly in his palm. Rory immediately knew by the feel it was one of his weapons the boys had brought with them. In less than a blink of an eye, he levelled the weapon on Max, took aim and fired.

The bullet hit true to its target.

Max's wrist instantaneously dropped and the pistol fell from his hanging hand to the ground.

A roar of pain, frustration, and so many other things emanated from Max as he grabbed at his mutilated wrist with his other hand.

Free from Max's hold, Katie lurched forward and quickly covered the ground to Pixie, launching herself into her sister's arms.

The boss moved closer to Max and waved the papers in front of his face as Max fell to his knees.

"I was at the marriage ceremony, Max, and the priest clearly said, 'What God has joined, man must not divide.' You're not God, Max, regardless of what you think. You're not even a close second." The boss held up the annulment and slowly ripped it to pieces in front of Max's broken face. Tears were streaming down Max's face and his body shook like a leaf in the breeze. He'd lost everything tonight, and the realisation was just starting to hit him.

He was a broken man and it showed.

"What, Max? No eloquent speeches left? How disappointing. Well, it's my turn now and I promise I'll keep it short. Tonight, Max, you've been judged and failed on all accounts. You've failed as a father, a brother, a son, an uncle, and a soldier. Tonight, you can state your case to God because that's where you're heading, you evil fucker, although I suspect you'll find yourself very soon trying to charm the devil. Best of luck, soldier."

Max's head slumped, and then the impossible seemed to happen. His torso shot up and he levelled a pistol at the boss.

Where had he pulled that from?

The one from his mangled hand was still on the ground.

There was the longest pause, as everyone in the barn seemed to hold his or her collective breaths.

"Rory, finish it now," the boss barked.

The boss hadn't even finished his sentence.

Without another thought, Rory had taken aim and pulled the trigger.

The bullet found its mark truly, and made a neat hole in Max's forehead.

His body slumped to the ground with a thud.

The duo of evil would trouble Pixie and her family no longer.

It was over.

Their eyes moved to the boss, still standing nonchalantly by Max's body.

"Well, that got a little bit exciting for a few moments." The boss turned and looked at them. "A little sloppy, boys. Looks like you could all use some more training."

Rory's eyes finally moved to Pixie, and he felt his gut clench in dread. As long as he lived, he'd never forget the look of horror on her beautiful face as she looked between Max's slain body and him.

Surely there was no way she'd forgive him for this.

What had he done?

The crack of the bullet being fired had instinctively jerked TJ's head upwards.

All she saw was Max crumple to the ground.

It was done. They were both out of her life forever.

Relief and a sense of loss overwhelmed her at once.

She'd just lost more family, regardless of how screwed-up in their thinking they were.

That hurt for some reason—although she willed it not to.

Family was very important. But at the same time, she knew they were evil to the core. There would never have been any peace until she either lived in servitude to Kelvin or she was dead.

One thing she knew emphatically: she had a lot of living to do.

Rory moved to her and pulled her hesitantly into his arms, bringing both Katie and her into his embrace.

"I've got you, Pixie," he whispered into her hair.

It felt as if she was home.

Tears flooded down her cheeks. She didn't know whether they were sad or happy tears. It didn't matter. She just wanted to soak up the feeling of being in his arms.

Katie clung to her and Rory all at the same time.

"Is it over?" Katie sobbed.

"Yeah, sweet thing, it is," Rory confirmed.

TJ lost track of how long they stood like this for.

A minute or five may have passed before the embrace was broken as Jazz moved to them, medical bag slung over shoulder.

"Rory, get TJ off that ankle, now. No more weight on it until it's assessed." Jazz was in full business mode. A chair appeared courtesy of Quade, and Rory helped her sit. Dylan had grabbed another and helped Katie onto it.

"Get the girls some blankets—it's freezing in here," Jazz ordered to no one in particular.

"Okay, honey, let's have a look at you," Jazz said, eyeing the hideous bruise on her cheek. "Any other injuries, TJ?"

"I fell and hit my head at the apartment; when I woke up, I was here. I've thrown up a few times and felt nauseous ever since and I've got the worst headache." She groaned. Exhaustion and the adrenalin letdown were starting to happen.

Rory growled at her admission of the injuries she'd sustained.

Quade passed Jazz the blanket and she wrapped it around TJ, covering her scantily clad body. The warmth was immediate. She didn't feel so exposed, even though she knew she was among friends.

"Quade, get those medics over here." Jazz grasped her lightly by the chin and looked directly into her eyes. "I can see some x-rays and probably an MRI and CT scan in your near future, TJ. I'm not taking any chances with a blow to the head."

TJ glanced at Rory and his face was shadowed with concern.

Jazz was still holding her chin.

"Do you have any other injuries that I need to know about?"

She was sure there was more to Jazz's question but for the life of her, she couldn't figure it out. Her head hurt too much. And she just didn't want to think. She wanted to cuddle up next to Rory for about a year. She reached for his hand and he immediately took hers.

"Were you sexually assaulted, honey?" Jazz's voice was barely above a whisper as she ran her eyes over her face.

She felt Rory tense. The anger started to radiate from him again.

"No," she whispered back. "I really need to lie down," she almost pleaded. Her frame didn't feel as if it would hold her upright at the moment and she didn't have the will to make it.

Rory scooped her into his arms once again and placed her gently on the stretcher that the medics had appeared with.

They wheeled her to the waiting ambulance and before she had to ask, he hopped in with her.

"Katie?" she whispered.

"She's fine, love. Jazz has Katie with her in the SUV. They'll meet us at the hospital."

She closed her eyes and was going to let sleep take her, when she felt a cool cloth wipe over her face.

"I'm sorry—we need you to stay awake," the ambulance officer informed her.

"I'll talk to you, Pixie," Rory assured her. "How about I start with I love you, even if you hate me for what I did." He gave her a sad but heartfelt smile.

What was he talking about?

Her fuzzy brain couldn't function to put the words together.

Chapter Thirty-Five

Jazz found him outside Pixie's room. He was leaning against the wall, head bowed low.

"Hey, come on, you could use a coffee. Now that we know she's going to be okay, we can let her sleep for a few hours." Jazz took his arm and moved him into the deserted lounge area.

She swiftly made coffees from the automated machine and sat in the chair across from him.

Operating on autopilot, he thanked her and wished the warmth from the cup would somehow seep into his veins. He'd felt icy cold ever since he'd seen the look on her face.

"Talk to me, Rory. What's got you knocked so low?" Jazz's voice was insistent and would allow no gap for him to escape.

"I've done it again and lost her, Jazz." His voice was not much more than a whisper and didn't sound like his own.

"Why do you think that, Rory?"

He put the cup down on the table separating them and moved to the window, looking out over the lights. The need to move had got too much; he couldn't just sit there.

Jazz said nothing, just waited him out.

"The look on her face. She looked from Max's crumpled body to me, and all I could see was horror written all over her beautiful face. My wife thinks I'm no better than the monster I shot." His voice trailed off as the enormity of what he'd done sunk in.

He'd ruined the best thing in his life.

"Are you sure that's what you saw, Rory?"

He spun and clenched his fists. "I know what I saw, Jazz. I'll never forget that look as long as I live. I told you, this is what I am. I'm nothing more than a cold-blooded killer. And again I feel nothing that Max is dead. I couldn't care less, in fact. All I'm glad is that he'll never terrorise Pixie or the kids again. Still think I'm honourable and good and all that now?"

He walked back to the chair and slumped down. Exhaustion flooded him. He wanted to sleep for a week but he knew sleep would never come, nor did he really want it. He deserved to feel like shit; he'd hurt her.

Jazz looked at him a long time before she spoke.

"Are you quite finished with the pity party?" He sat up straighter as if he'd been slapped. It was the last thing he'd been expecting to come out of Jazz's mouth. "I may have only known you a relatively short period of time, Rory, but we have been close through that. What I've seen is a guy who cares incredibly deeply for people, particularly his family. You always work to make people feel better; you hate for them to be in pain or hurting in any way. That's why you often joke around. You want people to relax and you inherently know that laughter and clowning around a bit makes people feel better. You also see things very clearly and can help others clarify their thinking too. Case in point—Brayden."

"What do you mean? What are you talking about?"

"I know you gave him a lot of advice and pointers where Rihanna was concerned. I also know you hung around to look out for Quade, and to help ease Rihanna into understanding the Centre and you guys better. They're the actions of someone who cares deeply and has a highly developed moral compass. I've been through this before; you're not a cold-blooded killer. You did your job tonight. You did what was right. More to the point, you followed orders. Tom's orders. He issued you an order and you followed it. Any other of the guys would have done the same. I would have done the same if I could have actually hit the target," she added, inflicting a little humour into the situation.

He thought on that for a few moments.

"But the look on her face was sheer horror." His plea was feeble.

"Have you spoken to her about it?"

"No." He shook his head.

"Then don't start second-guessing stuff that happened in a very dangerous and emotionally charged situation. Stop panicking and take the time to talk to your wife about it. You're assuming her feelings without giving her the benefit of expressing them." Jazz took a sip of coffee from her cup and just looked at him. "You know what I see before me?"

He looked up and shook his head in the negative.

"I see a guy who's jumping at shadows and probably creating something out of nothing. Take the time to talk to her before you torture yourself some more."

"But it's more than just tonight and you know it, Jazz. What have I done? I used her fear of Kelvin to push her into marrying me. That was calculating. I'm not good for her."

Jazz nodded her head and his stomach pitched. *Yep, even Jazz agreed it was.*

"So tell me this—when you asked her to marry you, did you love her?"

He didn't need to think on it. "Yes."

"So you're saying because you loved her and she was terrified of Kelvin, you pushed her into marrying you?"

"Yeah."

"And does she love you?"

"She says so but what if she's just saying that more from relief than really loving me? What if in a week or a month, she regrets this whole marriage thing and wants nothing to do with me?"

Jazz looked at him with a sad, knowing smile on her face. "Rory, for a guy you're almost far too much in touch with your feelings. Why are you trying to persecute yourself? You're a good person, a loving brother and husband. You don't need me blowing this sunshine. Stop thinking. Stop doubting yourself and TJ. It'll all be fine. And if it's any consolation, she loves you because she sees all the good in you. It only seems to be you who sees what you think are imperfections." Jazz broke out laughing, or more like giggling, actually.

"What's so damned funny?"

"You. For someone who can see everyone else so clearly, you really struggle deep down, don't you? Cut yourself some slack. Talk to her. Why on earth would you think you're not good for her?"

"Well, because it was all so sudden and you have to admit our world is quite different and she didn't know about any of that before I married her. It wasn't fair. Pixie deserved the right to choose whether she wanted to be with me knowing the truth."

"Okay, I can see your point and it's valid. But I ask you this question—did she have an issue with you having altered DNA? Did she feel as if she'd been betrayed in some way?"

He thought back to the night he'd told her. So much happened that night.

"No, she wasn't upset. In fact, she seemed more curious than anything else." Then he remembered what else she'd said and he must have smirked.

"Okay, now you have to tell me what that bit was."

"Can't a guy have any secrets with you?"

"Rory, you already know the answer to that one."

He let out a long sigh and he felt a little uncomfortable. "She told me how now she understood how I could be perfect."

Jazz just laughed.

"Yeah, she definitely loves you, big time. Any woman who would openly admit a man could be perfect must be madly in love with him. I'd give you a close to perfect but then I guess she knows you better than I do. So I'll take her word on it."

Rory felt his cheeks warm. He didn't normally ever feel embarrassment but this was such a weird conversation to be having.

"You've done it again, you know." She looked at him curiously. "You've gone and gotten everything out of me, and I didn't even feel a thing. In fact, I think I'm actually pleased to have someone to talk to."

She gave him a knowing smile. "Oh, I'm good. I've told you all more than once you can run but you can't hide. I will get it out of you in the end. It's up to you how much you want to fight."

"Quade doesn't stand a chance. When're you going to put the poor bloke out of his misery?"

"Who says I'm going to put him out of his misery?"

"Ah, Jazz, we heard the conversation earlier today, or was it yesterday? I have no idea what the time is."

"So? Just because I have an itch doesn't mean I'm going to scratch it. I've got a couple of scars from chicken pox I scratched when they itched like the bejeezus. I like to think I learn from my mistakes."

"The guy's going to have the worst case of blue balls."

"Rory, it's a medical fact that no man has ever died from blue balls."

"Yeah, but have a little mercy on us. We have to put up with his bad moods."

"I'll think about it. I'm not even sure what the organisational policy is on fraternisation with a co-worker but this discussion is not about me, and don't think I missed how you've skilfully transferred the conversation away from you."

He grinned a little sheepishly. She was onto him.

"Give her some time, Rory. Don't jump to conclusions. Talk to her about how she feels. I think you'll be surprised."

He nodded his head and finished his coffee. He really hoped Jazz was right, but surely they all couldn't have a happy ending?

A few hours later, Rory poked his head into Katie's hospital room. Nothing was physically wrong with her but as a precaution the doctors had decided to keep her here overnight. The poor kid had been through so much in the last few weeks. Last night had been tough on all of them. He could only begin to imagine how it must have been for a twelve-year-old girl.

She looked small, lonely, and lost sitting there all by herself.

"Hey, sweet girl. How're you doing this morning?" At his voice, her head sprang up and she looked at him and then promptly burst into tears. His gut lurched. What did he know about dealing with twelve-year-old, emotionally distressed females? He was way out of his comfort zone.

He took a deep breath, braced himself and moved towards the bed. *Guess he'd just have to wing it.*

"Don't look at me—I'm ugly when I cry," she sobbed.

The words knifed at his gut, the pain in her voice sounded so acute. "Oh sweetie, you could never be ugly. Anything but. You and your sister are the two most beautiful girls in the world to me." *God, he hoped that was the right thing to say.*

As he moved closer, she reached out and half lurched off the bed, almost throwing herself at him.

He caught her in his arms and settled them both on the bed. She burrowed her head into his chest and clung to him for grim death.

He tried to think of everything that had happened from her perspective. She had to be terrified, confused, and lost. Mostly lost—she'd lost so much. Her father, brother, mother, and now her uncle and cousin. And probably in her mind she'd lost Pixie, too.

Rory ran his hand over her hair. It had the same silkiness as Pixie's. She'd be a stunner in about four or five years— almost a carbon copy of Pixie, he guessed. And if he was around long enough, he'd have his hands full trying to keep the boys away. He really hoped it would come to pass.

"Hey Katie, you want to talk about what's got you so upset?" he asked gently.

She shook her head in the negative and sobbed a couple of more times.

"Sometimes it helps to talk about things, you know. Keeping it all bottled up can often make it worse than it really is. I'm guessing you don't feel like you have too many people to talk to right about now. But you're wrong—you can talk to any of us. All of us care very deeply for you, especially Pixie and me." He had no idea if he was saying the right thing. The words just seemed to keep rolling from his mouth.

"What's going to happen to me?" she finally squeaked out.

"What do you mean, honey?" he gently asked.

"Well, Pixie has you, but me and Marcus—there's nobody left for us. Aunt Clara can't look after us." Her young voice started to stammer and the sobbing came through. "Are we going to have to live somewhere else?" she choked out.

These Walsh girls were hell on his emotions.

They seemed with consummate ease to cut him to the core with their pain and their bravery all at once. Her scared little voice shook him more than he'd have thought possible. Her world was in turmoil.

Fuck, he should have been paying more attention.

He tightened his arms around her.

"No, baby girl, you're both going to be with Pixie and me. We've got to get you all well first, but we'll be together soon."

"But you sent us to Rihanna and Brayden's. You didn't want us," she argued in a low voice.

"No, Katie, honey, that's not how it was. We never meant for you to feel like that. You were all in a lot of danger, that's why we thought it best if you spent some time there. Brayden's house is very secure because he likes his privacy with the band and everything. It wasn't that we didn't want you. We both do—very much. Do you understand?"

She nodded slowly, moving her head against his chest. He could feel his T-shirt soaked through from her tears. The seconds passed and he let her absorb the comfort his holding her could provide. It wasn't much but if it made her feel better, he'd gladly sit here as long as she needed.

"Why did Uncle Max hate us so much and want to hurt us?" she finally asked.

Of all the questions—he wished he knew the answer to that one as well. One thing he did know was that the man was not right at the end.

"I'm not sure, sweetie. I think Max's issues stemmed from

a long time ago and over the years, he became so bitter and twisted about everything that his brain didn't work properly anymore. He started to make decisions that were cruel and hurtful. I think he had become what's known as a sociopath," Rory tried to explain.

"What's a sociopath?"

"Basically it's somebody who thinks only of their own gain and has lost the sense of what's right or wrong. There's a much bigger medical definition that I'm sure Jazz can explain to you but that's about the best I can do, sweetie. I'm just a mere male, after all." He tried to add a little humour. He wanted to see her smile.

She laughed. Then she sobered again.

He could feel the tension building in the air and he knew what she wanted to ask. How did he answer that question? What was the right answer? What was the truth?

"It's okay. You can ask me."

She raised her head off his chest and looked directly into his eyes. He felt so exposed. What was it with kids that they could just cut you to the core?

"Would Uncle Max really have shot me? Did you really have to kill Uncle Max?"

Rory doubted she'd fully come to terms with what the death meant just yet. Maybe she had. It couldn't have been much more graphic for her. Jazz needed to be doing this, not him. But he wouldn't let her down. She'd asked him.

He knew he had to answer her questions but what would she think of him after he told her the answers? How would she look at him?

"Katie, no young lady or anyone for that matter, should ever have to witness what you did last night. I'm not going to downplay it. You were there and you saw. The best I can do is try to explain what happened. Then we'll talk about how you feel about it."

She nodded briefly and snuggled into his chest again. At least she wasn't directly staring at him; that made it easier.

"First of all, you need to understand I didn't want to do what I did. I did it because it's my job and because I'd never let anything happen to you, your sister, or Marcus, if I could prevent it. I'd never let anything happen to anyone I care about if I could somehow stop it. Your Uncle Max had gone a bit crazy; he would have killed any of us there last night. And yes, I believe he would have killed you; he would have also killed my boss. There was no way I'd have let that happen." He didn't want to focus on her being his target too much but she'd needed to hear it just the same. "Your uncle was also trying to force Pixie to marry Kelvin. She didn't like Kelvin—he scared her and he's done some nasty things to her in the past."

"I didn't like him, either. He scared me, too. He started to look at me funny and it made me feel strange," she admitted.

"Remember that feeling, sweetie. That was your mind letting you know he was dangerous and that you should avoid him. If you ever get that feeling again with other people, you get yourself out of there and you tell Pixie or me. You don't ever stay around people who make you feel like that. Promise me, okay?"

He lightly pulled her chin up to look at him.

She nodded. "Okay, I promise."

"Thank you, Katie. I'll always look out for you but you've got to learn to look out for yourself as well. It's all part of growing up."

He let her chin go and her head sunk back to its spot on his chest.

"But did they really have to die?" she asked.

Oh God, what was the right answer to that question? A big part of him screamed, *hell, yes*. But it was him who had delivered the final death sentence. Did that make him any better than them?

"I couldn't see any other way out of it, Katie. Your uncle was insane. He wanted to kill anyone who he saw was in his path. You, me, the boss—even Pixie. He didn't care. I couldn't let him do that. I couldn't let him take you or Pixie away from me. I couldn't let him and Kelvin have you and her. I'm almost certain he would have hurt you both. I couldn't live with that. I'm sorry I had to kill him but I'm not sorry I did it. Does that make sense?"

"I hated him yesterday. I hated Kelvin, too. I wished them dead. And then it happened. I still can't believe what they said and did to us. So why do I feel so bad about hating them and wishing them dead? I'm sorry. " A fresh barrage of tears began to pour down her face.

"I know, sweetie. They were cruel and mean. They took advantage of their position and poisoned your love for them. They treated you badly. But they're your feelings and you've a right to feel whatever you want. You don't have to apologise to me for feeling the way you do. You've just got to learn to live with them. Even when it doesn't feel so good."

She clung to him, silent for a long time.

"I'm not sorry I did it, Katie. I'm just sorry that you're hurting because of it."

He said nothing more. There was nothing more to say. Katie needed to make up her own mind—pass her own judgement on what he'd done and how she felt about it.

Finally she looked up at him and smiled a little.

"Don't worry, Rory. You saved us. You made the right decision. If that cow had gorged you, that would have really made me upset."

He chuckled softly and let out the breath he didn't realise he'd been holding and she hugged him tighter. Kids were so black and white—simple. *When did we all start to screw things up in our heads?* he wondered.

"Thank you, Katie. I needed to hear that," he whispered. He doubted she'd ever know what she'd just given him. He wasn't sure he believed her but it was nice to hear it nonetheless.

And just like kids do, she brushed it off and went on to the next thing on her mind.

"So where are we going to live?" she asked, with more enthusiasm in her voice.

"Mmm, I don't know. Where do you want to live?" She had him curious now.

"Can we get a place at the beach? I hate living in the middle of nowhere," she whined.

He chuckled, seeing things through her eyes.

"Yeah, I think that might be doable. I'm kind of keen on the beach myself. Why don't we have a chat to Pixie about it? There's a lot we're going to have to work out over the next few months so I don't want you getting disappointed if we can't get it sorted out immediately. But I like the idea, and if Marcus and Pixie are on board with it, I think we should make it happen. We're all going to have to pull together as a team now to get us through all this. Can you do that?"

She smiled at him again and nodded. It warmed him through to know he could give her something bright and positive in her young life.

"Anything else you want to talk about?"

He could see her thinking for a moment.

"Nothing at the moment," she finally said.

There was something else he needed to say. Something that had been playing on his mind since he decided to marry Pixie, knowing very well she came as a package deal.

"Well, just so you know, you can come and talk to me anytime. I might not have all the answers but we'll work something out. I'm kind of new to this whole thing. It's a bit weird for me, you see. I'm not your father and I'm not your brother. I'm not quite sure where I fit. Sometimes, I'm going to have to set boundaries and you probably won't like me very much. That kind of comes with being the adult in this whole gig. Sometimes, I'm going to screw up at this. I won't mean to, but I will. I'll say something dumb and hurt your feelings. It's what us guys do. We don't mean it, but it happens. So I guess I'm asking you to be a bit patient with me until I can get my act together and figure out what you need me to be for you."

She looked at him with the most earnest look he'd ever seen on a twelve-year-old. *Oh shit! Had he just blown it all?*

Finally, she said, "Just be Rory." And gave him the warmest smile.

He hugged her tight one final time.

"That I can do, sweetheart. How about we go find Pixie?"

"Yeah, I've missed her."

"Well, we can't have that, can we?"

He helped her from the bed and passed her a light pullover that was beside the bed. It was chilly in the hospital.

For the first time in a long time, his heart felt lighter. How was it possible that a twelve-year-old kid could give him that?

He'd take it.

"How're you feeling this morning, TJ?" Jazz asked as she sashayed into her hospital room.

"Umm, a bit better. The nausea has gone and my headache is down to a dull throb rather than excruciating."

"Excellent. It was great news that all the scans and tests came back fine. Now you just need a lot of TLC and you'll be fine in a few days."

"That sounds good. I'm over being an invalid," she huffed, feeling annoyed at her inability to be active.

"Ah, TJ, you've hardly been that. But I can understand how you'd feel that way. You've been through the wringer physically, not to mention the emotional rollercoaster you've been on." Jazz hitched her hip on the bed and sat.

"Yeah, it has been insane. I guess in a lot of ways it hasn't really sunk in yet," TJ admitted. "How's Katie doing?"

TJ searched Jazz's face for answers. Rory had headed that way a while ago to check on her. TJ felt terrible how much she'd neglected Katie over the last little while. The poor kid must be going through hell.

"I think last night was very tough on her. She's got a lot on her mind. I had a bit of a chat to her but I don't think she was quite ready to talk to me yet."

"What should we do?" Her gut tightened and she started to worry.

"Nothing yet. We need to let her come to us when she's ready. All we need to do is let her know we're here for her when she wants to talk."

"It's my fault. I should have spent more time with her since Mum passed." TJ looked up at Jazz and she didn't seem too happy with her last comment.

"If you want to cast blame—at least level it where it's due. Max created all this mess; now you're going to have to pick up the pieces. And don't underestimate how many there will be for all of you, and they'll probably keep popping up for a while, particularly when you least expect it," Jazz warned.

"Thanks for your cheery words."

"Well, I think you've figured out by now I'm not going to sugar coat things just to make you feel better. I'm going to give you the truth so you know what you can expect and be prepared to deal with it."

"No, I picked up on that a while back." TJ grinned.

"Good."

TJ wriggled around uncomfortably. Something else was bothering her. Maybe Jazz could help, maybe not.

"Can I ask you something else?"

"Sure—you should know that." Jazz playfully mock frowned at her.

How did she put the words together that she needed to ask?

"How do I deal with Rory and what happened last night?"

Jazz looked at her squarely. "What exactly do you mean?"

TJ knew that Jazz had immediately jumped into protective friend mode around Rory and for that she was grateful on his behalf.

"I want to know how I help him get through pulling the trigger and killing Max. I saw the look on his face and he can hardly look at me. I know it affected him deeply."

Jazz looked at her for a moment and TJ knew she was being studied, tested maybe. Jazz was weighing up her words and trying to decide something.

"First of all, how do you feel about Rory shooting your uncle? That's what we need to work on first."

TJ didn't answer immediately. She looked away and searched her soul.

How did she really feel?

Sure, she felt loss because he was family, but that was all. Looking back, she realised that the loss she felt happened six years ago when he'd abandoned her that night. That had created the gaping wound and the fear she'd been carrying around in the years that had passed. Max and Kelvin's actions since the attack had just widened her wound and infected it more.

The thought of what he'd done to her father, brother, and mother made her sick to her stomach. She knew she'd shed a lot of tears over that in the future but not today. Today she wanted to take back her life and get things back in control and perspective.

The question hammered at her again—how did she really feel?

Finally she answered, not really thinking about the words, just speaking about how she felt. "I know it's probably wrong but I feel relieved. Lighter, probably even glad. If that makes me a bad person, then so be it. But that's how I feel. I'm glad they're gone. I'm not glad they're dead but I'm glad they're gone. I know I'll sleep easier knowing that they're not plotting to hurt me or my family ever again. It'll take me a while to get through what they did, especially Max, but I'll get there."

Jazz didn't say anything, just nodded.

TJ knew she was looking at her expectantly.

"If you're looking for my approval or disapproval, you'll get neither. You have to be comfortable in how you feel. And I think you are. So you don't blame him?"

"Blame him?" TJ felt the anger rise in her. "He came with the team and saved us from a fate worse than death. Why would I blame him?"

Jazz shrugged. "Well, that's the way I see it, too, but I just wanted to check that you shared that position. He needs to know you don't blame him."

Jazz looked away and TJ could see she was struggling with something. She hadn't seen Jazz quite so torn before.

"I'm not technically breaking any confidentiality because we were just having a 'chat.'" Jazz used her fingers to create air quotation marks. "But still I don't feel one hundred per cent comfortable giving you this information but I know you'll do the right thing with it." That tweaked TJ's interest.

"This is not the first time that Rory's job has required him to take a life." TJ knew Jazz was watching her closely for her reactions. She tried to keep her face as solemn as possible. The confirmation was still a shock even though she'd half expected it. These guys had a dangerous job to do. Things were going to happen from time to time, but she recognised his skill and that of his teammates.

"He killed a man a few months ago in a similar situation, only it was a gun to Rihanna's head that time. Rory took the shot. There have been other occasions as well. It's part of his job and he can do it very effectively when he needs to. This time was different, though. He killed a family member of yours. Regardless of whether the man deserved it or not, the outcome is still the same. Rory killed him, and both you and Katie witnessed that. That act in itself is going to play on his mind. I'm not sure he wants you being exposed to the darker side of his life. Personally he can deal with this aspect of his life well. It doesn't eat at him, but he worries how others perceive him because of it. That's where his fears stem from. Your perception of him will be his greatest concern."

TJ thought it through for a second.

"I could never think anything but the best about him. He's been so incredible to me, to us. That's him through and through. How could he even think that?" she asked, confused.

"Well, it may not seem logical to us but to him it is a very real concern. You need to tell him and make him understand. He's going to need to hear it from you."

She nodded, thinking through Jazz's words.

"Okay, I can do that. Thanks for the advice and trusting me with the insight."

Jazz just nodded. But TJ read it clearly as a *don't make me sorry I told you.*

"So what about you?" Jazz asked when she'd fallen silent for a second.

"What about me?"

"You're worried about everyone else. How do you feel about everything?"

"To tell you the truth, I actually feel better. Much better. I know it's probably wrong and I know I've got a heap of grieving still to do over the next few months but I don't feel trapped anymore. I know why my father and brother were killed. I know why my mother got cancer. And I now have an understanding why Kelvin and Max behaved like they did six years ago. I know it's so clichéd but they say *the truth will set you free* and that's kind of how I feel." She paused, surprised at how much she'd divulged, but she really meant what she'd said. "Now I just want to put it all behind us and get on with being happy. Surely we deserve some of that?"

Jazz giggled lightly and nodded.

"Honey, if there was ever someone who deserved all of that, it's you. But just so you know, I'm always here if you want to talk. You're probably going to end up hanging with the Centre crew a lot more in the future. It just seems easier because of you-know-what and I'd really like it if we could be friends. I feel that we've got close over the last few weeks and I value that."

"I'd like that, too, Jazz. I really appreciate everything you've done for us."

"That's what friends do, TJ. We're there for each other. Your time will come when I need a shoulder to cry on."

"Somehow I can't see that, Jazz." TJ shook her head slowly, unable to picture Jazz needing anyone's help.

"Oh, I can cry and become a mess with the best of them. Ask your husband. He's seen me at my lowest and he helped pick me back up. That's what the Centre's all about. We're an extended family. We all care. You only have to ask." Jazz giggled again and smiled a little sheepishly. "Well, actually you don't have to ask as we're probably going to butt in— me, particularly."

They were both laughing when Rory and Katie walked in.

"What's so funny?" he asked.

"I was just admitting to TJ how much I tend to butt into people's lives. Just don't tell Quade I admitted to it. He'll tease me worse than ever," Jazz explained.

Rory nodded and chuckled. "I'm cool with it being our secret, honey nose." He winked at her.

"Please, don't you start as well," Jazz begged.

"Okay but only because I like that you antagonise the hell out of the big guy. It does him good to get shaken up out of all that brooding." They all chuckled a little at that. It was such an apt description. Quade really was the walking poster boy for broody.

TJ saw his eyes cut to her. "So what's the prognosis, doc?" he asked Jazz.

"Well, we were just discussing that. A full recovery is definitely in the cards," she joked. "But I do prescribe she gets lots of TLC, which I'm leaving up to you to take care of."

He nodded and smiled. "That I can do and it would be my pleasure. What about her ankle?" None of them missed the innuendo but Jazz carried on.

"X-rays look good. No new damage, fortunately. She can start putting a little weight on it. Nothing more than a few steps, on flat ground only." Jazz turned to TJ. "I'll set up some physio as well, but I think you should have a fair idea how you need to rehab it. I mean, you were in your last year of training when you stopped school, weren't you?"

"Yeah, I was." TJ's mind wandered for a second. It seemed like a million years ago that she was at university studying to be a physiotherapist. *Wow, how things could change.*

They all looked at her expectantly when she said nothing.

"Sorry—just got lost in my thoughts." She didn't miss the look of concern that shot across Rory's face. She'd also noticed how Katie had attached herself to his arm. "So enough about me. How are you, Katie? I'm sorry that I haven't been down to see you but, Doctor Scary here's confined me to bed until she says differently."

"I'm okay." She looked a little unsure. Then she looked at Rory and he nodded at her; it seemed all Katie needed. She squared up her slight frame a little and smiled. "We talked for a bit about a lot of things and I feel better. Particularly now that we're moving to the beach." Katie shot Rory a mischievous grin.

"Katie, that's not quite what I said," Rory corrected with a slight edge to his voice. She watched her sister grin again.

"I know but she just has to agree. It's a great idea. Besides, if she doesn't, it's your job to change her mind," Katie decided.

"Oh, really, miss? So that's how it's going to be, hey?" He joined in her playfulness.

TJ looked to Jazz and Jazz looked back at her, just as confused.

"Ah, care to fill me in on what you two cooked up?" TJ asked, raising her eyebrows.

Katie smirked at Rory and he smiled back.

"You do it," Katie encouraged him.

"Oh, no. You decided to drop the bomb now. It's all yours. Besides, you've already said I'd have to do the convincing if she doesn't like the idea. I'd better not push my luck to start with, don't you think?"

Katie considered that for a few seconds. "Mmm, you're probably right."

She turned back to TJ. "We talked and I suggested we all move to the beach. Rory thought it was a great idea. We just need you and Marcus to agree, TJ."

TJ slapped on her most adult considered look and made sure she passed her gaze between both Rory and Katie. She curled her lip slightly and she saw Katie's eyes and heart sink—she was purposely playing out the tension.

"I think it's a great idea. I'm not sure how we'll do it, but we'll figure it out."

Katie looked for a second and then realised she'd been on board with the idea. Suddenly, Katie let out a high-pitched squeal.

TJ saw Rory flinch. She knew immediately that the squeal hurt his ears.

"Katie honey, one thing you need to know. I've got very sensitive ears. High-pitched squeals really hurt my ears. I'm not trying to take away from your excitement but if you could just squeal a little lower, I'd be eternally grateful."

Katie looked at him, all apologetic. "Sorry, Rory. Sure, I'll try to remember."

TJ looked between them. She wasn't sure what had happened when he'd gone to see her, but evidently something pretty monumental had gone down. Katie was engaged and dealing with everything much better than she'd expected.

Jazz looked over at her and raised her eyebrows. This time it was TJ's turn to shrug. Yep, she had no idea what they'd talked about either, but Katie was obviously feeling better. It was hardly surprising when she thought about it. Rory just had that way of making everything seem better.

Well, maybe things were really starting to look up. Time to really push her luck and see if she could blow this popsicle stand.

"When can I get out of here? I hate hospitals," she asked Jazz. TJ nearly added, *I've got entirely too many bad memories of them* but thought better of it with Katie in the room. Her sister's demeanour was positive at the moment. She didn't need to buy trouble by drawing attention to some of the hardships they'd experienced. It made TJ realise just how much she'd need to be on the lookout for her brother and sister. There was a lot on her plate. A lot of responsibility but she was confident they'd be able to make it through.

"I can understand that. Let's see how you're doing around lunchtime. If you're still on the improve, we'll bust you out of here," Jazz whispered conspiratorially.

TJ giggled at Jazz's antics and tried not to wince as the movement reminded her of exactly how much her head hurt.

Today they were okay. She hoped tomorrow would be even better.

Chapter Thirty-Six

TJ stretched out on the couch and just relaxed. Not only was it great to be home but it was so good to be able to just sit and "chill" without constantly wondering where the next threat was coming from. Now they could hopefully start to settle down into some sort of normal life, whatever that may be.

Rory walked in and placed a cup of tea on the table beside her. He then sat and pulled her legs across his thighs.

She opened her eyes slightly and peeked a look at him. It was a view she'd never get tired of. It was the first real chance they'd had to just be together since all "that Max stuff," as they now referred to it, happened.

They needed to talk. TJ had been worried ever since she'd seen the look on his face after he pulled the trigger. She was even more worried after she spoke to Jazz. They needed to sort out whatever was in Rory's head now before it became a real issue between them and started to impact on the solid relationship they'd been building.

Their relationship to date had been built on communication. He'd worked through her issues with physical intimacy, using compassion and understanding. Now it was her turn to help him.

"Rory, do you want talk about what happened with 'that Max stuff'?" she gently asked.

TJ saw him take a big breath and then slowly let it out. "Truthfully, not really, but I know we need to talk."

Yeah, it was really troubling him. But where did she start? What did she say? How did she start this conversation?

Ah, stuff it! She'd just dive right in.

He looked up at her strangely.

"What?" she asked.

"You're nervous about something. I can smell it. Just say it, Pixie."

"I'm worried about you. You haven't seemed like yourself since the shooting. I don't want you to blame yourself for what happened. It was Max's doing. He left you with no other choice." There, she'd said it.

"You're worried about me? But Pixie, I saw your face that night. I saw the look on your face after you realised I'd just put a bullet in your uncle." His words held a darkness and pain she'd never heard from him before. It tore at her heart.

Her mind raced back to the scene in the barn and she tried to remember what she'd felt. She knew she'd felt shock and horror at the gruesomeness of it. Of the cold hard reality of watching men die all around her. She'd realised that night, there was a big difference between watching death happen in a Hollywood blockbuster and watching it for real.

Watching it play out in front of her eyes was disturbing but not for the reasons he thought. The reality of it had shocked her to the core; she'd learned to accept death but not like this.

"Oh Rory, I think I need to explain. It was the surprise at seeing it play out before my eyes, not that you did it, that shocked me. I guess I've never been that close to the reality of sudden death like that. "

"Good try, my sweet Pixie, but I know what I saw. You were horrified and you looked directly at me like that, knowing that I sent your uncle to his death." He tried to move her legs from him but she pushed down on them, holding him in place.

"Rory, I need you to understand. I don't hold you responsible for what you did. You were protecting us all."

"Well, you should hold me responsible. I pulled the trigger." His voice was agitated and emotional; she knew this was really playing on his mind.

"Yes, you did. Because you had to. If you didn't, Max would have killed Tom, and who knows where he would have stopped then. It's a miracle he didn't kill Katie before.

If Max and Kelvin hadn't died last night, if you all hadn't stepped in, I'd be a slave to Kelvin and I hate to think what they'd have done to Katie in time. You stopped all of that. There was no other way. You had to end it. Max was never going to stop on his own."

"Yeah, I killed another man. I'm a killer, Pixie, sometimes even a cold-blooded one. Do you really want to have that in your life?"

She started to laugh, sat up, and moved closer to him.

He couldn't be for real, could he?

"Why are you laughing? This is so far from funny," he accused.

"Actually, it's hysterical. I can't believe you think that." She reached out and took his hand and moved it into her lap. "You look at me now and hear everything I'm about to say," she demanded of him. Reluctantly he obliged and met her eyes.

"I know you, Rory Stephen Southall. You seem so laid back but you're such a thinker. You consider everything and always make the right decisions. You go out of your way to make sure everyone's happy and feeling good about themselves. You are not a cold-blooded killer. You're my husband, the man I love, and I know you'd never do anything that didn't need to be done. You're the sort of man who can make the tough decisions because you can see clearly what needs to be done in the best interests of everyone. And if it takes me every day for the rest of my life to convince you of this then, I guess that's what I'll do. Because I will not have you thinking that rubbish about yourself for one day longer. You've obviously carried it for too long now.

"I love you because you are by far the best man I know and I'm proud to be your wife. So you need to lose whatever screwed-up ideas you think people have about you. I'm not the only one who feels this way about you. Ask any of the crew at the Centre—they'll all tell you the same thing. Nobody thinks you're a killer. You're a protector and a warrior for what's right. I'm not going to let you crucify yourself for nothing." She sucked in a breath after her little rant. TJ hoped he'd got the message and not just heard the words. If he needed to hear it every day, she'd gladly say it.

He was quiet for a long time, just breathing beside her.

Finally he turned a little and looked at her.

"Do you really mean it? Is that truly how you feel?"

She didn't hesitate. "Yes, it absolutely is. That is the honest to God truth and you know I don't joke or lie about stuff like that."

He looked a little sheepish again. "I don't know what to say."

"You don't need to say anything. You just need to stop crucifying yourself and driving a wedge between us for some perceived problem that's not there. I just need you to believe what I said and know that I believe in us. What happened that night changes nothing between us. All you did was eradicate a couple of parasites on society. It pains me that they were my family. Not what you did. And if you don't think I didn't consider killing him myself more than once that night, you're wrong. If I'd had the opportunity, I'd have done it, too. He deserved to die, Rory. Evil flowed through his veins. And he was going to keep hurting people." It was the most in his face she'd ever been but she was fighting for them and she was prepared to go all out. There was no way she was going to let his unfounded concerns drive them apart.

"Thank you, my love. I needed to hear that," he said solemnly.

"Yes, you did," she agreed. "You also need to remember it."

He nodded. "I hope you'll be here every day to remind me."

"I wouldn't want to be anywhere else." He hugged her tighter and she knew it was exactly the right thing he needed to hear.

"Are we good?" he finally asked.

"We're great and I'd like nothing more than to head to bed and cuddle up to my husband and sleep for about a week." She wriggled beside him until he got the message and hauled her gently into his lap.

"Is that so?"

"Yep. It is."

"Fair enough, but I have one other thing I want to talk to you about." He tightened his arms around her.

"Okay, what is it?"

"I've been wondering about how we're going to house the kids in the short term. We both know that we can't impose on Rihanna and Brayden much longer. Besides, the kids need to be with us." She nodded her agreement at his comments. "Moving them in here with us is the obvious short-term option, but there's only one spare bedroom and I don't think the kids sharing is ideal."

TJ hadn't even given it a thought. Again, Rory was one or ten steps ahead of her.

"You're right, here is our best option but the bedroom thing is a problem. I guess we'll just have to make do. Maybe we could convert the dining room into a bedroom?" TJ offered, thinking on the fly.

"Well, that's one option, but I have another idea. What if we closed in the back verandah? That way we aren't reducing the size of our living area at all."

She thought on that for about three seconds. "Let's do it."

"You sure?"

"Yes, but I should warn you, I know nothing about building." Then her face darkened and her heart fell as she thought it through some more.

"What, Pix?"

"On second thought, I think we'll have to come up with another idea because I can't afford the money for the materials right now. I had a look through the accounts this afternoon. I'm going to be juggling things as it is to pay off all the medical bills that still seem to keep coming."

"Stop worrying about it. I'll take care of the building costs and just give me the medical bills and I'll sort those out as well," he said, very matter of fact.

"No, Rory, they're my responsibility—not yours."

"Well, I guess it's time to have our discussion about finances that we never really got around to. I'm not exactly struggling, Pixie. The Centre has paid all my costs and provided me with a very handsome salary for the last fifteen years. I have a number of rental properties, a reasonable share portfolio and a good wad of cash in the bank." She gasped at his disclosure. "You and the kids are my family now. Let me take care of what's mine."

Pixie was a little taken aback by Rory's revelation. Although she could understand his point of view, she didn't want to be considered a charity case.

"It's very kind of you, Rory. I guess I'm just not comfortable with the idea."

He was quiet for a second.

"So let me get this straight. You're happy for me to live here rent free but you're not happy to let me help make the house we live in more comfortable for everyone?" The corner of his mouth curled up in a smirk. TJ knew this was going to be a tough one to win.

"But there's three of us and one of you."

"And the one of me happens to be an adult male who has solid means to provide. This adult male also knew what he was getting into when he asked you to marry him. I fully expected to take on the responsibility of the kids in every way. That includes financial." His voice and expression held such sincerity—it touched her heart. What she also picked up on was that he'd be offended if she didn't accept his offer.

"Okay," she finally whispered. She didn't want to sound ungrateful but it was difficult to accept help when she'd become so use to relying on herself for everything.

"That wasn't so hard, was it?" Rory tweaked her chin and pressed a kiss to her forehead.

TJ could feel the heat start to rise to her cheeks. She really didn't want to talk on this anymore. So she settled on shrugging her shoulders in answer.

"Umm, so we've established how we're going to fund the building. Any ideas how we're going to achieve it?"

"Easy—I'll sort it out and get it underway."

"Ah, Rory, I don't mean to sound doubtful but do you know anything about building? Because I certainly don't." She winced in mock concern.

"I guess it's a good thing that I do then." He chuckled.

She turned in his arms and looked at him. Yet another thing she was learning about her husband.

"Where did you learn about building?"

"My uncle owns a building company down south. I worked for him every holiday from when I was about thirteen till I was nineteen or twenty. I picked up a few skills."

She turned and kissed him playfully on the lips, before pulling back and smiling.

"Well, then I guess it's a good thing Tom gave you a couple of weeks off, because it looks as if you've got a project with your name on it."

"It does indeed. I'll get started in the morning."

TJ leant back against him and tried to stifle a yawn.

He stood with her in his arms.

"Come on, my love, time you were in bed cuddled up to me. I think we both got entirely not enough sleep last night. I don't enjoy spending the night in a chair, watching my wife sleep in a hospital bed."

She leant her head against his chest and looped her arms around his neck. Rory was definitely onto something and TJ had no plans of returning to hospital in a hurry.

Chapter Thirty-Seven

A week or so had passed and things were getting back to normal—whatever that was. Rory had certainly been making optimum use of the time off Tom had given him.

The very next day just after their discussion, Brayden, Dylan, Quade, Angelo, and Aaron all turned up dressed to work at barely six in the morning. Brayden had even bought Marcus with him. Rory had taken one of the trucks and disappeared even earlier. A few minutes after the Centre crew arrived, Rory pulled in with a truckload of building materials.

He promptly got out of the truck and walked to her.

"Pixie, Jazz is going to be here soon with Rihanna and Katie. Why don't you head out and order some carpet and pick out the furniture and the soft furnishings for the new room? I'm sure the girls would be up for a shopping trip."

Well, that was an invitation she was not going to refuse.

Not only did she pick out some new things for Marcus's room, she also decided the spare room could use a spruce up for Katie. TJ had wanted to give her sister something a little special as well.

She'd also had a totally carefree and fun day with Jazz, Rihanna, and Katie. Jazz and Rihanna were great fun and seemed to really welcome her into their little group with open arms. It felt nice to fit in and be wanted.

At the end of a couple of long days, they had two gorgeous new rooms for the kids.

To add to the excitement of finally having the kids home, they also got some really great news a couple of days ago.

TJ had been down at the yard finishing up for the day when Rory came into the office and flashed her his thousand-watt smile. That was always welcome and never failed to make her heart flutter and her panties damp.

"Guess what?" His excitement was just about bursting out of him.

"What?" TJ felt her own mood lighten. Rory's energy was infectious.

"Boss just rang. The insurance company is going to pay out on the truck and your father's life insurance."

It took a second to sink in.

When it did, she erupted from the chair and threw herself into his arms.

"Oh, Rory, that's incredible. How did it happen?" Relief flooded through her. Suddenly her money troubles were over. The business would be well into the black and they could use the money from her father's insurance money to set them up in a new house if they chose to. Even if they didn't sort the insurance on the family house, it wasn't such a big deal anymore.

For the first time in nearly two and a half years, she could breathe easy, financially. And to think all the time it was her own family who had put her in the predicament. The saying "blood makes you related but loyalty makes you family" couldn't have been truer.

The loyalty and support she'd felt and received from Rory and the Centre crew proved that statement one hundred per cent.

"The boss got onto them and presented the case. I'm not quite sure what he said or did but you'll have the money in your account tomorrow."

TJ was gobsmacked. She never dreamed she'd ever see that money.

"The man's a miracle worker."

Rory chuckled knowingly. "Let's just say he's persuasive when he wants to be."

Yeah, what a difference a week could make in your life!

The only thing that remained a mystery was the scent that Rory couldn't match to anyone. She figured it was one of

Max's paid goons because they hadn't been around since "the Max thing." Rory wasn't so sure and she knew without asking that he would remain vigilant.

She pushed all those thoughts aside.

Tonight, TJ had something else planned. During the week, she'd thought on it and decided it was something they both needed.

Her plans came together even easier when Brayden called and asked whether it was okay if he took the kids to a Steel concert. The kids were so excited.

The band was playing a benefit concert for charity up in Brisbane. The kids had begged her to let them go. She had absolutely no problem with them going with Brayden and Rihanna. TJ knew they'd keep them out of trouble. Jazz and Quade were apparently going as well. Rory and she had been invited, of course, but she'd declined, offering her ankle and moving through crowds as an excuse.

Really, she just wanted the opportunity to spend some uninterrupted, romantic time with Rory. The kids were going to stay with Brayden and Rihanna overnight to save them driving all the way out here and then back down to their place at the end of the night. The whole Centre crew were catching up at Brayden and Rihanna's tomorrow for a BBQ to celebrate the end to "the Max thing," the kids coming home, and a belated informal gathering for their marriage.

Rory took no convincing at all. He'd worked all day down at the depot and then come up looking hungry and just a little bit wild.

The presence of her husband alone heightened her need for him tenfold.

He was about to head off for a shower when she stopped him. She had specific plans for that later on.

Together they'd enjoyed a relaxed dinner she'd cooked. She didn't know whether you'd call it romantic but Rory seemed very happy.

It was one of the first meals she'd actually cooked from scratch for him.

"Pixie, I know you said you could cook but sweetheart—

you can seriously cook!" It was an exaggeration but yeah, she could more than hold her own in the kitchen.

"I'm glad you enjoyed it. It was only a roast."

"In case you haven't figured it out, my love, I'm just a simple guy. You can feed me a roast like that anytime and I'd be your devoted servant." He raised his eyebrows. "Actually, on second thought, you don't even need to worry about the dinner. I'm more than happy to be your servant."

After closing the dishwasher drawer, TJ walked towards him and circled her arms around his waist, pulling her body in tight to his. She laid her head against his chest.

"Well, in that case, I've got a few ideas about what my humble servant could do for me." She smiled up at him, her eyes holding a very blatant suggestion.

"Is that right?"

TJ felt the rapidly expanding bulge at her belly.

"More kissing, less talking, Surfer Boy," she playfully chastised.

He lowered his head to hers and their lips met. It seemed as if she'd been waiting forever for this, because she'd worked herself into such a frenzy this afternoon thinking through what she wanted to do with him.

Their kiss started slow, a sensual exploration and revision of the heat between them. His tongue teased along her lips and she surrendered to his request for access.

Oh, this is what she'd never get enough of, the exquisite pleasure that being close to Rory could unfurl in her. Her hands roamed over the solid muscles of his back and she wanted to be touching him, skin to skin—not through layers of clothing.

He entwined his tongue with hers and more sparks of pleasure rained through her. She loved the taste of him; she knew she'd never get enough in an entire lifetime. His hand came up and gently cupped the base of her skull, and he moved his mouth over hers, changing the angle of the kiss to explore some more of her mouth. Finally he drew away a little with a series of cheeky pecks and lip nibbles before he continued his playfulness down the side of her neck.

There it was—the spot that never failed to create goose bumps up and down her arms and cause her hips to wriggle, searching for him. She didn't want to wait any longer.

TJ reluctantly pulled away but she wanted to move things along. Tonight was going to be about her seducing him.

She took his hand and threw him a saucy look over her shoulder. It did amazing things to her confidence to watch his hungry gaze intensify with need for her. She led him the short distance to the bedroom and urged him to sit on the bed. Then she stepped back, glad she'd left the brace off her ankle this afternoon, and grasped the hem of her clingy T-shirt she'd worn to accentuate her curves. Her body rocked to an internal rhythm as she slowly drew the fabric up and over her head, leaving her standing in a very revealing jade coloured lace bra.

Her nipples were pebbled and the sensation of them rubbing against the lace was only adding to her need. She dipped her chin and shot him a coy smile, and then slid her hands down her trim stomach to the waistband of her skimpy black shorts. Her fingers fiddled with the top button, teasing him, and she blew him an air kiss on impulse.

The low growl that escaped his throat was more than enough reward and all the encouragement she needed to ham it up even more. She realised then that she didn't feel the least bit self-conscious; all she wanted was to excite him more.

Tonight she wanted him raw and primitive.

She wanted all of him.

She slid her left hand up and teased her index finger over her nipple, drawing his eyes to her movement.

"Ah, Pixie, when did you become such a temptress?" he groaned.

A light giggle escaped her lips.

"Since I realised how much I love having my incredibly hot and sexy husband make love to me. Since you erased a bad experience with passion and love."

"Well then, how about you strip off those shorts and let me see what else you've got for me." His voice was low and raspy. It sent more tingles up and down her spine.

TJ knew her words had affected him as much as her little striptease.

Her fingers slipped the button through the button hole and she slowly drew the zipper down. Then she hooked a thumb at each hip and shimmied the shorts down over her silky thighs and let them drop to the floor. She toed them off and then heard his breath hitch.

She took two steps forward and stood between his knees.

TJ picked up his hands and wrapped them around her back. "Would you be so kind as to help me with this clasp?"

"It would be my absolute pleasure."

His fingers deftly unfastened the clips at her back and then his fingertips trailed down her arms as he brought the straps with them. He flicked the bra onto the bed and grasped her around the waist. His mouth closed over her breast and he circled his tongue around her pebbled nipple.

It was the most exquisite torture.

A few seconds later, his hands slid under the waistband of her panties and he drew them down over her hips and off as well.

His mouth left her nipple and drew a slippery trail down over her quivering stomach.

"Enough!" She planted her hands on his shoulders and couldn't resist squeezing the solid mass before pushing back from him.

She motioned for him to stand and he immediately obliged. TJ's hands moved swiftly to the hem of his polo shirt and began to draw it upwards. With a little of Rory's help, it was dispensed with in just a second.

Her hands moved to his waistband and she made short work of removing them from him, increasing the efficiency by pulling his boxer briefs down at the same time.

TJ couldn't resist running her hands over his very full length and giving him a saucy squeeze, before she took his hand and led him into the adjoining bathroom.

As she leant in to run the shower, Rory hitched an arm around her waist and dragged her body back against his. There was no mistaking the need he had for her as his engorged length teased at her rounded bottom. The coarse hair of his groin brushing against her skin added to the sensation.

She stepped forward and he followed. Once in the shower, she turned in his arms and reached for the shower gel. TJ liberally smeared the gel all over his chest and then moved forward and rubbed her body against him.

It felt heavenly; the slight abrasion of his chest hair made her nipples ache even more. The throbbing need in her core was almost at an unbearable level. Her hand slid down between them and closed around his steely length. She rose up on tiptoe and slid his length between her legs, encouraging him to glide back and forth between her swollen feminine folds.

"Baby doll—you're killing me here." He lowered his head and sucked and nipped at her neck and the place where it joined her shoulder.

She was so close to the edge and he hadn't really even touched her yet. But today was about her taking control and there was something she'd been wanting to try, and today she was going to do it.

TJ pushed her body harder into him and urged him to step back and plant his back against the wall. She didn't miss the shudder that racked through him as his body responded to the cool tile against his heated flesh.

Her hands captured his hips and she slid down his body till she was on her knees. The water cascaded down over her back, making her feel all warm and needy. She looked up into his eyes, traced the tip of her tongue over her lips and then closed her mouth around the glorious plum coloured head of his cock.

A throaty growl escaped his lips as his hips pushed forward towards her face. His hands closed around her head and he drew himself back from her, almost to the point of leaving her lips but not quite.

"Sweetheart, I'll try to be still for you but you have to know your lips around my cock is one of my all-time favourite fantasies and it's just so fucking hot in reality, I'm not sure I'm going to be able stand it." He panted between words.

She smiled around his length and took him deeper into his mouth, using her tongue to massage and tease the protruding vein on the underside.

TJ licked and sucked and teased, all the time trying to learn and judge exactly what he liked best. She listened for his little breath hitches, the groans, and the shudders, and committed them all to memory. Experience at this was something she lacked, but she hoped enthusiasm and love would win the day.

It was a heady feeling being able to drive a man like Rory clear from his mind with her mouth, and she had solid intentions to do it regularly.

He was moving closer and closer to the edge and she started to tease him more. Sometimes sucking harder and rubbing her tongue along him more vigorously only to release the pressure and almost do nothing more than hold him in the velvet centre of her mouth. Very quickly she was learning it was fun to hold the power!

His hands tightened in her wet hair and she waited for the panic to come—but it didn't. This was Rory; she loved him and trusted him like no other.

"Pixie, you have to stop. I can't take it anymore. I'm going to come down your throat if you don't let up." His voice was ragged and edgy with the effort to form his thoughts into words.

"Do it. Tonight I want to see if all this talk about endurance is really true."

His low growl let her know in no uncertain terms that he thought he was up for the challenge.

She nodded her head around his length, hollowed her cheeks and he groaned again as she doubled her efforts.

A few short seconds later, his hips plunged towards her face; his flesh spasmed on her tongue and she swallowed his release. Her hands clutched at his rock solid butt and she was unable to resist the call to dig her fingernails in as the sharp burst of pleasure ripped through him.

The sound that escaped his throat was low and primal. TJ would have sworn it was a chorus of all his animal counterparts acknowledging his pleasure. Slowly the spasming lessened as he slipped from her mouth and he began to slump against the tiles more. He allowed his back to slide down the tiles till he was sitting on his butt across from her.

A few seconds later, his eyes returned to focus and he grinned at her.

"Well, aren't you the little surprise packet today, my love?"

She giggled and wasn't sure whether she blushed or whether it was the warmth of the water still caressing down over her.

"Oh, yeah—I can see you're very pleased with yourself," he teased.

She nodded cheekily, playing along.

"Well, turnabout is only fair and I'm suddenly feeling very hungry for some of your delicious honey."

TJ thought about that for a split second and then stood and stepped out of the shower and grabbed a couple of towels from the rack. She threw one around her shoulders and passed the other to him as he followed her out.

"Is that right? Well, I can probably accommodate that but it would be on my terms."

"Oh, the lady has terms, does she? And what might they be?" he asked between wipes with his towel.

"Well, today I'm in charge. You can taste all you want but we're doing it my way." She emphasised the words.

"Really?" She thought he was about to object and then he grinned and it turned into the big one and she almost came on the spot. "Well, now I'm intrigued and my love, I'm happy to let you lead anytime you want, if our prior activities are any indication of how you like to lead."

She looked at him from out under her long lashes. "It is fun for a change."

TJ threw her towel over the rail and turned to him, beckoning him closer with her index finger and a sexy smile as she backed towards the bed.

Rory followed along like a very willing and happy puppy.

What had gotten into her? he wondered for about the hundredth time in the last half an hour. His gorgeous, sexy wife had transformed into a siren and he liked it—a lot! She was completely uninhibited and by the pheromones she was letting off, incredibly aroused.

How did he get so lucky?

Rory watched her back up to the bed and let her thighs press back in against it before sinking her body down to come to rest with the bottom half of her legs dangling over the edge. It was just about the perfect spot for him to enjoy a feast at her pussy, but he'd wait and see what she had in mind.

She stretched her arms up, beckoning him towards her. He knelt between her thighs and covered her body with his. His mouth was at the perfect spot to enjoy her plump breasts or the satiny skin of her neck and shoulders.

"So, sweetheart, you're in charge—what are my instructions?" he asked, drawing a nipple into his mouth and swirling his tongue around it before sucking it sharply. Her back arched up off the bed and she moaned. He toyed with the little area above her areola and she hissed through her teeth this time.

Now who's controlling the shots? he thought to himself.

Rory lifted his eyes up and saw her fighting to form words; she was lost in the need her body was focused on.

"How about I just keep doing this until you decide what's happening next?" His mouth promptly returned to her other breast and he wriggled his hand down between them to stroke the wet feminine folds he could smell. He traced his fingers down each side of her labia before joining them together and slowly sinking them into the hot velvet depths of her channel.

A sharp whimper escaped her lips and her body would have shot from the bed if his weight didn't have her anchored firmly there. She was very close, very needy and he wanted her coming in his arms, under his body.

He flicked his thumb over her clit a few times and she cried his name as the orgasm ignited through her.

His fingers continued to stroke her folds and his mouth to nibble at her breasts until the very last shudder retreated. She was so beautiful, lost in passion.

Finally he rested his head on her chest and enjoyed listening to her heartbeat return to normal. Her hands running through his hair felt nice. It was both relaxing and a turn-on at the same time.

"Umm, I guess I'm not very good at this giving direction thing. I kind of forgot what I had planned." She giggled.

"Oh, I don't know about that. Why don't we try again? That was my fault you got distracted and came so beautifully for me." He was tracing a little path back and forth across her chin with his index finger. "So we'll chalk that one up to my bad."

"When you touch me, I just can't seem to hold back and I'd hardly call it 'a bad.'" She grinned languidly at him.

"Do I recall you mentioning something about endurance a few minutes ago?"

He nudged his hips forward and he knew there was no way Pixie could mistake how much he wanted her again.

"Well, given you seem ready to go again, there's something I've been wanting to try," she teased.

That had his interest.

"Oh, do tell, and just in case you forgot, I'm all on board if you want to talk dirty to me." He nipped at her ear and she squealed.

"Seriously, you really want me to talk dirty to you?"

"Try it and see what happens," he challenged.

He saw a slight frown form on her face as she tried to decide what to say. Swearing or crude language didn't come easy for his sweet Pixie.

Catching him slightly by surprise, she rolled, taking him with her. She wriggled up and straddled his hips. His cock, with a mind of its own, slammed up and pressed against her pussy, reminding her he was ready when she was.

"Rory." She looked at him accusingly.

"What?" He shrugged. "I can't be held responsible if my cock loves your pussy and wants to check out the interior decorating."

"Interior decorating, hey?" She giggled.

"Too lame?" he asked playfully.

Now she was all-out laughing and her wriggling on his hips was driving him even closer to distraction.

A few seconds later, she managed to control her laughing long enough to realise just how very turned on he was.

Fortunately, Pixie was a quick study.

She leant forward and whispered in his ear what she wanted him to do.

Oh yeah, he was on board with that!

Pixie sat up and looked down at him.

"Don't go all shy on me now, my love. My brain's already sent the message down below and I'm totally on board with it. Whenever you're ready, I'm ready, willing, and able," he joked with her.

She moved off him, turned the other way, and then straddled him again. Then the little minx had the audacity to arch her back and then hollow it before wriggling her curved bottom playfully at him.

Damn! His wife was definitely going to be some fun in the bedroom.

Yep, the universe loved him! All was good with the world.

Unable to resist, he slapped her lightly on her butt cheek and she shot forward in surprise and yelped. His reflexes were quicker and he caught her around the hips and dragged her back.

"Baby doll, you promised I could have some of your honey. I want it now." He settled himself under her hips and took a deep breath, filling his senses with her scent.

It was heavenly to him.

He could resist no longer; his tongue lapped along the folds of her sex, greedy for the taste of her sweet dew.

She wriggled a little at the first shock of his tongue connecting with her flesh and he grasped her hips more tightly. Pixie wasn't going anywhere until he had his fill.

Just as he was establishing a teasing rhythm with his tongue and mouth, her sweet lips closed over his long length and a sharp breath rushed from him, which in turn caused her to wriggle more and giggle around him. Which made him buck his hips and then she wriggled more.

It was the sweetest, funniest sort of pleasure/pain chain reaction they could have.

He sucked at her clit and she whimpered around his cock. The vibrations of her throat felt incredible against his sensitive length. *God, she was killing him.*

This was supposed to be her show but right about now, he needed her to come so he could change things up a bit. It was all he could do to hang on to his sanity with her luscious lips and mouth licking and sucking him for everything he was worth.

He drew a hand back from her hips and trailed his fingertips over the rounded globes of her butt. His wife had a gorgeous ass and he really needed to tell her.

The wet centre of her drew his fingertips and he couldn't resist running them through the soft, slippery flesh, coating them with her essence. He carefully parted the plumped folds and pushed a finger in, searching for that internal nerve centre that would increase her pleasure so much more.

Her breath was coming in quick pants and her hips were starting to thrust at him more erratically; he could feel the muscles of her thighs contracting against his arms.

She was close.

His erection slid from her mouth and he welcomed the slight reprieve from sensation; it allowed him to focus on his task.

"Rory, I'm about to come."

"I know, sweetheart, I can feel it."

"But what about you?"

"Forget about me for a minute. I'm not coming in your mouth twice tonight. Just relax for me and let me take you there."

She flicked her tongue out and licked over the rough skin of his balls. It wasn't quite what he'd had in mind when he'd said relax but he wasn't going to complain.

Pixie needed to come and he needed to be balls deep in her very soon, but before she came, there was something else he wanted to try.

He drew his fingers out of her, covered in her wetness, and traced them up the line dividing the perfect curves of her butt. When he reached her most secret rosette, he traced his index finger around the tight circle and applied just a tiny amount of pressure, letting her know he was there. Her initial reaction was to jerk forward but he held her at the hip and she surprised him more by wriggling back against his fingers once the initial shock had passed.

He nipped at her clit, and then licked it to soothe and she shattered around him. Her body collapsed onto him and spasmed against his as the waves of pleasure broke. Her hot panting breath tickled over his groin, reminding him how much he needed to be inside her.

A long few seconds passed and she rolled off him. Her belly still heaved from the exertion of the pleasure he'd given her.

Rory trailed his fingertips down her belly and round her distended nipples. She shivered as her body started to cool from the heat of just a few moments ago.

She looked up at him questioningly.

"Are you going to finish?"

"Oh yeah, that's my intention, if you're up for it."

"If it means I get to have you deep inside me, then I'm definitely up for it." Her voice had gone husky again at the thought of more intimacy.

"Excellent, 'cause what I have in mind will take me deep." He gave her a sexy little smile and wink and vaulted from the bed. He moved to the end and looked down at her. "I need you to turn around, if you're not too spent already."

TJ swung her legs around to oblige him. Her channel was already contracting at the thought of him soon being inside her. He hooked his arms under her knees and dragged her farther down the bed until her butt was right on the edge.

"Reach behind you and grab a couple of pillows. Put them under your lower back so it doesn't get sore when I start to thrust into you." His command was bossy, caring, and sexy at the same time. She did as he asked. Darn, he made her hot with just the slightest little things.

But she couldn't let him get away with everything—this was her show tonight, after all.

"Ah, Rory, I thought I was in charge," she reminded him, settling back, ready to have her world rocked again.

"And you were—you've come up with two excellent ideas. Now it's my turn to add another one to our repertoire. And this is one I've been wanting to try out since our first night together."

"Well, if you must." She pretended to huff.

"Oh baby, I must," he confirmed.

"Well, in that case, you have permission to rock my world again."

"Why, thank you, ma'am."

She giggled at the mock look of exasperation on his face.

The giggles were very short-lived and they soon became ahhhhhs as he moved even closer, if it was possible, and slowly fed his hungry cock into her. The sensation of him filling her, stretching her, claiming her was indescribable. He never failed to send her senses soaring and her brain to mush.

"Fuck, Pixie, I love being inside you. You're so tight and hot and wet for me—always."

His arms locked tighter around her legs and he closed his hands over her hips to grasp her tighter to him.

"Oh, Rory, it feels so good." She looked at him through half shut eyes, her eyelids no longer able to remain fully open.

The look of need and pleasure and passion on his face called to something deep within her. This was her husband she was sharing this with. It made it so much more special. They were one, a team.

"I'm so close again, can you go a bit harder...please?" she whimpered, needing to feel him own her body totally.

As she'd asked, he thrust at her harder and she felt him meet the barrier of her womb and all the other good bits between.

"Like that?" he growled out between thrusts.

"Yeah, like that. Perfect."

He thrust twice more.

"Reach down and stroke your clit for me, Pixie. I want to watch that while I feel you wrapped all around me."

Before she could think, her hand moved of its own accord and found her needy clit. She lightly rubbed at the little bead in time to his thrusts.

She felt her inner muscles clamp down on him and tighten even further around his girth. She was so near the edge.

"I sure hope you're close, sweetheart, because if you lock around me one more time like that, I'm going over."

His words were enough. The world crumpled beneath her and she was left floating on what seemed to be a never-ending roll of the most exquisite pleasure spasms. The next thrust and he caught up to her, joining in and sharing her pleasure with her.

Their bodies slammed together and rocked as passion overrode both of them.

Eventually they both collapsed on the bed in each other's arms as darkness began to fall outside.

A few moments later, when her brain was again able to function, she said, "I thought I was supposed to be in charge today."

"You are, even when you don't think you are."

"That sounds like some screwy logic."

"Mmm, maybe we could agree then to share it around."

"I could get on board with that," TJ acknowledged.

"Good, then that's settled. But promise me one thing." At his words, she rolled a little so she could look into his face, sensing that he was about to say something important. "Promise me we'll always have fun in the bedroom. Sure, we can do serious, but I really like this playful spontaneity thing we have going on."

She giggled. "Playful and spontaneous is just so you. There's no way I'd want you to be anything else. I love that we can just relax and have so much fun together."

"Me, too, sweet pea."

"Mmm, you know that thing I mentioned before about endurance?"

"Yeah," he said, looking at her a little warily.

"I think I'm going to be the problem. I really could use a little nap."

He cuddled her tighter.

"You take that nap, my love, and I'll be right here when you wake up, ready to continue our bedroom marathon," he joked. "But before you do—I need to tell you something else."

TJ looked at him, a little confused.

"You have a fantastic ass, my sweet, and I'm working up a whole new batch of fantasies involving it and the rest of your luscious body."

She giggled and snuggled in closer. "Let me know when you're ready to take them from the fantasy to the reality stage."

"Oh, you can bet on that. In fact, I might just have the first one sorted when you wake up."

She snuggled in closer. "I love you, Rory Southall— you're perfect to me and for me."

"I'm glad you think so. I love you, too, Teresa Jane Southall."

Mmm, and she got to go to sleep like this for the rest of her life. As Rory would say, *the universe really did love him* and now she was starting to think it may just love her as much.

Her eyes were already closed and she was drifting off as she thought she heard him mentioning something about needing to eat. She really hoped he meant food and not her, at least for the next hour. She so needed a nap.

Epilogue

Two Months Later

TJ leant back against the rear seat of the sleek bay cruiser that Selena was piloting. Katie was up front in the cut out bow, wind whipping through her hair. It was amazing to just lean back and relax. To actually be able to take the time to enjoy the smell of the salt water and the feel of the warm sun and the fresh air.

For the first time in a long time, she felt that her world was back on the right track. Since that night where they'd really talked, they'd laid in each other's arms many times and just enjoyed the closeness and talking with each other.

Rory had opened up a bit more about what really concerned him. He loved his job and what he shared with the Centre but sometimes he worried that he was losing himself in what he had to do. She could understand that. In fact, the last two and a half years had all been about responsibilities and hanging on. Now that it was over, she felt she could breathe, relax, and become more in touch with what she wanted out of life as a woman. She didn't need to be hellbent on driving herself and everyone else to keep the business afloat.

There'd been days when the grief hit her and she started crying for what seemed no reason. Katie and Marcus, to some extent, had been going through the same thing. Katie occasionally came to her but usually she sought Rory. He'd become her rock. From time to time, Rory mentioned that Marcus had shared stuff with him but she didn't really dig.

As long as Marcus felt comfortable talking to someone, who could be better than Rory?

Sure, she had new responsibilities with the kids but financially the drain was over. Now she could consider what she wanted to do. Initially, she'd just wanted to spend some time and settle into life with Rory and the kids.

As their strange little family unit, they'd talked and decided that although they'd never forget the past, they had to move on and they'd do it together. It was the first chapter of a brand-new book and it was exciting. Together they were making it happen. Things were getting easier every day.

The wind tugged at her jacket and she pulled the sides in. Sunlight hit the beautiful diamond on her left hand and she smiled at the memories of the impromptu wedding celebration they'd had at Brayden and Rihanna's after the first night she'd seduced her husband.

Jazz and Rihanna had been on the job and the house had been decorated to celebrate a wedding. It was more a relaxed party than anything else but it still had a wedding feel and it was perfect. TJ treasured the effort they all went to make her feel welcome among the group but also to help celebrate their marriage for the first real time.

Rory had surprised her when it was time to cut the cake. He'd dropped to one knee and taken her hand.

"Teresa Jane Southall, I know we're doing this all a little around the wrong way but I didn't want you to miss out on any important moments. I love you more than anything. And you make me so proud to be your husband." He pulled out the most beautiful solitaire diamond ring from his pocket. On closer look, she realised it was set with baguettes down each side of the band. It was not too big and not too small—just perfect.

He slid the ring onto her finger and then said, "I'd ask you to marry me but you already did." This drew a few chuckles from their gathered family. "So I'll ask instead that you love me for eternity just like I'll always love you."

It was the most romantic thing she'd ever heard and oh, so Rory. She'd leapt into his arms and held tight to him. It was the only place she'd wanted to be. It was a memory that would be no less vivid in fifty years' time.

Katie's shout of excitement broke into her thoughts and dragged her back to the here and now, albeit with a happy smile on her face.

"TJ, come look at this."

She rose and made her way carefully through the midsection of the twenty-three foot craft. Both Rihanna and Selena gave her a warm smile as she passed them at the helm and passengers seats. Rihanna was taking it easier in the boat today. Her very pregnant belly seemed to visibly grow by the day. That had to be expected towards the end with a multiple birth.

TJ took up the seat next to Katie.

"It's so cool, isn't it?" Katie's face was the picture of excitement. Pure joy. She was pointing out all the antics of the guys and girls messing about on the Jet Skis. Marcus was on the back with Rory. In another few months, he'd be old enough to get his licence and ride by himself. Wow, all those responsibilities now fell to Rory and her to oversee and guide them through.

Tears pricked at her eyes and she was glad for her oversized dark glasses. It was only then that TJ realised just how much she'd been holding her breath and hoping that Katie would be okay after what had happened.

Jazz had advised her that Katie would need time and she'd also need to know that the people around her loved her. Katie was easy to love. She had a sunny disposition and always tried hard at everything she did. Fact was, both Katie and Marcus were good kids. Now it was up to Rory and her to help them become just as good adults. Now that the initial shock had passed, she was actually enjoying spending time with both of them.

Her life had been about supporting the family for the last couple of years. Now she was able to enjoy her family.

She laughed when she heard a loud "Woohoo" over the purring of the large boat engine and the whine of the Jet Skis. Rory had launched himself and Marcus over the wake of a large cruiser they'd passed. The ski easily got airborne and flew through the air before kissing the waves again.

Rory had wanted her to join him on the back but she'd decided to let Marcus have the ride. It was winter and she didn't fancy pulling on a thick wetsuit to get on the ski. Sure, she would have loved to be pressed up against Rory but she'd get that tonight. Besides, this way she got to spend a little more time with Katie.

"Oh wow. We're heading for the bar," Katie yelled out, excited as they followed the Jet Skis out over the Southport bar.

TJ glanced back and noticed Selena grinning at Katie's excitement. The bar was very calm today with just a gentle swell running through, as was often the case in winter. The sleek craft they were riding in hardly moved at all as it cut through the waves.

Once past the spit, they headed north, skirting around South Stradbroke Island.

"Keep your eyes open for whales and dolphins. I heard a report that there have been a lot of sightings this week. You never know, we might get lucky and see some," Selena called to them.

"Really?" Katie shrieked as she began to train her eyes over to the right, looking for the mammals.

"Why don't we swap sides? That way you'll be able to see better," she suggested to Katie.

"Thanks, Pixie." Katie grinned cheekily.

TJ shook her head and laughed. "Oh no, not you, too?"

"Well, Rory calls you that, and it really seems to suit you. Besides, he hates it when people call you TJ."

"Oh, does he now? Or is he on some little mission just to change things the way he wants them?"

"No way," she yelled emphatically over the noise of the engines and ocean. "Rory wouldn't do that."

Great, she could feel a case of hero worship coming on and chuckled quietly to herself. He was damned near close to perfect.

A few minutes later, Katie half leapt from her seat and TJ reacted without thinking, grabbing hold of her warm wind jacket and dragging her back down.

"Whales, over there—look!" the young girl screamed.

Sure enough, the blow of a whale was visible not more than one hundred metres off the right side of the boat.

"Looks like we're in luck, ladies," Selena called and eased the throttles back to idle.

A few seconds later, the majestic creature rose up out of the ocean and breached, letting its massive body crash back to the water with an almighty splash. Its tail came up and slapped at the water as it dived again. A split second later, another massive whale rose up and they knew then they were witnessing a small pod making their way up the coast. The whales repeated the process over and over, obviously having a wonderful time playing and carousing around while making their way north for the winter.

Selena kept pace from a distance with the giants of the ocean. At times, it seemed like the whales were waving as they rolled and waggled their fins and slapped at the water.

They'd all been spellbound and it was an experience none of them would forget. The privilege to see something so large and beautiful up this close was breathtaking and it seemed to give them a real connection to the ocean environment they were out enjoying.

Finally they neared their destination. The guys had picked out a long deserted beach for them to enjoy a picnic and a bit of fun in the surf.

Katie launched herself over at TJ, wrapping her thin arms around her. TJ hugged her tight.

"I'm so glad you were with me when I saw my first whales, Pixie. I'll remember it forever." It was so evident that the experience had touched her sister deeply.

"I'm glad I could experience it with you, too, sweetie. It'll be one of our special moments that we can talk about when we're all old and grey," she teased.

"I'm never going to get old and grey." Katie laughed.

"Okay, if you say so."

"I do."

Katie sobered for a moment. "Do you think Mum sent them to us to check up on how we were doing?"

TJ looked out to the ocean, and for the second time today was fighting back the tears.

"Yeah, Katie, I think maybe she did. And I think we're doing pretty good, considering everything. What do you think?"

A look that was wise beyond her years crossed Katie's face, and then she nodded.

"I think you're right. We are doing pretty good. Mum and Dad would be proud of us."

"Yeah, they would, Katie."

Rory and Marcus moved over to the boat after beaching his ski and helped Selena pull the boat up and anchor it.

He offered his hand to Katie and she took it, scrambling over the front of the boat, eager to start her next adventure. She stepped forward and he reached up and grasped her around the waist, making it obvious he was keen to have her back close to him.

"Hey, sweet pea, weren't those whales something to see?"

"They were incredible. How lucky were we to see them so early in the season?" she agreed.

"Yeah, we sure were," he agreed. "Do you mind if I go catch a few waves? It seems I haven't been out on my board forever. Dylan's going to come out with me."

"Sure, I'd love to watch you surf. I think it's high time I got to see just how the name 'Surfer Boy' came about. But don't think you're going to use me to warm up when you're freezing your balls off." She gave him a lurid look, letting him know she knew sex would not be far from his mind.

"Oh, my love, that's half the fun of coming here. Seeing what we can get away with. Haven't you heard the story of how Rihanna got pregnant?"

"Rory—the kids are with us—not to mention most of your team."

"Okay, I might be able to behave for a few hours. Just try not to be too gorgeous." He leant forward and plopped a cheeky kiss against her lips. "I'll just grab my board out of the boat then I'll help you get settled."

A few minutes later, TJ was sprawled out on a bright beach towel. Admittedly she had a pullover on in defence to the winter chill, but still she felt very content with her lot in life. She could see Rory and Dylan out in the distance, paddling out on their boards. Their strong arms and legs made easy work of getting through the shore breakers. They both wore thick wetsuits to protect them from the cold, not that Queensland ever got really cold but still, out in the surf they'd eventually feel it.

Jazz wandered over and plonked herself down on the towel she'd laid out beside hers.

"So you two seem to have everything rocking along well. The kids seem happy." Jazz was never one to beat around the bush.

"Yep, we do. As a group, we have our moments but we're doing well. In fact, I'd even go as far to say that we're doing better than well."

"I'm so pleased for you all." Jazz's eyes cut to Katie, who was throwing a ball around with Marcus and some of the other guys and girls. "Katie's doing a lot better than I expected. I thought she'd take a lot more time to settle than what she seems to have."

"Oh, she has her moments, but I know she feels safe and wanted. Rory gives her that."

"Mmm, he does, but don't underestimate what you give her as well. You give her the best sort of role model she could have. You show her every day how to get up and get on with life when it deals you a shitty hand. And you do it with grace and without self-pity."

"Thanks, Jazz. It means a lot for you to say that. Yeah, I have had to deal with a lot of unpleasantness in my life but I'm also very fortunate that through it I've found a man I cherish, and that's not even mentioning how lucky I am that he comes with a very cool extended family." TJ nudged Jazz in the shoulder.

"Well, I'm glad you've recognised just how incredible we all are," Jazz flipped back in her best deadpan manner.

They both laughed like loons at each other.

Eventually TJ looked up and watched Rory spring up and ride a long wave nearly all the way to the shore. Seeing that, she understood. He loved the ocean and really needed to be near it. It was part of him.

"Wow, he's really good," Jazz said, impressed by watching Rory ride in.

"He is, isn't he? I guess that seals it. There's no way I could keep him from living by the beach now that I've seen him ride a wave like that."

"I don't think Rory would care where he lived as long as you're all with him."

"You're right but there's absolutely no reason we can't live at the beach. Now we have a manager in the trucking business. There's nothing holding us there. We don't need to be up at the crack of dawn to see trucks off. And the kids really do need to be closer to more interesting things. Besides, it will kind of be the last step of our new beginning."

TJ noticed how easily the "we" rolled off her tongue, without thought.

"Well, if that's what you think, you should do it!"

They chatted for a few more minutes about everything and nothing.

Finally, TJ noticed Jazz's eyes kept creeping back to Quade. Unlike everyone else, in defiance to the cold, he'd stripped down in the sun to his board shorts. His ripped body was very easy to look at and Jazz seemed to have no problem openly admiring it.

"That's one good-looking man."

"Ah ha," Jazz agreed.

"So what's between you two?"

"Not you as well? Everyone keeps asking. Ever heard of minding your own business?"

TJ laughed. *Jazz couldn't be serious, could she?* "In case it's escaped you, you're the nosiest person in this outfit. You mind everyone's business. You've got to expect that occasionally it's going to come back at you."

Jazz nodded good-naturedly. "I agree. But I thought I'd give it a go. The truth is I'm still in the resisting phase. I want to but I also don't want to give in. You should know by now I'm as stubborn as hell."

"Nope, completely escaped my notice."

Jazz playfully swatted at TJ's arm. "Smart arse."

Rory chose that moment to jog up the beach, all wet and looking incredibly hot from his surf. Her body responded as it always did. She wanted him—badly. His cheeky smirk let her know he'd not missed her aroused scent.

"So what are you lovely ladies up to?" he asked casually.

"Nothing really—we've just been admiring Quade's very hot body. Well, actually, Jazz has; I've just been agreeing. I've got my own hunk of manly hotness to snuggle up to whenever the mood strikes."

He leant down and kissed her on the lips. It was hot and playful and with no effort, they both knew it would be the start of something wild if they let it get that way.

"Well, as long as you remember that, my love."

"Oh, I'm counting on you reminding me very regularly." TJ batted her eyelashes at him.

"Count on it."

"Oh, come on guys," Jazz protested. "You're almost worse than Brayden and Rihanna. Give me a break. I'm all hot and horny over here and you're just making me jealous."

Quade had moved closer and they all heard the low growl he let out.

TJ and Rory couldn't hold the laughter back.

"Oh fuck—I forgot he could hear everything," Jazz chastised herself.

Quade strode up and grabbed Jazz by the hand and pulled her up.

"You and I need to take a walk and have a little chat," Quade demanded.

"I don't think so, you big oaf. You don't get to order me around like this," she started to protest, pulling away.

He leant down closer to her ear and spoke more quietly. "Shut up and walk, honey nose, or I'll carry you. I'm done with playing games. We're going to have this out." Something about his demands must have got through to her.

Jazz meekly took his offered hand and walked along beside him.

Rory and TJ smirked at each other. Things were really getting interesting there.

"So, Mrs Southall, could I interest you in a walk?"

"Maybe."

Rory peeled off his wetsuit and she sat back and enjoyed the view. She loved his muscled body and regularly spent hours cataloguing every single one. It was one of her favourite pastimes. Who needed a hobby when they had a husband as hot as hers?

He grabbed a towel from the big beach bag they'd brought along and quickly dried himself off before donning a T-shirt. Rory wrapped the towel around his waist and put his back slightly to the others. Not that they were paying attention. He dropped his board shorts and pulled on a dry pair all without losing the towel. It was impressive and obviously a practised move.

"What are you trying to do? Make me insane or something?" TJ complained.

"What? You were the one who wasn't keen on beach activities."

"I'm beginning to see the error of my ways."

He pulled her to her feet.

"Come on, let's take a walk." His arm came around her shoulders and he pulled her into his body. It was one of her favourite spots.

They walked in silence for a good while. Occasionally, they didn't want to have everyone eavesdropping on their conversation.

As they rounded a slight bend, Rory stopped and dropped down in front of her. He urged her to hop up on his back, piggyback style.

"What are you doing, you clown?" She giggled at his antics and obliged.

"We're going up there." He nodded with his head towards the little strand of native trees growing near the sand dune. "I thought I'd save you from clambering up the bank."

TJ thought better than to argue. He was much stronger and more athletic than her.

A few long strides later and he had her sitting on a grassy spot protected by the branches of the trees. The higher position gave her a perfect vantage point to enjoy the ocean view.

"It's so beautiful here, Rory."

"It is, my love."

Now was the perfect time to tell him.

"You never told me you were such a good surfer."

He shrugged offhandedly. "I grew up on the beach as a kid. Surfing was just part of the life."

"Well, you know I was keen on the idea of the move to the beach. Now I'm certain. After seeing you out there, I know it's right. Let's do it."

He hugged her close.

"Are you sure? I'm always happy near or on the ocean; it makes me feel centred. But I'm always going to be happier with you beside me and content."

"I'm sure. It's time to move on. I want to build something with you that's totally ours. Let's start looking."

He smirked a little.

"What aren't you telling me?"

"Well, the kids and I actually found a place we think will be perfect the other day. I was hoping you'd enjoy today and I could kind of break it to you gently. We all knew you were not opposed to the idea but you seem to feel the connection to the property more than the kids do."

"Oh Rory, that's true but I feel the connection to you and the kids a lot more. That's what matters to me. Home is where ever we make it. And I want to make it at the beach with you."

She leant over and kissed him passionately. He fell back and pulled her with him, encouraging her to move closer and over him.

It was fast moving from a kiss to something much more.

He broke away gently and pushed her back a little so he could see her face.

"There's something else I'd like to talk to you about."

She looked at him, puzzled.

"What?"

"I want you to go back to school and finish your final semester. I think you should finish what you set out to do. Even if you never practice physiotherapy, you'll have achieved one of your dreams. Something you wanted to do, not what you needed to do."

It never failed to amaze her just how astute he was.

"I swear, you read my mind sometimes. Just this morning, on the way over, I was thinking about going back to school."

"Well, do it, my love. If you hurry, you could probably make the enrolment for next semester which starts in a few weeks' time."

She ran her finger down the side of his cheek and pressed a peck on his lips. "You've given this more thought than you're letting on."

"Mmm, I have. I wanted to be sure I thought it was right before I suggested it. I didn't want you to feel like I was pushing you to do something you didn't want to." His hand closed in her hair and he took his turn at giving her a peck on the lips.

"Rory, you're not pushing me into anything I don't want to do." She trailed off, longing in her voice.

"Really, my love? In that case, let me revisit a little conversation we had when we arrived. Any chance you might have changed your mind about helping me warm up?"

"Oh, you're plenty warm from where I'm lying. In fact, I'd say you're smoking hot and I have no idea what I was thinking before. I was obviously confused. With further consideration, I'm liking your original plan a lot and I think you should put it into immediate action." She touched her lips to the tip of his nose.

"Is that right?"

"Yep, it is."

"Well, in that case, I can hardly refuse. But I'm leading..."

"But you led this morning..." she whined at him, playing the part.

"Stop talking and use that gorgeous mouth to kiss me, Pixie."

She could do that. It was no hardship at all.

The End

I hope you enjoyed reading the second Centre Games novel, Finding Judgement. All the gang will be back for Dylan and Vanessa's story, Finding Justice.

Acknowledgements

It's been a hellfire few months since I released Finding Trust back in late February. In March, I realised I'd set myself an almost impossible deadline to get Finding Judgement written (1st June). I'd barely started on Finding Judgement and essentially I had three months to make it happen.

Somehow I did it, while working through one of the busiest times in my life. I think the biggest motivator for me was Rory and TJ. Their story grabbed hold of me and wouldn't let go. (142,500 words later it's done). And Rory is just so damned nice—how could I refuse him anything?

It was also the praise and encouragement from my readers of Finding Trust that drove me hard. I work in IT and over the last twenty years of successfully doing so, I can count the times on one hand anyone has ever complimented me on what I do. Just doesn't happen in IT. It seems if you write a book that people enjoy, they let you know.

I'm stunned at how much pleasure I get from somebody telling me they couldn't put the book down. Or the excitement and anticipation I see when someone asks me about when the next book will be available. To be able to give someone a few hours pleasure and enjoyment is a very special thing. Thank you to my readers for taking a chance on me and giving me that privilege.

To the ladies at The Killion Group—Kim, Jen, and Em, you've come through for me again. Amazing cover and branding! Love working with you ladies. Onto the next book!

To Faith Williams, my editor—again you've ploughed through the mammoth task and made my job easy. Thanks for being so efficient and wonderful to work with.

Dr Patrick See—Firstly, thank you for the medical advice for this novel, definitely your turf! And thanks for just being an all-round great guy. I enjoy your wisdom, level-headed approach to life, and friendship.

To Colin, you've made working in IT enjoyable again. If I'm going to do it—I wouldn't want to do it with anyone else! Thanks for your support through these last few months. You're a great friend, travel buddy, and business partner. The good times are ahead!

Kim, my number-one fan and beta reader, I know I put you through hell every time. I give you drops of the novel and leave you hanging. Our late-night chats are the best! Let's see what we can do for Dylan now.

To Pati, my new American friend and beta reader—I may not have met you in person yet but you've given me so much support, encouragement, and advice. You make me want to do better. Thank you so much.

To my mum and dad, thanks for helping keep my life on track and the household running when I'm swamped with work, writing, and travel. You both play such an important part in my life.

And lastly to my husband and kids, another one done, guys! I actually think we did okay through this. We've got the routine happening. Thanks for just being you and letting me be me. I look forward to the day we publish your first book super duper! Your twenty-page effort at six just astounds me. Love you guys so much.

Hope you enjoy reading Rory and TJ's story as much as I have enjoyed writing it.

Nat

About the Author

I recently discovered those school vocational assessments are really interesting and probably correct! Who would have thought, hey? You see, I clearly remember taking one of those in Year 11 (for my US friends, I think that equates to junior year in high school). Anyway, semantics. Well, the results came back indicating that I should pursue a career in writing and something else. What that something else was I can't remember but the writing thing stuck in my mind.

Sure, I'd always liked English and had already developed a ravenous appetite for romance novels by the age of sixteen—but who becomes a writer straight out of school? So to cut a long story short, I went to Uni and studied Business and ended up managing large-scale IT projects shortly after.

I can't complain: it's been a great career. I've done some awesome projects and met some incredible people and I won't be giving it up anytime soon. Anyway, I've messed around with a couple of "secret" novels over the years and I finally decided to get serious and finish one. Hence *"Finding Trust"* came about. And about twenty years later, I've finally proved a vocational assessment correct, because I love writing!

As to some other stuff about me: I live on the Gold Coast, Australia. I love spending time with my family and friends. When I'm not sitting behind a screen playing with IT or writing, you might find me down the beach playing in the waves on a Jet Ski or a bogey board (both are uber cool). When the weather turns a bit cooler (doesn't really happen on the Gold Coast), we like to head for the snow. I've discovered I have two kids who are kamikaze skiers—they must take after their father. He's always at me to "release the handbrake." Apparently I'd ski so much better. I call it a healthy understanding of self-preservation and gravity!

I like to think I can fit in a few workouts and martial arts classes each week. This tends to be a figment of my imagination more than reality, unfortunately. I am trying to remedy this, but those damn characters just keep demanding to have their stories told and, well, there's always another good book to read!

I hope you enjoy mine.

Please drop me a line. You can find me at my website, www.nataliegayle.com. I'm active on Facebook, Twitter, and via email Natalie@nataliegayle.com.au. I'd love to know what you think of my books and well, let's be truthful—I love talking about books, whether they're mine or someone else's. Fiction is just so much more fun than reality!!!

Happy Reading
Natalie Gayle

www.ingramcontent.com/pod-product-compliance
Lightning Source LLC
Chambersburg PA
CBHW051433260626
47162CB00001B/79